PRAISE FOR THE TRIUMPHANT SERIES BY W.E.B. GRIFFIN . . .

BADGE OF HONOR

A powerful and dramatic look inside today's urban police forces—from the cop on the street, to the detectives, to the chief of police. Here are the men and women of outstanding courage who have taken on one of the hardest jobs on earth . . .

"Readers will feel as if they're part of the investigations, and the true-to-life characters will soon feel like old friends. Excellent reading!"
—Dale Brown, bestselling author of *Day of the Cheetah* and *Hammerheads*

"Gritty, fast-paced . . . authentic."
—Richard Herman, Jr., author of *The Warbirds*

"Griffin is a natural storyteller . . ."
—*Publishers Weekly*

"Damn effective."
—Tom Clancy, bestselling author of *The Hunt for Red October*

Turn the page for reviews of W.E.B. Griffin's other bestselling series . . .

THE CORPS

The *New York Times* bestselling saga—a stunningly authentic portrait of the Marine Corps, the brave men and women who fought, and loved, in the sweeping turmoil of World War II . . .

BROTHERHOOD OF WAR

The magnificent *New York Times* bestselling saga that made Griffin a superstar of military fiction—the epic story of the U.S. Army, from the privates to the generals, in the world's most harrowing wars . . .

"Griffin is a storyteller in the grand tradition, probably the best man around for describing the military community. BROTHERHOOD OF WAR . . . is an American epic."
—bestselling author Tom Clancy

"Extremely well-done . . . First-rate."
—*The Washington Post*

"Absorbing . . . fascinating descriptions of weapons, tactics, Army life and battle."
—*The New York Times*

"A major work . . . magnificent . . . powerful."
—William Bradford Huie, author of *The Execution of Private Slovik*

"A crackling good story. It gets into the hearts and minds of those who . . . fight our nation's wars."
—William R. Corson, Lt. Col. (Ret.) U.S.M.C., author of *The Betrayal* and *The Armies of Ignorance*

W.E.B. GRIFFIN

THE
WITNESS

FOURTH IN THE <u>BADGE OF HONOR</u> SERIES

J

JOVE BOOKS, NEW YORK

For Sergeant Zebulon V. Casey
Internal Affairs Division
Police Department, Retired, the City of Philadelphia.
He knows why.

BADGE OF HONOR: THE WITNESS

A Jove Book / published by arrangement with the author

PRINTING HISTORY
Jove edition / January 1992

ISBN: 0-515-10747-6

Jove Books are published by The Berkley Publishing Group,
200 Madison Avenue, New York, New York 10016.
The name "JOVE" and the "J" logo
are trademarks belonging to Jove Publications, Inc.

PRINTED IN THE UNITED STATES OF AMERICA

10 9 8 7 6 5

ONE

The Day After New Year's Day Reception given by Taddeus Czernich, who was the police commissioner of the City of Philadelphia was considered by Staff Inspector Peter F. Wohl as a lousy idea whose time had unfortunately come.

New Year's Eve is not a popular festive occasion so far as the police of Philadelphia are concerned. For one thing, almost no police are free to make merry themselves, because they are on duty. On New Year's Eve all the amateur drunks are out in force, with a lamentable tendency to settle midnight differences of opinion with one form of violence or another, and/or to run their automobiles through red lights and into one another, which of course requires the professional services of the Police Department to put things in order.

New Year's Day is worse. Philadelphia greets the New Year with the Mummer's Parade down Broad Street. There are massive crowds of people, many of whom have ingested one form of antifreeze or another, to control. Pickpockets and other thieves, who have been anxiously awaiting the chance to ply their trades, come out of the woodwork.

1

For a very long time, the Day After New Year's Day was a day on which every police officer who did not absolutely have to be on duty stayed home, slept late, and tried to forget how he had spent New Year's Eve and New Year's Day.

But then, during the reign of Police Commissioner Jerry Carlucci, that all changed. Jerry Carlucci had decided that it behooved him to make some gesture to the senior commanders of the Department in token of his appreciation for their faithful service during the past year.

He would, he decided, have a Commissioner's Reception at his home, and invite every captain and above in the Department. It would have been nice to invite all the white shirts, but there were just too many lieutenants; they would have to wait until they got themselves promoted. Since New Year's Day was out of the question, because everybody was working, the Day After New Year's Day was selected.

By the time Commissioner Czernich had assumed office, following the election of Jerry Carlucci as mayor of the City of Brotherly Love, the Commissioner's Reception on the Day After New Year's Day had become a tradition.

The wives, of course, loved it. Because their husbands had been working, they hadn't had the chance to do anything special on New Year's Eve. Now, through the gracious invitation of the commissioner, they had the opportunity to get all dressed up and meet with the other ladies in a pleasant atmosphere.

If the senior officers of the Philadelphia Police Department, who had really looked forward to doing nothing more physically exerting than walking from the bedroom to their chair in front of the TV in the living room, didn't like it, too bad.

Marriage was a two-way street. It was not too much to ask of a husband that he put on either his best uniform (uniforms were "suggested") or his good suit and spend three hours in the company of his spiffed-up spouse, who had spent New Year's watching the TV.

What wives thought of the affair was not really germane for Staff Inspector Wohl, who did not have one, had never had one, and had absolutely no desire to change that situation anytime soon.

There was a Mrs. Wohl at the reception however, in the role of wife. She was Mrs. Olga Wohl, whose husband was Chief Inspector Augustus Wohl, Retired.

Mrs. Wohl had actually said to Staff Inspector Wohl, "Peter, if you were married, your wife would be here with you. She would love it."

Peter Wohl had learned at twelve that debating his mother was a no-win arrangement, so he simply smiled at her.

"And you should have worn your uniform," Mrs. Wohl went on. "You look so nice in it. Why didn't you?"

Wohl was wearing a nearly new single-breasted glen plaid suit, a light blue, button-down collar shirt, and a striped necktie his administrative assistant had told him was also worn by members of Her Britannic Majesty's Household Cavalry. He was a pleasant-looking thirty-five-year-old who did not much resemble what comes to mind when the term "cop" or "staff inspector" comes up.

"It didn't come back from the cleaners."

That was not the truth, the whole truth, and nothing but the truth. Staff Inspector Wohl's uniform was hanging in one of his closets. He had bought it when he had been promoted to lieutenant, and the epaulets were adorned with a golden bar. Now the epaulets carrried the golden oak leaf (like an army major's) of a staff inspector, but the uniform still looked almost brand-new. He had seldom worn it as a lieutenant, or as a captain, and he rarely wore it now. He had last worn it six months before at the inspector's funeral Captain Richard F. "Dutch" Moffitt had earned for himself by getting killed in the line of duty. It would not have bothered Staff Inspector Wohl if his uniform remained in his closet, unworn, until the moths ate it down to the last button hole.

"Well, you certainly have no one to blame but yourself for that."

"You're right, Mother," he said, reaching for another shrimp.

The food at the Commissioner's Day After New Year's Day Reception was superb. This was less a manifestation of either Commissioner Czernich's taste or his generosity toward his guests but rather of the high esteem in which Commissioner Czernich and the police generally were held by various citizens of the City of Brotherly Love.

This, too, was a legacy from the reign of Jerry Carlucci as police commissioner. At the very first Commissioner's Reception to which then Sergeant Wohl had gone (under the mantle of then active Chief Inspector Wohl), the food had been heavily Italian in flavor. When the mayor's many friends in the Italian community had heard that Jerry was having a party for the other cops on the Day After New Year's Day, it seemed only right that they sort of help him out.

You can say a lot of things, many of them unpleasant, about Jerry Carlucci, but nobody ever heard of him taking a dime. And on what he's making as commissioner, he can't afford to feed all them cops. Angelo, call Salvatore, and maybe Joe Fierellio, too, and tell them I'm gonna make up some pasta and a ham, and maybe some pastry, and send it out to Jerry Carlucci's house, for the Day After New Year's Day cop party he's giving, and ask them maybe they want to get in on it.

By the time Commissioner Carlucci's Second Annual Day After New Year's Day Reception was held, the Commissioner's many friends in the other ethnic communities of the City of Brotherly Love had learned what the Italians had done. The repast of the Second Reception had been multinational in scope. By the time of Commissioner Carlucci's last Day After New Year's Day Reception (three years before; two days after which he had to resign to run for mayor), being *permitted* to make a little contribution to the Commissioner's Day After New Year's Day Reception carried a certain cachet among the city's restauranteurs, fish mongers, pastry bakers, florists, and wholesale butchers.

"When did you start drinking that?"

"Right after the waiter filled the glass."

"I mean, start drinking champagne?"

"As soon as I heard it was free, Mother."

"Don't be a smarty-pants, Peter. It gives me a headache, is what I mean."

"Then if I were you, I wouldn't drink it."

A tall, muscular, intelligent-faced young man, who looked to be in his late twenties, walked up to them.

"Good afternoon, Inspector," he said, and nodded at Olga Wohl. "Ma'am."

"Hello, Charley," Wohl said. "Do you know my mother?"

"No, I don't. I know Chief Wohl, ma'am."

"Mother, this is Sergeant Draper. He's Commissioner Cohan's driver."

"Nice to meet you," she said. "Are you having a nice time?"

"Yes, ma'am. Inspector, when you have a minute, the commissioner would like to have a word with you."

"Which commissioner, Charley?" Wohl asked. "Your commissioner, or that one?"

He raised his glass in the direction of half a dozen men gathered in a knot. One of them was the Hon. Jerry Carlucci. The others were Chief Inspector Augustus Wohl, Retired, Chief Inspector Matt Lowenstein, Chief Inspector Dennis V. Coughlin, Captain Jack McGovern, and Police Commissioner Taddeus Czernich.

"Mine, sir," Sergeant Draper said, a little chagrined. "Commissioner Cohan is over thataway." He pointed with an inclination of his head.

"Tell him I'll be right with him."

"Yes, sir."

"Where, by the way," Olga Wohl asked as soon as Draper was out of earshot, "is your driver?"

"I don't have a driver, Mother. I am a lowly staff inspector."

"You know what I mean. The Payne boy. Your father likes him."

"Oh, you mean, my *administrative assistant?*"

"You know very well what I meant. Shouldn't he be here?"

"I believe Officer Payne is having dinner with his parents."

"He should be here. He could meet people."

"He already knows people."

"I mean the *right* people."

"He already knows the right people. He told me that he and his father were going to play golf with H. Richard Detweiler and Chadwick T. Nesbitt this morning."

"Really?"

Chadwick T. Nesbitt III and H. Richard Detweiler were chairman of the board and president, respectively, of Nesfoods, International, which had begun more than a century before as Nesbitt Potted Meats and was now Philadelphia's largest single employer.

"Now if *I* were interested in social climbing, I probably could have talked myself into an invitation."

"You don't play golf."

"I could learn."

"He's a policeman now, Peter. It doesn't matter who his family is."

"Mother, I have no intention of telling them, but I'll bet

you a dollar to a doughnut that if Jerry Carlucci or the commissioner knew where Matt is, they would be delighted.''

Mrs. Wohl sniffed; Peter wasn't sure what it meant.

"I'd better go see what Cohan wants," Wohl said. "Can I trust you to go easy on the booze?''

"You ought to be ashamed of yourself, Peter Wohl!''

"I'll be right back," Wohl said. "I hope.''

Deputy Commissioner-Administration Francis J. Cohan was a fair-skinned, finely featured, trim man of fifty or so. He was dressed in a suit almost identical to Peter Wohl's, but instead of the blue button-down collar shirt and striped necktie, he wore a stiffly starched white shirt and a tie bearing miniature representations of the insignia of the International Association of Chiefs of Police.

"Happy New Year, Commissioner," Wohl said. "You wanted to see me, sir?''

"Happy New Year, Peter," Cohan said, smiling and offering his hand. "Yes, I did. Why don't we get ourselves a fresh drink and find a quiet corner someplace? What is that, champagne?''

"Yes, sir.''

"When did you start drinking that?''

"As soon as I saw the bottles with 'Moet et Chandon' on them. This is first-class stuff.''

"It gives me a headache.''

"May I say I admire your taste in suits, Commissioner?''

Cohan chuckled. "I noticed," he said. "Makes us look like the Bobbsey Twins, doesn't it?''

"Did you ever notice, sir, that when a man goes someplace and sees someone else with a suit like his, he thinks, 'Well, he certainly has good taste,' but if a woman sees somebody with a dress like hers, she wants to go home?''

"Don't get me started on the subject of women," Cohan said, and put his hand on Wohl's arm and led him to the bar. "Sometimes I think the Chinese had the right idea. Just keep enough for breeding purposes and drown the rest at birth.''

Commissioner Cohan ordered a fresh Scotch and water. "And bubbly for my son here. You'd better give him two. Those look like small glasses, and this may take some time.''

The bartender served the drinks.

"Tad Czernich said he has a little office off the hall; that we could use that," Cohan said. "Now let's see if we can find it."

I sense, Peter Wohl thought, *that while this little chat is obviously important—Czernich knows about it—it doesn't concern anything I've either done wrong or have not done.*

Commissioner Czernich's home office was closet-sized. There was barely room for a desk, an upholstered "executive" chair, and a second, straight-backed, metal chair. Wohl thought, idly, that it was probably used by Czernich only to make or take telephone calls privately. There were three telephones on the battered wooden desk.

Cohan sat in the upholstered chair.

"Have you got room enough to turn around and close the door?" he asked.

"If I suck in my breath."

Wohl closed the door behind him and sat down, feeling something like a schoolboy, in the straight-backed chair.

"Peter, the sequence in which this happened was that I was going to talk to you first, then, if you were amenable, to Tad, and if *he* was amenable, *then* to the mayor. It didn't go that way. I got here as the mayor did. He wanted to talk to me. I had to take the opportunity; he was in a good mood. So the sequence has been reversed."

Which means that I am about to be presented with a fait accompli; Carlucci has apparently gone along with whatever Cohan wants to do, and whether I am amenable or not no longer matters.

"You're aware, I'm sure, Peter, that the great majority of FBI agents are either Irish or Mormons?"

"I know one named Franklin D. Roosevelt Stevens that I'll bet isn't either Irish or Mormon," Peter said.

Cohan laughed, but Peter saw that it was with an effort.

"Okay," Cohan said. "Strike 'great majority' and insert 'a great many.' "

"Yes, sir. I've noticed, come to think of it."

"You ever hear the story, Peter, about why is it better to get arrested by an Irish FBI agent than a Mormon FBI agent?"

What the hell is this, a Polish joke?

"No, sir. I can't say that I have."

"Let's say the crime is spitting on the sidewalk, and the punishment is death by firing squad. You know they really do that, the Mormons in Utah, execute by firing squad?"

"Yes, sir. I'd heard that."

"Okay. So here's this guy, spitting on the sidewalk. If the Mormon FBI guy sees him, that's it. Cuff him. Read him his Miranda and stand him up against the wall. The law's the law. Spitters get shot. Period."

"I'm a little lost, Commissioner."

"Now, the Irish FBI agent: He sees the guy spitting. He knows it's against the law, but he knows that he's spit once or twice himself in his time. And maybe he thinks that getting shot for spitting is maybe a little harsh. So he either gets something in his eye so he can't identify the culprit, or he forgets to read him his rights."

"And therefore, be nice to Irish FBI agents?"

"What follows gets no further than Czernich's closet, okay?"

"Yes, sir."

"You know Jack Malone, don't you?"

"Sure."

Before Chief Inspector Cohan had been named a deputy commissioner, Sergeant John J. Malone had been his driver. Wohl now remembered that Malone had been on the last lieutenant's list. He couldn't remember where he had been assigned. If, indeed, he had ever known.

"And?"

"What do I think of him? Good cop. Smart. Straight arrow."

"Not always smart," Cohan said.

"Oh?"

"Assault is a felony," Cohan said carefully. "A police officer who is found guilty of committing any crime, not just a felony, is dismissed. A Mormon FBI guy would say, 'That's the law. Fire him. Put the felon in jail.' "

But you're Irish, right?

"You may have noticed, Peter, that I'm Irish," Cohan said.

"Who did he hit?"

"It's not important, but you'd probably hear anyway. A lawyer named Howard B. Candless."

Wohl shrugged, signaling he had never heard of him.

"Jack did quite a job on him," Cohan said. "Knocked a couple of teeth out. Caused what the medical report said were 'multiple bruises and contusions.' They kept Candless in the hospital two days, worrying about a possible concussion."

"Why?" Wohl asked. "That doesn't sound like Malone."

"And when he was finished with the lawyer, Jack had a couple too many drinks and went home and slapped his wife around."

"On general principles?"

"Jack is a very simple guy. He believes that when a woman marries one man, she should not get into another man's bed."

"Jesus Christ!"

"They kept her in the hospital overnight; long enough to make Polaroid pictures of her bruises and contusions. That's important."

"But he's not going to be charged? Or did I get the wrong impression?"

"It took some doing. He wasn't charged."

Malone wasn't charged because Deputy Commissioner Cohan is his rabbi. Every up-and-coming police officer has a rabbi. My father was Jerry Carlucci's rabbi. Jerry Carlucci was Denny Coughlin's rabbi. Denny Coughlin, it is said, is my rabbi. Even Officer Matthew M. Payne has a rabbi, I have lately come to realize—me.

The function of a rabbi is to select a young officer and guide him through the mine fields of police department politics, try to see that he is given assignments that will broaden his areas of expertise and enhance his chances of promotion. And, of course, when he gets in trouble, to try not only to fix it, so he doesn't get kicked off the cops, but to try to insure that he won't do what he did again.

"He was lucky to have you as a friend," Wohl said.

"He's a good man," Cohan said. "And a good cop."

"Yes, sir, I think so."

"I had him assigned to Major Crimes Division, to the Auto Squad," Cohan said. "And I arranged for him to stay there after he made lieutenant. All this took place, you understand, right around the time they were making up the lieutenant's list. If there had been an Internal Affairs report—"

"I understand," Wohl said. "What's his status with his wife?"

"They were divorced. I was a little slow on that one, Peter. A little naive. I thought the lawyer had gone along with withdrawing the assault charges because he was either ashamed of what he had done, didn't want the story repeated around the courtrooms, and/or didn't want to have any scandal floating around Mrs. Malone, who he intended to marry."

"But?"

"It would not have solved his purpose to have Jack locked up or even fired. That might have tended to make the judge feel a little sympathetic toward Jack when he got him in court and showed the judge the color photos of Mrs. Malone's swollen, black-and-blue face. And, Jesus, tell it all, the bruises on her chest and ass. Jack literally kicked her ass all over the house."

"Oh, Christ! Who was the judge?"

"Seymour F. Marshutz," Cohan said. "Marshutz cannot conceive of a situation—don't misunderstand me, I'm not defending what Jack did, not for a minute—where slapping a wife around is not right up there with child molesting. I tried to talk to him, I've known Sy Marshutz for years, and got absolutely nowhere."

"And?"

"She got everything, of course. The only reason he didn't give her alimony is because we don't have alimony in Pennsylvania, but he gave her everything else they owned but his clothes and an old junk car. Custody, of course, because the way Sy Marshutz sees it, while playing the whore is bad, it's not as bad as violence, and Jack has limited visitation privileges."

I wonder what I'm supposed to do with Lieutenant Jack Malone. That's obviously what this is about; this is not marital notes from all over.

"I had a long talk—lots of long talks—with Jack. I chewed his ass. I held his hand. For all I know, if Marilyn had done to me what his wife did to Jack, maybe I'd have taken a swing at her too. Anyway, I told him his life wasn't over, and that if I were him, I'd give everything I have to the job for a while, that thinking about what happened was only—you know what I mean, Peter."

"Yes, sir."

"So he took me literally. He's working all the time. He's got a room in a hotel, the St. Charles, on Arch at 19th?"

"Faded grandeur," Wohl said without thinking.

"Yeah," Cohan said. "Okay. Anyway. All he does is work and watch TV in the hotel room."

"No booze?"

"A little of that. We had a talk about that too. I think he's had more to drink in the last year than he's had up to now. That isn't a problem.''

''But there is one.''

''Yeah. Now he sees a car thief behind every bush.''

''I don't follow you, sir.''

''All work and no play hasn't made Jack a dull boy, Peter,'' Cohan said solemnly, ''it's put his imagination in high gear, out of control.''

''Is this any of my business, sir?''

''He thinks Bob Holland is a car thief.''

Bob Holland was Holland Cadillac Motor Cars. And Bob Holland Chevrolet. And Holland Pontiac-GMC. And there was a strong rumor going around that Broad Street Ford and Jenkintown Chrysler-Plymouth were really owned by Robert L. Holland.

''Is he?''

''Come on, Peter,'' Cohan said. ''You're not talking about some sleaze-ball used car dealer here.''

''I gather Jack has nothing but a hunch to go on?''

''He went to Charley Gaft and asked for permission to surveil all of Holland's showrooms,'' Cohan said. ''And when Gaft turned him down, he came to me. Ten minutes after Bob called me and told me he was worried about him.''

Captain Charles B. Gaft commanded the Major Crimes Division.

''I'm afraid to ask what all this has to do with me, Commissioner. What do you want me to do, have Highway Patrol keep an eye on Bob Holland's showrooms? Or sit on Jack Malone?''

''Peter,'' Cohan said, almost sadly, ''your mouth has a tendency to run away with itself. It's only because I've known you, literally, since you wore short pants and because I know what a good police officer you are that I don't take offense. But there are those—people of growing importance to you, now that you're moving up—who would think that was just a flippant remark and unbecoming to a division commander.''

Oh, shit!

''Commissioner, it was flippant, and I apologize. I have no excuse to offer except the champagne.''

''Now, I already said, I understand your sense of humor, Peter. But maybe you'd better watch that champagne. It sneaks up on you.''

"Yes, sir. But I do apologize."

"It never happened. Getting back to Jack. He's under a strain. He's working too hard. But he's a fine police officer and worth saving, and that's why I'm asking you for your help."

I'll be a sonofabitch. He rehearsed that little speech. That's what he planned to say to me to see if I would stand still for whatever he wants. It was supposed to be delivered before he went to see Czernich and Carlucci.

"Whatever I can do, Commissioner."

I say nobly, aware that I have absolutely no option to do or say anything else.

"I knew I could count on you, Peter. What I'm going to do is send Jack over to you—"

Shit! But what else did I expect?

"—and have Tony Lucci transferred to Jack's job on the Auto Squad in Major Crimes."

Lieutenant Anthony J. Lucci, who had been Mayor Carlucci's driver as a sergeant, had been sent to Special Operations on his promotion to lieutenant. It was a reward for a job well done, which by possibly innocent coincidence gave His Honor the Mayor a window on the inner workings of Special Operations, reports delivered daily.

Every black cloud has a silver lining. I get rid of Lucci. What's that going to cost me? Is he telling the truth about Malone not having a bottle problem, or am I going to have to nurse a drunk?

"Now, I have no intention of trying to tell you how to run your division, Peter, or what to do with Jack Malone when you get him—"

But?

"—but if you could find something constructive for him to do that would keep him from thinking he's been assigned to the rubber-gun squad, I would be personally grateful."

"So far as I'm concerned, Commissioner, even after what you've told me, Jack Malone is a good cop, and I'll find something worthwhile for him to do."

"What was Lucci doing?"

"He's my administrative officer. He also makes sure the mayor knows what's going on."

Cohan looked sharply at Wohl, pursed his lips thoughtfully for a moment, and then said, "So I've heard. Jack won't feel any obligation to do that, Peter."

"Thank you, sir."

"Your father is in good spirits, isn't he?" Cohan said. "I had a pleasant chat with him a couple of minutes ago."

Our little chat is apparently over.

"I think he'd go back on the job tomorrow, if someone asked him."

"The grass is not as green as it looked?"

"I think he's bored, sir."

"He was active all his life," Cohan said. "That's understandable."

Cohan pushed himself out of the seat and extended his hand.

"Thank you, Peter," he said. "I knew I could count on you."

"Anytime, Commissioner."

GENERAL: 0565 01/02/74 FROM COMMISSIONER PAGE 1

of 1

************ CITY OF PHILADELPHIA ***********

************ POLICE DEPARTMENT ***********

TRANSFERS:

EFFECTIVE 1201 AM JANUARY 3, 1974

LIEUTENANT ANTHONY S. LUCCI: REASSIGNED FROM SPECIAL OPERATIONS DIVISION TO MAJOR CRIMES DIVISION AS COMMANDING OFFICER AUTO SQUAD.

LIEUTENANT JOHN J. MALONE: REASSIGNED FROM AUTO SQUAD, MAJOR CRIMES DIVISION TO SPECIAL OPERATIONS DIVISION.

TADDEUS CZERNICH

POLICE COMMISSIONER

TWO

The day began for Police Officer Charles McFadden at five minutes before six A.M. when Mrs. Agnes McFadden, his mother, went into his bedroom, on the second floor of a row house on Fitzgerald Street, near Methodist Hospital in South Philadelphia, snapped on the lights, walked to his bed, and rather loudly announced, "Almost six. Rise and shine, Charley."

Officer McFadden, who the previous Tuesday had celebrated his twenty-third birthday, was large-boned and broad-shouldered and weighed 214 pounds.

He rolled over on his back, shielded his eyes from the light, and replied, "Jesus, already?"

"Watch your mouth, mister," his mother said sharply, and then added, "if you didn't keep that poor girl out until all hours, you just might not have such trouble getting up in the morning."

With a visible effort Charley McFadden hauled himself into a sitting position and swung his feet out of bed and onto the floor.

"Mom, Margaret didn't get *off work* until half past ten."

"Then you should have brought her straight home, instead of keeping her up all night," Mrs. McFadden said, and then marched out of the room.

Margaret McCarthy, R.N., a slight, blue-eyed, redheaded young woman, was the niece of Bob and Patricia McCarthy, who lived across Fitzgerald Street and had been in the neighborhood, and good friends, just about as long as the McFaddens, and that meant even before Charley had been born.

Margaret and Charley had known each other as kids, before her parents had moved to Baltimore, and Agnes remembered seeing her after that, on holidays and whenever else her family had visited, but she and Charley had met again only a couple of months ago.

Margaret had gone through the Nurse Training Program and gotten her R.N. at Johns Hopkins Hospital in Baltimore, and now she was enrolled at Temple University to get a college degree.

As smart as Margaret was, Agnes McFadden wouldn't have been at all surprised if she wound up as a doctor.

Anyway, Charley and Margaret had bumped into each other and started going out, and there was no question in Agnes's mind that it was only a matter of time until Charley popped the question. She wouldn't have been surprised if they were waiting for one of two things, Margaret finishing her first year at Temple, or Charley taking the examination for detective. Or maybe both.

Agnes and Rudy McFadden approved of the match. She wasn't sure that the McCarthys were all that enthusiastic. Bob McCarthy was the sort of man who held a grudge, and Agnes thought he was still sore at Charley for taking out the windshield of his brand-new Ford with a golf ball, playing stickball in the street, when Charley was still a kid.

And Agnes knew full well all the nasty things Bob McCarthy had had to say about Charley when Charley had first gone on the cops and they'd made him work with the drug people.

The truth was, Agnes realized, that Charley did look and act like a bum when that was going on. He wore a beard and filthy, dirty clothes, and he was out all night, every night, and he'd hardly ever gone to church.

Anybody but Bob McCarthy, Agnes often thought, would have put that all behind him, and maybe even apologized, after

Charley had caught the drug addict who had shot Captain Moffitt, and gotten a citation from Police Commissioner Czernich himself, and they'd let him wear a uniform like a regular cop. But people like Bob McCarthy, Agnes understood, found it very hard to admit they were wrong.

Charley McFadden took a quick shower and shave and splashed himself liberally with Bahama Lime aftershave, a bottle of which had been Margaret's birthday gift to him.

He put on fresh underwear, went to the head of the stairs, and called down, "Don't make no breakfast, Mom. We're going out."

"I already made it," she said. "Why don't you bring her over here? There's more than enough."

"We're meeting some people," Charley replied.

That was not true. But he wanted to have breakfast with Margaret alone, not with his mother hanging over her shoulder.

There was a snort of derision from the kitchen.

Charley went into his room and put on his uniform. There was a blue shirt and a black necktie (a pretied tie that clipped on; regular ties that went around the neck could be grabbed), breeches, motorcycle boots, a leather jacket, a Sam Browne belt from which were suspended a holster for the service revolver, a handcuff case, and an attachment that held a nightstick. Finally, bending his knees to get a good look at himself in the mirror over his chest of drawers, Charley put squarely in place on his head a leather-brimmed cap. There was no crown stiffener.

This was the uniform of the Highway Patrol, which differed considerably from the uniform of ordinary police officers. They wore trousers and shoes, for example, not breeches and boots, and the crowns of their brimmed caps were stiffly erect.

Highway Patrol was considered, especially by members of the Highway Patrol, as the elite unit of the Philadelphia Police Department.

In the ordinary course of events, a rookie cop such as Officer McFadden (who had been a policeman not yet two years) would be either walking a footbeat or working a van in a district, hauling sick fat ladies down stairwells for transport to a hospital, or prisoners between where they were arrested and the district holding cell and between there and the Central Cell Room in the Roundhouse. He would not ordinarily be trusted to ride around in a district radio patrol car. He would be working under close supervision, learning the policeman's profession. The one thing a rookie cop would almost certainly not be doing would be putting on a Highway Patrolman's distinctive uniform.

But two extraordinary things had happened to Officer Charles McFadden in his short police career. The first had been his assignment, right from the Academy, to the Narcotics Bureau.

Narcotics had learned that one of the more effective—perhaps the most effective—means to deal with people who trafficked in proscribed drugs was to infiltrate, so to speak, the drug culture.

This could not be accomplished, Narcotics had learned, by simply putting Narcotics Division police officers in plainclothes and sending them out onto the streets. The faces of Narcotics Division officers were known to the drug people. And bringing in officers from districts far from the major areas of drug activity and putting them in plainclothes didn't work either. Even if the vendors of controlled substances did not recognize the face of an individual police officer, they seemed to be able to "make him" by observing the subtle mannerisms of dress, behavior, or speech that, apparently, almost all policemen with a couple of years on the job seem to manifest.

There was only one solution, and somewhat reluctantly Narcotics turned to it. One or two young, brand-new police officers were selected from each class at the Police Academy and asked to volunteer for a plainclothes and/or undercover assignment with Narcotics.

A cop with a week on the job (or, less often, just graduated-from-the-Academy rookie) was not going to be recognized on the street because he had not been on the street. Nor had he been a cop long enough to acquire a cop's mannerisms.

Few rookies, whose notions of police work were mostly acquired from television and the movies, refused such an opportunity to battle crime. When asked, Officer Charley McFadden had accepted immediately.

Some, perhaps even most, such volunteers don't work out when they actually go on the streets. The tension is too much for some. Others simply cannot physically stomach what they see in the course of their duties, and some just prove inept. They are then, if they hadn't graduated from the Academy, sent back to finish their training, or, if they have graduated, sent to a district.

Charley McFadden proved to be the exception. He was a good undercover Narc virtually from almost the first day, and got even better at it with experience, and after he had grown a beard, and come to look, in his mother's description, "like a filthy bum."

After three months on the job, he was paired with Officer Jesus Martinez, a slight, intense Latino who had been on the job for six months longer than Charley, and had learned the mannerisms of a successful middle-level drug dealer to near perfection.

They were an odd couple, the extra large Irishman and the barely over the height and weight minimums Latino. Behind their backs, they were known by their brother Narcotics Bureau officers as Mutt & Jeff, after the cartoon characters.

But they were good at what they did, and not only their peers understood this. Their lieutenant at the time, Dave Pekach, led them to believe that if they kept up the good work, he would do his very best to keep them in Narcotics even when their identities had become known on the street.

That was important. They didn't tell the rookies at the time they were recruited, but what usually happened when undercover Narcs became, inevitably, known on the street was that they were reassigned to a district. There, they picked up their police career where it had been interrupted. That is to say they now got to work a wagon and haul sick fat ladies down narrow stairways and prisoners down to Central Cell Room.

The way to become a detective in the Philadelphia Police Department was not the way it was in the movies, where a smiling police commissioner handed a detective's badge to the undercover rookie who had just made a really good arrest. In Philadelphia, it doesn't matter if you catch Jack the Ripper with the knife in his hand, you wait until you have two years on the job, and then you take the examination for detective, and if you pass, when your number comes up, then, and only then, you get to be a detective.

What Lieutenant Dave Pekach had offered them, instead of being sent to some damned district to work school crossings and turn off fire hydrants, was a chance to stay in Narcotics as plainclothes officers until they had their time in to take the detective exam.

Charley and Jesus would have killed to convince Lieutenant Pekach what good undercover Narcs they were, what good plainclothes cops they could be, if that would keep them from going out to some damned district in uniform.

And it almost came to that.

Captain Richard F. Moffitt, off duty and in civilian clothing, had walked in on a robbery in progress in a diner on Roosevelt Boulevard.

The doer, to Captain Moffitt's experienced eye, was a strung-out junkie, a poor, skinny, dirty Irish kid who had somehow got hooked on the shit and was, with a thirty-dollar Saturday Night Special .22 revolver, trying to score enough money for a hit, or something to eat, or probably both.

"I'm a police officer," Captain Moffitt said gently. "Put the gun down, son, before somebody gets hurt."

The doer, subsequently identified as a poor, skinny Irish kid who had somehow gotten hooked on a pharmacist's encyclopedia of controlled substances, and whose name was Gerald Vincent Gallagher, fired every .22 Long Rifle cartridge his pistol held at Captain Moffitt, and managed to hit him once.

That was enough. The bullet ruptured an artery, and Captain Richard F. Moffitt died a minute or so later, slumped against the wall of the diner.

The killing of any cop triggers a deep emotional response in every other policeman. And "Dutch" Moffitt was not an ordinary cop. He was a captain. He was the son of a cop. His brother had been a cop, and it was immediately recalled that the brother, a sergeant, had been shot to death while answering a silent alarm.

And Captain Dutch Moffitt had been the commanding officer of Highway Patrol. Highway Patrol had been organized years before to do what its name implied. The first Highway Patrolmen had patrolled the highways throughout the city on motorcycles. The breeches, boots, and leather jackets of Highway Patrol motorcylists were still worn, although radio patrol cars now outnumbered motorcycles.

Highway Patrol had become, beginning with the reign of Captain Jerry Carlucci (and later with the blessing of Inspector Carlucci, and Chief Inspector Carlucci, and Deputy Commissioner Carlucci, and Commissioner Carlucci, and now Mayor Carlucci), a special force.

Although the Philadelphia *Ledger*, which did not approve of much that Mayor Carlucci did, was prone to refer to the Highway Patrol as "Carlucci's Commandos" and even as his "Jackbooted Gestapo,'' just about everyone else in Philadelphia recognized Highway Patrol and its officers, who rode two men to an RPC, and who did most of their patrolling in high-crime areas of the city, as something special.

Getting into Highway was difficult. As a general rule of thumb, an officer had to have four or five years, good years, on the job. It helped to be about six feet and at least 175 pounds, and it helped if you had come to the attention of someone who was (or had been) a Highway supervisor—that is, a sergeant or better—and he had decided that you were a better cop than most. An assignment to Highway was seen by many as a good step to take if you wanted to rise above sergeant elsewhere in the Police Department.

Every police officer in Philadelphia reacted emotionally to the murder of Captain Dutch Moffitt—*If the bad guys can get away with shooting a cop, what's next?*—but it was taken as a personal affront by every man in Highway.

The result was that eight thousand police officers, most especially including every member of the Highway Patrol, were searching for Gerald Vincent Gallagher.

He was found by two rookie cops, working undercover in Narcotics, whose names were Charley McFadden and Jesus Martinez. And it wasn't a question of just stumbling onto the dirty little scumbag, either. On their own time, not even getting overtime, they had staked out Pratt Street Terminal, where Charley McFadden had an idea the miserable pissant would eventually show up.

And he had, and Charley and Jesus had chased the scumbag down the elevated tracks until Charles Vincent Gallagher had slipped, fallen onto the third rail, fried himself, and then been cut into many pieces under the wheels of a train.

Once they'd gotten their pictures in the newspaper, of course, Jesus's and Charley's effectiveness as undercover Narcs came to an end. And at a very awkward time for them, as Lieutenant David Pekach, having been promoted to captain, had been transferred out of Narcotics, and his replacement, a real shit heel, in their judgment, immediately made it clear that he felt no obligation to honor Lieutenant Pekach's implied promise to keep them in Narcotics in plainclothes if they did a good job on the job.

They had, however, also come to the attention of Chief Inspector Dennis V. Coughlin, who was arguably the most influential of the seven chief inspectors in the Department. Denny Coughlin saw in Charley McFadden something of himself. In other words, a good, hardworking Irish Catholic lad from South Philadelphia who was obviously destined to be a better than average cop. And Coughlin knew that once a rookie had worked the streets undercover, he regarded being put back in uniform as a demotion.

So he arranged for Officer McFadden to be assigned, temporarily, to the 12th District, in plainclothes, to work on an auto burglary detail. Chief Coughlin felt no such kinship for Officer Martinez—for one thing, the little Mexican didn't look big enough to be a real cop, and for another, Coughlin was made vaguely uneasy by someone who had the same name as the Son of God himself—but fair was fair, and he arranged for Jesus Martinez to be similarly assigned.

Then when Mayor Carlucci had set up Special Operations and given it to Peter Wohl, the problem of what to do with McFadden and Martinez was, as far as Denny Coughlin was concerned, solved. He sent them over to Special Operations. Peter Wohl was a smart cop; he'd figure out something useful for them to do.

The subordination of Highway Patrol to the new Special Operations Division had been regarded by many, most, Highway guys as bullshit. It was wondered, aloud, why the mayor, who *was* a real Highway guy, had let the commissioner get away with it.

Giving command of Special Operations (and thus, Highway) to Staff Inspector Peter Wohl made it even worse. Everybody knew what staff inspectors did. Not that locking up judges and city commissioners and other big shots like that on the take wasn't important, but it wasn't the same thing as being out on the street, one-on-one, with the worst scumbags in Philadelphia.

Wohl seemed to prove what a Roundhouse asshole he was when he was reliably quoted as saying that anyone who willingly got on a motorcycle wasn't playing with a full deck. Every Highway Patrolman had to go through extensive motorcycle training ("Wheel School") and prove he could really ride a motorcycle, and they didn't like some Roundhouse politically savvy supercop making fun of that.

That was all bad enough, but what really pissed people off, the straw that broke the fucking camel's back, so to speak, was

Wohl's probationary Highway Patrolman idea. Wohl said that he would approve the transfer into Highway of outstanding young cops who didn't have four or five years on the job. He would put them to work under a Highway supervisor for six months. At any time during the six months, the supervisor could recommend, in writing, that the rookie be transferred out of Highway. But he had to give his reasons. In other words, if the rookie didn't screw up, he was in. He would get himself sent to Wheel School and if he got through that, he could go buy himself a pair of boots, breeches, and a crushed-crown brimmed cap.

The first two probationary Highway Patrolmen were Officers Jesus Martinez and Charles McFadden.

Officer Charley McFadden pulled open the top left-hand drawer of his dresser and took his Smith & Wesson Military & Police .38 Special caliber service revolver from under a pile of Jockey shorts and slipped it into his holster.

Then he went down the stairs two at a time.

"See you later, Mom!" he called at the bottom.

"Ask Margaret if she'd like to come to supper," Agnes McFadden said. "If you can spare the time for your mother."

"I'll ask," Charley said, and went out the door.

He ran across Fitzgerald Street, down two houses, and up the steps to the porch. The door opened as he got there.

Margaret was wearing her nurse suit. Sometimes she did, and sometimes she didn't. Charley wasn't sure exactly how that worked, but he did know that she was a real knockout in her starched white uniform. Not that she wasn't in regular clothes too, of course. But there was something about that white uniform that turned Charley on.

"Hi!" she said.

"Hi!"

She stood on her toes and kissed him. Chastely, but on the lips.

She had an armful of books.

"How come the books?"

"Classes in the morning," she said. "Then I agreed to fill in at the emergency room from one to seven."

"I get off at four," he said, disappointed.

"I need the money," she said, and then corrected herself. "*We* need the money. And I'm getting double-time."

They went down the stairs. Charley unlocked the door of his Volkswagen.

"Good morning, Margaret!" Agnes McFadden called from the white marble steps in front of her door.

"Morning, Mrs. McFadden."

"Why don't you come to supper?"

"I'd love to, but I can't. I'm working. Can I have a rain-check?"

"Yeah, sure."

Charley closed the door after her, and then went around the front and got behind the wheel.

"So what are you going to do today?"

"I got court," Charley replied. "Which means I get off at four."

"I told you, they're paying me double-time."

"How come?"

"Because it's less than twenty-four hours since my last over-time tour. I got overtime yesterday too."

"You're not getting enough sleep," Charley said.

"So tonight, after I meet you in the FOP at seven-fifteen, and we have dinner, I go to bed early."

The Fraternal Order of Police, on Spring Garden Street, was just a couple of minutes walk from Hahnemann Hospital on North Broad Street in downtown Philadelphia.

"Yeah," he said. "This isn't a hell of a lot of fun, is it?"

"Most people are broke when they get married, and have to go in debt. We won't be."

"To hell with it. Let's get married and go in debt."

She laughed and leaned over and kissed him again.

They had breakfast in the medical staff cafeteria at Temple Hospital. The food was good and reasonable and there was a place to park the Volkswagen. As long as she was wearing a nurse's uniform and her R.N. pin, she could eat there. When she was in regular clothes, for some reason, they wouldn't let her do that.

Charley sometimes felt a little uncomfortable when he was in his Highway uniform and they ate there. He had the feeling that some of the medical personnel had started believing the bullshit the Philadelphia *Ledger* had been printing about the cops generally, and Highway specifically. The *Ledger* had re-ally been on Highway's ass, with that "Carlucci's Commandos'' and "Gestapo" bullshit, so it wasn't really surprising. People believe what they read.

He thought that if he was really a Highway guy, maybe he wouldn't be so sensitive about it. Nobody in the world knew it but Margaret, but the truth was, he didn't like Highway. What he really wanted to be was a detective.

If I was in here in plainclothes, nobody would give me a second look; they would think I was a doctor, or a pill salesman, or something.

When they finished breakfast, Charley got in the Volkswagen and drove to Highway headquarters at Bustleton and Bowler Streets in Northeast Philadelphia.

There, he met his partner, Police Officer Gerald "Gerry" D. Quinn, who was thirty-three, had been on the job eleven years and in Highway for five years.

The very first day he and Quinn had gone on patrol together, they had stopped a '72 Buick for speeding. It had turned out to be stolen. The case was finally coming up for trial today.

They stood roll call, and then drew a car, Highway 22, a year-old Chevrolet with 97,000-odd miles on its odometer. If by some miracle the trial went off as scheduled, they could then go on patrol. They drove downtown to City Hall at the intersection of Broad and Market Streets and parked just outside the southeast corner entrance.

Just off the southeast stairwell is Court Attendance, an administrative unit of the Police Department, which tries to keep track of which police officer is to testify at what time in which courtroom. They checked in there, learned where they were supposed to go to testify, and then went to the stairwell itself, where a blind concessionaire brewed what most police agreed was the worst coffee in the Delaware River Basin. They shot the bull with other cops for a while, and then went upstairs to their courtroom to wait for their case to be called.

The day began for Staff Inspector Peter Frederick Wohl at about the same time, a few minutes before six, as it had for Officer Charles McFadden.

Wohl was wakened by the ringing of one of the two telephones on the bedside table in his bedroom in his apartment. His over-a-six-car-garage apartment had once been the chauffeur's quarters of a turn-of-the-century mansion on the 800

block of Norwood Street in Chestnut Hill. The mansion itself
had been divided into luxury apartments.

"Inspector Wohl," he said, somewhat formally. The phone
that had been ringing was the official phone, paid for by the
Police Department.

"Six o'clock, sir. Good morning."

It was the voice of the tour lieutenant at Bustleton and Bowler. The voice was familiar, and so was the face he could put
to it—that of a lieutenant newly assigned to Special Operations—but he could not come up with a name.

"Good morning," Wohl said, as cheerfully as he could
manage. "How goes the never-ending war against crime?"

The lieutenant chuckled.

"I don't know about that, sir. But I can report your car is
back from the garage. Shall I have someone run it over to
you?"

For the first time, Wohl remembered what had happened to
his car, an unmarked nearly brand-new Ford LTD four-door
sedan. The sonofabitch had just died on him. He had been
stopped by the red light at Mount Airy and Germantown Avenue on the way home from Commissioner Czernich's soiree,
and when the light changed, the Ford had moved fifteen feet
forward and lurched to a stop.

When he tried to start it, the only thing that happened was
the lights dimmed. The radio still worked, happily. He had
called for a police tow truck, and then asked Police Radio to
have the nearest Highway or Special Operations car meet him.

By the time the tow truck reached him, a Highway RPC, a
Highway sergeant, and the Special Operations/Highway lieutenant were already there. The lieutenant had driven him home.

Wohl sat up and swung his feet out of bed, hoping to clear
his brain.

"Let me think," he said.

If they sent somebody over with his car, it would be someone who should be out on the street, or someone who was
going off-duty, and thus should not be doing a white shirt a
favor.

On the other hand, he was reluctant to drive his personal car
over to Bustleton and Bowler for a number of reasons, not the
least of which was that it might get "accidentally" bumped by
a Highway Patrolman who believed Peter Wohl to be the devil
reincarnate.

Peter Wohl's personal automobile was a twenty-three-year-old Jaguar XK-120 drophead roadster. He had spent four years and more money than he liked to think about rebuilding it from the frame up.

And even if I did drive it over there, he finally decided, *when the day is over I will be back on square one, since I obviously cannot drive both the Jag and the Department's Ford back here at the same time*.

"Let me call you if I need a ride, Lieutenant," Wohl said. "If you don't hear from me, just forget it."

"Yes, sir. I'll be here."

Wohl hung up the official telephone and picked up the one he paid for and dialed a number from memory.

"Hello."

"Peter Wohl, Matt. Did I wake you?"

"No, sir. I had to get out of bed to take a shower."

"You sound pretty chipper this morning, Officer Payne."

"We celibates always sleep, sir, with a clear conscience and wake up chipper."

Wohl chuckled, and then asked, "Have you had breakfast?"

"No, sir."

"I'll swap you a breakfast of your choice for a ride to work. The Ford broke last night. They fixed it and took it to Bustleton and Bowler."

"Thirty minutes?"

"Thank you, Matt. I hate to put you out."

"You *did* say, sir, *you* were buying breakfast?"

"Yes, I did."

"Thirty minutes, sir."

THREE

Officer Matthew M. Payne had just about finished dressing when Wohl called. Like Wohl, he was a bachelor. He lived in a very nice, if rather small, apartment on the top floor of a turn-of-the-century mansion on Rittenhouse Square. The lower floors of the building, owned by his father, now housed the Delaware Valley Cancer Society.

A tall, lithely muscled twenty-two-year-old, Payne had graduated the previous June from the University of Pennsylvania and had almost immediately joined the Police Department. He was assigned as "administrative assistant" to Inspector Wohl, who commanded the Special Operations Division of the Philadelphia Police Department. It was a plainclothes assignment.

He put the telephone back into its cradle and then walked to the fireplace, where he tied his necktie in the mirror over the mantel. He put his jacket on and then went back to the fireplace and took his Smith & Wesson "Undercover" .38 Special five-shot revolver and its ankle holster from the mantelpiece and strapped it to his ankle.

Then he left the apartment, went down the narrow stairs to

the fourth floor, and got on the elevator to the parking garage in the basement.

There he got into a new silver Porsche 911, his graduation present from his father, and drove out of the garage, waving at the Holmes Security Service rent-a-cop as he passed his glassed-in cubicle. For a long time the rent-a-cop, a retired Traffic Division corporal, was the only person in the building who knew that Payne was a policeman.

There had been a lot of guessing by the two dozen young women who worked for the Cancer Society about just who the good-looking young guy who lived in the attic apartment was. He had been reliably reported to be a stockbroker, a lawyer, in the advertising business, and several other things. No one had suggested that he might be a cop; cops are not expected to dress like an advertisement for Brooks Brothers or to drive new silver Porsche 911s.

But then Officer Payne had shot to death one Warren K. Fletcher, thirty-one, of a Germantown address, whom the newspapers had taken to calling "the Northwest serial rapist" and his photograph, with Mayor Jerry Carlucci's arm around him, had been on the front pages of all the newspapers, and his secret was out.

He was not an overly egotistical young man, but it seemed to him that after the shooting, the looks of invitation in the eyes of the Cancer Society's maidens had seemed to intensify.

There were two or three of them he thought he would like to get to know, in the biblical sense, but he had painful proof when he was at the University of Pennsylvania that *"hell hath no fury like a woman scorned"* was more than a cleverly turned phrase. A woman scorned who worked where he lived, he had concluded, was too much of a risk to take.

Matt Payne drove to Peter Wohl's apartment via the Schuylkill Expressway, not recklessly, but well over the speed limit. He was aware that he was in little danger of being stopped (much less cited) for speeding. The Schuylkill Expressway was patrolled by officers of the Highway Patrol, all of whom were aware that Inspector Wohl's administrative assistant drove a silver Porsche 911.

Wohl was waiting for him when Payne arrived, leaning against one of the garage doors.

"Funny, you don't look celibate," Wohl said as he got in the car.

"Good morning, sir."

"Let's go somewhere nice, Matt. I know I'm buying, but the condemned man is entitled to a hearty meal."

"I don't think I like the sound of that," Matt replied.

"Not you, me. Condemned, I mean. They want me in the commissioner's office at ten. I'm sure what he wants to know is how the Magnella job is going."

Officer Joseph Magnella, twenty-four, had been found lying in the gutter beside his 22nd District RPC (radio patrol car) with seven .22 bullets in his body. Mayor Carlucci had given the job to Special Operations. A massive effort, led by two of the best detectives in the department, to find the doers had so far come up with nothing.

"Nothing came up overnight?" Matt asked softly.

"Not a goddamned clue, to coin a phrase," Wohl said bitterly. "I told them to call me if anything at all came up. Nobody called."

Payne braked before turning onto Norwood Street.

"How about The Country Club?" he asked.

The Country Club was a diner with a reputation for good food on Cottman Avenue in the Northeast, along their route to Bustleton and Bowler.

"Fine," Wohl said.

Wohl bought a copy of the *Ledger* from a vending machine as they walked into the restaurant, glanced at the headlines, and then flipped through it until he found what he was looking for.

"Somewhat self-righteously," he said, handing the paper to Matt, "the *Ledger* comments editorially on the incompetence of the Police Department, vis-à-vis the murder of Officer Magnella."

The waitress appeared and handed them menus.

"Breakfast steak, pink in the middle, two fried eggs, sunny side up, home fries, an English muffin, orange juice, milk, and coffee," Payne ordered without looking at the menu.

"If you're what you say you are, where do you get the appetite?" Wohl said, and added, "Toast and coffee, please."

"I have high hopes," Payne replied. "You have to eat, Inspector."

"Who do you think you are, my mother?"

"Think of the starving children in India," Payne said. "How *they* would love a breakfast steak."

"Oh, Jesus," Wohl groaned, but after a moment added, "Okay. Do that twice, please, miss."

Payne read the editorial and handed the newspaper back.

"You didn't expect anything else, did you?" Payne asked.

"I can ignore those bastards when they're wrong. But it smarts when they're right."

"Harris and Washington will come up with something."

"He said, not really believing it."

"I believe it."

"As a matter of fact, the longer they don't come up with something, the greater the odds are that they won't," Wohl said.

The waitress delivered the coffee, milk, and orange juice, sparing Payne having to respond. He was grateful; he hated to sound like a cheerleader.

Wohl ate everything put before him, but absently. He volunteered no further conversation, and Payne decided he should keep his mouth shut.

They were halfway between The Country Club and Special Operations headquarters when Wohl decided to tell Payne about Lieutenant Jack Malone.

"We're getting a new lieutenant this morning," he said. "And Lucci's being transferred out."

"That sounds like bad news-good news."

"Lieutenant Malone used to be Commissioner Cohan's driver. Cohan is behind the transfer."

"Then it's good news-good news?"

"Not necessarily," Wohl said. "Cohan sprung this on me at Commissioner Czernich's reception. Malone's had some personal problems, and in a manner of speaking has been working too hard. Cohan wants to take some of the pressure off him. He's had the Auto Squad in Major Crimes; that's where Lucci's going. It's a good job. Cohan's afraid that Malone will think he's been shanghaied to us. Which means that I have—"

"Has he?" Payne interrupted. "Been shanghaied to us?"

"I used the wrong word. *Punished* would be better. He's been shanghaied in the sense that he didn't ask for the transfer, and probably doesn't like the idea, but I'm not really sure if he just needs some of the pressure taken off, or whether Cohan is sending him a message. Cohan made it plain that he expects me to put him to work doing something worthy of his talent."

"What did he do?" Payne asked.

Why the hell did I tell him any of this in the first place?

"He caught his wife in bed with a lawyer and beat them up."

"Both of them?"

"Yeah, both of them. But that's not why he's being sent to us, I don't think. The pressure began to affect his work."

"I don't think I understand."

And aside from that, the problems, personal or professional, of a lieutenant are really none of the business of a police officer. But I started this, didn't I? And Payne is really more than a run-of-the-mill young cop, isn't he?

"He's got a wild idea that Bob Holland is involved in auto theft," Wohl said.

"Holland Cadillac?" Matt asked, a hint of incredulity in his voice.

"Yeah."

"Is he?"

"I don't know. It strikes me as damned unlikely. If I had to bet, I'd say no. Why should he be? He's got a dealership on every other corner in Philadelphia. Presumably, they're making money. He sold the city the mayor's limousine. Hell, my father bought his Buick from him; he gives a police discount, whatever the hell that is. And Commissioner Cohan obviously doesn't think so; he thinks that the pressure got to Malone and his imagination ran away with him."

"He was at the club yesterday. I saw him in the bar with that congressman I think is light on his feet."

"Holland?" Wohl asked, and when Payne nodded, he went on, "Which club was that?"

"We played at Whitemarsh Valley."

"So Holland has friends in high places, right? Is that what you're driving at?"

"It would explain why the commissioner wants him out of the Auto Squad."

"Yeah," Wohl agreed a moment later. "Well, if Holland is doing hot cars, that's now Lucci's concern, not Malone's."

And I will make sure that Lieutenant Jack Malone clearly understands that.

"What are you going to do with him?" Payne asked.

"We now have a plans and training officer," Wohl said. "His name is Lieutenant John J. Malone."

"What's he going to do?"

"I haven't figured that out yet," Wohl said.

When Payne pulled into the parking lot, it was half past seven. The cars of Captain Mike Sabara, Wohl's deputy, and Captain Dave Pekach, the commanding officer of Highway Patrol, were already there. Payne wondered if Wohl had sent for them—the normal duty day began at eight—or whether they had come in early on their own.

Once inside the building, Wohl, Sabara, and Pekach went into Wohl's office and closed the door. Payne understood that his presence was not desired.

He told the sergeant on the desk that if the inspector was looking for him, he had gone to park his car and to get the inspector's car.

When he came back and sat down at his desk, Wohl's phone began to ring.

"Inspector Wohl's office, Officer Payne."

"My name is Special Agent Davis of the FBI," the caller said. "Inspector Wohl, please."

"I'm sorry, sir, the inspector is tied up. May I have him call you back?"

"I wonder if you would please tell him that Special Agent in Charge Davis wants just a moment of time, and see if he'll speak to me?"

There was a tone of authority in Davis's voice that got through to Matt.

"Hold on, please, sir," he said, and walked to the closed door. He knocked and then, without waiting, opened it.

"Sir, there's a Special Agent Davis—'Special Agent in Charge' is actually what he said—on twenty-nine. He said he wants 'just a moment of your time.' You want to talk to him?"

"For your general information, Officer Payne, Special Agent in Charge Davis is the high priest of the FBI in Philadelphia," Wohl said. "Yes, of course, I'll talk to him." He picked up the telephone, pushed one of the buttons on it, and said, "Hello, Walter. How are you?"

Payne closed the door and went back to his desk.

When he got out of bed, at quarter past seven, John J. "Jack" Malone almost immediately learned that among a large number of other things that had gone wrong recently in his life he could now count the plumbing system of the St. Charles Hotel, where he resided. Specifically, both the hot and cold taps in his bathroom ran ice-cold.

While he fully understood that the St. Charles was not in the league of the Bellevue-Stratford or the Warwick, neither was it a flea bag, and considering what they were charging him for his "suite" (a bedroom, a tiny sitting room, and an alcove containing a small refrigerator, a two-burner electric stove, and a small table), it seemed to him that the least the bastards could do was make sure the hot water worked.

There was no question that it was not working. That, until he just now had been desperately hoping, it was not just the time required to get hot water up from the basement heater to the tenth floor. The damned water had been running full blast for five minutes and it was just as ice-cold now as it had been when he first turned it on.

A shower, under the circumstances, was clearly out of the question. Shaving was going to be bad enough (he had a beard that, even with a hot-towel preshave soak, wore out a blade every time he sawed it off); he was not going to stand under a torrent of ice water.

At least, he consoled himself, he had nobly kept John Jameson in his bottle last night. He had not so much as sniffed a cork for forty-eight hours, so he would not reek of old booze when he presented himself to Staff Inspector Peter Wohl and announced he was reporting for duty. All he would smell of was twenty-four hours worth of flaking skin plus more than a little nervous sweat. It was possible that a liberal sprinkling of cologne would mask that.

Possible or not, that was his only choice.

He had slept in his underwear, so he took that off, rubbed his underarms briskly with a stiff towel, and then patted himself there and elsewhere with cologne. The cologne, he was painfully aware, had been Little Jack's birthday gift to Daddy. Little Jack was nine, Daddy, thirty-four.

Three weeks before, the Honorable Seymour F. Marshutz of the Family Court had awarded Daddy very limited rights of visitation (one weekend a month, plus no more than three lunch or supper visits per month, with the understanding that Jack would give Mrs. Malone at least three hours notice, preferably longer, of his intention to exercise the lunch/supper privilege) in which to be Daddy.

He tore brown paper from around three bundles from the

laundry before he found the one with underwear in it, and then put on a T-shirt and boxer shorts. Then he went to the closet for a uniform.

The uniform was new. The last time he'd worn a uniform, he had been a cop in the 13th District. He'd worn plainclothes as a detective in South Detectives, and then when he'd made sergeant, he'd been assigned as driver to Chief Inspector Francis J. Cohan, another plainclothes assignment. When Chief Cohan had been made deputy commissioner-Operations, as sort of a reward for a job well done, Cohan had arranged for Jack Malone to be assigned to the Major Crimes Division, still in plainclothes. When he'd made lieutenant, four months before, he had gone out and bought a new uniform, knowing that sooner or later, he would need one. As commanding officer of the Auto Squad, it was up to him whether or not to wear a uniform; he had elected not to.

Sooner had come much quicker than he expected. Captain Charley Gaft, who commanded Major Crimes, had called him up yesterday and told him he was being transferred, immediately, to Special Operations, and suggested he use the holiday to clean out his desk in Major Crimes.

"Can I ask why?"

"Career enhancement," Captain Gaft replied, after a just barely perceptible hesitation.

That was so much bullshit.

"I see."

There had been a tone in his voice that Captain Gaft had picked up on.

"It could be a number of things," Gaft offered.

"Sir?"

"You know Tony Lucci?" Gaft asked.

"Yes, sir."

Tony Lucci, as a sergeant, had been Mayor Jerry Carlucci's driver. When he had made lieutenant (four places under Jack Malone on the list), he had been assigned to Special Operations. The word was that he was the mayor's spy in Special Operations.

"He's taking over for you here, and you're replacing him at Bustleton and Bowler. I was told about both transfers, not asked, but it seems possible to me that the mayor may have been interested in seeing that Tony got an assignment that would enhance his career."

"Oh, it was *his* career enhancement you were talking about?"

"Maybe Lucci knows when it's best to back off, Jack."

"Are we talking about Holland here?"

"I'm not. I don't know about you."

Malone did not reply.

"You're being *transferred*, Jack," Captain Gaft went on. "You want a little advice, leave it at that. Maybe it was time. Sometimes people, especially people with personal problems, get too tied up with the job. That sometimes gets people in trouble. That didn't happen to you. Maybe if you weren't being transferred, it would have. Am I getting through to you?"

"Yes, sir."

He's really a good guy. What I really did was go over his head. If you go over a captain's head, even if you're right, you'd better expect trouble. I went over his head, and nobody thinks I'm right, and it could be a lot worse. There are a lot of assignments for a lieutenant a lot worse than Lucci's old job in Special Operations—whatever Lucci's job was.

Gaft didn't stick it in me, although everybody would have understood it if he had. Or Cohan took care of me again. Or both. More than likely, both. But there is sort of a "this is your last chance, Malone, to straighten up and fly right" element in this transfer.

"You're expected at Bustleton and Bowler at eight-thirty. In uniform. Maybe it would be a good idea to clear out your desk here today. Any loose ends we can worry about later."

"Yes, sir," Malone had said. "Captain, I enjoyed working for you."

"Most of the time, Jack, I enjoyed having you work for me. When you get settled out there with the hotshots, call me, and we'll have lunch or something."

"I'll do that, sir. Thank you."

"Good luck, Jack."

Malone had bought only one new uniform when he'd made lieutenant. There had not been, thanks to his lawyer's money-up-front business practice, enough money for more than one. Now he would need at least one—and preferably two—more. But that was his problem, not the Police Department's. He would just have to take the one he had to a two-hour dry cleaners, until, by temporarily giving up unimportant things, like eating, he could come up with the money to buy more. EZ-

Credit was something else that had gone with Mrs. John J. Malone.

Malone examined himself in the none-too-clear mirror on the chest of drawers. He did not especially like what he saw. Gone was the trim young cop, replaced by a lieutenant who looked like a lieutenant.

Chubby, Malone thought. *Hairline retreating. A little pouchy under the eyes. Is that the beginning of a jowl?*

He left his suite and walked down the narrow, dimly lit corridor to the elevator, which, after he pushed the button, announced its arrival with an alarming combination of screeches and groans.

He stopped by the desk, which was manned by a cadaverous white male in a soiled maroon sports coat.

"There's no hot water."

"I know, they're working on it," the desk clerk said, without raising his eyes from the Philadelphia *Daily News.*

"If it's not fixed by the time I get home from work, I'll blow up the building," Malone said.

The desk clerk raised his eyes from the *Daily News.*

"I didn't know you were a cop," he said.

"Now you do. Get the hot water fixed."

Malone found his car, on the roof of which someone had left two beer cans and the remains of a slice of pizza. It was a seven-year-old Ford Mustang. There had once been two cars registered in his name, the other a 1972 Ford station wagon. Ellen now had that.

I should have the station wagon. And I should have the house. She was the one fucking around. She should be living in that goddamned hotel and driving this piece of shit.

Look on the bright side. No alimony. And, what the hell, she needed something to carry Little Jack around in.

He knocked the beer cans and pizza off the roof and got in. He went east to North Broad Street, and then out North Broad to Roosevelt Boulevard. Eight blocks down Roosevelt Boulevard he made a lane change that did not meet the standards of a brother police officer.

There was the growl of a siren, and when he looked in the mirror, he saw a cop waving him over.

A Highway Patrol car. Only Highway RPCs had two cops in them.

He nodded his head to show that he understood the order, and as soon as he could safely do so pulled to the side.

The Highway Patrolman swaggered over to the Mustang, only at the last moment noticing that there was a gold bar on the epaulets of Malone's blue jacket.

"Good morning, sir," the Highway Patrolman said.

"Good morning."

"Lieutenant, your turn signal's inoperative. I thought you'd like to know."

"Yes. Thank you very much. I'll have it checked."

The Highway Patrolman saluted and walked back to his car.

Malone moved the turn signal lever.

The goddamn thing really is broken. Did I use the sonofabitch, and it didn't work, or was I just weaving through traffic in this rusty piece of shit, and he stopped me for that?

Moot point, Lieutenant. Either today, or tomorrow, or the day after that, one of those two guys is going to see me at Bustleton and Bowler, and I will become universally known as the New Lieutenant Who Drives Not Only Recklessly But in a Real Piece of Shit of an Ancient Mustang.

Malone hadn't been to Highway Patrol Headquarters, at Bustleton and Bowler Streets, not far from the North Philadelphia Airport, in a long time. It had been busy then, he remembered, because it shared the building with the headquarters of the 7th District, but it had been nothing like it was now.

There were the cars and vans of the 7th District; the cars and motorcycles of Highway Patrol; a flock of cars, marked and unmarked, that obviously belonged to Special Operations; and even a stakeout van. His hope of finding a parking space reserved for LIEUTENANTS or even OFFICIAL VISITORS had been wishful thinking. He had trouble just driving through the parking lot. The only empty space he saw was marked RESERVED FOR COMMISSIONER.

He drove around the block and tried again. This time a turnkey (an officer assigned to make himself useful in the parking lot) waved him down and pointed out a parking spot reserved for a sergeant.

It was crowded inside too, but finally he managed to give his name to a sergeant at a desk just inside a door marked HEADQUARTERS, SPECIAL OPERATIONS.

"Welcome to the circus, Lieutenant," the sergeant said. "I saw the teletype. The inspector's office is through that door."

On the other side of the door was a small room, barely large enough for the two desks it held back-to-back. One of them was not occupied. There was a sign on it, CAPTAIN MICHAEL J. SABARA.

There was a young plainclothes cop at the other one. When he saw Malone he stood up.

"Lieutenant Malone?"

"Right."

"The inspector's expecting you, sir. I'll see if he's free."

"Thank you."

The plainclothes cop stuck his head in an interior door, and Malone heard his name spoken.

Then the door opened and Staff Inspector Peter Wohl came out. Malone had seen him around before, but now he was surprised to see how young he was.

He's no older than I am. And not only a staff inspector, but a division commander. Is he really that good? Or is it pull?

"I'm Inspector Wohl, Lieutenant," Wohl said. "Now that I see you, I know we've met, but I can't remember where."

"Yes, sir."

"I hate to make you cool your heels, but I've got something that really won't wait. Officer Payne will get you a cup of coffee. Be careful he doesn't pour it in your lap."

"Yes, sir."

Payne? Oh, hell, yes! This is the kid who blew the brains out of the Northwest serial rapist.

Wohl disappeared behind his door again.

"How do you take your coffee, Lieutenant?"

"In a cup, please, if that's convenient," Malone said.

"Yes, sir," Payne said, chuckling.

"I don't know why I said that," Malone said. "I wasn't trying to be a smart-ass."

"I think you'll be right at home around here, Lieutenant," Payne said.

Payne went to a coffee machine sitting on top of a file cabinet and a moment later handed Malone a steaming china cup.

"There's sugar and what is euphemistically known as non-dairy creamer," he said.

"Black's fine," Malone said. "Thank you."

He remembered a story that had gone around the Department about the time Captain Dutch Moffitt had been shot, and Special Operations had been formed and given to Peter Wohl.

Dutch Moffitt's deputy had been a well-liked lieutenant named Mike Sabara. It was presumed that, after the scumbag killed Dutch, Mike Sabara would take over as Highway commander. Instead, the job went to newly promoted Captain Dave Pekach. Sabara was named Wohl's deputy commander of Special Operations. It quickly went around Highway that Wohl had told Sabara he could either wear plainclothes or a regular uniform, but he didn't want to see him in Highway breeches and boots. And then Wohl had announced a new recruiting policy for Highway, outstanding young cops who didn't have four, five years on the job. The first two "probationary" Highway Patrolmen were the two Narcs who got the critter who killed Captain Moffitt.

The idea that just anybody could get into Highway had enraged most Highway Patrolmen.

Well, maybe the two guys who caught the scumbag who shot down Captain Dutch Moffitt were entitled to a little special treatment, but letting just about anybody in Highway—

A delegation, someone had told Malone, three Highway sergeants and two long-time Highway Patrolmen, went to see Captain Sabara: Couldn't Sabara have a word with Wohl and tell him how what he was doing was really going to fuck Highway up? Nothing against the inspector personally; it's just that he just doesn't *know* about *Highway*.

Captain Sabara, a phlegmatic man, announced he would think about it.

Two days later one of the sergeants who had gone to Captain Sabara to ask him if he could have a word with Staff Inspector Wohl had to go see Captain Sabara again. His emotional state was mingled fury and gross embarrassment.

"I wouldn't bother you with this, Captain, but nobody knows where Captain Pekach is."

"What's the problem?"

"You know about the parade? Escort the governor to Constitution Hall?"

Sabara nodded. "Twelve wheels. At the airport no later than eleven-thirty. Something wrong?"

"Captain, we brought the bikes here. We went inside for a cup of coffee, before the inspection. When we went back out, there was only ten wheels."

"You're not telling me somebody stole two Highway bikes?"

"Stole, no. Some wiseass is fucking around. When I find out who, I'll have his ass. But what do we do now?"

"Everybody else is outside, where they're supposed to be?"

"Yes, sir."

Captain Sabara, with the sergeant following, strode purposefully out of his office and then out the side door of the building, where he found ten Highway motorcycles lined up neatly, their riders standing beside them.

"Whose wheels are missing?" he demanded.

Two Highway Patrolmen, holding their plastic helmets in their hands and looking more than a little sheepish, stepped forward.

"What did you do, leave the keys in them?"

One patrolman nodded, embarrassed. The second began to explain, "Captain, who the hell's going to steal a Highway—"

He was stilled in midsentence by one of Captain Mike Sabara's nearly legendary frosty glances.

Sabara kept up his icy look for about thirty seconds, and then there came the sound of two motorcycles, approaching at high speed.

"Who the fuck—?" the sergeant asked, only to find that Captain Sabara's cold eyes were now on him.

Two Highway wheels, ridden by guys in complete Highway regalia, including plastic helmets with the face masks down, appeared just outside the parking lot on Bustleton Street, and slid to a stop on squealing tires. Now their sergeant's stripes were visible.

They sat there a moment, revving the engines, and then, one at a time, entered the parking lot, where, simultaneously, they executed a maneuver known to the motorcycling fraternity as a "wheelie." This maneuver involves lifting the front wheel off the ground and steering by precisely adjusting the balance of what is now a powered unicycle by shifting the weight of the body.

It is a maneuver that only can be successfully accomplished by a rider of extraordinary skill. In the interest of rider safety and vehicle economy, the maneuver is forbidden by the Police Department except for instructional purposes by Wheel School instructors.

After passing one way through the parking lot, the two cyclists dropped the front wheel gently back onto the ground, simultaneously negotiated a turn, and then simultaneously executed another wheelie, in the other direction. A final gentle lowering on the front wheel, a final gentle, precise turn, and then the two rode to the center of the parked motorcycles and stopped. They revved the engines a final time, kicked the kick stands in place in a synchronized movement, and then swung off the machines.

The first rider raised his face mask and then removed his helmet.

Jesus H. Christ, it's Pekach! I knew he had been in Highway, but I didn't know he could ride a wheel that good!

"For obvious reasons," Captain Pekach announced solemnly, "I think I should remind all of you that Departmental regulations require that the keys to motorcycles be removed when they are left unattended."

The second rider now raised his mask and removed his helmet.

"Anyone who willingly gets on one of those things," Staff Inspector Peter Wohl announced, "is obviously not playing with a full deck."

Then he and Captain Pekach walked into the building.

Captain Sabara had turned to the sergeant who had reported the missing wheels to him.

"Did I ever tell you, Sergeant, that when I first came to Highway the sergeant I replaced was Inspector Wohl?"

Then he turned and walked into the building.

Malone thought it was a great story. But it was more than that. Wohl knew how to deal with people. After the wheelie demonstration, and after the word had spread that Wohl had been the youngest sergeant ever in Highway, there had been no more bitching that he didn't understand how things were in Highway.

And, Malone thought, it had been a nice touch for Wohl to come out of his office himself to apologize for being tied up. Most division commanders wouldn't have done that; they would have told their driver to have the newcomer wait.

And what Payne had said, "you'll be right at home around here," was interesting too.

Maybe this Special Operations assignment will turn out all right after all.

FOUR

At five minutes past one that afternoon, Abu Ben Mohammed
pushed open one of the double doors giving access to the business premises of Goldblatt & Sons Credit Furniture & Appliances, Inc., which occupied all of a three-story building on
the north side of South Street, between South 8th and South
9th Streets in South Philadelphia.

Abu Ben Mohammed, according to police records, had been
born, as Charles David Stevens, at the Temple University Hospital, in North Philadelphia, twenty-four years, six months,
and eleven days earlier. On the occasion of his most recent
arrest, he had been described as a Negro Male, five feet nine
inches tall, weighing approximately 165 pounds, and with no
particular deformities or scars.

Goldblatt & Sons had a doorman, Albert J. Monahan, who
was fifty-six. Red Monahan had been with Goldblatt & Sons
for thirty-eight years. He went way back to when it had been
Samuel Goldblatt Fine Furniture, when Mr. Joshua Goldblatt
(now treasurer) and Mr. Harold Goldblatt (now secretary) had
been in short pants, and Mr. Samuel Goldblatt, Jr., (now pres-

ident) then known as "Little Sammy," had been just another muscular eighteen-year-old working one of the trucks delivering merchandise alongside Red.

Before he'd had his heart attack, three years before, Red Monahan had worked his way up to warehouse supervisor. In addition to the portions of the third floor and of the basement of the building on South Street used to warehouse, there was a five-story warehouse building on Washington Avenue two blocks away.

Red had been responsible for checking merchandise as it came in, filling orders from the store to be loaded on trucks, and in moving merchandise back and forth between the store and the warehouse.

Old Mr. Goldblatt had still been alive when Red had his heart attack, although he was getting pretty fragile. But he insisted on being taken to the hospital to see Red, and Young Mr. Sam had, nervously, loaded him into his Buick and taken him.

Old Mr. Goldblatt had told Red that he was too mean an Irishman to die, or even to stay sick for very long, and anyway not to worry. The store had good hospital insurance and what that didn't pay, the store would. And he could consider himself retired, at full pay, from that moment. Anyone with thirty-five years with the store was entitled to take it easy when the time came.

Red told Old Mr. Goldblatt that he didn't want to retire; everybody he knew who retired was dead in a year or eighteen months. And what the hell would he do, anyway, sit around the house all day?

Old Mr. Goldblatt told Red that there would be a job for him at the store as long as he wanted one, and then when he was back in the Buick he told Young Mr. Sam that he was to figure out something for Red to do that wouldn't be a strain on him, but that would also keep him busy.

"No make work. Red's got pride."

"Jesus Christ, Pop!"

"Just do it, Sammy. Let me know what you come up with."

What Young Mr. Sam came up with was what he called "floor walker." When he was a kid, there had been floor walkers in Strawbridge & Clothier, John Wanamaker's, and other top-class department stores. What they did was literally walk the floor, keeping an eye on customers, stock, and employees.

Goldblatt & Sons had never had such people, but once he thought of it, it struck Young Mr. Sam as a pretty good idea. For one thing, Red was a genial Irishman, charming, silver-haired. People liked him. For another, nobody knew more about the stock than Red did. If when people came through the door, Red could be there to greet them with a smile and find out whether they were interested in a bedroom suite, or a re-frigerator, or a rug, or whatever, then he could point them in the right direction. "Appliances are on the second floor, right up the stairs." "Carpets are on the third floor, you'll find the elevator right over there."

The first problem was to think of a new term to describe what he would be doing. Young Mr. Sam didn't think Red would like to be a floor walker. He finally came up with "mer-chandise counselor." Red's face stiffened when he heard that, but he heard Young Mr. Sam out, listening to Sam explain what would be expected of him.

"You mean like a doorman, Sam, right? To make sure the customers don't get away?"

"Yeah."

"That sounds like a pretty good idea," Red had said.

Having Red Monahan working as the doorman turned out to be a very good idea, better than Young Mr. Sam would have believed when he first thought of it.

Red started out by telling people, "Bedroom suites are in the front of the third floor. Take the elevator and when you get up there ask for Mrs. Lipshutz." Or "Wall-to-wall carpeting is in the back of the store. Ask for Mr. Callahan."

The next step was to have the salespeople waiting downstairs near the door. Red would march the customer over to Mrs. Lipshutz or whoever and introduce her with a naughty little wink: "Mrs. Lipshutz is our bedroom expert."

And when somebody came in sore because the Credit De-partment hadn't credited their account, or because the leg had come off a kitchen chair, or something, Red would be the soul of sympathy and calm them down.

And he kept the undesirables out. There were a lot of drunks around South Street, particularly on Friday nights, when the store was open until nine P.M. and he discouraged them from coming in the store. And he kept the religious loonies from bothering the customers too. The ones who just wanted to pass out their literature were bad enough, but the ones who just about demanded money to plant trees in Israel, or save souls for Jesus in the Congo, or to buy tickets for the Annual Picnic of the 3rd Abyssinian Baptist Church, things like that, had been, pre-Red the Doorman, a real pain in the ass.

Now Red either discouraged them before they got through the doors, or got rid of the really determined ones with a couple of bucks from a roll of singles he got, as needed, from petty cash.

Abu Ben Mohammed, when Red Monahan greeted him at the door, told him he wanted to see about some wall-to-wall carpet.

"You saw the ad in the paper, I guess?" Red asked.

"Huh?"

"We're having a special sale," Red explained. "Twenty-five percent off everything we have in stock, plus free pad and installation."

"No kidding?"

"Absolutely," Red said. "You picked the right day to get yourself some carpet."

He guided Abu Ben Mohammed over to where Phil Katz, who was Old Mr. Sam's nephew, was sitting with the other salespeople on the tufted blue velvet couch and matching armchairs that a sign advertised as "Today's Special! Three-Piece Suite! $99 Down! No Payment Until March!"

"Mr. Katz," Red began, which caused Phil Katz to break off his conversation with Mr. Callahan in midsentence and get to his feet with a smile in place.

"Mr. Katz," Red went on, "this is Mr.—I didn't catch your name?"

"I didn't tell you," Abu Ben Mohammed replied.

"This gentleman," Red Monahan went on, "is interested in some wall-to-wall carpeting."

"Well, this is your day," Mr. Katz said, "we're running a special sale. Why don't we ride up to the carpet department and let me show you what we have?"

Mr. Katz thought he might have a live one. He had, of course, noticed that Abu Ben Mohammed was wearing what he thought of as African clothes. Over a purple turtleneck sweater and baggy black trousers, Abu Ben Mohammed was wearing a brightly colored dashiki. Perched on the back of his head was sort of a black yarmulke, neatly and rather brightly embroidered in a yellow and green pattern. He was also wearing a trench coat over his shoulders. Maybe they didn't have overcoats in North Africa, Mr. Katz thought, or maybe this guy just didn't have an African coat to handle the chill of January in Philadelphia.

What was important was that he was into the African thing, and the Africans were deep into carpets. They put them two and three deep on the floors, and sometimes they even upholstered their walls with them.

What was just about as important was that he had come into the store today. The furniture business just about died after Christmas; it was Phil Katz's personal opinion that the store was just pissing money down the toilet with their advertisements in the Philadelphia *Daily News* for ''After Christmas'' and ''New Year's'' sales. People had spent their money (or used up their credit, which was the same thing) buying Christmas presents. They had no money to do anything but start paying the bills they had run up for Christmas.

But there were exceptions to every rule, and this guy in the dashiki just might be one of them. Mr. Katz had heard that the blacks who had become Muslims had to stop drinking and smoking and gambling, which meant this guy might just have the money to cover the floors of his apartment with carpet.

He led Abu Ben Mohammed to the elevator, slid the door shut, and took him up to the third floor.

Five minutes after Abu Ben Mohammed entered the store, a man subsequently identified as Hector Carlos Estivez, twenty-four, five feet nine inches tall, and weighing 140 pounds, and again with no distinguishing marks or features, came in.

He told Red Monahan that he wanted to look at a washer-drier combination, and was turned over by Red to Mrs. Emily Watkins, who was forty-eight, and had worked for fifteen years in the Credit Department of Goldblatt & Sons before deciding, three years before, that she could make more money on the floor, on a small salary plus commission, than she could at her desk. She had asked Young Mr. Sam for a chance to try, and to his surprise, she had done very well, probably, he had finally decided, because women did most of the buying of washers and driers and other appliances, and probably trusted another woman more than they would a man.

Mrs. Watkins led Mr. Estivez up the stairs to the second floor, and then to the rear of the building, where the washer-driers were on display. She was not nearly as enthusiastic about her chances to make a sale to her potential customer as Mr. Katz had been about his. She had been in the credit business a long time, and had a feel for who would have credit and who wouldn't. Mr. Estivez did not strike her as the kind of man who held a steady job. But on the other hand, he might have hit his number or something and might have the cash.

In a similar manner, over the next twenty minutes, seven more potential customers pushed open the door from South Street into Goldblatt & Sons Credit Furniture & Appliances, Inc., were greeted by Red Monahan and turned over to a member of the sales force.

One of them, the third to come in the store, was a woman. She was later identified as Doris M. (Mrs. Harold) Martin, fifty-two, of East Hagert Street in Kensington. She had come in to look at carpet for her upstairs corridor and bedrooms after having seen the Goldblatt & Sons advertisement in that day's *Daily News*. Red Monahan introduced Mrs. Martin to Mrs. Irene Dougherty, who took her by elevator to the third floor.

The other six people to come in were all men. Two of them wore clothing suggesting they were either Muslims or at least had some connection with an African culture. All of them were, according to the race codification then in use by the Philadelphia Police Department, Negroid. Two of them, however, had such pale skin pigmentation that there was some question whether they were "really colored" or "maybe Puerto Rican or Mexican, or something like that."

The last of the six men to enter the store, at approximately 1:32 P.M., described as a "black male, approximately six feet tall, thirty years of age, and weighing approximately one hundred seventy-five pounds," was wearing a "dark blue, waist-length woolen jacket similar in appearance to the U.S. Navy pea coat."

Immediately upon entering Goldblatt & Sons, this suspect, subsequently identified as Kenneth H. Dorne, aka "King," aka Hussein El Baruca, turned and began to bolt the door shut.

"Hey, friend," Red Monahan asked as he walked up to him, "what are you doing?"

"Shut your face, motherfucker!" Hussein El Baruca replied, simultaneously drawing a large, blue in color, large-caliber semiautomatic pistol (probably a Colt Model 1911 or 1911A1 .45-caliber service pistol) and pointing it at Red Monahan.

"Hey, you don't really want to do this—" Red Monahan said, whereupon Hussein El Baruca struck him, with a slashing backward motion of his right arm, in the face with the pistol, with sufficient force to knock him down and, it was subsequently learned, to cause a crack in Mr. Monahan's full upper denture.

Then he raised the pistol to a nearly vertical position and fired it three times. One of the bullets struck a fluorescent lighting fixture on the ceiling, smashing a bulb, which caused broken glass and then a cloud of powder, from the interior coating of the bulb, to float down from the ceiling. Then, the fixture itself tore loose at one end, causing a short-circuit in the wiring. There was a flash of light, and then that entire line of lighting fixtures, one of two running from the front of the store to the rear, went off, reducing the light on the ground floor by half.

"On your fucking bellies or I'll blow your fucking heads off!" Hussein El Baruca ordered.

The three salespeople, two men and a woman, waiting for customers in the living-room suite, and Red Monahan complied with the order. The woman crossed herself, and her lips moved in prayer as she got onto her knees and then laid on the floor.

Hussein El Baruca then turned back to the double doors and closed the venetian blinds on them. There was a large display window on either side of the entrance. A complete bedroom set was on display in one window, and a complete bedroom set in the other. The "walls" behind the furniture in each window blocked the view of the interior of the store to passersby, and with the blinds on the doors now closed, there was no way anyone on South Street could look into Goldblatt & Sons Credit Furniture & Appliances, Inc.

The sound of the three pistol shots fired by Hussein El Baruca was muffled somewhat by the upholstered furniture on the ground floor, and because the store was open from the front to the rear, where the Credit Department was located. But it was loud enough to be heard on the second floor, where it was correctly interpreted by Hector Carlos Estivez as the signal he had been expecting.

He took what was probably a Smith & Wesson Military & Police .38 Special caliber revolver from where he had concealed it in the small of his back, held it in both hands at arm's length, and fired two shots at the glass viewing port of a Hot-point drier that was sitting on the floor approximately six feet from him, and two feet to the left of Mrs. Emily Watkins.

Mrs. Watkins yelped and covered her mouth with both hands.

Hector Carlos Estivez when he saw that he missed the glass viewing port with one of his shots, and that the second had cracked but not smashed or penetrated the glass, said, "Shit!" and fired a third time. This time the thick, tempered glass of the viewing port broke.

"On the floor, bitch!" Hector Carlos Estivez said, and Mrs. Watkins, now whimpering, dropped to her knees and then spread herself on the floor.

The shots from Estivez's revolver were audible to Abu Ben Mohammed on the third floor, where Phil Katz was explaining to him that trying to get by with bottom-of-the-line cheap carpet was really not economy at all.

"It's just like tires," Mr. Katz was saying, "what you're really buying is wear. You— What the hell was that?"

"You're being robbed, motherfucker, that's what it is," Abu Ben Mohammed said, taking a large-caliber, single-action, Western-style revolver with plastic "pearl" grips from beneath his dashiki. He pushed the hammer back, cocking the pistol, and then fired at a three-foot-tall, stainless-steel cigarette receptacle that had been placed beside the elevator door.

A hole appeared near the top of the receptacle, which then slowly tilted to one side, as if in a slow-motion picture, and then fell, dislodging a sand-filled glass tray, which shattered upon striking the metal elevator threshold.

"Jesus H. Christ!" Phil Katz said.

"Lay down on the floor," Abu Ben Mohammed ordered.

"What?"

"On the fucking floor, you heard me."

"Yes, sir."

The executive offices of Goldblatt & Sons Credit Furniture & Appliances, Inc., those of Mr. Samuel Goldblatt, Jr., and Mr. Harold Goldblatt, the secretary, and their secretary, Mrs. Blanche Steiner, forty-four, were at the right rear of the building. Mr. Joshua Goldblatt, the treasurer, maintained his office in the Credit Department on the ground floor.

The sound of Abu Ben Mohammed's pistol shot attracted the attention of Mr. Samuel Goldblatt, Jr., who looked up from the work on his desk, and then stood up. When the executive offices had been built, one-way glass panels providing a view of the third-floor showroom had been installed. But they had never really worked, and eventually had been almost entirely covered up by a row of filing cabinets. The only way to see what was going on on the floor was to open the door and look.

Mr. Goldblatt did so, and found himself looking into the barrel of Abu Ben Mohammed's revolver.

"Hands up, honky!"

"Yes, sir," Mr. Goldblatt said.

"Oh, my *God!*" Mrs. Steiner said, thereby attracting Abu Ben Mohammed's attention.

"Out here, bitch!"

"Do what he says, Blanche," Mr. Goldblatt said.

Abu Ben Mohammed then took careful aim at Mrs. Steiner's IBM typewriter and fired. The machine seemed to lift slightly off the desk and then settled back. There was a faint screeching noise, and then, a short-circuit within the typewriter having caused a fuse to blow, the overhead lights in the executive office went out. Desk lamps on Mr. Goldblatt's and Mrs. Steiner's desks continued to burn and produced sufficient light to see.

"Oh, my *God!*" Mrs. Steiner wailed.

"Please don't hurt anyone," Mr. Goldblatt pleaded. "We'll do whatever you want us to do."

Abu Ben Mohammed then struck Mr. Goldblatt on the head, with a downward slashing motion of his pistol, causing him to fall to his knees and also causing a small cut on the (bald) top of his head.

"Get the money and some rope," Abu Ben Mohammed ordered.

"What?" Mrs. Steiner asked.

"There's no money up here," Mr. Goldblatt said. "Honest to God there isn't!"

"Bullshit!" Abu Ben Mohammed said. "Get the fucking money!"

Mr. Goldblatt reached into the hip pocket of his trousers and came out with his wallet that he handed to Abu Ben Mohammed.

"Take this," he said.

Abu Ben Mohammed took the wallet, and from it not less than one hundred twenty dollars and not more than two hundred dollars and put the bills in a pocket of his dashiki. Then he threw the wallet at Mr. Goldblatt.

"Give him your purse, Blanche," Mr. Goldblatt said.

"Go get it," Abu Ben Mohammed said to Mrs. Steiner, and then added to Mr. Goldblatt, "If you're lying to me, if we find any money in that office, I'm going to blow your fucking honky head off."

"I swear to God, believe me, we don't keep any money up here."

"Then what's that fucking safe for?"

"Business papers. Look for yourself."

"Don't you tell me what to do, you honky motherfucker!" Abu Ben Mohammed said, and swung his pistol at Mr. Goldblatt's head again. Mr. Goldblatt was able to ward off most of the force of this blow with his hands, suffering only a minor bruise to his left hand.

Mrs. Steiner took her purse from a desk drawer and offered it to Abu Ben Mohammed. A coin purse contained approximately sixteen dollars in bills, and there was approximately sixty dollars in her wallet. Abu Ben Mohammed removed these monies and placed them in a pocket of his dashiki.

On the second floor, meanwhile, Hector Carlos Estivez had startled Mrs. Emily Watkins by ordering her to remove her shoes and stockings. When she had done so, he used one of the stockings to bind her hands behind her back. He then told her to lie down again, on her stomach, and when she failed to so quickly enough to satisfy him, he pushed her so that she fell.

A minute or so later Mrs. Watkins was ordered to get up, and when she was not able to get to her feet quickly enough to satisfy Hector Carlos Estivez, he kicked her in the side, and then jerked her to an upright position.

She saw then for the first time Mr. Ted Sadowsky, a Goldblatt employee specializing in televisions and stereo equipment, who had been in the front part of the building. He was being held at gunpoint, probably a Colt Police Positive .38 Special caliber snub-nosed revolver (or the Smith & Wesson equivalent) by a suspect subsequently identified as Randolph George Dawes, aka Muhammed el Sikkim, Negro Male, twenty-four, five feet nine inches, 160 pounds.

"Tie the cocksucker up," Hector Carlos Estivez said to Muhammed el Sikkim, and handed him Mrs. Watkins's other stocking.

Muhammed el Sikkim tied Mr. Sadowsky's hands behind his back with Mrs. Watkins's stocking, and then led the two of them to the stairway between the passenger and freight elevators and took them to the third floor, where he ordered them to get on the floor on their stomachs.

"No fucking rope and no fucking money," Abu Ben Mohammed said to Muhammed el Sikkim.

"Use stockings. Tell that kike bitch to take hers off."

Mrs. Steiner was then forced to remove her panty hose, which were torn apart at the crotch and one part of them then used to tie her arms behind her back. Mr. Samuel Goldblatt was then tied in a similar manner, with the other leg of Mrs. Steiner's panty hose, and he and Mrs. Steiner were then forced to lay on their stomachs beside Mr. Sadowsky and Mrs. Watkins.

Within the next five minutes, all Goldblatt employees, plus the one customer in the store, Mrs. Doris Martin, were brought to the third floor by the perpetrators. These included the three employees on duty in the first-floor Credit Department, the remaining salespeople, and Mr. Monahan.

From this point, inasmuch as all Goldblatt employees (including Mr. Samuel Goldblatt, Jr.) and Mrs. Martin were lying on their stomachs on the floor of the third floor of the Goldblatt Building with their arms bound behind them, the only witnesses to the perpetrators' actions on the first and second floors of the Goldblatt Building were the perpetrators themselves.

What is known is that three (or four) of the perpetrators (almost certainly including Abu Ben Mohammed, and probably including Hector Carlos Estivez and Muhammed el Sikkim) went to the Credit Department on the first floor and

(a) Removed approximately four hundred eighty dollars in bills and coins-in-rolls from the cashier's cash drawer.

(b) Broke into the interior compartments (three) of the safe. The safe itself was open at the time the robbery began. There was no cash in the safe.

(c) Emptied the contents of a wastebasket (mostly waste paper) into the safe and set it afire.

Sometime during this period, Mr. John Francis Cohn, forty-nine, of Queen Lane in East Falls, supervisor of the Maintenance Department of Goldblatt & Sons Credit Furniture &

Appliances, Inc., apparently entered the building via a door on Rodman Street, the narrow alley at the rear of the building. This self-closing door was closed to the public and was normally locked. Mr. Cohn had a key.

Apparently, Mr. Cohn then descended to the basement of the store by the stairwell between the freight and passenger elevators. He then uncrated (or completed uncrating) a special, demonstration model Hotpoint washing machine, constructed of a plastic material so that the interior of the apparatus was visible, and, using a hand truck, put the machine onto the freight elevator.

He then apparently ascended to the second floor, where he had received instructions to install the machine in the Washer and Drier Department.

He moved the machine to the rear of the second floor, and then apparently became aware that there were no salespeople on duty. (Or possibly wished to ascertain precisely where he was to set up the machine.) He then got back onto the freight elevator and descended to the first floor, and opened the door and the elevator gate.

At this point, apparently, he saw the perpetrators and attempted to flee by moving the elevator. At this point, the perpetrators saw him, and at least two of them then fired their weapons at him.

Mr. Cohn was struck by four bullets, two of .38 Special caliber and two of .45 Colt Automatic Pistol caliber. Three additional .38 Special caliber and one additional .45 ACP bullets were later found in the woodwork of the elevator.

Mr. Cohn fell inward into the elevator.

The perpetrators then entered the stairwell and went to the third floor. They reported to the others that they "had blown away a honky motherfucker on the elevator," and that the cash register had contained "only a lousy five hundred fucking dollars."

A conversation, within hearing, but out of sight of the victims, was then held, during which one of the perpetrators announced he had found an inflammable fluid and soaked some carpet with it, and that he was going to "burn the fucking place down, and the honkies with it."

Another perpetrator was heard to say, "It's time to get the fuck out of here."

The perpetrators then, without further discussion, apparently ignited the inflammable fluid that had been poured upon a stack of carpet, descending to the first floor by means of the stairwell between the freight and passenger elevators, exited the building via a fire door in the rear of the building opening onto the alley (Rodman Street).

Opening of the fire door set off an alarm, which both caused bells mounted on the front and rear of the building and in the finance and executive offices to begin to ring, and was connected with the Holmes Security Service. A Holmes employee then

(a) Telephoned the Police Radio Room,

(b) Attempted to telephone the Goldblatt Building to verify that the alarm had not been accidentally triggered, and on failing to have anyone answer the telephone,

(c) Contacted a Holmes patrol unit in the area, informing him of the triggering of the alarm in the Goldblatt Building.

The Radio Room of the Philadelphia Police Department is on the second floor of the Police Administration Building at Eighth and Race Streets in downtown Philadelphia.

"Police Emergency," the operator, a thirty-seven-year-old woman named Janet Grosse, said into her headset.

"This is Holmes," the caller said. "I have a signal of a fire door audible alarm at Goldblatt Furniture, northwest corner, 8th and South."

The call from Holmes Security Service was treated exactly as any other call for help would be treated, except of course that Mrs. Grosse, who had worked in Police Radio for eleven years, seemed to recognize the voice of the Holmes man and made a subconscious decision from the phrasing of the report that it was genuine, and not coming from someone who got his kicks sending the cops on wild goose chases.

"Got you covered," she said, which was not exactly the precise response called for by regulations.

Eighth and South streets, Mrs. Grosse knew, was in the 6th Police District, which has its headquarters at 11th and Winter Streets. She looked up at her board and saw that Radio Patrol Car 611 was available for service.

She opened her microphone.

"Six Eleven, northwest corner, 8th and South, Goldblatt's Furniture, an audible alarm."

RPC 611 was a somewhat battered 1972 Plymouth with more than 100,000 miles on its odometer. When the call came, Officer James J. Molyneux, Badge Number 6771, who had been on the job eighteen years, had just turned left off South Broad Street onto South Street.

He picked up his microphone.

"Six Eleven, okay."

Officer Molyneux turned on his flashing lights, but not the siren, and held his hand down on the horn button to clear the traffic in front of him.

At just about this time, the ringing of the alarm bell had attracted the attention of Police Officer Johnson V. Collins, Badge Number 2662, who was then on foot patrol (Beat Two) on South Street between 10th and 11th Streets.

Officer Collins was equipped with a portable radio, and heard Mrs. Grosse's call to RPC 611. He took his radio from its holster and spoke into it.

"Six Beat Two," he said. "That's on me. I've got it."

Mrs. Grosse immediately replied, "Okay, Six Beat Two. Six Eleven, resume patrol."

Officer Molyneux, without responding, turned off his flashing lights, but, having nothing better to do, continued driving down South Street toward Goldblatt & Sons Credit Furniture & Appliances, Inc.

Officer Collins walked purposefully (but did not run or even trot; audible alarms went off all the time) down South Street to the Goldblatt Building. It was only when he found the doors closed and the venetian blinds closed that he suspected that anything might be out of the ordinary. Business was slow, but Goldblatt's shouldn't be closed.

He glanced up the street and saw RPC 611 coming in his direction. Now trotting, he went to the corner of South and South Ninth Streets, stepped into the street, and raised his arm to attract the attention of the driver of 611. He recognized Officer Molyneux.

He made a signal for Molyneux to cover the front of the building, and when he was sure that Molyneux understood what was being asked of him, Collins trotted down South Ninth Street to Rodman Street, which was more of an alley than a street, and then to the rear of the Goldblatt Building.

The fire door had an automatic closing device, but it had not completely closed the door. Collins was able to get his fingers behind the inch-wide strip of steel welded to the end of the door to shield the crack between door and jamb and pull the door open.

He took several steps inside the building, and then saw the body lying in the freight elevator and the blood on the elevator's wall.

"Jesus, Mary, and Joseph!" he breathed, and reached for his radio.

"Six Beat Two, Six Beat Two, give me some backup here, I think I've got a robbery in progress! Give me a wagon too. I've got a shooting victim!"

Then, suddenly remembering that portable radios often fail to work inside a building, he went back into the alley and repeated his call.

"What's your location, Six Beat Two?" Police Radio replied.

"800 South Street. Goldblatt Furniture."

The first response was from Officer Molyneux.

"Six Eleven, I'm on the scene. In front."

He was drowned out by the Police Radio transmission. First there were three beeps, and then Mrs. Grosse announced, "800 South Street. Assist officer. Holdup in progress. Report of shooting and hospital case."

Then there came a brief pause, and the entire message, including the three beeps, was repeated.

The response was immediate:

"Six A, in." Six A was one of the two 9th District sergeants on duty. He was responsible for covering the lower end of the district, from Vine Street to South Street. The other sergeant (Six B) covered the upper end of the district from Vine to Poplar Streets.

"Six Oh One, in." Six Oh One was one of the 9th District's two-man vans.

"Highway Twenty-Two, in on that."

"Six Ten, in," came from another 6th District RPC.

"Six Command, in," came from the car of the 6th District lieutenant on duty, who was responsible for covering the entire district.

Officer Collins replace his radio in its holster, drew his service revolver, and, with his mouth dry and his heart beating almost audibly, went, very carefully, back into the building.

FIVE

Officers Gerald Quinn and Charles McFadden had spent all of the morning hanging around the sixth-floor hallway outside Courtroom 636 in City Hall waiting to be called to testify. The assistant DA sent word, however, that they probably would be, and asked them not to leave the building until he gave them permission or until the court broke for lunch.

That meant that in addition to the lousy coffee served by the concessionaire in the stairwell, they would have to eat lunch in some crowded greasy spoon restaurant nearby.

They went back to Courtroom 636 a few minutes before two. The assistant district attorney told them they would not be needed. By the time they had gone back downstairs and checked out through Court Attendance, it was a few minutes after two.

They went out and found their car. Quinn got behind the wheel and cranked the battered Chevrolet. The radio warmed almost immediately, and came to life:

"BEEP BEEP BEEP. 800 South Street. Assist officer. Holdup in progress. Report of shooting and hospital case.

"BEEP BEEP BEEP. 800 South Street. Assist officer. Holdup in progress. Report of shooting and hospital case."

Quinn had the siren howling and the lights flashing even before McFadden could pick up the microphone.

When he had it in his hand, he said, "Highway Twenty-Two in on that."

Mrs. Janet Grosse's—Police Radio's—second call about the robbery of Goldblatt & Sons Credit Furniture & Appliances, Inc.—

Beep Beep Beep. 800 South Street. Assist officer. Holdup in progress. Report of shooting and hospital case.

—was also picked up by one of the several police frequency radios in an antennae-festooned Buick, a new one, registered to one Michael J. O'Hara of the 2100 block of South Shields Street in West Philadelphia.

Mr. O'Hara had just a moment before entered the Buick after having taken luncheon (a cheese-steak sandwich, a large side order of french fries, and three bottles of Ortleib's beer) at Beato's on Parrish Street, in the company of Sergeant Max Feldman, of the 9th District.

When the call came, Mr. O'Hara was filling out a small printed document that he would, on Friday, turn into the administrative office of the Philadelphia *Bulletin*, the newspaper by which he was employed. It would state that in the course of business he had entertained Sergeant Feldman at luncheon at a cost of $23.50, plus a $3.75 tip, for a total of $27.25. In due course, a check would be issued to reimburse Mr. O'Hara for this business expense.

Actually, Mr. O'Hara had not paid for the lunch, and indeed had no idea what it had cost. Sergeant Feldman's money was no good at Beato's, and the management had picked up Mr. O'Hara's tab as a further courtesy to Sergeant Feldman.

But several months before, Casimir J. Bolinski, LLD, had renegotiated Mr. O'Hara's contract for the provision of his professional services to the *Bulletin*. Among other stipulations, the new contract required the *Bulletin* to reimburse Mr. O'Hara for whatever expenses he incurred in carrying out his professional duties, specifically including the entertainment of individuals who, in Mr. O'Hara's sole judgment, might prove useful to him professionally.

Since Casimir had gone to all that trouble for him, it seemed to Mr. O'Hara that it would be ungrateful of him not to turn in luncheon expense vouchers whether or not cash had actually changed hands. Anyway, Mr. O'Hara reasoned, if Beato's hadn't grabbed the tab, he *would* have paid it.

Mr. O'Hara's profession was journalism. Specifically, he was the *Bulletin*'s top crime reporter. Arguably, he was the best crime reporter in Philadelphia or, for that matter, between Boston and Washington.

Dr. Bolinski had enjoyed a certain fame—some said "notoriety"—as a linebacker for the Green Bay Packers professional football team before hanging up the suit and joining the bar and entering the legal specialization field of representing professional athletes.

Bull Bolinski had surprised a lot of people, including Mickey O'Hara, who had known him since they were in the third grade at Saint Stephen's Parochial School at 10th and Butler, with his near-instant success at big-dollar contract negotiations.

"What it is, Michael," The Bull had once explained to him over a beer, "is that the fuckers think I'm just a dumb fucking jock. That gives me a leg up on the bastards."

The Bull was the only person in the world except Mickey's mother who called Mr. O'Hara "Michael." Mickey, similarly, was the only person in the world save Mrs. Bolinski who called The Bull "Casimir." The Bull's mother didn't even call him Casimir; usually it was Sonny, but often she called him "Bull" too.

That went back to Saint Stephen's too, where Sister Mary Magdalene, the principal, had a thing about Christian names. You either used the name you got when you were baptized, or you took a crack across the hand, bottom, or a stab into the ribs from Sister Mary Magdalene's eighteen-inch steel-reinforced ruler.

Casimir had been in town eight months before and had been deeply shocked to learn how little Michael was being compensated for his services by the *Bulletin*.

"Jesus, Michael, you got a fucking Pulitzer Prize, and that's all those cheap bastards are paying you? That's fucking outrageous!"

"Casimir, you may have been a hot shit ball player, and you may be a hot shit lawyer now, but you don't know your ass from left field about newspapers."

"Trust me, Michael," The Bull had said confidently. "I can handle those bastards."

Somewhat uneasily, Mr. O'Hara had placed the financial aspects of his career into Dr. Bolinski's hands. To his genuine surprise, the *Bulletin* was now paying him more money than he had ever expected to make, and there were fringe benefits like the Buick (previously he had driven his own car and been reimbursed at a dime a mile) and the expense account.

While it would not be fair to say that Mickey O'Hara was happy to hear that someone had been illegally deprived of their property at gunpoint, or that somebody had gotten themselves shot, neither would it be honest to say that he was beside himself with vicarious sorrow.

It had been a damned dull week, so far, and so far the line of type reading, *"By Michael J. O'Hara, Bulletin Staff Writer"* had not appeared on the front page of the *Bulletin*. A good shooting would probably fix that.

Mickey finished filling out the expense account chit, shoved the pad of forms back into the glove compartment, and got the Buick moving.

Mickey knew the streets of the City of Philadelphia as well as any London taxi driver knows those of the city on the Thames. He turned left onto 26th Street and headed south toward the Art Museum and moved swiftly down the Benjamin Franklin Parkway toward City Hall. The pedestrian traffic around City Hall was frustrating, but his pace picked up as he headed south on Broad Street toward South Street. As he turned east on South Street, he could see flashing lights a few blocks ahead.

He drove expertly. That is to say, he was not reckless. But he paid absolutely no attention to the posted speed limits, and paused for red lights only long enough to make sure he could get across the intersection without getting hit.

He was not worried about being cited for violation of the Motor Vehicle Code. His chances of being charged with speeding or running a red light or reckless lane changing were about as great as those of Mayor Jerry Carlucci's.

Mickey O'Hara was regarded by the Police Department as one of their own. To be sure, there was always some stiff-necked prick who would point out that all Mickey O'Hara was, was a goddamn civilian and entitled to no special privileges. But for every one of these, there were two or three cops, driving RPCs or walking beats, or captains and inspectors, who had known Mickey for twenty years and had come to believe that he was on the side of the cops, and told the prick where to head in.

When the Emerald Society had a function, and there was a head table, Mickey O'Hara was routinely seated at it. The Fraternal Order of Police club, downtown, off North Broad Street, had an ironclad rule that the only way a civilian could get past the door was in the company of a member. Except for Mickey O'Hara, who could be expected to drop in once a night for a beer, sitting at a stool near the cash register that might as well have had his name on it, because it was tacitly reserved for him.

The thing about Mickey, it was said, was that he never betrayed a confidence. If you told him something was out of school, you would never see it in the newspaper.

There was a white-capped (Traffic Division) cop diverting traffic away from South Street onto South 9th Street when Mickey O'Hara's Buick appeared.

He waved Mickey through, winked at him as he passed, and then furiously blew his whistle at the car behind him, who thought he wanted to follow Mickey.

Mickey pulled up behind a car he recognized as belonging to Central Detectives. Some of the chrome letters that had once spelled out CHEVROLET had fallen off; now it read CHE RO   T. He had seen it the night before downtown; a lawyer from Pittsburgh had been mugged and stabbed coming out of a bar. The detective had told Mickey what had happened, and when Mickey had asked him, "What do you think?" the detective had said, "It's a start, but the bastards breed like rabbits."

Mickey took a 35-mm camera from the passenger side floor and got out. He saw that South Street was jammed with police vehicles of all descriptions. There were three 6th District RPCs, cars assigned to one of the 6th District sergeants and the 6th District lieutenant captain, a Highway RPC, a 6th District van and two stakeout vans, the Mobile Crime Lab vehicle, and a number of unmarked cars. One of the unmarked cars was a brand-new Chevrolet Impala, telling Mickey that a captain (or better) with nothing more important to do had come to the crime scene, and was more than likely getting in the way. The other unmarked cars were battered; that meant they were from Central Detectives.

Obviously (people were standing around) whatever had happened here was over. The stakeout vans, which are manned by specially trained policemen who are equipped with special weapons (rifles, shotguns, machine guns, et cetera) and equipment, and called into use in situations where ordinary armament (handguns) is likely to be inadequate, were not going to be needed.

Then Mickey saw a familiar face, that of Homicide Detective Joe D'Amata, and knew that something serious had happened. The "hospital case" in the Police Radio call hadn't needed a hospital.

Mickey stepped over the Crime Scene barrier and walked toward another familiar face. He now knew who was driving the new Impala.

"I didn't know they let old men like you go in on real jobs," Mickey said.

Chief Inspector Matt Lowenstein, a short, stocky man with large, dark eyes, who commanded the Detective Division, took a black, six-inch cigar from between his lips and looked coldly at Mickey.

"If there's one thing I can't stand, it's a laugh-a-minute Irishman," he said. "I knew if I didn't get out of here, something unpleasant, like you showing up, would happen."

"Things a little slow at the Roundhouse, are they? Or are you trying to recapture your youth by patrolling the streets?"

"I was driving by, all right? Up yours, O'Hara."

Despite the exchange, they were friends. Matt Lowenstein met Mickey O'Hara's criteria for a very good cop. Not all senior supervisors did. O'Hara admired Lowenstein for being an absolute straight arrow, who protected his men like a mother hen.

On Lowenstein's part, he not only respected O'Hara professionally, but when his son had been bar mitzvahed, not only had Mickey shown up (his gift had been *The Oxford Complete Dictionary of the English Language*) but the event had been reported on the front page of the Sunday Social Section, complete with a three-column picture of Lowenstein and his son via Mickey's influence at the *Bulletin*.

"So before you go back to the rocking chair, you going to tell me what happened? Why are you here?"

"I told you, I was nearby and heard the call," Lowenstein said. "It's a strange one, Mickey. Six, eight guys, A-rabs—"

"Real Arabs?" Mickey interrupted.

"They kept saying 'motherfucker.' That's Arabian, isn't it?"

Mickey chuckled. "I think so," he said solemnly.

"They came in the place one at a time, spread out through the building, and then pulled guns. They shot up the place, God only knows why, and then tried to set some rugs on fire. The maintenance man walked in while it was going on, and they killed him."

"He try to do something or what?"

Lowenstein shrugged.

"Don't know yet. You want to have a look?"

"I'd like to, Matt," Mickey said.

Lowenstein pursed his lips. A surprisingly loud whistle came from between them. A dozen people turned to look, including the uniformed cop guarding access to the Goldblatt crime scene.

"He's okay," Lowenstein said, pointing to Mickey O'Hara.

"Thanks," Mickey said.

"Sylvia said if you can watch your filthy mouth, you can come to dinner."

"When?"

"How about tonight?"

"Fine. What time and what can I bring?"

"Half past six. You don't have to bring anything, but take a shave and a shower."

"Didn't The Dago tell you you were supposed to cultivate the press?"

"No. But I'll tell you what I did hear: You finally found some girl willing to be seen in public with you. Bring her, if you want."

"Okay. I was going to anyway," Mickey said, and touched Lowenstein's arm and walked past the cop into Goldblatt & Sons Credit Furniture & Appliances, Inc.

As Michael J. O'Hara walked into Goldblatt & Sons Credit Furniture & Appliances, Inc., on South Street, four blocks away, on 11th Street, near Carpenter, three law enforcement officers in civilian clothing were having their lunch in Shank & Evelyn's Restaurant.

They were Staff Inspector Peter Wohl and Officer Matthew Payne of the Philadelphia Police Department, and Walter Davis, a tall, well-built, well-dressed (in a gray pin-striped, three-piece suit) man in his middle forties, who was the special agent in charge (the "SAC") of the Philadelphia Office of the Federal Bureau of Investigation.

Shank & Evelyn's Restaurant was not the sort of place Walter Davis had had in mind when he had telephoned Wohl early that morning to ask if he was free for lunch. Davis had had in mind the Ristorante Alfredo, in downtown Philadelphia, in part because the food was superb and the banquettes would provide what he considered to be the necessary privacy he sought, and also because he thought it would provide an opportunity to needle the management a little.

There was no question in Davis's mind (or for that matter in the minds of any peace officer with the brains to find his rear end with both hands) that Ristorante Alfredo was owned by persons connected with organized crime, otherwise known as "the Mob" and sometimes as "the Mafia."

Davis was sure that there would be someone in the restaurant who would recognize him and Wohl, whom Davis believed to be as bright and competent a Philadelphia cop as they came, and note and report to his superiors that they had been taking lunch together.

If that had caused Ricco Baltazari, who held the restaurant license for Ristorante Alfredo, or Vincenzo Savarese, "the businessman" who actually owned it, some uncomfortable moments wondering what the head of the FBI and the head of Special Operations were up to, together, that would have added a little something to the luncheon.

But that had not come to pass. Wohl had accepted the invitation, and said that since he would be at the Roundhouse at about lunchtime, he would just stop by the FBI office when he was finished with his business and pick Davis up.

The Administration Building of the Philadelphia Police Department, at 8th and Race Streets, was universally called "the Roundhouse" because its architect had been fascinated with curves, and everything in the building was curved, right down to the elevators.

Wohl's own office was at Bustleton and Bowler Streets in Northeast Philadelphia, from which he commanded the Special Operations Division, which consisted of the Highway Patrol and a newly formed, somewhat experimental unit of above-average uniformed and plainclothes cops.

The original idea was that Special Operations, which like

the Highway Patrol had city-wide responsibility, would move into high-crime areas of the city, and overwhelm the problem with manpower, special equipment and techniques, and an arrangement with the district attorney to hustle the arrested through the criminal justice procedure.

That was being done, but politics had inevitably entered the picture almost immediately. First, there had been the murder of Jerome Nelson, whose father, Arthur J. Nelson, was chairman of the board of the Daye-Nelson Corporation, which owned (among other newspapers and television stations) the Philadelphia *Ledger* and WGHA-TV.

When a Homicide Division lieutenant, Edward M. DelRaye, had been truthfully tactless enough to inform the press that the police were looking for a Negro Male, Pierre St. Maury, a known homosexual known to be living with young Nelson in his luxury Society Hill apartment, in connection with the killing, the *Ledger* and its publisher had declared war on both the Police Department and the Hon. Jerry Carlucci, mayor of the City of Philadelphia.

Mayor Carlucci had "suggested" to Police Commissioner Taddeus Czernich that the investigation of the Nelson murder be turned over to Peter Wohl's Special Operations Division.

The case had more or less solved itself when two other Negro Homosexual Males had been arrested in Atlantic City in possession of Jerome Nelson's Visa and American Express cards, and had been charged by New Jersey authorities with the murder of Pierre St. Maury, whose body had been found near Jerome Nelson's abandoned Jaguar in the wilds of New Jersey.

SAC Davis knew that, for reasons that could only be described as political, Mayor Carlucci had "suggested" to Commissioner Czernich that Peter Wohl's Special Operations Division be given responsibility for three other situations that had attracted a good deal of media attention, much of it (all of it, in the case of the *Ledger*) unfavorable.

The first of these, a serial murder-rapist in Northwest Philadelphia, had been resolved, to favorable publicity, when a police officer assigned to Special Operations had not only shot the murder-rapist to death, but done so when the villain actually had his next intended victim tied up, naked, in the back of his van.

The other two highly publicized cases had not gone at all

well. One was the apparently senseless murder of a young police officer who had been on patrol near Temple University. A massive effort, still ongoing, hadn't turned up a thing, which gave Arthur Nelson's *Ledger* an at least once-a-week opportunity to run an editorial criticizing the Police Department generally, Special Operations specifically, and Mayor Carlucci in particular.

Davis was sure that the pressure on Wohl to find the cop killer must be enormous.

The third case had been that of a contract hit of a third-rate mobster, Anthony J. DeZego, also known as "Tony the Zee," on the roof of a downtown parking garage. Ordinarily, the untimely demise of a minor thug would have been forgotten in twenty-four hours, but this particular thug had been in the company of a young woman named Penelope Detweiler when someone had opened up on him with a shotgun. The Detweiler girl's father was president of Nesfoods International and one of the rocks upon which the cathedral of Philadelphia society had been built. Not only had this young woman been wounded during the attack on Mr. DeZego, but it had come out that she was not only carrying on with Tony the Zee but also addicted to heroin.

Obviously, since it wasn't their fault that their precious child had not only been shacking up with a married thug, but had been injecting and inhaling narcotics, it had to be somebody's fault. Since the police were supposed to stop that sort of thing it was obviously the fault of the police. For a few days, the influence of Nesfoods International had allied itself with Mr. Nelson and his newspaper in roundly condemning the Police Department and the mayor.

But then that had stopped, with Mr. Detweiler making a 180-degree turn. Davis had no idea how Mayor Carlucci (or possibly Peter Wohl) had pulled that off, but what had happened was that Detweiler had made a speech not only praising the police, but also starting, with a large contribution of his own, a reward fund to catch whoever had murdered the young cop in his patrol car.

Special Agent Davis knew that Mr. Detweiler's change of heart had nothing to do with the cops having caught whoever had killed DeZego and seriously wounded his daughter. That was never going to happen. The DeZego murder and the Detweiler aggravated assault cases would almost certainly never be officially closed.

There had been a report from the FBI's Chicago office that a known contract hit man meeting the description of the DeZego killer had been found in the trunk of his car with three 45-caliber bullets having passed through his cranial cavity. There was little question in anyone's mind that the DeZego/Detweiler hit man had himself been hit, probably to shut his mouth, but knowing something and being able to prove it were two entirely different things.

Special Agent in Charge Davis had been meaning to have lunch with Peter Wohl, to chat, out of school, about these cases, even before he had learned, within the past forty-eight hours, that the Nelson case was not, in something of an understatement, over. It was in fact the reason he had asked Staff Inspector Wohl to break bread with him, preferably in some quiet restaurant, like Ristorante Alfredo, where they could talk in confidence.

Davis had been summoned to Washington two days before and informed that after a review of the facts, the United States Attorney for the Eastern District of Pennsylvania had brought the case of the two Negro Males who had kidnapped Pierre St. Maury, taken him against his will across a state border, and then shot him to death before a federal Grand Jury and secured an indictment against them under the Lindbergh Act.

Davis had been informed that it behooved him to do whatever he could to assist the deputy attorney general in securing a conviction. He had been told that the case had attracted the interest of certain people high in the Justice Department. Davis did not need to be reminded that the deputy attorney general of the United States, before his appointment, had been a senior partner of the law firm that represented the Daye-Nelson Corporation.

Davis had been on the telephone when Wohl had appeared at his office, and Wohl consequently had had to cool his heels for fifteen minutes before Davis could come out of his office to greet him, and apologize for getting hung up.

This would have annoyed Peter Wohl in any case, when all things were going fine in his world. Today that wasn't the case. He had just come from the Roundhouse, where he had had a painful session with Mayor Carlucci and Commissioner Czernich, witnessed by Chief Inspectors Matt Lowenstein (Detective Division) and Dennis V. Coughlin concerning the inability of the Special Operations Division to come up with even *one* fucking thing that might lead them to find whoever had put four .22 Long Rifle bullets into the chest, and one into the leg, of Police Officer Joseph Magnella.

He had not been in the mood to be kept waiting by anybody, and Special Agent Davis had seen this on his face.

It was unfortunate, Davis had thought, that Wohl first of all looked too young to be a staff inspector of police, (he was, in fact, Davis had recalled, the youngest staff inspector in the Department) and second, he seemed to have a thing about not introducing himself by giving his rank or even identifying himself as a police officer unless it was absolutely necessary.

If he had told the receptionist that he was "Staff Inspector Wohl," Davis thought, *she would certainly have taken him into the staff coffee room as a professional courtesy. But apparently, he had not done so; the receptionist had said, "There's a man named Wohl to see you." And so she had pointed out a chair in the outer office to him and let him wait.*

And then, no sooner had Davis put on his topcoat and hat, as they were literally walking out of the reception room to the elevators, there had been another "must-take" telephone call.

"Peter, I'm sorry."

"Why don't we try this another time? You're obviously really too busy."

"Wait downstairs, I'll only be a minute."

It had been at least ten minutes. When he walked out onto the street, Wohl had been leaning against the fender of his official Plymouth, wearing a visibly insincere smile.

"Well, Walter, here you are!"

"You know how these things go," Davis replied.

"Certainly," Wohl said. "I mean, my God, FBI agents aren't expected to have to eat, are they?"

"How does Italian sound, Peter?"

"Italian sounds fine," Wohl replied and opened the back door of the car for him. Only then did Davis see the young man behind the wheel of the Ford.

A plainclothesman, he decided. *He's too young to be a detective.*

He realized that the presence of Wohl's driver was going to be a problem. He didn't want to talk about the murder-kidnapping case, especially the political implications of it, in front of a junior police officer.

Wohl slammed the door after Davis and got in the front seat.

"Shank & Evelyn's, Matt," he ordered. "Eleventh and Carpenter."

"Yes, sir," the young cop said.

"Officer Payne, this is Special Agent—Special Agent *in Charge*, excuse *me*, Davis."

"How do you do?" Payne said.

"Nice to meet you," Davis said absently, forcing a smile. He had begun to suspect that the luncheon was not going to go well. "Peter, I was thinking about Alfredo's—"

"That's a Mob-owned joint," Wohl said, as if shocked at the suggestion. "I don't know about the FBI, but we local cops have to worry about where we're seen, isn't that so, Officer Payne?"

"Yes, sir, we certainly do," the young cop said, playing straight man to Wohl.

"Besides, the veal is better at Shank & Evelyn's than at Ristorante Alfredo, wouldn't you say, Officer Payne?"

"Yes, sir, I would agree with that."

"Officer Payne is quite a gourmet, Walter. He really knows his veal."

"Okay, Peter, I give up," Davis said. "I'm sorry about making you wait. I really am. It won't happen again."

"I have no idea what you're talking about, Walter. Anyway, Officer Payne and I don't have anything else to do but wait around to buy the FBI lunch, do we, Officer Payne?"

"Not a thing, sir."

"I'm buying the lunch," Davis said.

"In that case, you want us to go back and stand around on the curb for a while?"

"So, how are things, Peter?" Davis said, smiling. "Not to change the subject, of course?"

"Can't complain," Wohl said.

Davis had seen that they had turned left onto South Broad and were heading toward the airport.

"Where is this restaurant?" Davis asked.

"In South Philly. If you want good Italian food, go to South Philly, I always say. Isn't that so, Officer Payne?"

"Yes, sir," Officer Payne replied. "You're always saying that, sir."

"So tell me, Officer Payne, how do you like being Inspector Wohl's straight man?"

Officer Payne turned and smiled at Davis. "I like it fine, sir," he said.

Nice-looking kid, Davis thought.

A few minutes later Payne turned off South Broad Street, and then onto Christian, and then south onto 11th Street. A 3rd District sergeant's car was parked in a Tow Away Zone at a corner.

"Pull up beside him, Matt," Wohl ordered, and, when Payne did so, rolled down the window.

What Davis thought of as a real, old-time beat cop, a heavy-set, florid-faced sergeant in his fifties, first scowled out of the window and then smiled broadly. With surprising agility, he got out of the car, put out his hand, and said, "Goddamn, look who's out slumming. How the hell are you, Peter—Inspector?"

He saw me, Davis thought, *and decided he should not call Wohl by his first name in front of a stranger, who is probably a senior police official.*

"Pat, say hello to the headman of the FBI, Walter Davis," Wohl said. "Walter, Sergeant Pat McGovern. He was my tour sergeant in this district when I got out of the Academy."

"Hello, sir, an honor I'm sure," McGovern said to Davis.

"How are you, Sergeant?"

McGovern looked at Payne, decided he wasn't important, and nodded at him.

"Anything I can do for you?" McGovern asked.

"Where can we find a place to park?" Wohl asked.

"Going in Shank & Evelyn's?"

"Yeah."

"You got a parking place," Sergeant McGovern said. He raised his eyes to Matt Payne. "Back it up, son, and I'll get out of your way."

"Good to see you, Pat."

"Yeah, you too," McGovern said as he started to get back in his car. "Say hello to your old man. He all right?"

Davis remembered that Wohl's father was a retired chief inspector.

"If anything, meaner."

"Impossible," McGovern said, and then got his car moving.

Payne moved into the space vacated, and Davis and Wohl got out of the car.

"Peter," Davis said quietly, touching Wohl's arm. "Could we send your driver someplace else to eat?"

"Is this personal, Walter?"

Davis hesitated a moment before replying.

"No. Not really."

"He's good with details," Wohl said, nodding toward Payne.

Which translates, Davis thought, a little annoyed, *that Wohl's straight man doesn't go somewhere else to eat.*

Shank & Evelyn's Restaurant was worse for Davis's purposes than he could have imagined possible. The whole place was smaller than his office, and consisted of a grill, a counter with ten or twelve stools, and half a dozen tables, at the largest of which, provided they kept their elbows at their sides, four people could eat.

What I should have done, Davis thought, annoyed, *was simply get in my car and drive out to Wohl's office at Bustleton and Bowler. This is a disaster.*

They found seats at a tiny table littered with the debris of the previous customers' meals. A massively bosomed waitress with a beehive hairdo first cleaned the table and then took their orders. Wohl ordered the veal, and somewhat reluctantly, Davis ordered the same.

"Sausage, *hot* sausage, and peppers, please, extra peppers," Matt Payne said.

"Frankie around?" Wohl asked her.

"In the back," the waitress said.

Wohl nodded.

A minute or so later, a very large, sweating man in a chef's hat, T-shirt, and white trousers came up to the table, offering his hand.

"How the hell are you, Peter?"

"Frankie, say hello to Walter Davis and Matt Payne," Wohl said. "This is Frankie Perri."

Frankie gave them a callused ham of a hand.

"Matt works for me," Wohl went on. "Walter runs the FBI. He said he'd never met a Mob guy, so I said I could fix that and brought him here."

"He's kidding, I hope you know," Frankie said.

"Yes, of course," Davis said uncomfortably.

"With a name like Frankie Perri, the FBI figures you have to be in the Mafia," Wohl said.

"Kiss my ass, Peter," Frankie Perri said, punching Wohl affectionately on the arm. "I'm going to burn your goddamn veal."

He put out his hand to Davis, and nodded at Matt.

"Nice to meet you, Mr. Davis. Come back. Both of you."

"Thank you," Davis said, and then when he was gone, he said, "What do you call that, Peter, community relations?"

"What's on your mind, Walter?"

"The government is going to try Clifford Wallis and Delmore Travis for murder/kidnapping under the Lindbergh Act."

"Who?" Matt Payne asked.

Wohl glanced at him, a flicker of annoyance in his eyes.

"New Jersey's got them," Wohl said, "with a lot of evidence, on a murder one. They might plea bargain that down to manslaughter one, but no further. That's good for twenty-to-life, anyway. Why?"

"They violated federal law, Peter."

"Come on."

"Let us say there is considerable interest in this case rather high up in the Justice Department."

"You mean that Arthur Nelson wants them prosecuted," Wohl said.

Davis, who had been sitting back in his chair with his left hand against his cheek, moved the hand momentarily away from his face, a tacit agreement with Wohl's statement.

"Why?" Wohl asked, visibly thinking aloud.

"People get paroled on a state twenty-to-life conviction after what, seven years?" Davis said.

"And he wants to make sure they do more than seven years for the murder of his son. You got enough to try them?"

"We have enough for a Grand Jury indictment."

"That's not what I asked."

"I grant, it's pretty circumstantial," Davis said. "That's why I'm turning to you for help, Peter."

"Would you think me cynical to suspect that someone's leaning on you about this, Walter?"

"Yes," Davis said, smiling. "But they called me to Washington yesterday, and both of the telephone calls that delayed this little luncheon of ours concerned this case."

The waitress with the beehive hairdo delivered three large

plates with sliced tomatoes and onions just about covering them.

When she had gone, Wohl took a forkful, chewed it slowly, and then asked, "So how can I help, Walter? More than the established, official routine for cooperation with the FBI would be helpful?"

"I need what you have as soon as I can get it, and I want everything you have, not just what a normal request for information would produce."

The waitress delivered three round water glasses, now scarred nearly gray by a thousand trips through the dishwasher. She half filled them, from a battered stainless-steel water pitcher, with a red liquid.

"Frankie said his grandfather made it over in Jersey," the waitress said.

Wohl picked up his glass, then stood up, called "Frankie," and, when he had his attention, called "Salud!" and then sat down again.

Walter Davis, thinking, *Oh, God, homemade Dago Red!* took a swallow. It was surprisingly good.

"You're almost certainly drinking an alcoholic beverage on which the applicable federal tax has not been paid," Wohl said. "Does that bother you?"

"Not a damned bit, to tell you the truth," Davis said. He stood up, called "Frankie" and then "Salud!" and then sat down, looking at Wohl, obviously pleased with himself.

Wohl chuckled, then looked at Matt Payne.

"Matt, when we get back to the office, round up everything in my files on the Nelson murder case. Make a copy of everything. Then go to Homicide and do the same thing. Then find Detective Harris and photocopy everything he has. Have it ready for me in the morning."

"Yes, sir," Matt Payne said.

"I'll take a look at it, see if anything is missing, and then you can take it to the FBI. Soon enough for you, Walter?"

"Thank you, Peter. 'Harris,' you said, was the detective on the job? Any chance that I could talk to him?"

"You, or one of your people?"

"Actually, I was thinking of one of my people."

"Tony Harris is the exception to the rule that most detectives really would rather be FBI agents, Walter. I don't think that would be very productive."

"I thought everybody loved us," Davis said.

"We all do. Isn't that so, Officer Payne?"

"Yes, sir. We all love the FBI."

The waitress with the beehive hairdo delivered their meal.

The veal was, Walter Davis was willing to admit, better than the veal in Ristorante Alfredo. And the homemade Chianti was nicer than some of the dry red wine he'd had at twenty-five dollars a bottle in Ristorante Alfredo.

But he knew that neither the quality of the food nor its considerably cheaper than Ristorante Alfredo prices were the reasons Peter Wohl had brought him here for lunch.

SIX

Under the special agent in charge (the "SAC") of the Philadelphia Office of the Federal Bureau of Investigation were three divisions, Criminal Affairs, Counterintelligence, and Administration. Each division was under an assistant agent in charge, called an "A-SAC."

It was SAC Davis's custom to hold two daily Senior Staff Conferences, called "SSC"'s, each business day, one first thing in the morning, and the other at four P.M. Participation at the SSCs was limited to the SAC and the three A-SACs. The conferences were informal. No stenographic record was made of them, except when the SAC could not be present, and one of the A-SACs was standing in for him. The SAC naturally wanted to know what he had missed, so a steno was called in to make a written record.

If one of the A-SACs could not make a SSC, one of his assistants, customarily, but not always, the most senior special agent in that division, would be appointed to stand in for him.

This was very common. The A-SACs were busy men, and it was often inconvenient for them to make both daily SSCs,

75

although they generally tried to make at least one of them, and took especial pains not to miss two days' SSCs in a row.

But it was a rare thing for SAC Davis to find, as he did when he returned to his office from lunch with Staff Inspector Wohl and Officer Payne, all three A-SACs waiting outside his office for the afternoon SSC.

He was pleased. In addition to whatever else would be discussed, he intended to discuss the upcoming trials of Clifford Wallis and Delmore Travis. The political aspects were mind-boggling. Washington was going to be breathing down his neck on this one, and not only the senior hierarchy of the FBI, joining which was one of SAC Davis's most fond dreams, but the higher—*highest*—echelons of the Department of Justice.

If he handled this well, it would reflect well upon him. If he dropped the ball (or someone he was responsible for dropped it), there would be no chance whatever that he would be transferred to Washington and named a deputy inspector. And from what he had seen of the situation, there was a saber-toothed tiger behind every filing cabinet, just waiting to leap and bite off somebody's ass.

This sort of a case was the sort of thing one should discuss with the A-SACs personally, not with one of their subordinates. With all three of the A-SACs present at this SSC, it would not be necessary to call a special SSC.

Davis waited until he had heard all the reports of what was going on in the Criminal, Administrative, and Counterintelligence Divisions, and made the few decisions necessary before getting into what he was now thinking of as the "Wallis/Travis Sticky Ball of Wax."

Then he gave a report, the essentials and the flavor, of both the personal conference he had had in Washington the day before and the two telephone calls he had had that morning before going off to lunch with Staff Inspector Wohl and his straight man.

"I had lunch today with Staff Inspector Wohl of the Philadelphia Police Department," he announced. "Everybody know who Wohl is?"

The three A-SACs nodded.

"I didn't go through you, Glenn," he explained to Glenn Williamson, A-SAC (Administration), "I know Peter Wohl, and this was unofficial. But I think you should open a line of communication with Captain— What's his name?"

"Duffy. Jack Duffy, Chief," Williamson furnished. Williamson was a well-dressed man of forty-two who took especial pains with his full head of silver-gray hair.

"—Duffy of—what's his title, Glenn?"

"Assistant to the commissioner, Chief."

"—whatever—as soon as possible. Either this afternoon, or first thing in the morning," Davis finished.

For reasons SAC Davis really did not understand, cooperation between the Philadelphia Police Department and the Federal Bureau of Investigation was not what he believed it should be. Getting anything out of them was like pulling teeth. When he had found the opportunity, he had discussed the problem with Commissioner Czernich. Czernich had told him that whenever he wanted anything from the Department, he should contact Captain Duffy, who would take care of whatever was requested. It had been Davis's experience that bringing Duffy into the loop had served primarily to promptly inform Czernich that the FBI was asking for something; it had not measurably speeded up getting anything. The reverse, he thought, might actually be the case.

But now that Duffy was in the loop, Duffy would have to be consulted.

"Yes, sir."

"You might mention I had an unofficial word with Wohl. Whatever you think best."

"Yes, sir. How did it go with Wohl, sir?"

"Very interesting man. He had his straight man with him. I was thinking of lunch at Alfredo's, and we wound up in a greasy spoon in South Philadelphia."

"His straight man, sir?" A-SAC (Criminal Affairs) Frank F. Young asked. Young was a redhead, pale-faced, and on the edge between muscular and plump.

"His driver. A young plainclothes cop named Payne. They have a little comedy routine they use on people Wohl's annoyed with. I had to keep Wohl waiting twice, you see—"

"Oh, you met Payne, Chief?" A-SAC (Counterintelligence) Isaac J. Towne asked. He was a thirty-nine-year-old, balding Mormon, who took his religion seriously, a tall, hawk-featured man who had once told Davis, perfectly serious, that he regarded the Communists as the Antichrist.

"You know him?" Davis asked, surprised.

"I know about him," Towne replied. "Actually, I know a

good deal about him. Among other things, he's the fellow who blew the brains of the serial rapist all over his van.''

''Oh, really?'' A-SAC Young asked, genuine interest evident in his voice. Davis knew that Young had a fascination for what he had once called ''real street cop stuff''; Davis suspected he was less interested in some of the white-collar crime that occupied a good deal of the FBI's time and effort.

''How is it you know 'a good deal about him,' Isaac?'' Davis asked.

''Well, when I saw the story in the papers, the name rang a bell, and I checked my files. We had just finished a CBI on him.'' (Complete Background Investigation.)

''He'd applied for the FBI?''

''The Marine Corps. He was about to be commissioned.''

''Apparently he wasn't?''

''He flunked the physical,'' Towne said. ''His father, his *adoptive* father, is Brewster Cortland Payne.''

''As in Mawson, Payne, Stockton, McAdoo and whatever else?''

''And Lester. Right, Chief.''

SAC Davis found that fascinating. He was himself an attorney, and although he had never actively practiced law, he was active in the Philadelphia Bar Association. He knew enough about the Bar in Philadelphia to know that Mawson, Payne, Stockton, McAdoo & Lester was one of the more prestigious firms.

''His 'adoptive' father, you said?''

''Yes, sir. His father was a Philadelphia cop. A sergeant. Killed in the line of duty. His mother remarried Payne, and Payne adopted the boy.''

That would stick in your mind, Davis thought, *a street cop killed in the line of duty.*

''I wonder why he became a cop?'' Davis wondered aloud, and then, without waiting for a reply, asked, ''You say he was the man who shot the serial rapist?''

''Right, Chief. In the head, with his service revolver. Blew his brains all over the inside of his van.''

And that, too, would stick in your mind, wouldn't it, Isaac?

''I seem to remember seeing something about that in the papers,'' Davis said. ''But as I was saying, Wohl, once he'd made his annoyance with me quite clear, was very cooperative.

He's going to photocopy everything in his files and have this Payne fellow bring it over here tomorrow."

The three A-SACs nodded their understanding.

"I just had a thought," Davis went on. "Do you happen to recall precisely why Payne failed the Marine Corps physical?"

Isaac Young searched his memory, then shook his head. "No."

"Can you find out?" Davis ordered. "The FBI is always looking for outstanding young men."

"Right, Chief," Isaac Young said.

"And when Officer Payne delivers the material from Inspector Wohl, I think one of us should receive it. Tell the receptionist. Make sure she understands. Show him around the office."

"Right, Chief," Young said.

I mean, after all, Davis thought, *why would a bright young man of good family want to be a cop when he could be an FBI agent?*

And if that doesn't turn out, it can't hurt to have a friend—especially a kid like that, who must hear all sorts of interesting things in the Department.

Matt Payne, feeding documents into the Xerox machine, jumped when Peter Wohl spoke in his ear.

"I have bled enough for the city for one day," Wohl announced. "I am going home and get into a cold martini or a hot blonde, whichever comes first."

"Yes, sir." Matt chuckled. "I'll see you in the morning."

"One of the wounds from which I'm bleeding has to do with what you're doing—"

"Sir?" Matt asked, confused.

"I just got off the phone with Commissioner Czernich," Wohl went on. "I don't know what Davis's agenda really is, and I wondered why he came to me with the request for all that stuff. One possibility was that he didn't want the commissioner to know he was asking for it. With that in mind, I called the commissioner and told him where and with whom we had lunch—" He saw the confused look still on Payne's face and stopped.

"I'm—I don't follow you, Inspector," Matt said.

"For reasons I'm sure I don't have to explain, we are very careful what we pass to the FBI," Wohl said.

I haven't the faintest idea what he's talking about.

"Yes, sir."

"Nothing goes over to them unless the commissioner approves it. Denny Coughlin or Matt Lowenstein might slip them something quietly, but since career suicide is not one of my aims, I won't, and Davis must know that."

"So why did he ask you?"

"Right. So I called the commissioner. The commissioner told me I had done the right thing in calling him, and that I should use my good judgment in giving him whatever I felt like giving him."

"Okay," Matt said thoughtfully.

"Two minutes after I hung up, Czernich called back. 'Peter,' he said, 'I've been thinking it over, and I think I know why Davis went directly to you.' So I said, 'Yes, sir?' and he said, 'It's because you and the Payne kid look more like FBI agents than cops. Hahaha!' And then he hung up."

"Jesus!" Matt said.

"It may well be Polish humor," Wohl said. "But I'm paranoid. The moral to this little story is that I want you to clearly understand you are to pass nothing to the FBI, or the feds generally, unless I tell you to. Clear?"

"Yes, sir."

"Okay. Then I will say good night."

"I'll see you in the morning, sir."

"God willing, and if the creek don't rise," Wohl said solemnly, and walked out of the room.

Matt Payne finished making copies of the documents he had taken from the file, stuffed the copies into a large manila envelope, and then returned the originals to their filing cabinet.

It was quarter to four. He would still have to see Detective Tony Harris, and then go downtown to Homicide and see if their files contained something he hadn't found, or would get from Harris. He would not be able to quit at five.

Tony Harris was not in the closet-sized office he shared with Detective Jason Washington. Washington, he knew, had taken the day off; he had a place at The Shore that always seemed to need some kind of emergency repair.

He really should, he thought, talk to Washington about the file Wohl wanted to pass to the FBI. Washington had worked with Harris on the Nelson job. He remembered overhearing

Washington telling Wohl he would be back sometime in the afternoon.

The tour lieutenant, Harry Jensen, a Highway guy, said that Harris was out on the street somewhere. Both he and Washington were running down increasingly less promising leads to find whoever had shot down Joe Magnella, the young 22nd District cop. Wohl, Matt thought, had not really been kidding when he had said he had bled enough for the city for one day; the pressure on him to find the Magnella doers was enormous.

Payne went to Special Operations communications and tried to raise Harris on the radio. There was no reply, which meant that Harris was either working and away from his car, or that he had hung it up for the day.

That left Homicide, and opened the question of how to get there. He could go to the sergeant and get keys to one of the Special Operations cars. Or he could see if he could catch a ride downtown in either a Special Operations car or a Highway car. In either case, when he was finished at the Roundhouse, that would leave him downtown and his personal car here.

There was no reason for him to come back here, except to get his car, because it would be long past quitting before he finished at Homicide and finally ran Harris down, if he managed to do that.

He went back to Lieutenant Jensen and told him that if Inspector Wohl called for him, to tell him that he had gone to Homicide in his own car, and was going to quit for the day when he finished there.

"The inspector know where to reach you?"

"I'll either be home or I'll call in," Matt said.

"But you *are* going to Homicide?"

"Yes, sir."

Lieutenant Jensen, Matt suspected, was one of a large number of people, in and out of Highway, who nursed a resentment toward him. That a rookie should have a plainclothes assignment as administrative assistant to a division commander was part of it; and part of it, Matt knew, was that he had about as powerful a rabbi, in the person of Chief Inspector Dennis V. Coughlin, as they came.

He had once discussed this with Detective Jason Washington, who had said it was clear to him that the only option Matt had in the circumstances was to adopt a "fuck you" philosophy.

"You didn't ask for the assignment, Matt, the mayor set that up. And it's not your fault that Denny Coughlin looks on you as the son he never had. If people can't figure that out for themselves, fuck 'em."

In time, Matt hoped, the resentment would pass.

He drove downtown via North Broad Street, and was surprised, until he considered the hour, to find a spot in the parking area behind the Roundhouse.

If I were a cynical man, he thought, *I might be prone to suspect that not all of the captains, inspectors, and chief inspectors who toil here in The Palace scrupulously avoid leaving their place of duty before five* P.M.

He entered the Roundhouse by the rear door, waved his ID at the corporal behind the thick plastic window, and the corporal pushed the button that triggered the solenoid in the door to the lobby.

He got in one of the curved elevators and rode it up one floor, and then walked down the curved corridor to the Homicide Bureau.

He had been here often before, and twice under more or less involuntary conditions. The first time, which ranked among the top two or three most unpleasant experiences of his life, had been an eight-hour visit following his shooting of Warren K. Fletcher, aka the Northwest serial rapist.

He had been "interviewed" by two very unpleasant Homicide detectives, under the cold eye of a Homicide captain named Henry Quaire, all three of whom seemed to feel that the shooting was not a good shooting. It had not helped at all that both Peter Wohl and Denny Coughlin had established themselves in Quaire's office during the "interview." By the time the "interview" was over, Matt was beginning to wonder whose side the Homicide guys were on.

The second time was when an asshole Narcotics sergeant had actually suspected (with nothing more, really, to go on than the Porsche) that Matt was (a) involved with drugs, and therefore (b) connected with the shotgun slaying of a Mafia guy named Tony DeZego.

That was all the bastard had. And all Matt had done to arouse his suspicion was to have driven onto the crime scene a minute or two after the shooting had taken place. You didn't have to be Sherlock Holmes to figure out that if Matt had been involved, he wouldn't have been the one who had sent his date to call the *shooting, hospital case* in.

This afternoon, however, all was sweetness and light. He had no sooner got to the railing barring access to the interior of the Homicide Bureau when he heard his name being called, and then saw Captain Quaire smiling and waving him inside.

Quaire offered his hand.

"How are you, Payne? Inspector Wohl called. We've been expecting you."

"How are you, sir?"

"I had them pull the files," Quaire said, tapping a stack of folders on his desk.

"I appreciate that," Matt said.

"I would have them Xeroxed," Captain Quaire said, "but I didn't know what you already had."

"I got a bunch," Matt said, holding up the well-stuffed manila envelope.

Quaire picked up the folders on his desk and carried them to an unoccupied desk in the outer office and sat there as Matt went through the Homicide files on the Nelson murder.

There were only three things—none of which looked important—in the Homicide files that Matt hadn't already found at Bustleton and Bowler, but it took half an hour to find them.

"I didn't think there'd be much," Captain Quaire said as Matt was making copies. "Anything else we can do for Special Operations?"

"I need to use the phone, sir," Matt said. "I'm supposed to see if Mr. Harris has anything."

"Oh, yes, *Mr.* Harris," Quaire said, dryly sarcastic. "*Mr.* Harris used to work here, you know."

"He's told me," Matt said, smiling.

Quaire laughed.

"Help yourself," Quaire said, pointing at a telephone.

Matt called Harris's number at Special Operations. There was no answer. Then he called Police Radio and asked the operator if she could contact W-William Four and ask him to call Homicide.

A minute later she reported there was no response from W-William Four.

"Thank you," Matt said, and hung up.

"For your general information, Officer Payne," Captain Quaire said, "in my long experience with *Mr.* Harris, when he worked here, you understand, it is often difficult to establish contact with him at the cocktail hour.''

"Thank you, sir. I'll remember that.''

"Why don't you try him at his apartment in an hour or so?''

"I will," Matt said.

Two detectives walked into the room. One of them, a slightly built, natty, olive-skinned man, Matt recognized. He was a Homicide detective, Joe D'Amata. The other one, a large, heavy, round-faced man, he didn't know.

"What have you got, Joe?" Captain Quaire said.

"High noon at the OK Corral, Captain," D'Amata said.

"Whaddaya say, Payne? How are you?''

"Hello, Joe.''

"He calls Tony Harris 'Mr.' " Captain Quaire said. "That tell you anything?''

"Tony Harris is much older than I am," D'Amata said, grinning. He turned to the other detective. "You know Payne, don't you?''

The other detective shook his head no.

"Jerry Pelosi, Central Detectives, Matt Payne, Special Operations, also known as 'Dead Eye.' ''

"I know *who* he is, I just never met him. How are you, Payne?" Pelosi said, offering Matt a large, muscular hand and a smile.

"Hi," Matt said, and then, to keep D'Amata from making further witty reference to the shooting, he asked, "What's this 'OK Corral' business?''

" 'High Noon at the OK Corral,' " D'Amata corrected him. "The current count of bullets fired and found at Goldblatt's, not counting what the medical examiner will find in Mr. Cohn—three, maybe four—is twenty-six.''

"Jesus," Captain Quaire said.

"And they're still looking.''

"What's Goldblatt's?" Matt asked.

"Furniture store on South Street," Pelosi explained. "Robbery and murder. Early this afternoon.''

"And a gun battle," Matt offered.

"No," D'Amata said, as much to Captain Quaire as to correct Payne. "Not a gun battle. Nobody took a shot at them. Nobody even had a gun. The doers just shot the place up, for no reason that I can figure.''

Quaire looked between the two detectives. When his eyes

met Pelosi's, Pelosi said, "What *I* can't figure, Captain, is why they hit this place in the first place. They never have much cash around, couple of hundred bucks, maybe a thousand tops. They could have hit any one of the bars around there, and got more. And why did they hit it now? I mean, right after the holidays, there's no business?"

"You have any idea who the doers are?" Quaire asked.

"No, but we're working on that," D'Amata said. "The victims are still a little shaky. I want them calm when I show them some pictures."

Quaire nodded.

"I'd better get out of here," Matt Payne said, suspecting he might be in the way. "Thank you for your help, Captain. And it was nice to meet you."

"Same here," Pelosi replied.

"Anytime you want to sell that piece of shit you drive around in, Payne, cheap, of course, call me," D'Amata said, punching Matt's shoulder.

Matt got as far as the outer door when Captain Quaire called his name. Matt turned.

"Yes, sir?"

"If you manage to find him," Quaire said. "Give our regards to *Mr.* Harris. Tell him we miss his smiling face around here."

"Yes, sir," Matt said. "I'll do that."

On the way to the lobby in the elevator, Matt thought first, *If they didn't like me, they would not tease me.* Teasing, he had learned, was not the police way of expressing displeasure or contempt.

And then he thought, *Shit, I'll be out all night looking for Harris.*

And then a solution to his problem popped into his mind. He crossed the lobby to the desk and asked the corporal if he could use the telephone.

"Business?"

"No, I'm going to call my bookie," Matt said.

The corporal, not smiling, pushed the telephone to him. Matt dialed, from memory, the home telephone of Detective Jason Washington.

SEVEN

Detective Jason Washington was sitting slumped almost sin-fully comfortably in his molded plywood and leather chair, his feet up on a matching footstool, when the telephone rang. The chair had been, ten days before, his forty-third birthday gift from his daughter and son-in-law. He had expected either a necktie, or a box of cigars, or maybe a bottle of Johnnie Walker Black. The chair had surprised him to begin with, and even more after he'd seen one in the window of John Wanamaker's Department Store with a sign announcing that the Charles Eames Chair and Matching Footstool was now available in Better Furniture for $980.

A glass dark with twelve-year-old Scotch rested on his stom-ach. Whenever anything disturbing happened, it was Jason Washington's custom to make himself a drink of good whiskey. He would then sit down and think the problem over. During the thought process, he never touched the whiskey. The net result of this, he sometimes thought, was that he wasted a lot of good whiskey.

"Hello," he said to the telephone. He had a very deep,

melodious voice. When she was little, his daughter used to say he should be on the radio.

"Mr. Washington, this is Matt."

Officer Matthew M. Payne had the discomfiting habit of calling Detective Washington "Mr." At first, Washington had suspected that Payne was being obsequious, or perhaps even, less kindly, mocking him in some perverse manner known only to upper-class white boys. He had come to understand, however, that Matt Payne called him "Mr.," even after being told not to, as a manifestation of his respect. Washington found this discomfiting too.

"Hello, Matt."

"I hate to bother you at home, but I have a little problem. Is this a bad time for me to call?"

I am sitting here alone with a bottle of Johnnie Walker Black Label, just hoping for something to brighten my day.

"What is it, Matt?"

"The feds are going to try the two guys who carved up Jerome Nelson."

What the hell is he talking about?

"Run that past me again?"

"The inspector and I had lunch with the FBI SAC, Mr. Davis. He told the inspector the feds are going to try the doers of the Nelson job for kidnapping. He asked the inspector for what we have on the job. The inspector told me to Xerox everything we have in the files, what Homicide has, and to check with Mr. Harris. I just left Homicide. I can't find Harris. The inspector wants it all on his desk first thing in the morning."

The first thought Jason Washington had was, *Has Wohl lost his mind? If Czernich finds out he has been slipping material to the FBI, he'll be on the phone to Jerry Carlucci two seconds later, and ten seconds after that, Wohl will be teaching "Police Administration" at the Academy.*

This was immediately followed by the obvious rebuttal: *Either Czernich is in on this, or Wohl has his own agenda; the one thing Peter Wohl is not is a fool.*

And then: *Interesting, the way he calls the FBI guy "Mr."; Wohl "the inspector"; and, the first time, Harris "Mr." But that title of respect dropped off the second time he got to Tony. Since he knows that Tony is a first-rate detective, it has to be something else. A little vestigial Main Line snobbery, because Tony dresses like a bum? Or has the kid figured out that Tony has a bottle problem? One possibility is that he called Tony at home—if a furnished room can be called a home—and Tony was incoherent, and he'd rather not deal with that.*

"Why don't you bring what you have here, Matt? I'll have a look at it; see if it's all there."

"Yes, sir," Matt Payne said. "Thank you. I'm on my way."

Washington broke the connection with his finger and dialed Tony's number. There was no answer.

Meaning he's not there. Or that he's there, passed out.

He took a well-worn leather-bound notebook from his pocket, found the number of the Red Rooster, Tony Harris's favorite bar, and dialed it. Tony wasn't there. Washington left word for him to call him at home. It was possible, even likely, that Wohl would want to see him in the morning. Wohl, being Wohl, probably knew all about Tony's bottle problem, but it would not do Tony any good if Wohl saw him with the shakes.

He hung up, looked at the drink he had left sitting on the table beside his chair, and took the first swallow from it.

Jason and Martha Washington lived in an apartment on the tenth floor of a luxury building on the parkway. A wall of ceiling-to-floor windows in the living room gave them a view of the Art Museum, the Schuylkill River, and West Philadelphia.

Martha Washington was a commercial artist who made just about as much money as he did. Now that their daughter, Barbara, was gone, married to a twenty-five-year-old electronics engineer at RCA, across the Delaware in Jersey, who made as much money as his in-laws did together, the Washingtons were, as Jason thought of it, "comfortable."

Not only did they have the condo at The Shore, but Martha had a Lincoln; the furniture in the apartment was all they wanted; and Martha was starting to buy (and sell at often amazing profit) art. It had been a long time, he thought, since there had been an angry or hurt look in Martha's eyes when he walked in wearing a Tripler or Hart, Shaffner & Marx new suit.

They no longer had to think about the costs of getting Barbara a good education. That need had been removed from the financial equation when the graduate student of engineering had snatched her from her cradle the week before he graduated and RCA started throwing money at him.

Ten minutes later the doorman announced that a Mr. Payne was calling.

"If he's wearing shoes, send him up, please."

Washington timed his walk to the door precisely; he opened it as Matt got off the elevator.

"Sorry to bother you with this at home," Matt said.

"Come on in, Matt. I am drinking from the good stuff; make yourself one."

"What's the occasion?"

"Let me see what you have," Washington said, putting out his hand for the manila envelope. "You know where the booze is."

Matt headed for the liquor cabinet.

He is, with the possible exception of Peter Wohl, the only one of my brothers in blue who is not awed and/or made uncomfortable by this apartment.

Washington sat down on a leather upholstered couch and took the photocopies from the envelope and went through them. Payne sat in an armchair watching him.

"I think everything's there, Matt," Washington said, finally.

"Thank God," Matt said. "Thank you."

"You couldn't find Tony, you said?"

"He didn't answer the radio—twice, and he didn't answer the phone at his apartment."

"You ever been to his apartment?"

Matt shook his head no.

Then he hasn't found Tony mumbling incoherently into his booze. Moot point, he will learn eventually.

"Anything interesting going on at Homicide?"

"They had a murder of a guy during a robbery at a furniture store on South Street."

"I heard the call," Washington said.

The *officer needs assistance shooting hospital case* call had been on the air when he switched on the police radio in his unmarked police car as he came off the Benjamin Franklin Bridge into Philadelphia from New Jersey. By the time he reached the parkway, he had heard Matt Lowenstein calling in that he was at the scene. That too was very interesting. The chief of the Detective Division would ordinarily not go in on a robbery, or even a murder. Neither was uncommon in Philadelphia. He finally decided that Lowenstein had coincidentally been somewhere near without anything else important to do.

The car issued to Jason Washington by the Philadelphia Police Department was a new, two-tone (blue over gray) Ford LTD four-door sedan. It had whitewall tires, elaborate chrome wheel covers, and powder blue velour upholstery. There were only eight thousand odd miles on the odometer, and the car still even smelled new.

Detectives (like corporals, only one step above the lowest rank in the Police Department hierarchy) are not normally given brand-new cars to drive, much less to take home after work, but Jason Washington was not an ordinary detective.

Until recently, he had been able to take more than a little pride in his reputation of being the best detective in the Homicide Bureau, which was tantamount to saying that he was arguably the best detective in the entire Philadelphia Police Department, as it is generally conceded that the best detectives are assigned to Homicide.

Washington had not willingly given up his assignment to Homicide. He had been transferred (he thought of it as "shanghaied") to the just-then-formed Special Operations Division over his somewhat bluntly stated desire not to be transferred.

There had been a number of advantages in being assigned to Homicide. There was of course the personal satisfaction of simply knowing that you *were* a Homicide detective. That satisfaction was of course buttressed if you could believe that you were probably the best Homicide detective in the Bureau.

Jason Washington was not plagued with extraordinary humility. While he was perfectly willing to admit there were a number of very good detectives in Homicide, he could not honestly state that he knew of any who were quite as professionally competent as he was.

And the money was good, because of overtime. As a Homicide detective, he had taken home as much money as a chief inspector. Chief inspectors, he knew, often put in as many hours as he did, but under Civil Service regulations, they didn't get paid for it; they were given "compensatory time off" that they never seemed able to find time to take.

And chief inspectors (and other Police Department supervisors) spent a good portion of their time handling administrative matters that had little to do with catching critters, marching them through the judicial process, and seeing them sentenced and packed off to the pokey.

In Homicide, all Jason Washington had had to do was catch critters, either on jobs that had come to him via the Wheel, or on jobs that the Wheel had given to others, but on which he had been asked to "assist."

(The Wheel wasn't really a wheel, but rather a piece of lined paper, on which, at the beginning of each tour, each Homicide detective's name was written. As each homicide came to the attention of the Homicide Bureau, the job was given to the detective whose name was at the head of the list. He would not be given another job until every other detective listed on the Wheel had, in turn, been given one.)

While Jason Washington was at least as good as any other Homicide detective while working the crime scene, and certainly at least as knowledgeable as any other Homicide detective in the use of the high-tech techniques now available to match fibers, determine that a particular bullet had been fired from a particular weapon, and so on, his real strengths, he believed, were psychological and intellectual.

He believed, with more than a little reason, that he had no peers in interrogation. He could play, with great skill, any number of roles when interviewing a suspect. If the situation demanded it, Washington, who stood well over six feet and weighed 220 pounds, could strike terror into the heart of most human beings who had previously believed they were not afraid of the Devil himself. Or, with equal ease, he could assume the role of sympathetic uncle who understood how, through no fault of his own, the suspect had found himself in a situation where striking the deceased in the forehead with a fire axe had seemed a perfectly reasonable thing to do under the circumstances, and that the decent thing to do now was put the whole unfortunate incident behind him (or her) by making a clean breast of it.

Intellectually, Washington believed that both by natural inclination (perhaps genetic) and by long experience, he had no equal in discovering anomalies. An anomaly, by definition, is a deviation, modification, mutation, permutation, shift, or variation from the norm. If there was one tiny little piece of the jigsaw puzzle that didn't fit, Jason Washington could find it.

He had, in other words, been perfectly happy as the acknowledged best detective in Homicide when Jerome Nelson had been found in his apartment on Society Hill dead of multiple wounds probably inflicted by one of his own matched set of teak-handled Solingen kitchen knives.

The Wheel had assigned the case to Detective Anthony C. "Tony" Harris, who was not only a good friend of Washington's, but, in Washington's judgment, the second-best detective in Homicide. As soon as the case had come in, and as soon as Jerome Nelson's position in society had become known, Jason Washington had felt sure that he would soon be involved with it himself. Tony certainly would want some help, and would naturally turn to Jason Washington, or Captain Henry C. Quaire, who commanded the Homicide Bureau, would order him to work with Tony.

It hadn't happened quite that way. The Honorable Jerry Carlucci, mayor of the City of Brotherly Love, had taken the job away from the Homicide Bureau and given it to the newly formed Special Operations Division. Jason Washington's initial reaction to that had mirrored that of Captain Quaire and Chief Inspector Matt Lowenstein, who commanded the Detective Division that included the Homicide Bureau: righteous indignation that once more The Dago had put his goddamn nose in where it had no business.

Mayor Carlucci's notorious penchant for issuing orders directly to various divisions (for that matter, to individual officers) of the Police Department, instead of letting the commissioner run it, was, in a sense, understandable. Before winning, in his first bid for elective office, the mayoralty, The Dago had been police commissioner. He had, in fact, held every rank in the Philadelphia Police Department except police woman. He therefore believed that he knew at least as much about running the Police Department as anyone else. And he had read the statutory functions of the mayor, which quite clearly stated that he was responsible for supervising "the various departments of the city."

On a secondary level, his parochial indignation as a Homicide detective aside, Jason Washington had thought that he understood The Dago's game plan, and that it would work. The Dago had turned out to be a better politician than anyone ever thought he would be.

Jason Washington and Jerry Carlucci went way back together. Carlucci had done a year in Homicide as a lieutenant, before he passed the captain's examination and moved to Highway Patrol. It was only fair to acknowledge that Carlucci had been a good lieutenant—he had been an all around good cop, no one ever denied that—one proof of which being that even back then he had been smart enough to exercise only the barest minimum of supervision over Detective Jason Washington.

When, rarely, they bumped into each other, Washington could count on a bear hug and being greeted either by his Christian name or as "Ol' Buddy," or both. Jason Washington, who did not like to be hugged by anyone except his wife and daughter, and disliked being called "Ol' Buddy" by anyone, always smiled and referred to The Dago as "Mr. Mayor."

The way Washington had seen the assignment of the Nelson job to Special Operations seemed to make sense. Carlucci had just set up Special Operations. It was his. What had become a big deal murder in the newspapers, because of the victim, was actually just a routine homicide. The odds were that the job would be closed in a week or two by Homicide. But that would not earn The Dago any favorable space in the newspapers. That's what Homicide was supposed to do, solve homicides.

But if Jerry Carlucci's Special Operations solved the Nelson job, His Honor the Mayor could, and would, claim the credit.

And Washington had seen that The Dago had carefully hedged his bet: Special Operations was commanded by Peter Wohl, who not only had been a sergeant in Homicide, but was, in Washington's judgment (and that of a lot of other knowledgeable people), one of the smartest cops in the Department. Before The Dago had formed Special Operations and given it to Peter Wohl, Wohl had been the youngest (ever) staff inspector in the department.

Staff inspectors ranked immediately above captains. With the exception, now, of Wohl, they operated within the Internal Affairs Division, and were charged with, primarily, investigations of corruption within and outside the Police Department. Wohl, just before being given Special Operations, had sent two judges and a city councilman to the state penitentiary for some rather imaginative income augmentation.

Washington had reasoned that Carlucci had decided that Wohl would have no trouble finding who had punctured Jerome Nelson so thoroughly, and that Special Operations—thus the mayor—would get the credit.

Washington had underestimated both Carlucci and Wohl. To

make sure that Wohl did indeed catch the critters who had punctured Nelson with his own imported butcher knives, he gave him blanket authority to transfer to Special Operations anybody he thought he needed. Wohl had immediately decided that he needed Detectives Washington and Harris, and over howls of protest from the chief inspector of the Detective Division, the commanding officer of the Homicide Bureau, and Detectives Harris and Washington, they had been transferred to Special Operations.

Wohl was not only a good cop, but a good guy, and he had assured both Washington and Harris that he would see they could make as much overtime money as they had in Homicide, and done other things to soothe their ruffled feathers. They would work directly for him (and his deputy, Captain Mike Sabara) rather than under some sergeant, and had even arranged for the both of them to draw brand-new cars (normally reserved for at least captains) from the Police Garage.

He would not, however, promise (as Washington asked) to return them to Homicide once they caught whoever had murdered Jerome Nelson.

That job had just about solved itself when two critters had been caught by the cops in Atlantic City using Nelson's credit cards, but by then a looney tune in Northwest Philadelphia had started abducting and then carving up women, and the process had been repeated: Jerry Carlucci had called a press conference to announce he had given the job of apprehending the Northwest serial rapist to Special Operations, and Wohl had given it to Washington and Harris.

Washington and Harris had just about identified the psychopath who was carrying women off in the back of his van when, in one of those lucky breaks that sometimes happen, his van had been spotted by the rookie cop Wohl had had dumped in his lap by Chief Inspector Dennis V. Coughlin and was using as his driver.

Denny Coughlin, in what some people would call blatant nepotism but which Jason Washington felt perfectly sensible, had sent Officer Matthew M. Payne right out of the Police Academy to Special Operations, his intention clearly being to keep the kid from getting hurt before he came to his senses and quit the cops.

The kid had been born Matthew Mark Moffitt, three months after his father, Sergeant John Xavier Moffitt, had gotten himself shot to death answering a silent alarm. Sergeant Moffitt and Denny Coughlin had gone through the Academy together, and Coughlin had wept shamelessly at his funeral and when he had become the baby's godfather three months later.

Washington had always had the private opinion that Denny Coughlin had been more than a little sweet on the widow. If he had been (or, for that matter, if he still was; he had never married), he hadn't been able to do anything about it, for six months after Sergeant Moffitt had been killed, his widow got a job working as a trainee-secretary for Lowerie, Tant, Foster, Pedigill and Payne, a large and prestigious law firm. She hadn't worked more than a month or so when, pushing the kid in a stroller by the Franklin Institute on a Sunday afternoon, she met Brewster Cortland Payne II, walking his kids.

Payne recognized her vaguely from work; she was one of the girls in the typing pool. He spoke to her, and Patty Moffitt replied, because she had seen him at work too. He was the only son of one of the two founding partners of the law firm.

Within half an hour, Brewster Cortland Payne II learned that Mrs. Moffitt was a widow, and Patty Moffitt learned that his kids were motherless: Mrs. Payne had been killed in an auto accident returning from the Payne lodge in the Poconos some months before.

A month later Patricia Moffitt, enraging her family, her late husband's family, and the Payne family establishment, became Mrs. Brewster C. Payne II. Nice Irish Catholic Widows do not marry Main Line WASPs in an Episcopal Church, nor let their fatherless children be adopted by WASPs, nor become Episcopalians.

Similarly, Main Line WASPs, scions of distinguished families, and heirs apparent to prestigious law firms, do not consort with—much less marry—little Irish typists from Kensington. Brewster C. Payne II resigned from the family law firm and set up his own practice in a two-room office with his bride functioning as his secretary.

That was twenty-odd years ago. Mrs. Brewster C. Payne II (who had borne Mr. Payne two additional children) was now a Main Line Matron of impeccable reputation, and Brewster C. Payne, Attorney At Law, was now the presiding partner of Mawson, Payne, Stockton, McAdoo & Lester, Lawyers, whose offices and eighty-four junior partners and associates occupied two entire floors of the Philadelphia Savings Fund Society

Building, and were arguably the most successful and unquestionably one of the two or three most prestigious law firms in the city.

Mrs. Payne had done what she could (in Jason Washington's opinion, taken the extra step, and then a couple more) to see that her son did not lose contact with either her late husband's family or with her late husband's best friend, Dennis V. Coughlin.

Her late husband's family were cops. John X. Moffitt's father and grandfather had been cops, and his brother (Richard C., known as "Dutch") was a cop. Her ex-mother-in-law, known as Mother Moffitt, a formidable German/Irish lady in her late sixties, had a father and two brothers who had retired from the Department.

Seven months before, when Captain "Dutch" Moffitt had been given a police funeral presided over by the cardinal archbishop of Philadelphia at Saint Monica's Church, Mother Moffitt had let the world know that she had not forgiven her ex-daughter-in-law for leaving Holy Mother Church and taking her son with her. Patricia Moffitt Payne's name had been conspicuously absent not only from the list of family members entitled to sit in a reserved pew but from the list of Friends of the Family as well.

When Denny Coughlin had told the inspector working the door that the entire Payne family was to be seated inside and up front in Saint Monica's if that meant evicting members of the City Council, Mother Moffitt had pretended Patty Payne and her husband and their kids were invisible.

Three days later Matthew M. Payne had walked into the City Administration Building across from City Hall, taken the exam, and joined the cops.

There was nothing that either Brewster C. Payne or Chief Inspector Dennis V. Coughlin could do about it. The two, who over the years had become friends, had a long talk over lunch at the Union League Club. They agreed that Matt's motives were fairly obvious: The fact that his Uncle Dutch had been killed obviously had a lot to do with it, and so did the results of a physical examination that found something wrong with his eyes and would keep him from becoming a second lieutenant in the Marine Corps when he graduated from the University of Pennsylvania.

He could prove his challenged masculinity by becoming a cop, in the footsteps of his real father, uncle, and grandfather.

Adoptive father and godfather agreed that what Matt really should do was go on to law school, but they also agreed that he was just as hardheaded as his mother when he wanted to do something, and could not be talked out of joining the cops.

It was to be hoped that when the emotions caused by Dutch's death and the Marine Corps rejection had time to simmer down, he would come to his senses. They were both agreed that Matt was a more levelheaded kid than most. With a little bit of luck that would happen before he was close to graduating from the Police Academy.

It didn't happen. He did well in the Academy.

Dennis V. Coughlin, as a sergeant, had gone to Patricia Moffitt's apartment to tell her that her husband had just been shot to death. He had no intention of going to Patricia Moffitt Payne to tell her her son had just been killed as a cop. The most influential of the seven chief inspectors had a word with the chief of Personnel, and Officer Payne was assigned to Special Operations.

There, after Denny Coughlin had a quiet word with Peter Wohl, Officer Payne was assigned duties as a sort of clerk/driver, the hope now being that when he saw what police work was really like, he would finally come to his senses, quit the cops, and go to law school.

What Jason Washington hadn't already known of Matt Payne's background had been filled in by Peter Wohl when he gave him Payne as a gofer. The investigation of the Northwest Philadelphia serial rapist/murderer had become very intense. Washington needed someone to run errands, make telephone calls, and otherwise save his time.

Payne had gone with Washington to Bucks County, where the body of the latest victim had been found. Washington had gotten a description of the man, his van, the license plate number, and had made plaster casts of the van's tire tracks. Within hours, they would know who they were looking for.

Washington had sent Payne back to Philadelphia with the tire casts and orders to tell Peter Wohl of the latest developments before he quit for the day. Payne had dropped off the tire casts at the laboratory in the Roundhouse, and then turned in the unmarked police car he had been driving at Special Operations headquarters at Bustleton and Bowler Streets.

In his own car, on the way to Wohl's apartment in Chestnut Hill, Payne had spotted the van. There was no way he could call for backup. In the very first time he had ever attempted to exercise his authority as a police officer, Payne had walked up to the van.

The driver had then tried to run him over. Payne had jumped out of the way, but the van had wiped out the rear end of Payne's Porsche 911 and then raced away.

Payne had fired five shots, all the cylinder of his snub-nosed Smith & Wesson Undercover held. One bullet, in what Jason Washington believed (and, more importantly, Payne realized) was blind luck, had struck the van driver in the back of the head.

The van had crashed into a tree. When Payne jerked the door open, he found the looney-tune's next intended victim, already stripped naked and trussed up like a Christmas turkey, under a tarpaulin in the back.

When Police Radio had put out the *beep beep beep, assist officer, shots fired, hospital case* the second response had been "M-Mary One in on the shots fired."

M-Mary One was the radio call assigned to Jerry Carlucci's official Cadillac. The mayor had been on the way to his Chestnut Hill home after speaking at a dinner in South Philadelphia.

The lifelong cop in Jerry Carlucci could no more resist responding to an *assist officer shots fired* than he could pass up a chance to speak to a group of potential voters. Then, too, he sensed that there were a lot of voters out there who liked to see pictures in the newspapers, or on television, of their mayor at a crime scene, personally leading the war against crime.

Mickey O'Hara had also been working the streets that night. The next morning's *Bulletin* had a three-column picture of Mayor Carlucci, standing so that the snub-nosed revolver on his belt was visible under his jacket, with his arm around Officer Payne's shoulder. In the accompanying story by Michael J. O'Hara, *Bulletin* Staff Writer, Officer Payne was described by the mayor as both "administrative assistant" to Peter Wohl and as "the type of well-educated, dedicated, courageous young police officer" now, under his direction, being recruited for the Police Department.

The mayor's description of Matt Payne as Wohl's administrative assistant had erased any notions Wohl might have had to transfer Officer Payne someplace else.

He had joked about it to Washington: "Thank God for our mayor. I didn't even know what an administrative assistant was, and now I have one." But Washington sensed that Wohl was really not at all displeased.

For one thing, a "driver," analogous to an aide-de-camp for a general officer in the military services, was a perquisite of inspectors, chief inspectors, and deputy commissioners. Wohl was only a staff inspector, but he was also the only division commanding officer who was not at least an inspector. Before the mayor's off-the-cuff designation of Matt Payne as his "administrative assistant," Wohl had not had a driver, and there would have been cracks about delusions of glory from the corps of inspectors and chief inspectors, more than a few of whom thought they should have been given command of Special Operations, if he had asked for one.

But most important, Washington thought, was that Wohl needed not only a driver, but one like Matt Payne. It may have sounded like bullshit when The Dago said it for the papers, but Washington could find nothing wrong with the notion of young police officers who were in fact well educated, dedicated, and courageous.

"Detective D'Amata said it was 'high noon at the OK Corral' at the furniture store," Matt Payne said.

There he goes again. "Detective D'Amata," said with respect, instead of just D'Amata, or for that matter "Joe." Joe D'Amata would not be at all annoyed to be called by his first name by Matt. So far as D'Amata's concerned, Matt stopped being a rookie when he shot the serial rapist.

"Meaning what?"

"He said the doers really shot the place up. He said they found twenty-six bullets."

"There was a gun battle?"

"No. That's what he said was interesting. They just shot off their guns. Not even the victim had a gun."

"There was just the one victim?"

"He was the maintenance man; he walked in on it."

"They have a lead on the doers?"

"I think Detective D'Amata has a good idea. He said that the witnesses were still pretty shaky; he wanted them to calm down a little before he showed them pictures."

"That may work, and it may not," Washington said. "A lot of people, with good reason, are nervous about having to go to court and point their fingers. Particularly at scumbags like these, a gang of them.''

''Yes, sir,'' Matt said.

Washington met his eyes.

''I am not going to tell you anymore not to call me 'sir,' '' he said.

''Sorry,'' Matt said, throwing up his hands. ''It just slips out.''

''Let me show you what the postman brought today,'' Washington said. He went to the table by the door and returned with a postcard and handed it to Matt.

It was a printed form, Number 73–41, (Revised 3/72) issued by the Personnel Department of the City of Philadelphia, headed FINAL RESULTS OF EXAMINATIONS. It informed Jason Washington that his Final Average on the Examination for Police Sergeant was 96.52 and that his Rank on List was 3.

''Jesus!'' Payne exclaimed happily.

''You asked what the occasion was,'' Washington said.

''Well, congratulations!'' Matt said enthusiastically. ''I didn't even know you had taken the examination.''

''I'd almost forgotten I had,'' Washington said.

Matt looked at him with curiosity in his eyes, but did not ask.

''Two days after Wohl shanghaied me to Special Operations,'' Washington explained, ''I put my name in. I almost didn't take it. I never cracked a book.''

''But you came in third,'' Matt said.

''As I said, Officer Payne, you may now call me 'sir.' ''

''Well, I think this is splendid!''

Spoken like a true Main Line WASP. ''Splendid.''

''Splendid?'' Washington asked dryly.

''I think so.''

''Thank you, Matt,'' Washington said.

''So what happens to you now? Will they transfer you?''

''I devoutly hope so,'' Washington said. ''Back to Homicide.''

''I'd hate to see you go.''

Now that I think about it, I'm not so sure I want to go back to Homicide. Not as a sergeant.

''I don't think Peter Wohl will let me go anywhere until we catch the cop killer,'' Washington said.

''Is that the way that works? It's up to the inspector?''

"No. The way it works is that assignments of newly promoted people are made by Personnel. They evaluate the individual in terms of vacancies, his future career, and the good
of the Department. After a good deal of thought and paper-
pushing, they reach a decision, and the promotee—is that right,
'promotee'?"

"Why not?" Matt chuckled.

"—the *promotee* gets his new assignment. Providing of
course, that certain members of the hierarchy, Denny Coughlin, for example, and Matt Lowenstein, people like that, and,
of course, our own beloved commander, P. Wohl, agree. If
they don't like the promotee's assignment, they somehow manage to get it changed to one they do like. The operative words
are 'for the good of the Department.' "

"I think I understand," Matt said.

There was the sound of a key in the door. Jason Washington
started toward it, but it opened before he could reach it.

It was a very tall, sharply featured woman, her hair drawn
tight against an angular skull.

She looks, Matt thought, *like one of the Egyptian bas-reliefs
in the museum.*

Martha (Mrs. Jason) Washington, wearing a flowing pale
green dress, stepped into the apartment. Behind her was the
doorman, carrying a very large framed picture, wrapped in
kraft paper.

"Take that from him, please," she ordered.

Washington put his hand in his pocket, gave the doorman a
couple of dollar bills, and relieved him of the picture.

"Hello, Matt," Martha Washington said.

"Good evening," Matt said.

"What's this?" Jason asked.

"I thought you could tell from the shape," she said. "It's a
bathtub."

Jason Washington tore the kraft paper away. It was a turn-
of-the-century oil painting of a voluptuous nude, reclining on
her side.

"Finally, some art I can understand and appreciate," Washington said.

"Inspector Wohl's got one almost just like that," Matt said.

"That figures," Martha said. "That's to sell, Jason, not for
you to ogle; don't get attached to it. I found it in one of those
terribly chic places off South Street. I think he needed the

money to pay the rent. I bought it right, and I think I know just where to get rid of it."

"Well, *I* like it," Matt said. "How much do you want for it?"

"You're too young," she said. "And besides, it would enrage your liberated female girlfriends."

"Yeah," Matt said, considering that. The prospect seemed to please him.

She seemed to see his whiskey glass for the first time.

"Are we celebrating something?" she asked.

"Yes, indeed," Matt said.

"Good evening, Matthew," Jason Washington said. "Nice of you to drop by."

"Just what's going on here?"

"Good night, Mrs. Washington," Matt said.

"Jason?" Mrs. Washington asked. There was a hint of threat in her voice.

"I took the sergeant's exam," Jason said.

"Well, it's about damned time," she said. "And you think you passed? Is that what you're celebrating?"

"Not exactly," Matt heard Jason Washington say as he pulled the door closed after him.

EIGHT

Chief Inspector Matt Lowenstein lived in a row house on Tyson Avenue, just off Roosevelt Boulevard in Northeast Philadelphia, with his wife, Sarah, and their only child, Samuel Lowenstein, who was fifteen.

It was the only home they had ever had. The down payment had been a wedding gift from Sarah's parents. The Lowensteins had been married three weeks after Matt, with three years on the job, had been promoted to detective. His first assignment as a detective had been to Northeast Detectives, not far away at Harbison and Levick Streets.

Sarah, at the time of her marriage, had been employed as a librarian at the Fox Chase Branch of the Philadelphia Public Library. Shortly afterward, she had become librarian at Northeast High School, at Cottman and Algon, and had held that job, with the exception of the three years she had taken off to have their son, ever since.

Sarah was active in women's affairs of Temple Sholom, a reformed congregation at Large Street and Roosevelt Boulevard, but had long since given up hope of getting Matt to take a more active role in the affairs of the synagogue.

While what Matt said—that he did not have an eight-to-five, five-day-a-week job, but was on call twenty-four hours a day seven days a week, and thus could really not get involved like somebody who had a regular job—was true, Sarah suspected that if he did have a regular job, he would have found another excuse not to get involved.

There was absolutely no pressure from Rabbi Stephen Kuntz, who had replaced the retiring Rabbi Schneider just before Samuel was born, for Matt to take a greater role in the affairs of the congregation, which, in the beginning, had surprised Sarah, for Matt and the new young rabbi had quickly become close. And then she came to understand that *was* the reason.

The rabbi had a surfeit of homes offering him sumptuous meals on tables set with silver and the good china, with everyone on their good behavior, listening with polite attention as he discoursed on the moral issues of the day. Her home, she was sure, was the only home in the rabbi's congregation where he was greeted by the man of the house calling out, "Lock up the booze, the rabbi's here."

She didn't think the rabbi sat with his tie pulled down and his shoes off in anyone else's basement, sucking beer from the bottleneck watching the fights on TV, or arguing politics loudly, or laughing deep in his belly at Lowenstein's recounting of the most recent ribald story of the *schwartzes* or the Irishers or the wops in the Roundhouse.

The rabbi needed a respite from the piety of the congregation, and Matt gave it to him. That was a contribution to the congregation, too, more important, Sarah had come to understand, than having Matt serve on the Building Committee or whatever.

And it worked the other way too. When Matt had been a lieutenant in the 16th District, and had to shoot a poor, crazy hillbilly woman who had already used a shotgun to kill her husband and was about to kill a cop with it, and was as distraught as Sarah had ever seen him, Rabbi Steve had gone off with him and Denny Coughlin to the Jersey shore for four days.

All three of them had bad breath and bloodshot eyes when they came back, but the terrible look was gone from Matt's eyes and that was all, Sarah thought, that really mattered.

Rabbi Kuntz had "dropped by" ten minutes before Lowenstein came home, fifteen minutes late, to announce that he had run into Mickey O'Hara and invited him and his girlfriend for supper.

"You could have called," Sarah said. "They have telephones all over. What time's he coming?"

"*They.* He's bringing his girlfriend. I told him half past six."

"If I had a little warning, I could have made a roast or something. Now I don't know what I'm going to do."

"Go to the deli," Lowenstein said, grinning at Kuntz. "Mickey's a smart Irisher. He likes Jew food."

"You're terrible," Sarah said. "You think that would be all right?"

"Of course it would," Lowenstein said. "Get cold cuts and hot potato salad."

"Well, all right, I suppose."

"You really like that coffee, or would you rather have a beer? Or a drink?"

"I think I'll finish the coffee and go," the rabbi said.

"Don't be silly. Mickey's always good for a laugh. You look like you could use one."

"I'd be in the way."

"Beer or booze?"

"Beer, please."

"Don't be polite. I'm going to have a stiff drink. It's been a bad day."

"Beer anyway."

"Samuel's not home yet, so don't go in the basement," Sarah said as she took her coat off a hook by the rear door. "You wouldn't hear the doorbell."

"Where is he?"

"He called and said he would be studying with the Rosen girl, Natalie."

"That's what they call that now, 'studying'?"

"He must have had a bad day, Rabbi, excuse him, please," Sarah said, and went out the door.

"A bad bad day?" Kuntz asked. "Or an ordinary, run-of-the-mill bad day?"

Lowenstein took a bottle of beer from the refrigerator and handed it to Kuntz, and then made himself a stiff Scotch, with very little ice or water, before replying.

"Maybe in the middle of that," Lowenstein said, raising his drink and adding *"Mazeltov."*

"*Mazeltov,*" the rabbi replied.

"I spent a painful hour and a half—closer to two, really—before lunch with the commissioner and the mayor," Lowenstein said. "Most of it strained silence, which is actually worse than an exhibition of his famous Neapolitan temper."

"What about?"

"That young Italian cop who got himself shot down by Temple University. You know what I'm talking about?"

Kuntz nodded. "It's been in the papers."

"Has it really?" Lowenstein said bitterly. "There was another editorial in today's *Ledger*, you see that one?"

Kuntz nodded.

"We have no idea who shot him or why," Lowenstein said. "Not even a hunch. And the mayor, who is angry at several levels, first, giving him the benefit of the doubt, as a cop, and then as an Italian, and then, obviously, as a politician, getting the flack from the newspapers, and not only the *Ledger*, is really angry. Frustrated, maybe, is the better word."

"Which makes him angry."

"Yeah."

"And he's holding you responsible?"

"He took the job away from me—technically away from Homicide, but it's the same thing—and gave it to Special Operations. I think he now regrets that."

"Special Operations isn't up to the job?"

"You know Peter Wohl? Runs Special Operations?"

Kuntz shook his head no.

"Very sharp cop. His father is a retired chief, an old pal of mine. Peter was a sergeant in Homicide. He was the youngest captain in the Department, and is now the youngest staff inspector. Just before Carlucci gave him Special Operations, he put Judge Findermann away."

"I remember that," Kuntz said. "So why can't he find the people who did this?"

"For the same reason I couldn't; there's simply nothing out there to find."

"But wouldn't you have more resources in the Detective Division? More experienced people?"

"Wohl took the two best homicide detectives away from Homicide, with the mayor's blessing," Lowenstein said. "And I passed the word that anything else he wants from the Detective Division, he can have. The way it works is that if you don't get anything at the scene of the crime, then you start ringing doorbells and asking questions. Wohl's people have run out of doorbells to ring and people to question. Hell, there's a twenty-five-thousand-dollar reward out—Nesfoods International put it up—and we haven't gotten a damned thing out of that, either.''

"And the mayor knows all of this?''

"Sure. And I think one of the reasons he's so upset is that he knows he couldn't do any better himself. But that doesn't get the newspapers off his back. I had a very unkind thought in there this morning: The only reason Carlucci isn't throwing Peter Wohl to the wolves—''

"This man Wohl was there?''

"Yeah. Wohl and Denny Coughlin too. As I was saying, the only reason he hasn't already thrown Wohl to the wolves is because he knows that whoever he would send in to replace him wouldn't be able to do a damned thing Wohl hasn't already done. And he—Carlucci—would look even worse if his pinch hitter struck out.''

"Yes, I see.''

"Shooting a cop is like shooting the pope,'' Lowenstein said. "You just can't tolerate it. So you throw all the resources you can lay your hands on at the job. We've done that, and that hasn't been good enough. But there's other crimes in the city, and you can't keep it up. Not even if it means that for the first time in the history of the City of Philadelphia, a cop killer will get away with it.''

"Really? This has never happened before?''

"Never,'' Lowenstein said. "Not once. And, at the risk of repeating myself, you can't let anyone get away with shooting a cop.''

"So what will happen?''

Lowenstein shrugged his shoulders and threw up his hands in a gesture of helplessness.

"And two other little items to brighten my day came to my attention,'' he said. "One connected to the Magnella—that's the name of the young cop—job. Interesting problem of ethics. You know Captain Frieberg, Manny Frieberg?''

"Sure.''.

"He's got the 9th District. One of my boys. Good cop. There are those that say I'm his rabbi.''

"I've heard the term,'' Rabbi Kuntz said with a chuckle.

"He came to see me just before I went to see the mayor. At half past three this morning, one of his cars answered a call about a body in a saloon parking lot. It wasn't a body. It was a passed-out drunk. Specifically, it was one of the hotshot homicide detectives I mentioned a moment ago, who were transferred from Homicide to Peter Wohl. He passed out, fortunately, between the barroom door and his car, so he didn't have a chance to run into the cardinal archbishop or a station wagon full of nuns."

Kuntz chuckled, and then asked, "Does he have a drinking problem?"

Lowenstein ignored the question.

"When they tried to wake him up," he went on, "he got belligerent, so they took his gun away from him and locked him up in a district holding cell. When Manny came in, he turned him loose and then came to see me."

"You said 'ethical problem'?"

"If he worked for me, I'd know how to deal with him. I'd tell him if I heard he had so much as sniffed a cork for six months, he would be on the recovered stolen car detail forever."

"I don't know what that means."

"Two kinds of stolen cars are recovered. The ones some kids took for a joy ride and ditched, or ones that somebody has stripped and abandoned. In either case, it has to be investigated. Lots of forms that no one will ever see again have to be filled out. It's the worst job a detective can get. For a Homicide detective, it would be the worst thing that could possibly happen to him."

"But?"

"He doesn't work for me. So what do I do, go tell Peter Wohl? Since he doesn't work for me, it's none of my business, right? And I don't know how Peter would handle it. He's under a hell of a lot of pressure, and he would not be pleased to hear that one of the two men he's forced to rely on has a bad bottle problem."

"Is that what it is? The man is an alcoholic?"

"Maybe not yet, but almost. What happened is that his wife caught him in the wrong bed. The judge awarded the wife everything but his spare pair of socks. He's living in a cheap room out by the University, eating baked beans out of the can. And the ex-wife is using his money to support a boyfriend."

"How sad," Kuntz said.

The doorbell played "Be It Ever So Humble."

"That's O'Hara," Lowenstein said, looking at his watch. "He has only one virtue, punctuality. The subject we were on is now closed, okay?"

Kuntz nodded.

Lowenstein left the kitchen and returned in a moment leading Mickey O'Hara, who had a bottle in a brown bag in his hand, and a young woman.

"If I knew the rabbi was going to be here, I'd have brought two of these," Mickey said, handing the bag to Lowenstein. He pulled a bottle of Johnnie Walker Black Label Scotch from it.

"Hello, Mickey, how are you?" Kuntz said.

"I won't say you shouldn't have done this, because you should have," Lowenstein said.

"Don't let it go to your head, the *Bulletin*'s paying for it."

The young woman with Mickey O'Hara, Kuntz thought (almost simultaneously realizing that it was not a kind thought), was not what he would have expected. She was—he searched for the word and came up with—wholesome. More than that. She was tastefully, conservatively dressed, with just the right amount of makeup. She had a full head of well-coiffured dark brown hair.

And she was, Kuntz saw, more than a little surprised, even shocked, at the exchange between Lowenstein and O'Hara.

"I'm Stephen Kuntz," he said.

"Eleanor Neal," she said. "How do you do?"

"If you understand that these two are old friends," Kuntz said, "it explains a good deal."

She smiled. "And is there a reason Mickey called you a rabbi?"

"I happen to be a rabbi," Kuntz said.

"Oh?" she said.

"I'm Matt Lowenstein. Don't mind Mick and me. Welcome to Chez Lowenstein."

"Thank you for having me," Eleanor said.

"I just got to ask this," Lowenstein said.

"No, you don't," Mickey said.

"Mick!" Eleanor protested.

"What he's going to ask is 'what is a nice girl like you doing going out with me?' "

"Well, I don't think he would have asked that, but if he did, I would have said that finally you're introducing me to your friends."

"What I was going to ask," Lowenstein said, more than a little lamely, "was how is it he's never brought you here before?"

"Why haven't you, Mick?" Eleanor asked.

"Well, you're here now, and that's all that counts," Kuntz said.

"And if you'll make us a drink, I'll give you something else," O'Hara said.

"Excuse me," Lowenstein said, sounding genuinely contrite. "What can I fix you, Miss Neal?"

"Eleanor, please," she said. "Would you happen to have any white wine?"

"Absolutely," Lowenstein said, and took a bottle from the refrigerator.

"No, I don't mind helping myself to the Scotch, thank you very much," O'Hara said.

"There's an open bottle," Lowenstein said.

"Yeah, but you've refilled it with cheap hootch so often the neck is chipped," O'Hara said, and pulled the cork from the bottle he had brought.

Kuntz laughed.

"Hey, you're supposed to be on my side," Lowenstein protested.

"I am a simple man of God trying my very best to bring peace between the warring factions," Kuntz said piously.

"I think you have your work cut out for you," Eleanor said.

Lowenstein handed her a glass of wine, and then turned to O'Hara.

"Okay. What else have you got me that somebody else paid for?"

O'Hara took an envelope from his inside jacket pocket and handed it to him. Lowenstein, suspiciously, took it from the envelope and unfolded it. Then his expression changed.

"What the hell is this?"

"It was delivered to the *Bulletin*, left with the girl downstairs in an envelope marked 'urgent.' "

"Where's the envelope?" Lowenstein snapped.

"With the original. You *did* notice that was a copy?"

"Where's the original?"

"I had a messenger take it, and the envelope, to Homicide."
Lowenstein handed the sheet of paper to Kuntz.

ISLAMIC LIBERATION ARMY

There Is No God But God,
And Allah Is His Name

PRESS RELEASE:

Be advised that the events at Goldblatt's Furniture Store today were conducted by troops of the Islamic Liberation Army.
It was the first battle of many to follow against the infidel sons of Zion, who for too long have victimized the African Brothers (Islamic and other) and other minorities of Philadelphia.
Death to the Zionist oppressors of our people!
　Freedom Now!
　Muhammed el Sikkim
　Chief of Staff
　Islamic Liberation Army

"What in the world is this?" Kuntz asked when he had read it.

"There was a robbery, and a murder, at Goldblatt's furniture store on South Street this afternoon," Lowenstein said.

"But what's *this*?"

"The Islamic Liberation Army just confessed to the job," O'Hara said dryly.

"What's the Islamic Liberation Army?" Kuntz asked.

"Offhand," Lowenstein said, "I would guess it's half a dozen *schwartzer* stickup artists who saw Malcolm X on TV, smoked some funny cigarettes, and then went to Sears, Roebuck and bought themselves bathrobes."

Kuntz saw the look of confusion on Eleanor's face.

"May I show her this?" he asked.

"Sure," O'Hara said. "It's not like it's a secret or anything."

"Did the other papers get this, Mickey, do you think, or just Philly's ace crime writer?" Lowenstein asked.

"I didn't ask, but I'll bet they did."

"What's a—what did you say before, 'Schwartz'?" Eleanor asked.

"*Schwartzes,*" Lowenstein explained. "It's Yiddish. Means 'blacks.' "

"I don't understand," Kuntz confessed.

"Offhand, Rabbi," O'Hara said, "it's obviously one of two things: a group of master criminals cleverly trying to get Sherlock Holmes here and his gumshoes off their trail, or the opening salvo of the Great Race War."

"What the hell *is* it, if you're so smart, wiseass?" Lowenstein asked.

"Or it could be a couple of guys named O'Shaughnessy and Goldberg, college kids, maybe, trying to pull the chain of the newspapers," O'Hara said.

"You really think so?" Lowenstein asked, his tone of voice making it clear that possibility had not occurred to him.

"I really don't know what to think, Matt," Mickey replied.

"What did you *write*?"

"About the Islamic Liberation Army, you mean?"

"Yes."

"Nothing."

"*Nothing?*"

"Just because somebody sends me a piece of paper that says they're the Islamic Liberation Army and that they've declared war on the Jews doesn't make it so. *You* tell me you think the Islamic Liberation Army shot up Goldblatt's and murdered that maintenance man, and I'll write it. But not until."

"You got that after the robbery, right?"

"Of course," O'Hara said. "And Joe D'Amata told me that the Central Detective is on the job, Pelosi?"

"Jerry Pelosi," Lowenstein furnished.

"He's got a damned good idea who the doers are. And he doesn't think they're a bunch of looney-tune amateur Arabs."

Lieutenant Jack Malone was not equipped with the necessary household skills for happy bachelorhood. He was the fourth of five children, the others all female. Jack and his father (a Fire Department captain) had met what the Malone family perceived to be the responsibility of the male gender: They moved furniture, washed the car, cut the grass, painted, and even moved the garbage cans from beside the kitchen door to the curb, and then moved them back.

But the other domestic tasks in the house were clearly feminine responsibilities, and Mrs. Jeannette Malone and her daughters shopped, cooked, laundered, ironed, made beds, set and cleaned the table, and washed the dishes.

This arrangement lasted until, a week after he graduated from North Catholic High School, Jack enlisted in the Army. For four years thereafter, except for the making of his bunk in the prescribed manner and shining of boots and brass, the Army took over for his mother and sisters. He ate in mess halls. Once a week he carried a bag full of dirty clothing to the supply room and picked up last week's laundry, now washed, starched, and pressed by an Army laundry for a three-dollar-a-month charge.

When he got out of the Army, he immediately took both the Fire Department and Police Department tests. The Police Department came up first, and he became a cop. He really had not wanted to be a fireman, although, rather than hurt his father's feelings, he would have joined the firemen if that test had come back first.

He lived at home until, fifteen months after he got out of the Army, he had married Ellen Fogarty. Ellen had been reared under a comparable perception of the roles and responsibilities of the sexes in marriage. The man went to work, and the woman kept house. The only real difference, aside from the joys of the marriage bed, in living with Ellen as opposed to living with his mother and sisters was that Ellen put some really strange food on the table. Mexican, Chinese, even *Indian*-Indian, things like that.

He had pretended to like it, and after a while had even grown used to it.

When he had reentered the single state, he was for the first time in his life forced to fend for himself. Obviously, he could not move back into his parents' house. For one thing, his sister Deborah had married a real loser who couldn't hold a job for more than three months at a time, and Charley and Deborah and their two kids were "until things worked out for Charley" living in the house.

But that wasn't the only reason he couldn't live there. His father had made it clear that he believed he wasn't getting the whole story about what had gone wrong with Jack and Ellen. Good Catholic girls like Ellen from decent families don't suddenly just decide to start fucking some lawyer; there are two sides to every story, and since he wasn't getting Ellen's that was because Ellen was too decent to tell anybody what Jack had done that made her do it.

The only time in ten years and four months of marriage that Jack had laid a hand on Ellen was that one time, after he'd knocked Howard Candless around, and then gone home to tell her, and ask her why, and she had screamed, so mad that she was spitting in his face, that because whenever he touched her, she wanted to puke.

He couldn't be any sorrier about that than he was, sorry and ashamed, but it had happened, and there was no taking it back. And it had happened only once.

His mother had cried when she heard about it, which was even worse than having her yell at him, and his sisters, every damned one of them, had made it plain they believed the reason Ellen had done what she had done was because he had been regularly knocking Ellen around all the time, and she'd finally had enough.

That had really surprised him and made him wonder about his brothers-in-law. Was the reason his sisters were so quick to jump on the idea that he was regularly knocking Ellen around because they were regularly getting it from their husbands? It wasn't such a far-out idea when he thought about it. If his sisters were getting slapped around, they would have kept it to themselves, knowing full well that their father and their brother would have kicked the living shit out of their husbands.

And if that was the case, Jack Malone reasoned, that would explain why they were almost happy to find out that Jack Malone was no better than their husbands.

And Ellen had jumped on that, and made it sing like a violin. When she had taken Little Jack to see Grandma, she had told Grandma she didn't think it would do anyone any good, least of all Little Jack, to dwell on what had happened between them. All she thought was that Little Jack's father needed help, and she really hoped he could get it.

In the eyes of Grandma and his sisters, that made Ellen just about as noble as the Virgin Mary.

So not only could he not move back into his parents' house, he really hated to go over there at all.

So into the St. Charles Hotel. In some ways, it was like when he made sergeant in the Army and he had gotten his own room. The big differences were that he couldn't get his laundry done for three bucks a month, and there was no mess hall passing out free "take all you want, but eat what you take" meals.

The one uniform Jack had bought when he made lieutenant came with two pair of pants, so he still had a freshly pressed pair to wear on the job tomorrow. Tomorrow night, depending on whether he spilled something on the jacket or not, he would have to have it at least pressed, but that wasn't a problem for tonight.

What he would have liked to do tonight was go out and have a couple of beers, beers hell, drinks, and then a steak with a glass of red wine or two with that, and then maybe a nightcap or something afterward.

What he did was what he could afford to do. He went to Colonel Sanders's and bought the special (a half breast, a leg, a couple of livers, a roll, and a little tub of cole slaw) for $1.69 and took it back to the St. Charles. There he took off his clothes and ate it in his underwear, watching the TV, washing it down with a glass of water from the tap.

He fell asleep watching a rerun of *I Love Lucy* and woke up to the trumpets and drum roll announcing *Nine's News at Nine*.

He could taste all of the Colonel's Seventeen Secret Herbs and Spices in his mouth, and his left leg had gone to sleep. He hobbled around the room flexing and shaking his left leg.

He put the remnants of the $1.69 Special in the wastebasket under the sink in the toilet, and then tested the water. It ran rusty red for a couple of seconds, burped, and then turned hot.

He took a hot shower, thinking that simply because there was hot water now there was no guarantee that there would be hot water in the morning.

He was now wide awake. He knew that even if he could force himself to go to sleep, he would almost certainly wake up at say half past four and, if that happened, never get back to sleep.

He put on a pair of blue jeans and a sweatshirt and a pair of sneakers and left the room.

There was a tavern on the corner of 18th and Arch. He certainly could afford a beer.

He pushed open the door and looked inside and changed his mind. A bunch of losers sitting around staring into the stale, getting warm beer in their glasses. Nobody was having a good time.

He acted like he was looking for somebody who wasn't there, and went back out onto 18th Street.

He knew where he wanted to go, and what he wanted to do, and walked to where he had parked his car and got in it.

Am I doing this because I didn't want to belly up to the bar with the other losers, or is this what I really wanted to do in the first place?

He drove up North Broad Street until he came to the Holland Pontiac-GMC showroom. The lights were on, but there was no one in the showroom. They closed at half past nine.

He turned left and made the next left, which put him behind the Pontiac-GMC showroom building and between it and a large concrete block building on which was lettered, HOLLAND MOTOR COMPANY BODY SHOP.

It was a factory-type building. The windows were of what he thought of as chicken wire reinforced glass. They passed light, but you couldn't see through them.

The Holland Motor Company Body Shop was going full blast.

It was a twenty-four-hour-a-day, seven-days-a-week operation. Part of this was because they fixed the entire GM line of cars in this body shop, not just Pontiacs and GMCs. And part of it was because, to help the working man who needed his car to drive to work, you could bring your crumpled fender to the Holland Motor Car Body Shop in installments, leaving it there overnight and getting it back in the morning. They would straighten the fender one night, prime it the second, and paint it the third night, or over the weekends.

And the other reason they were open twenty-four hours a day, seven days a week, Lieutenant Jack Malone was convinced, was because the Working Man's Friend had a hot car scam of some kind going.

Malone had no facts. Just a gut feeling. But he *knew.*

I don't care if he and Commissioner Czernich play with the same rubber duck, the sonofabitch is a thief. And I'm going to catch him.

He circled the block, and then found a place to park the rusty old Mustang in the shadow of a building where he would not attract attention, and from which he could keep his eyes on the door to the Holland Motor Company Body Shop.

Something, maybe not tonight, maybe not this week, maybe

*not this fucking year, but something, sometime, sooner or later,
is going to happen, and then I'll know how he's doing it.*

He lit a cigarette, saw that it was his next to last—

Fuck it, I smoke too much anyway—

—and settled himself against the worn-out and lumpy cushion and started to look.

NINE

When Officer Charles McFadden finished his tour at four, he went looking for Officer Matthew Payne. When he went through the door marked HEADQUARTERS, SPECIAL OPERATIONS, Payne was not at his desk. And there was no one sitting at the sergeant's desk either.

Charley sat on the edge of Payne's desk, confident that one or both of them would turn up in a minute; *somebody* would be around to answer the inspector's phone.

A minute or so later, the door to the inspector's office opened and a slight, fair-skinned, rather sharp-featured police officer came out. He was in Highway regalia identical to Officer McFadden's, except that there were silver captain's bars on the epaulets of his leather jacket. He was Captain David Pekach, commanding officer of Highway Patrol.

McFadden pushed himself quickly off Payne's desk.

"Hey, whaddaya say, McFadden?" Captain Pekach said, smiling, and offering his hand.

"Captain," McFadden replied.

"Where's the sergeant?" Pekach asked.

"I don't know," Charley said. "I came in here looking for Payne."

"The inspector's got him running down some paperwork. I don't think he'll be back today. Something I can do for you?"

"No, sir, it was— I wanted to see if he wanted to have a beer or something."

"You might try him at home in a couple of hours," Pekach said. "I really don't think he'll be coming back. Do me a favor, Charley?"

"Yes, sir."

"Stick around for a couple of minutes and answer the phone until the sergeant comes back. He's probably in the can. But somebody should be on that phone."

"Yes, sir."

"The inspector's gone for the day. Captain Sabara and I are minding the store."

"Yes, sir," McFadden said, smiling. He liked Captain Pekach. Pekach had been his lieutenant when he had worked undercover in Narcotics.

The door opened and a sergeant whom McFadden didn't know came in.

"You looking for me, sir?"

"Not anymore," Pekach said, tempering the sarcasm with a little smile.

"I had to go to the can, Captain."

"See if you can find Detective Harris," Pekach said. "Keep looking. Tell him to call either me or Captain Sabara, no matter what the hour."

"Yes, sir."

Pekach turned and went back into the office he shared with Captain Mike Sabara. Then he turned again, remembering two things: first, that he had not said "So long" or something to McFadden; and second that McFadden and his partner had answered the call on the shooting at Goldblatt's furniture.

He reentered the outer office just in time to hear the sergeant snarl, "What do you want?" at McFadden.

"Officer McFadden, Sergeant," Pekach said, "for the good of the Department, you understand, was kind enough to be standing by to answer the telephone. Since, you see, there was no one else out here."

The sergeant flushed.

"Come on in a minute, Charley," Pekach said. "You got a minute?"

"Yes, sir."

Pekach held the door open for Charley and then followed him into the office.

Captain Michael J. Sabara, a short, muscular, swarthy-skinned man whose acne-scarred face, dark eyes, and mustache made him appear far more menacing than was the case, looked up curiously at McFadden.

"You know Charley, don't you, Mike?" Pekach asked.

"Yeah, sure," Sabara said, offering his hand. "How are you, McFadden?"

At least this one, he thought, *looks like a Highway Patrolman.*

The other one, in Captain Sabara's mind, was Officer Jesus Martinez; the *other* of the first two probationary Highway Patrolmen. Jesus Martinez was just barely over Departmental height and weight minimums. It wasn't his fault, but he just didn't look like a Highway Patrolman. He looked, in Captain Sabara's opinion, like a small-sized spic dressed up in a cut-down Highway Patrol uniform.

"Charley, you went in on that shots fired, hospital case at Goldblatt's, didn't you?" Pekach asked.

"Yes, sir. Quinn and I were at City Hall when we heard it."

"What did you find?"

"Nothing. They were long gone—they had stashed a van out in back—when we got there."

"You hear anything on the scene about the doers?"

"Spades in bathrobes," McFadden said, "Is what we heard. Dumb spades. They—Goldblatt's—don't keep any real money in the store."

"What do you think about this?" Captain Sabara said, and handed him a photocopy of the press release that had been sent to Mickey O'Hara at the *Bulletin*.

"What the hell is it?" McFadden asked.

"What do you think it is, Charley?" Pekach asked.

"I think it's bullshit. *If* this thing is real, and they're going to have a war with the Jews, how come the guy they shot was an Irishman?"

"Good question," Pekach said. "If you had to guess, Charley, what would you say?"

"Jesus, Captain, I don't know. I don't think this Liberation Army is for real—is it?"

"That seems to be the question of the day, Charley," Pekach said, and then changed the subject. "I don't seem to see you much anymore. How do you like Highway?"

"It's all right, I guess," Charley replied. "But sometimes, Captain, I sort of miss Narcotics."

"Narcotics or undercover?" Pekach pursued.

"Both, I guess."

"If you don't catch up with Payne tonight, I'll tell him you were looking for him," Pekach said.

McFadden understood he was being dismissed.

"Yes, sir. Good night, Captain." He faced Sabara and repeated, "Captain."

Sabara nodded and smiled.

When McFadden had closed the door behind him, Sabara said, "There are three hundred young cops out there with five, six years on the job who would give their left nut to be in Highway, and that one says, 'It's all right, I guess.' "

"But *your* three hundred young cops never had the opportunity to work for *me* in *Narcotics*," Pekach said.

"Oh, go to hell," Sabara chuckled. "You're no better than he is."

"He wasn't much help, was he?"

"No, he wasn't. Did you think he would be?"

"Wohl said he thought we should find out what we could about Goldblatt's. I was trying."

"You really think Special Operations is going to wind up with that job?"

"I wouldn't be surprised. Carlucci probably sees a story in the newspapers, 'Mayor Carlucci announced this afternoon that the Special Operations Division arrested the Islamic Liberation Army—' "

"All eight of them," Sabara interrupted. "That's if there *is* an Islamic Liberation Army. And anyway, Highway could handle it without the bullshit."

"That's my line, Mike. Write this on your forehead: '*Pekach is Highway, I'm Special Operations.*' "

Sabara chuckled again. "What the hell is Wohl up to?"

"I guess he's just trying to cover his ass," Pekach replied. "In case he does—in other words, we do—get that job."

• • •

Charley McFadden drove home, took a bottle of Schlitz from the refrigerator, carried it into the living room, sat on the couch, and dialed Matt Payne's apartment. It rang twice.

"Matthew Payne profoundly regrets, knowing what devastating disappointment it will cause you, that he is not available for conversation at this time. If you would be so kind as to leave your number at the beep, he will know that you have called."

"Shit!" Charley said, laughing, and hung up.

"Watch your mouth, Charley!" his mother called from the kitchen.

Charley hoisted himself out of the couch and went up the stairs, two at a time, to his bedroom. He took his pistol from its holster, put it in the sock drawer of his dresser, and took his snub-nosed Colt .38 Special and its holster out of the drawer. Then he took off his uniform. He rubbed the Sam Browne belt and its accoutrements with a polishing cloth, took a brush to his boots, and then arranged everything neatly in his closet, where, with the addition of a clean shirt, it would be ready for tomorrow.

Then he dressed in blue jeans and a sweatshirt that had WILDWOOD BY THE SEA and a representation of a fish jumping out of the water painted on it. He slipped his feet into loafers and completed dressing by unpinning his badge from his leather jacket and pinning it to a leather badge and ID case and putting that in his left hip pocket, and by slipping the spring clip of the Colt holster inside his trousers just in front of his right hip.

He went down the stairs three at a time, grabbed a quilted nylon zipper jacket from a hook by the front door, and, quickly, so there would be no opportunity for challenge, called out, "I'm going down to Flo & Danny's for a beer, Ma. And then out for supper."

Flo & Danny's Bar & Grill was on the corner. He slid onto a bar stool and Danny, without a word, drew a beer and set it before him.

"How they hanging, kid?"

"One lower than the other."

Charley looked at his watch. It was quarter to six. He had to meet Margaret at the FOP at seven. It would take fifteen minutes to drive there. There was plenty of time.

Maybe too much. She doesn't like it when I smell like a beer tap.

"Danny, give me an egg and a sausage," he said.

Harry fished a purple pickled egg and a piece of pickled sausage from two glass jars beside the cash register and delivered them on a paper napkin. Charley took a bite of the egg, and walked to the telephone and put the rest of his egg in his mouth as he dropped a dime in the slot and dialed a number.

"Hello."

"You and your goddamn wiseass answer machine messages. Where have you been?"

"Running errands."

"You want to have a beer or something?"

"Just one. I got a date."

"Me too. At seven."

"You want to come here? Where are you?"

"Home. FOP?"

"Fifteen minutes?"

"Good."

Matt Payne hung up.

Charley paid for the beer, the egg, and the sausage, and got in his car and drove to the FOP. Matt Payne's Porsche was already in the parking lot, and he found him at the bar.

There was just time to order a beer and have it served when he heard Margaret's soft voice in his ear.

"Hi!"

"Well, as I live and breathe, Florence Nightingale," Matt said, smiling.

"Hello, Matt."

"You're early," Charley said.

"You make it sound like an accusation," Matt said.

"Get off early?" Charley asked.

"Not exactly."

"What's that mean?"

"I mean, I went in, and they said they really needed me from midnight till six."

"They told you to come in," Charley said indignantly.

"And I get an hour, at time-and-a-half, just for coming in," Margaret said. "Plus double-time for midnight to six."

"You're not really going to go in at midnight?" Charley asked incredulously.

"Yes, of course, I am," Margaret said. "I told you, it's double-time."

"If I were you, I'd tell them where to stick their double-time."

"Charley!"

"May I make a suggestion?" Matt asked.

"Huh?" Charley asked.

"What, Matt?" Margaret asked, a touch of impatience in her voice.

"If you're going to fight like married people, why don't you go get married?"

"I'm with him," Charley said.

"We just can't, Matt," Margaret said. "Not right now."

"It is better to marry than to burn," Matt quoted sonorously. "Saint Peter."

"No, it's not," Margaret said. "Saint Peter, I mean."

"It was one of those guys," Matt said. "Saint Timothy?"

"So what do we do now?" Charley asked.

"I don't know about you, but I'm going home to get some sleep. You can stay with Matt."

"I'll take you home," Charley said flatly. "He's got a date."

"You don't have to take me home."

"I'll take you home, *and* to work."

"You don't have to do that."

"You're not going walking around North Broad Street alone at midnight."

"Don't be silly."

"Listen to him, Margaret," Matt said.

"Oh, God!" she said in resignation.

Charley got off the bar stool.

"Let's go," he said.

"We'll have to get together real soon, Margaret, and do this again," Matt said.

"You can go to hell too," Margaret said, but she touched his arm before she left.

Matt watched as the two of them walked across the room, and then signaled for another drink.

He did not have a date. But when Charley had called, he had realized that he did not want to sit in a bar somewhere and watch television with Charley.

What he wanted to do was get laid. He had been doing very poorly in that department lately. If he was with Charley, getting laid was, now that Charley had found Margaret, out of the question. Charley was a very moral person.

The trouble, he thought, as he watched the bartender take a bill and make change, *is that men want to get* laid *and women want a* relationship. *Since I don't want a relationship, consequently, I'm not getting laid very much.*

As he took his first sip of the fresh drink, he considered the possibility of hanging around the FOP and seeing what developed. There were sometimes unattached women around the bar. Some of them had a connection with either the police or the court establishment, clerks, secretaries, girls like that. And some were police groupies, who liked to hang around with cops.

Rumor had it that the latter group screwed like minks. The trouble there was the groupies, so to speak, had their groupies, cops who liked to hang around with girls who screwed like minks.

The demand for their services, Matt decided, *overwhelmed the supply. If I try to move in on what looks to be someone else's sure thing for the night, I'm liable to get knocked on my ass.*

And the others, the secretaries and the clerks, the nice *girls, some of whom seemed to have been looking at me with what could be interest, were, like the vast majority of their sisters, not looking to get laid, but rather for a* relationship.

Back to square one.

And if I have another of these, I am very likely to forget this calm, logical, most importantly sober analysis of the situation and wind up either in a relationship, *or engaged in an altercation with a brother officer in the parking lot, or, more likely, right here on the dance floor, which altercation, no matter who the victor, would be difficult to explain when, inevitably, Staff Inspector P. Wohl heard about it.*

He finished his drink, picked up his change, and walked across the room to the stairs leading up to the street.

Was that really invitation in that well-stacked redhead's eyes or has my imagination been inflamed by this near-terminal case of lakanookie?

He got in the Porsche and drove home. There were, he noticed when he drove in the underground beneath the building that housed both the Delaware Valley Cancer Society and Chez Payne, far more cars in it than there normally were at this hour of the night. Ordinarily, it was just about deserted.

Parking spaces twenty-nine and thirty, which happened to

be closest to the elevator, had been reserved by the management for the occupant of the top-floor apartment. The management had been instructed to do so by the owner, less as a courtesy to his son, who occupied the top-floor apartment, than, the son had come to understand, because a second parking spot was convenient when the owner's wife or other members of the family had some need to park around Rittenhouse Square.

Tonight, a Cadillac Fleetwood sedan was parked in parking space twenty-nine, its right side overflowing into what looked like half of parking space thirty. The Payne family owned a Cadillac Fleetwood, but this wasn't it.

Matt managed to squeeze the Porsche 911 into what was left of parking space thirty. But when he had done so, there was not room enough between him and the Cadillac to open the Porsche's driver's side door. It was necessary for him to exit by the passenger side door, which, in a Porsche 911, is a squirming feat worthy of Houdini.

He got on the elevator and rode it to the third floor and got off. The narrow corridor between the elevator and the stairs to his apartment was crowded with people.

A woman he could never remember having seen before in his life rushed over to him, stuck something to his lapel, cried, "Oh, I'm so glad you could come!" and handed him a glass of champagne.

"Thank you," Matt said. The champagne glass, he noticed, was plastic.

"We're circulating *downward* tonight," the woman said.

"Are we?"

"Yes, isn't that clever?"

"Mind-boggling," Matt replied.

The woman walked away.

Nice ass for an old woman; I wonder if there's anybody here under, say, thirty?

"Hello, Mr. Payne."

It was one of the Holmes Security rent-a-cops. Matt knew he was a retired police sergeant, and it made him a little uncomfortable to be called "Mr." by a sergeant.

"I bet you know what's going on here," Matt said, smiling at him.

The retired cop chuckled. "I saw the look on your face. This is a party for the people who worked on the Cancer Society Ball."

"I have no idea what that means, but thanks anyway."

"You know, the ones who sold tickets, did all the work. And, of course, gave money."

"Oh," Matt said.

He saw a very pretty face, surrounded by blond hair in a pageboy. She was looking at him with unabashed curiosity. All he could see was the head and shoulders. The lady was on her way down the narrow stairway to the second floor.

Oh, that's what she meant by "circulating downward."

"I just came from the FOP," Matt said. "I wondered where everybody had come from."

"This is better than the FOP," the Holmes man said. "Here the booze is free. There's a bar in the lobby."

"But I don't belong."

"They don't know that. That lady gave you a badge, and you got by me. *I* keep the riffraff out."

The pretty face in the blond pageboy was no longer in sight.

"Well, maybe I *should* do my part for the noble cause," Matt said.

You're wasting your time. But on the other hand, nothing ventured, nothing gained.

The blonde was not on the second floor. He went down to the lobby and saw the bar.

What I will do is get a drink, and then go upstairs.

There was a small wait in line, and then he found himself facing the bartender.

"Scotch, please. Water."

"Any preference?"

Matt looked and saw that whatever else it did, the Opera Ball Club or whatever the hell it was really served fine booze.

"Famous Grouse, please. Easy on the water."

He became aware, in less time than it takes to tell, first of an exotic perfume, then of an expanse of white flesh that swelled with exquisite grace before disappearing beneath a delicate brassiere, and then of warm breath on his ear.

"I hope you won't be offended by my saying so, but your gun is showing," the voice behind the warm breath on his ear said in almost a whisper.

It was the blonde in the pageboy.

For the first time he noticed that she was wearing a hat.

If half an ounce of black silk and silk netting can be called a hat, he thought.

What the hell did she say about a gun? God, I bet she has nice teats!

"I beg your pardon?"

She smiled, and laughed softly, and tugged on his arm, pulling his head down.

"Your gun," she said. "It's showing."

This time when he smelled her breath, he picked up the smell of alcohol. Gin, he thought. He looked down at his leg and saw that his trouser leg was hiked up, caught by the butt of the pistol in his ankle holster.

Shit!

When I had to climb out of the goddamn car because of that asshole in the Cadillac in both my parking places, that's when it happened.

He squatted and rearranged his trouser leg.

"Thank you."

"I don't think anybody else noticed," she said. "It was only because I was going downstairs that I saw it. You know what I mean?"

"Thank you for telling me."

"Could I ask you a question? Out of pure idle—there being not much else to think about around here—curiosity?"

"Sure?"

"How many of you are there here tonight?"

What the hell is that supposed to mean?

"How many do you see?"

"That's why I'm asking," she said, laughing. "I'm curious."

Matt held up three fingers.

"Let's start with the easy things. How many fingers?"

"Three, wise guy," she said. "And I only see one of you. That's why I'm asking how many others there are of you. Just out of idle curiosity."

"As far as I know, I am the only one like me here tonight."

"The only one in regular clothes, you mean."

"What?"

"I mean not counting him," she said, pointing to a Holmes Security man taking invitations by the door, "and the one I saw you talking to upstairs."

"Oh. I'm not a rent-a-cop. I had no idea what you were talking about."

"Then what are you doing walking around with a gun strapped to your leg? Your *ankle*?"

"I'm a cop."

"Are you really?"

He nodded.

"A detective, you mean? There are police here, too, in addition to—what did you say, the rent-a-cops?"

"No. Not a detective. A cop. Off duty."

"You're pulling my leg. Aren't you?"

"Boy Scout's honor," Matt said, holding up three fingers.

"And you're active in, a sponsor, of the Cancer Society Ball?"

"Regretfully, no."

"Then what are you doing here?"

"You mean, *here*?" Matt said, and nodded his head to take in the lobby.

"Yes."

"I got off the elevator and a lady told me she was so glad I could come, pinned this thing on me, and handed me a glass of champagne."

She laughed and took his arm, which caused contact between his elbow and her bosom.

"All right, wise guy," she said. "What were you doing getting off the elevator?"

"I live here," Matt said.

"You live here?"

He nodded. "In what Charles Dickens would call the 'garret.'"

She let go of his arm and stepped in front of him and looked at him intently.

"And your name is Matt—*Matthew*—Payne, right?"

"Guilty," Matt said. "You have the advantage, mademoiselle, on me."

"Don't go away," she said, and then asked. "What is that?"

"Famous Grouse."

He watched as she went to the bar and returned with another drink for him, and what, to judge by the gin on her breath, was a martini on the rocks.

She handed him the Scotch and took a swallow of her martini.

"I needed that," she said. "The way they were talking about

you—'Poor Patricia's *Boy*'—I thought you'd have acne and wear short pants.''

''Who was talking about me?''

''It was the only interesting conversation I heard here tonight. You'll never guess who lives upstairs: Poor Patricia Payne's Boy, they sent him to UP and he paid them back by joining the cops right after he graduated. He's the one who shot the serial rapist in the head.''

''Oh.''

''And it's madam, not mademoiselle, by the way. I'm sort of married.''

''What does 'sort of married' mean?''

''Among other things, that he's not here tonight,'' she said. ''Can we let it go at that?''

''Sure.''

''Did you really?''

''Did I really what?''

''Shoot that man in the head?''

''Jesus!''

''I'll take that as a yes,'' she said, and took another sip of her martini. ''Is that the gun you did it with?''

''Does it matter?''

''Answer the question.''

''Yes, as a matter of fact, it is. Can we change the subject to something more pleasant, like cancer, for example?''

''So you live upstairs, do you? In what Charles Dickens would call the 'garret'?''

''That's right.''

''Are you going to ask me if I want to go to your apartment and look at your etchings, Matthew Payne?''

''I don't have any etchings,'' he said.

''I'll settle for a look at your gun,'' she said.

''I beg your pardon?''

''You heard me,'' she said. ''You show me what I want to see, and I will show you what you—judging by the way you've been looking down my front—want to see.''

''Jesus!''

''Actually, it's Helene,'' she said, and took his hand. ''Deal?''

''If you're serious,'' he said. ''The elevator is over there.''

''With a little bit of luck, there will be no one on it but you and me,'' Helene said. "Do you have some gin, or should I bring this with me?''

"I have gin,'' he said.

She put her glass down, put her hand under his arm, and steered him to the elevator.

When it stopped at the lobby floor, the tiny elevator already held four people, but they squeezed on anyway. Matt was aware of the pressure of her breasts on his back, and was quite sure that it was intentional.

On the third floor, he unlocked the door to his stairwell and motioned for her to precede him. At the top, when he had turned on the lights, she turned to him and smiled.

"Dickens would have said 'tiny garret.' ''

"And he would have been right.''

"Make me a drink—martini?''

"Sure.''

"But first, show me the gun.''

He squatted, took the revolver from its holster, opened the cylinder, and ejected the cartridges.

"Those are the bullets, the same kind?''

"Cartridges,'' he corrected automatically.

"Let me see one.''

He dropped one in her hand. She inhaled audibly as she touched it, and then rolled it around in the upturned palm of her hand.

"Show me how it goes in,'' she said.

He took the cartridge back and dropped it in the cylinder.

"It takes five,'' he said.

He unloaded it again, dropped the cartridge in his pocket, and handed her the revolver.

As he poured gin over ice in his tiny kitchen, he could see her looking at the gun from all angles. Finally, she sniffed it, and then sat down, disappearing from sight behind the bookcase that separated the "living area'' from the "dining area,'' at least on the architect's plans.

When he went into the living area, she was sitting on the edge of his couch. The pistol was on the coffee table. She was running her fingers over it. To do so, she had to lean forward, which served to give him a good look down her dress.

"I found that very interesting,'' she said, reaching up for her drink. " 'Exciting' would be a better word.''

"We try to please,'' he said. He picked up the pistol and

carried it to the mantel over the fireplace. He was now more than a little uncomfortable. He didn't like her reaction to the pistol, and suspected that she was somehow excited by the knowledge that he had killed someone with it.

There's a word for that, and it's spelled P E R V E R S E.

When he turned around, she was on her feet, walking toward him.

"How old are you, Poor Patricia Payne's Boy Matthew?"

"Twenty-two."

"I'm pushing thirty," she said. "Which does pose something of a problem for you, doesn't it?"

"I don't know what you mean."

She laughed, just a little nastily.

"As does the fact that I am behaving very oddly indeed about your gun, not to mention the fact that I am married. Right?"

He could think of nothing whatever to say.

"So we will leave the decision up to you, Matthew Payne. Do I say good night and thank you for showing me your etchings, or do I take off my dress?"

"Do what you want to do," Matt said.

She met his eyes, and pushed her dress off one shoulder and then the other, and then worked it down off her hips.

Then she walked to him, put her hands to his face, and kissed him. And then he felt her hand on his zipper.

When Margaret McCarthy got in Charley McFadden's Volkswagen he could almost immediately smell soap. He glanced at her and saw that her hair was still damp.

Charley immediately had—and was as immediately shamed by—a mental image of Margaret naked in her shower.

"You didn't have to do this, you know," Margaret said.

"What? You got some guy waiting for you at the hospital?"

"Absolutely, and in my uniform we're going to a bar somewhere."

"I'll break his neck," Charley said.

"What I meant, honey," Margaret said, "was that you didn't have to stay up just to drive me to work."

I really like it when she calls me "honey."

"I don't want you wandering around North Broad Street alone at midnight," Charley said. "Are we going to argue about this again?"

"No, Charley."

"Call me 'honey' again," Charley said. "I like that."

"Just 'honey.' Not 'sugar'? How do you feel about 'saccharine'?"

"Now, you're making fun of me."

"No, honey, I'm not," Margaret said, and leaned over and kissed him on the cheek.

"I like that too," he said.

"Well, I'd do it more often if I didn't wear lipstick. When I go on duty, no lipstick, and you get a little smooch."

"Now you know why I had to drive you to work," Charley said.

She laughed.

"What are you going to do now? Go home? Or go back to the FOP and have a couple of beers with Matt?"

"If I went to the FOP and Payne was still there, I would have to carry him home. Anyway, he had a date."

"A date? He doesn't have a girl, does he?"

"He has lots of them. Jesus, with that car, what did you expect?"

"A lot of girls, including this one, don't really care what kind of a car a fellow drives."

"There's not a lot of girls like you."

"Is that the voice of experience talking?"

"Maybe, maybe not. Matt was really bananas about one girl. A rich girl, like him. He met her when Whatsername, the girl whose father owns Nesfoods, got married."

"What happened?"

"She was a rich girl. She thought he was nuts for wanting to be a cop. Instead of like, a lawyer, something like that."

"So why does he want to be a cop?"

"I thought a lot about that. What it is, I think, is that he likes it. It's got nothing to do with him not getting in the Marines, or that his father, his real father, was killed on the job. I think he just likes it. And he's working for Inspector Wohl. He gets to see a lot of stuff. I don't think he'd stick around if they had him in one of the districts, turning off fire hydrants."

"You really like him, don't you?"

"Yeah. We get along good."

"You going to ask him to be your best man when we get married?"

Charley had not thought about a best man.

"Yeah," he said. "I guess I will, if I live that long."

"Are we going to start on that subject again?"

"I'm not starting anything. That's just the truth."

"We want to have some money in the bank when we get married."

"I'd just as soon go in hock like everybody else," Charley said. "Jesus, baby, I go nuts sometimes thinking about you."

"Like when, for example?"

"Like now, for example. Since you asked. I smell your soap, and then I—"

"Then you what?"

"I think of you taking a shower."

"Those are carnal thoughts."

"You bet your ass they are," Charley said. "About as carnal as they get."

There was a long silence.

"I guess I shouldn't have said that. Sorry."

"You think you could live six weeks the way things are?"

"What happens in six weeks?"

"The semester's over. I could skip a semester. I wouldn't want to be a just-married, and work a full shift, and try to go to school. But I could skip a semester."

"Jesus, baby, you mean it?"

"I'll call my mother in the morning and tell her we don't want to wait anymore."

"Jesus! Great!"

"I get those thoughts too, honey," Margaret said. She reached over and caught his hand.

At the hospital, when she kissed him, she kissed him on the mouth and gave him a little tongue, something she didn't hardly ever do.

Where the fuck am I?

I was thinking about that, and what she said about her having those kind of thoughts, carnal thoughts too, and drove right across Broad Street without thinking where I'm supposed to be going.

"Shit!" he said, and slowed abruptly, and made the next left.

There's Holland's body shop. That means I'm behind Holland Pontiac-GMC, just a block off North Broad. That's not so bad. I could have wound up in Paoli or somewhere not thinking like that.

And then something wrong caught his eye. There was a guy sitting in a beat-up old Mustang in an alley.

If I hadn't been looking to see where the fuck I was, I would never have seen him.

What's wrong about it? Well, maybe nothing. Or maybe he's drunk. Or dead. Or maybe not. Now that I think of it, he was smoking a cigarette. People don't sit in alleys smoking cigarettes at midnight. Not around here.

He made the next right, and the next, and pulled to the curb.

Fuck it, McFadden. It ain't any of your business, and you ain't Sherlock Holmes.

Fuck fuck it!

Charley turned off the headlights and got out of the car. He took his wallet ID folder from his pocket and folded it back on itself, so the badge was visible, and then he took the snub nose from its holster, and held it at arm's length down along his leg so that it would be kind of hard to see.

Then he went in the alley, and sort of keeping in the shadows walked down close to the Mustang.

Piece of shit, that car.

Moving very quickly now, he walked up to the driver's window. He tapped on the window with his badge.

He scared shit out of the guy inside, who jumped.

The window rolled down.

"Excuse me, sir. I'm a police officer. Is everything all right?"

"I'm a Three-Six-Nine," the man said. "Everything's okay. On the job."

Oh, shit. He's probably a Central Detective on stakeout. Why didn't you mind your own fucking business?

Fuck fuck fuck it. Maybe he ain't.

"Let me see your folder, please," Charley said, and pulled the door open so the light would come on. It didn't.

Lieutenant Jack Malone thinking, *This big fucker, whoever he is, smells something wrong, and he's got his gun out,* very slowly and nonthreateningly found his badge and photo ID and handed it to Officer Charles McFadden.

"Lieutenant, I'm sorry as hell about this."

"Don't be silly. You were just doing your job. I suppose I did look a little suspicious."

"I didn't know what the fuck to think, so I thought I'd better check. Sorry to bother you, sir."

"No problem, I told you that," Malone said. "But I don't want this on the record. You call it in?"

"No, sir. I'm in my own car. No radio."

"Just keep this between ourselves. What did you say your name was?"

"McFadden, sir."

"You work this district?"

"No, sir. I'm Highway."

"Well, I'll certainly tell Captain Pekach how alert you were. But I don't want anyone else to know you saw me here. Okay?"

"Yes, sir. I understand. Good night, sir."

Charley stuffed his pistol back in its holster and walked back up the alley.

Nice guy. I really could have got my ass in a crack doing that. But he understood why I did it. Malone was his name. I wonder where he works. He said he knows Captain Pekach.

And then he got back in the Volkswagen, and there was still a faint smell of Margaret's soap, and he started to think about her, and her in the shower, and what she had said about her having those kinds of thoughts too, and Lieutenant Malone and the rusty piece of shit he was driving were relegated to a far corner of his mind.

TEN

The time projected on the ceiling by the clever little machine that had been Amelia Payne, M.D.'s birthday present to her little brother showed that it was quarter past eleven.

It should be later than that, Matt thought, *considering all that's happened.*

He bent one of the pillows on the bed in half and propped it under his head. Then he reached down and pulled up the blanket. The sheet that covered him wasn't enough; he felt chilled.

He could hear the shower running in the bath, and in his mind's eye saw Helene at her ablutions, and for a moment considered leaping out of the bed and getting in the shower with her.

He sensed that it would be a bad idea, and discarded the notion.

Three times is a sufficiency. At the moment, almost certainly, the lady is not burning with lust.

Well, two and a half, considering the first time was more on the order of premature ejaculation than a proper screw.

With an effort, she had been very kind about that. He was not to worry. It happened sometimes. But she had been visibly pleased at his resurgent desire, or more precisely when El Wango had risen phoenixlike from the ashes of too-quickly burned passion.

And clearly done his duty: There is absolutely no way that she could have faked that orgasm.

Orgasms?

Passion followed by sleep, followed by slowly becoming delightedly aware that what one is fondling in one's sleep is not the goddamn pillow again, but a magnificent real live boob, attached to a real live woman.

One who whispered huskily in the dark "Don't stop!" when, ever the gentleman, I decided that copping a feel was perhaps not the thing to do under the circumstances.

And El Wango, God bless him, had risen to the occasion, giving his all for God, Mother, and Country, as if determined to prove that what good had happened previously was the norm, and that "oh, shit" spasm earlier on a once-in-a-century aberration.

She had said, "I'll be sore for a week," which I understand could be a complaint, but which, I believe, I will accept as a compliment.

The drumming of the shower died, and he could hear the last gurgle as the water went down the drain, and he could hear other faint sounds, including what he thought was the sound of his hairbrush clattering into the washbasin.

And then she came out. In her underwear, but still modestly covering herself with a towel.

"You're not leaving?" Matt said. "The evening is young."

"The question is what about the Opera Ball people?"

She sat on the edge of the bed, keeping the towel in place.

I was right. Thrice, or even twice and a half, is a more than a sufficiency, it is a surfeit.

"I haven't heard the elevator in a while. I guess they're all gone. Would you like me to take you home?"

"I have a car."

"Where?"

"In the garage in the basement."

"Parked right next to the elevator?"

"How did you know that?"

"You're the Cadillac in my parking spot. Spots. The gods—

the Greco-Roman ones, who understand this sort of thing—obviously wanted us to get together.''

''I don't know about that, but I do know what got us together. It's spelled G I N. As in, I should know better than to drink martinis.''

''Are you sorry?''

''Yes, of course, I'm sorry,'' Helene said. ''I expect you hear this from all your married ladies, but in my case it's true. I normally don't do things like this.''

''Well, I'm glad you made an exception for me,'' Matt said. ''And just for the record, you're my first married lady. I would like to thank you for being gentle with me, it being my first time.''

She laughed, and then grew serious.

''I would like to say the same thing,'' she said. ''But you're the third. And I decided just ninety seconds ago, the last.''

''I didn't measure up?''

''That's the trouble. You—left nothing to be desired. Except more of you, and that's obviously out of the question.''

''Why is it obviously out of the question?''

She got up suddenly from the bed, dropped the towel, and walked out of the bedroom, snapping, ''I'm married,'' angrily over her shoulder.

She'll be back, Matt thought confidently. *She will at least say good-bye.*

But she did not come back, so he picked up the towel she had dropped and put it around his waist and went looking for her.

She was gone.

I don't even know what her last name is.

During his military service Staff Inspector Peter F. Wohl had learned that rubber gloves were what smart people wore when applying cordovan shoe polish to foot wear, otherwise you walked around for a couple of days with brown fingernails. When the last pair had worn out, the only rubber gloves he could find in the Acme Supermarket had been the ones he now wore, which were flaming pink in color and decorated in a floral pattern. At the time, their function, not their appearance, had seemed to be the criteria.

Now he was not so sure. Mrs. Samantha Stoddard, the 230-pound, fifty-two-year-old Afro-American grandmother who cleaned the apartment two times a week had found them under the sink and offered the unsolicited opinion that he better hope nobody but her ever saw them. "*I know* you like girls, Peter. Other people might wonder."

Mrs. Stoddard felt at ease calling Staff Inspector Wohl by his Christian name because she had been doing so since he was four years old. She still spent the balance of the week working for his mother.

When the telephone rang, at ten past seven in the morning, Wohl was standing at his kitchen sink, wearing his pink rubber gloves, his underwear, an unbuttoned shirt, and his socks, examining with satisfaction the shine he had just caused to appear on a pair of loafers. At five past seven, as he prepared to slip his feet into them, he had discovered that they were in desperate need of a shine.

From the sound of the bell, he could tell that it was his official telephone ringing. He headed for the bedroom, hurriedly removing the flaming pink rubber gloves as he did so. The left came off with no difficulty; the right stuck. Before he got it off, he had cordovan shoe polish all over his left hand.

"Shit!" he said aloud, adding aloud. "Why do I think this is going to be one of those days?"

Then he picked up the telephone.

"Inspector Wohl."

"Matt Lowenstein, Peter. Is there some reason you can't meet me at Tommy Callis's office at eight?"

"No, sir."

"Keep it under your hat," Lowenstein said, and hung up.

Wohl replaced the handset in its cradle, but, deep in thought, kept his hand on it for a moment. Thomas J. Callis was the district attorney. He could think of no business he—that is to say Special Operations, including Highway Patrol—had with the district attorney. If something serious had happened, he would have been informed of it.

A wild hair appeared—Tony Harris was on a spectacular bender; he could have run into a school bus or something—and was immediately discarded. He would have heard of that too, as quickly as he had learned that they had held Tony overnight in the 9th District holding cell.

He shrugged, and dialed the Special Operations number. He told the lieutenant who answered that he would be in late. He did not say how late or where he would be. Lowenstein had told him to keep the meeting at the DA's office under his hat.

He looked at his watch, then shook his head. There was no time to go somewhere for breakfast.

He returned to the kitchen, put a pot of water on the stove to boil, and got eggs and bread from the refrigerator. He decided he would not make coffee, because that would mean having to clean the pot, technically a brewer his mother had given him for Christmas. It made marvelous coffee, but unless it was cleaned almost immediately, it turned the coffee grounds in its works to concrete and required a major overhaul.

When the water boiled, he added vinegar, then, with a wooden spoon, swirled the water around until it formed a whirlpool. Then, expertly, he cracked two eggs with one hand and dropped them into the water. By the time they were done, the toaster had popped up. He took the eggs from the water with a slotted spoon, put them onto the toast, and moved to his small kitchen table. Time elapsed, beginning to end: ten minutes.

"If I only had a cup of coffee," he announced aloud, "all would be right in my world."

Then it occurred to him that if he was to meet with the district attorney, a suit would be in order, not the blazer and slacks he had intended to wear. And if he wore a suit, shoes, not loafers, would be in order.

The whole goddamn shoe-shining business, including the polish-stained left hand, had been a waste of time and effort.

He returned to the sink, and washed his hands with a bar of miracle abrasive soap that was guaranteed to remove all kinds of stain. The manufacturers had apparently never dealt with cordovan shoe polish.

Or, he thought cynically, *they knew damned well that very few people would wrap up a fifty-cent bar of soap and mail it off to Dubuque, Iowa, or wherever, for a refund. Particularly since they wouldn't have the address in Iowa, having thrown the wrapping away when they took the soap out.*

He took his pale blue shirt off, replaced it with a white one, and put on a dark gray, pin-striped suit.

"Oh, you are a handsome devil, Peter Wohl," he said as he checked himself in the mirror. "I wonder why you don't get laid more than you do?"

He arrived downtown at the district attorney's office with

five minutes to spare, having exceeded the speed limit over almost all of the route.

As he looked at his watch, he thought the hour was odd. He didn't think the district attorney was usually about the people's business at eight A.M. Had Callis summoned Lowenstein at this time? Probably not. If Callis had wanted to see them, somebody would have called him too. The odds were that Lowenstein had called Callis and told him he had to see him as soon as possible, and then when Callis had agreed, Lowenstein had called him.

Why?

Chief Inspector Matt Lowenstein, Detective Joe D'Amata of Homicide, and another man, obviously a detective, were in Callis's outer office when Peter walked in.

"I was getting worried about you," Lowenstein greeted him.

"Good morning, Chief, I'm not late, am I?"

"Just barely," Lowenstein said. "You know Jerry Pelosi, don't you?"

"Sure. How are you, Pelosi?"

They shook hands.

The mystery is over. Pelosi's the Central Detectives guy working the Goldblatt job. This is about that.

There was no chance to ask Chief Lowenstein. A large, silver-haired, ruddy-faced man, the Hon. Thomas J. Callis, district attorney of Philadelphia, swept into his outer office, the door held open for him by Philadelphia County Detective W.H. Mahoney. The district attorney had in effect his own detective bureau. Most of them, like Mahoney, were ex-Philadelphia Police Department officers. A detective bodyguard-driver was one of the perks of being the district attorney.

"Hello, Matt," Callis said. "How the hell are you?"

A real pol, Wohl thought. Wohl did not ordinarily like politicians, but he was of mixed emotions about Callis. He had worked closely with him during his investigation—

In those happy, happy, days when I was just one more staff inspector—

—of Judge Findermann and his fellow scumbags, and had concluded that Callis was deeply offended by the very notion of a judge on the take, and interested in the prosecution for that reason alone, not simply because it might look good for him in the newspapers.

"And Peter," Callis went on, "looking the fashion plate even at this un-godly hour."

"Good morning, Mr. Callis."

"Tommy! Tommy! How many times do I have to tell you that?"

"Tommy," Wohl said obediently.

"Detective D'Amata I know, of course, but I don't think I've had the pleasure—"

"Detective Jerry Pelosi," Lowenstein offered, "of Central Detectives."

"Well, I'm delighted to meet you, Jerry," Callis said, sounding as if he meant it, and pumping his hand.

Callis turned and faced the others, beaming as if just seeing them gave him great pleasure.

"Well, let's get on with this, whatever it is," he said. "Are we all going in, Matt?"

"Why not?" Lowenstein said, after a just perceptible pause. "Mahoney knows when to keep his mouth shut, don't you, Mahoney?"

"Yes, of course he does," Callis said. "Well then, come on in. Anybody want some coffee?"

"I would kill for a cup of coffee," Wohl said.

"Figuratively speaking, of course, Peter?"

"Don't get between me and the pot," Wohl replied.

"Black, Inspector?" Mahoney asked.

"Please," Wohl said.

"My time is your time, Matt, providing this doesn't last more than thirty minutes," Callis said.

"You heard about the Goldblatt job?" Lowenstein asked.

"You mean the—what was it?—'Islamic Liberation Army'? It was all over the tube. The *Ledger* even ran a photo of their press release on the front page of the second section. Who the hell are these nuts, Matt?"

"Between Pelosi and D'Amata we have a pretty good idea who they are," Lowenstein said.

"Good idea or names?"

"Names. On almost all of them, anyway."

"Witnesses?"

"There were twenty-odd people in Goldblatt's," Lowenstein replied.

"That's not what I asked."

"We have one *good* witness," Lowenstein said carefully.

"A Goldblatt employee. Worked like sort of a doorman. Albert J. Monahan. Pelosi showed him pictures and he positively identified all of them."

"A moment ago you said there were twenty-odd people in Goldblatt's."

"They don't want to get involved. In other words, they're scared. That press release and the way the press swallowed it, hook, line, and sinker, made things worse."

"So if you catch these guys, you have *one* witness?"

"There's no question of 'if' we catch them, Tommy," Lowenstein said. "The question is how, and what we do with them."

"Let's cut to the chase," the district attorney said.

"Okay. Two things bug me about this job," Lowenstein said. "First, something that's been building up the last couple of years. Witnesses not wanting to get involved. A lot of scumbags are walking around out there because witnesses suddenly have developed trouble with their memories."

Callis nodded. "They're afraid. I don't know what to do about it."

"In a minute, I'll tell you. The second things is I don't like the idea of a bunch of *schwartzer* thugs dressing up like Arabs—"

"Americans of African descent, you mean, of course, Chief?" Callis interrupted softly.

"—and announcing they're not really stick-up artists—in this case, murderers—but soldiers in some liberation army."

"And blaming the Jews for all their troubles?"

"Yeah. Blaming *us* Jews for all their troubles," Lowenstein said. "That bothers me personally, but I'm here as the chief inspector of Detectives of the City of Philadelphia. Okay?"

"No offense, Matt."

"I called Jason Washington last night—" Lowenstein said, and then interrupted himself. "I tried to call you, Peter, but all I got was your answering machine. Then I called your driver, and all I got there was a smart-ass message on his answering machine. So I gave up and called Washington without checking with you. I hope you're not sore. I thought it was necessary."

"Don't be silly," Wohl said. "But if you are referring to Officer Payne, he is my administrative assistant, not my driver. Only full inspectors and better get drivers."

"I don't think it will be too long, Chief," Callis said, "before Peter is a full inspector, do you?"

"What about Washington, Chief?" Wohl asked.

"He has a relationship with Arthur X," Lowenstein went on. "I asked him to call him."

Arthur X, a Negro male, thirty-six years of age, 175 pounds, who shaved his head, and wore flowing robes, had been born Arthur John Thomlinson. He had replaced Thomlinson with X on the basis that Thomlinson was a slave name. Arthur X was head of the Philadelphia Islamic Temple, which was established in a former movie palace on North Broad Street.

He had converted an estimated three thousand people to his version of Islam. The men wore suits and ties, and the women white robes, including headgear that covered most of their faces.

"And?" Tommy Callis asked.

"He told Jason he never heard of the Islamic Liberation Army."

"Did Jason believe him? Do you?"

"Yeah."

"Why?"

"He and Jason have an understanding. He doesn't lie to Jason, and Jason doesn't lie to him. Jason said he had the feeling that Arthur didn't like their using the term 'Islamic.' That's his word."

"He didn't volunteer who he thought these people might be, by any chance?"

"Jason didn't ask. He said if he asked, and Arthur told him—Jason said he didn't think Arthur knew, but he certainly could find out—then we would owe him one. I told you, Tommy, we already know who they are."

"So why did you have Washington call Arthur X?"

"To make sure that when we go to pick these scumbags up, we wouldn't be running into the Fruit of Islam screaming religious and/or racial persecution."

The Fruit of Islam was a group, estimated to be as many as one hundred, of Arthur X's followers, all at least six feet tall, who served as Arthur X's bodyguard.

"So when are you going to pick these people up?" Tommy Callis asked.

"That's what I wanted to talk to you about," Lowenstein said. "I want to do it like Gangbusters."

"I don't know what that means, Matt," Callis said carefully.

"I want warrants issued for all the people that Mr. Monahan has identified from photographs. I want them—this is where Peter and the Highway Patrol come in—picked up all at one time, say tomorrow morning at six. I then want Mr. Monahan to pick them out of a lineup, one at a time, as soon as possible, after the arraignment, before the preliminary hearing. I want them charged with first degree murder and armed robbery. Then I want to run them past a municipal court in the Roundhouse who is not going to release them on their own recognizance or on two-bit bail. I want you to run them past the Grand Jury just as soon as that can be arranged, and then I want them on the docket just as soon as that can be arranged. Unless there is some reason not to, I want them all tried together, and I want one of the best assistant DAs in the Homicide Unit, preferably the head man, to prosecute. I would not be unhappy if you could find the time to prosecute yourself, Tommy."

Tommy Callis thought that over a minute.

"You have *one* witness."

"He's a good one. Credible."

"One," Callis repeated.

"You're suggesting those thugs would get to him?"

"What have they got to lose? It's already murder one. And he could get sick, or drop dead or something."

"That's where Peter comes in again. Right now, I've got a couple of Northwest Detectives on Mr. Monahan. That's just to be sure. Just as soon as this thing starts, I want Peter to *conspicuously* protect Mr. Monahan."

"Meaning what?"

"A Highway car parked around the clock in front of his house. If he insists on going to work, Highway will take him back and forth, and park in front of Goldblatt's while he's working."

"He could still have a heart attack, or something."

"And he could get struck by lightning," Lowenstein said. "Anything's possible. I think it's more possible that we could come up with a couple, maybe six, eight, ten more witnesses."

"Explain that to me, Matt."

"Peter will also put Highway people on the other witnesses."

"What for?" Callis asked, without thinking.

''To protect them, of course. We are dealing with dangerous people here. While the witnesses, if they are to be believed, can't identify the doers, the doers don't know that.''

''Christ, Matt, I don't know,'' Callis protested.

''Once they come to understand that they are in some danger whether or not they testify, they may decide that the only way they can *really* protect their asses is by making sure these scumbags are put away. An assistant DA, with good persuasive skills, might be able to jolt their memories a little. I also thought I would ask Peter to have Washington have a word with the witnesses.''

''The Afro-American witnesses, you mean?''

''All of them. Jason is a formidable sonofabitch, in addition to being very persuasive.''

''You're suggesting, 'Here is this big black *good* guy, who will protect me from the *bad* black guys'?'' Callis asked.

''Why not?'' Lowenstein said. ''And I'm going to suggest to Peter that when we make the arrests, it might be a good idea to use black Highway guys. A couple of them, anyway, at each site.''

''Yeah,'' Wohl said thoughtfully. ''Good idea.''

Callis thought about that a moment.

''I presume Commissioner Czernich thinks this is a good idea?'' he asked, finally.

''I haven't had the opportunity to discuss this with the commissioner,'' Lowenstein said.

''What?'' Callis asked disbelievingly.

''Commissioner Czernich is a very busy man,'' Lowenstein said. ''And besides, he won't fart unless The Dago tells him to. Or authorize anything that's not in the book. If I went to Tad Czernich, he would check with The Dago before he said anything. And I know, and so do you, Tommy, that the mayor would rather not know about this until it was over.''

Callis looked at his watch.

''My God, and it's only quarter after eight!''

''The early bird gets the worm,'' Lowenstein said.

''You haven't said much about this, Peter.''

''I haven't had anything to say.''

''Well, what *do* you think about this?''

''If Special Operations is called upon by Chief Lowenstein to assist the Detective Division, we would of course do so.''

Callis picked up his coffee cup and found that it was empty.

He held it up impatiently and Sergeant Mahoney quickly went to take it from him.

He tapped his fingertips together impatiently for a moment, said "Christ!" and then picked up one of the two telephones on his desk.

"Ask Mr. Stillwell to come in here, please," he said. "Tell him it's—just ask him to come in right away, please."

Wohl glanced at Lowenstein, whose eyebrows rose in surprise. When he saw Wohl looking at him, he gave a barely perceptible shrug.

Farnsworth Stillwell was an assistant district attorney. Generally speaking, there were three kinds of assistant district attorneys, young ones fresh from law school, who took the job to pay the rent and gain experience, and left after a few years; the mediocre ones who had just stayed on because the hoped-for good offer had not come; and the ones who stayed on because they liked the job and were willing to work for less than they could make in private practice.

Farnsworth Stillwell did not fall into any of the three categories. He came from a wealthy, socially prominent family. He had gone from Princeton into the Navy, become a pilot, and earned the Distinguished Flying Cross and some other medals for valor flying off an aircraft carrier off Vietnam. He had been seriously injured when he tried to land his damaged aircraft on returning to his carrier after a mission.

There had been six months in a hospital to consider what he wanted to do with his future now that a permanently stiff knee had eliminated the Navy and flying. He had decided on public service. He'd gone to law school, found and married a suitable wife, and then decided the quickest way to put himself in the public eye was by becoming an assistant district attorney.

He was, in Peter Wohl's judgment, smart—perhaps even brilliant—in addition to being competent. He was tall, thin, getting gray flecks in his hair, superbly tailored, and charming.

Wohl had come to know him rather well in the latter stages of the Judge Findermann investigation, and during the prosecution. There had been overtures of friendship from Stillwell. Without coming out and saying so, Stillwell had made it clear that he thought that he and Wohl, as they rose in the system, could be useful to each other.

Obviously, Stillwell was going places, and Wohl was fully aware of the political side of being a cop, particularly in the upper ranks. But he had, as tactfully as he could manage, rejected the offer.

There was something about the sonofabitch that he just didn't like. He couldn't put his finger on it, and vacillated between thinking that he just didn't like politicians, or archetypical WASPs, (and that consequently he was making a mistake) and a gut feeling that there was a mean, or perhaps corrupt, streak in Stillwell somewhere. Whatever it was, he knew that he did not want to get any closer to Farnsworth Stillwell, professionally or personally, than he had to.

He wondered now, as they waited for Stillwell to show up in Callis's office, what Matt Lowenstein thought of him.

"You wanted to see me, boss?" Stillwell called cheerfully as he strode, with an uneven gait, because of his knee, into Callis's office.

Then he saw Lowenstein first, and then Wohl, D'Amata, and Pelosi.

"Chief Lowenstein," he said. "How nice to see you. And Peter!"

He went to each and pumped their hands, and then turned to D'Amata and Pelosi.

"I'm Still Stillwell," he said, putting out his hand.

"Joe D'Amata, of Homicide," Lowenstein offered, "and Jerry Pelosi of Central Detectives."

"Sit down," Callis ordered, tempering it with a smile. "Matt's got a wild idea. I want your reaction to it."

"Chief Lowenstein is not the kind of man who has wild ideas," Stillwell said. "*Unusual*, perhaps. But not wild."

Nice try, Wohl thought, somewhat unkindly, *but a waste of effort. Matt Lowenstein wouldn't vote Republican if Moses were heading the ticket.*

"Tell the man about your *unusual* idea, Matt," Callis said.

Lowenstein laid out, quickly but completely, what he had in mind.

"What do you think of the chief's idea, Peter?" Stillwell asked.

Covering your ass, Still?

"We know what we think about it," Callis said. "What we want to know is what *you* think about it."

Thank you, Mr. District Attorney.

"All right. Gut reaction. Off the top of my head. I love it."

"Why?" Callis asked.

" 'District Attorney Thomas J. Callis announced this afternoon that he will bring the six, eight, whatever it is, members of the gang calling themselves the Islamic Liberation Army before the Grand Jury immediately, and that he is confident the Grand Jury will return murder and armed robbery indictments against all of them.' "

"You *were* listening when Lowenstein said they have just the one witness?"

"Yes. And I was also listening when he said he thought other witnesses might experience a miraculous return of memory."

"You want to put your money where your mouth is?" Callis asked.

"Am I going to be allowed to take part in this?"

"It's yours, if you want it," Callis said.

"I've got a pretty heavy schedule—"

"Meaning you really don't want to get involved, now that you've had ten seconds to think it over?"

"Meaning, I'll have to have some help with my present calendar."

"No problem," Callis said. "That can be arranged."

Callis, Wohl thought unkindly, but with a certain degree of admiration, *has just pulled a Carlucci. If this works, he will take, if not all, at least a substantial portion of the credit. And if it goes wrong, that will be Farnsworth Stillwell's fault. Or mine.*

Or Matt Lowenstein's fault. Or mine.

Probably the latter. When you get to the bottom line, Farnsworth Stillwell is smarter than either Lowenstein or me. Or at least less principled. Or both.

"Keep me up-to-date on what's going on," Callis said. "And later today, Still, I'll want to talk to you about the municipal court judge."

"Right, Chief," Stillwell said. "Gentlemen, why don't we go into the conference room and work out some of the details?"

"Thank you, Tommy," Lowenstein said.

Callis grunted. When he gave his hand to Peter Wohl, he said, "You'd better hope your people can protect Mr. Monahan, Peter. For that matter you'd better hope he doesn't have a heart attack."

When Officer Matthew Payne walked into the Special Operations Office, the sergeant had given him the message that Inspector Wohl had called in at 7:12 to say that he would not be in until later, time unspecified.

Officer Payne sat down at his desk and opened the *Bulletin*. He had just started to read Mickey O'Hara's story about the robbery and murder at Goldblatt & Sons Credit Furniture & Appliances, Inc., when, startling him, the newspaper was snatched out of his hands.

Officer Charles McFadden was standing there, looking very pleased with himself.

"Jesus Christ, Charley!"

"Gotcha, huh?"

"Why aren't you out fighting crime?"

"Need a favor."

"Okay. Within reason."

"Be my best man," Charley said.

"I have this strange feeling you're serious."

"Margaret's going to call her mother this morning; we're going to get married in six weeks."

"Yeah, sure, Charley. I'd be honored."

"Thank you," Charley said very seriously, shook Matt's hand enthusiastically, and walked out of the office.

When he was gone, Matt picked up and read the *Bulletin* and then the *Ledger*. Both carried stories about the robbery of Goldblatt's. The *Ledger* story was accompanied by a photograph of a press release from the Islamic Liberation Army, claiming responsibility. Mickey O'Hara's story in the *Bulletin* hadn't mentioned the Islamic Liberation Army.

Matt found that interesting. He allowed himself to hope that the press release was a hoax, on which the *Ledger* had bit, and which would show them up for the assholes they were.

The society pages of both newspapers (called "LIVING" in the *Ledger*) carried stories of the festivities of the Delaware Valley Cancer Society on Rittenhouse Square, complete with photographs of some of the guests, standing around holding plastic champagne glasses. Matt hoped that he would find Helene's picture, and then, in the caption, her last name. He examined each of them carefully but was unable to find a picture of Helene.

Of course not. While this momentous occasion was being photographed for posterity, Helene and I were thrashing around in our birthday suits on my bed. It's a shame I don't have a picture of that for my memory book.

The telephone rang.

"Good morning. Inspector Wohl's office, Officer Payne."

"You're remarkably cheerful," Wohl's voice said.

"Yes, sir. Every day, in every way, things are getting better and better."

"I gather you were not alone in your monastic cell last night?"

"Yes, sir. That's true."

"I'm in the DA's office, Matt. Get word to Pekach and Sabara that I want to see them in my office at half past eleven. Tell them to keep lunch free too."

"Yes, sir."

"In the upper right drawer of my desk, you'll find a ring of keys. They're to the elementary school building at Frankford and Castor."

"Yes, sir?"

"Get a car and take Lieutenant Malone over there. Tell him I want his assessment of the building as a headquarters—listen carefully: for Special Operations headquarters and Special Operations; for Special Operations headquarters and Highway; and for Special Operations headquarters, Special Operations, *and* Highway. All three possibilities. Got it?"

"Yes, sir. I understand."

"Don't help him," Wohl said.

"Sir?" Matt asked, confused.

"I want to know what you think too, separately," Wohl said. "Get him back in time for the eleven-thirty meeting."

"Yes, sir. What would you like me to do with the stuff for the FBI?"

"You have it all?"

"Yes, sir. I couldn't run Mr. Harris down, but I asked Mr. Washington to have a look at it, and he said I found everything they'd want."

"Leave it on my desk. Maybe I'll have time—I'll have to make time—to look at it before eleven-thirty. You have to be damned careful what you hand the FBI. Call them, and tell them they'll have it this afternoon."

"Yes, sir."

"And see if you can get word to Washington to be there at half past eleven."

"Just Mr. Washington?"

"Just Mr. Washington" Wohl repeated, and hung up.

Matt called Captain Sabara, Captain Pekach, Detective Washington—*now Sergeant Washington*—and finally the FBI office. He got through to everybody but SAC Davis, who was not available to come to the telephone. Matt left word that the material Inspector Wohl was sending would be there that afternoon.

Then he went to the Special Operations dispatcher and asked for a car. When he had the keys, he went and looked for Lieutenant Malone.

ELEVEN

The building at Frankford and Castor Avenues, according to what was chiseled in stone over the front door and on a piece of granite to the left of the door, had been built in 1892 as the Frankford Grammar School.

Plywood had been nailed over the glass portion of the doors and many of the ground-floor windows, the ones from which, Matt Payne decided, the local vandals had been successful in ripping off the wire mesh window guards.

The front doors were locked with two massive padlocks and closing chains looped around the center posts of the door. When Matt finally managed to get one padlock to function, he turned to Lieutenant Jack Malone.

"Why don't we just stop here and go back and tell the inspector that a detailed survey of these premises has forced us to conclude they are unfit for human habitation?"

"They obviously are, but we are talking about *police* habitation," Malone said. "The standards for which are considerably looser."

Matt jerked the door open. It sagged and dragged on the ground; the top hinge had pulled loose from the rotten frame.

He bowed and waved Malone past him.

Malone chuckled. From what he had seen of Payne, he liked him. He was not only a pleasant kid, but he'd already proven he was a cop. And Malone had heard the gossip. He knew that Payne's father had been a sergeant, killed on the job, and that he had a very important rabbi in Chief Inspector Dennis V. Coughlin.

Not that he needed one, Malone thought, as close as Payne was to Inspector Wohl. Wohl was a powerful man in the Department. In his present uncomfortable circumstances, that could mean he could get his career back on track, or begin thinking of leaving the Department as soon as he had his twenty in, or maybe even before.

And since Payne was close to Wohl, the same thing applied to him. He could help, or he could hurt. Malone had waked up wondering what kind of trouble he was already in, thanks to that zealous Highway cop who had spotted him keeping an eye on Holland's body shop.

Wohl hadn't said anything to him about keeping his nose out of Auto Squad's business now that he was assigned to Special Operations. Malone knew that he was supposed to be smart enough to figure that out himself. There was little chance that Wohl hadn't heard about it, however.

They didn't send me to Special Operations without talking to Wohl about Poor Jack Malone, who has personal problems, and who incidentally had somehow acquired the nutty idea that Robert L. Holland, respectable businessman and pal of everybody important from Mayor Jerry Carlucci down, was a car thief.

The smart thing for me to have done was just forget the whole damned thing and make myself useful around Special Operations. A good year on this job, and the word would get around that I had gotten through my personal problems and could now, again, be trusted not to make an ass of myself and the Department. That word, coming from Wohl, would straighten everything out.

The worst possible scenario would be for the Highway cop, McFadden, he said his name was, to tell his lieutenant that he had checked out a suspicious car parked near Holland's body shop and found the new lieutenant, Malone, in it. If that hap-

pened, there was a good chance that the lieutenant would "mention" that to either Sabara or Pekach. Or maybe to Inspector Wohl himself. In any event, Wohl would hear about it.

At that point, Wohl would have to call me in and tell me to straighten up and fly right or find myself another home. Wohl was not about to put himself in a position where the brass would jump on his ass for letting Poor Jack Malone run around making wild accusations about a friend of the mayor's.

I think I could probably talk myself out of the first time. Yes, sir. I'm sorry, sir. I realize I was wrong, sir. It won't happen again, sir.

And I couldn't let it happen again, which would mean that sonofabitch would continue to get away with it.

That's the worst possible scenario. That doesn't mean it will go down that way. For one thing, the odds are, because McFadden probably walked away thinking he had made a fool of himself, that he had walked into, and almost fucked up, a stakeout where he had no business, that McFadden won't mention what happened to anybody, least of all his lieutenant.

That, I suppose, is the best possible scenario. What will really happen is probably somewhere in between. Whatever it is, since I can't do a fucking thing about it, there's no point in worrying about it.

That puts me back to what I do next. The smart thing to do obviously, since I nearly got caught doing something that really threatens my career, is don't do that no more.

But I'm a cop, and Holland is a thief, and what cops are supposed to do is lock up thieves.

Maybe Wohl, if I went to him, would understand. He understands that some thieves are fucking pillars of the community. Christ, he locked up Judge Findermann, didn't he?

You're dreaming, Poor Jack Malone. You don't have anything to go on except a gut feeling, and if you said that to Wohl, you'd soon be commanding officer of the rubber-gun squad.

Inside the outer doors was a small flight of stairs. Malone went up that, and then through a second set of doors. He heard scurrying noises that experience told him was the sound of rats.

I wonder what the hell they eat in here? It doesn't look like anybody has been in here in years.

He waited for a moment, to let his eyes adjust to the dim

light, and then went left down a corridor. The ancient hardwood floor squealed and creaked under his weight. There was a sign with PRINCIPAL still lettered on a door. He pushed that open and looked inside.

There was a counter inside, and several open doors, through which he could see rooms that could be used as Wohl's and Sabara's office.

"We could put the boss in there, I suppose," he said.

"Jesus!"

"And you, Officer Payne," Malone said. "I can see your desk right there by the hole in the wall."

"Do they really think we can use this place?" Payne asked.

"I think the inspector is desperate," Malone said. "We're sitting in each other's laps at Bustleton and Bowler."

"Well, there's a big enough parking lot. Already fenced in. We could start with that, I suppose, and build on it."

"Where?" Malone asked, and then went to a window and looked out where Payne pointed.

"I was reading the grant, and there's—"

"What?"

"The Justice Department Grant," Payne said. "That's where we got the money for Special Operations. A.C.T. It stands for Augmented Crime Teams."

Interesting. He's probably the only guy in Special Operations besides Wohl and Sabara who ever heard of the grant, much less read it.

"You were saying?"

"There's money in there, available on application, for capital improvement. About a hundred grand, if I remember correctly. The question is, would fixing this dump up be considered a 'capital improvement'?"

"I don't know," Malone said. "It's a thought."

"I'll mention it to the inspector," Payne said.

Malone went back in the corridor and down it and into another room. It was a boys' room.

"Well, there's something else we could start with and build on," Malone said. "I saw a Highway guy this morning who's small enough to use one of those urinals."

"Hay-zus," Payne chuckled.

"What?"

"Hay-zus—Jesus—Martinez. He's a quarter of an inch and maybe two pounds over Department minimums."

"How did he get in Highway? Most of those guys are six feet something?"

"He was one of the two of the inspector's first probationary Highway Patrolmen. He was a Narc. He and his partner were the ones who caught the guy who killed Dutch Moffitt. The inspector gave him a chance to see if he could make Highway, and he did."

"Oh, yeah. I remember that. The doer got himself run over by an elevated train, right?"

"Right."

"I remember Dutch Moffitt too. He was a real pisser. Big, good-looking guy. He screwed everything in skirts. What did they say?—'that he'd screw a snake if he could get it to hold still.' Did you know him?"

So that's why I have not been wallowing in Episcopalian remorse for having taken someone else's wife into my bed! My Moffitt genes have overwhelmed all my moral training.

"Dutch was my uncle," Payne said.

"Oh, Christ!" Malone said. "Payne, I'm sorry. I meant no offense."

"None taken," Payne said. "Dutch was—Dutch."

"If I'd have known he was your uncle, I wouldn't have—"

"Lieutenant, it's all right," Matt said. "But I would like to make a suggestion."

"Shoot."

"I think we have seen enough of this ruin to know that without spending a hell of a lot of money on it, it's useless. Why don't we go back and tell the inspector that? Maybe there is money in the grant we could get."

"Agreed. I'm freezing."

"Presuming we can get the door to shut, let's go find a cup of coffee."

Inspector Wohl was walking to the door of the building at Bustleton and Bowler as Matt Payne and Jack Malone drove up. He saw them and waited for them to get out of their car.

"Well, if it isn't the real estate squad," Wohl greeted them. "How did that go?"

"Well, we cut it sort of short, sir," Payne said. "The building is falling down. Unless we can get the money to fix it from ACT Capital Improvement, I think we should tell the City 'thank you, but no thank you.'"

He did not get the smile he expected.

"How many rooms?" Wohl asked. "Did you find someplace that could be used as a holding cell? Will the roof take antennae?"

"We didn't get that far, sir," Payne said.

"Go that far this afternoon when you come back from the FBI," Wohl said. "I didn't send you over there for a casual look. The building is ours, and there is money in the ACT Grant."

"I'm sorry, sir," Matt said.

"It's my fault, Inspector," Malone said.

"No, it's not," Wohl said flatly. "Matt, for Christ's sake, do me the courtesy of listening carefully to what I'm saying in the future."

"Yes, sir," Matt said.

"We'll take care of it, sir," Malone said.

"No, 'we' won't," Wohl said. "*He* will. *He* will come in in the morning with a sketch of the building, including dimensions. Indicate on it where people might fit. See what shape the furnace is in. *If* there is a furnace. You get the idea, and I don't care if you're there all night, Matt."

"Yes, sir."

"I don't see Jason Washington's car. Did you get in touch with him?"

"Yes, sir. He said he would be here."

"I want you in on this, Malone," Wohl said, and walked ahead of them into the building.

Well, the kid fucked up, sorry about that was the first thing Malone thought. This was immediately followed by, *Now he has to do it all himself,* and finally with a sudden insight: *If Wohl knows the kid can examine that building by himself, then there was no reason for him to send me over there in the first place. Except maybe to compare what the both of us had to say; in other words, to see if I am as smart as the kid. I'll be a sonofabitch.*

Jason Washington was standing by the door to Wohl's office.

"Got a minute, Inspector?" he asked.

"Yeah, sure," Wohl said. He looked over his shoulder. "You two go on in."

Captain Mike Sabara and Captain Dave Pekach were in Wohl's office, sitting on the couch in front of a small coffee table.

"Slide over, Dave, and make room for Malone," Sabara said, "otherwise we'll have Washington on here with us. Malone isn't nearly as broad in the beam."

"Your pal McFadden was looking for you, Payne," Pekach said as he made room for Malone. "Did he find you?"

"When was he looking?"

"Last night."

"Yeah. And he came looking for me again this morning. I am to be the best man at his wedding."

Christ, Malone thought, *maybe I'll get the worst possible scenario. If McFadden and Payne are pals, that's just as dangerous as McFadden telling his lieutenant he saw me staking out Holland's body shop. Damn!*

"Are you going to ask me to be your best man, David?" Sabara asked innocently.

"What?"

"Well, a nice Polish boy like you can't just go on living in sin indefinitely, can you?"

"Fuck you, Mike!" Pekach flared.

What the hell is that all about?

"If you feel that way, you can just get somebody else to be your best man," Sabara said.

"Goddammit, knock it off!"

"Play nice, children," Wohl said, coming into the room.

"He's always on my ass about Martha," Pekach said.

"Get off Captain Pekach's ass about Martha, Captain Sabara," Wohl said.

"Yes, sir," Sabara said, seemingly chastised. "What time is it, David?"

Without thinking, Pekach held up his wrist and opened his mouth.

"Nice watch, Dave," Sabara said innocently. "Where did you say you got it?"

"You sonofabitch!" Pekach flared.

It was too much for Wohl; he started to laugh, and when he did, Payne joined in.

Pekach looked like he was about to erupt, but finally started to laugh too, shaking his head.

"You bastards!"

"Show Malone your watch, Dave," Wohl said.

Pekach looked uncomfortable, but finally held up his wrist.

Around it was a heavy gold strap attached to a gold Omega chronograph.

Jesus, Malone thought, *that's worth three, four thousand dollars!*

"My—lady friend—gave it to me," he explained. There was a touch of pride in his voice. "These guys are just jealous."

"I certainly am," Jason Washington said. "That's worth thirty-nine ninety-five if it's worth a dime."

There was more laughter, and then Wohl ended it. "Recess is over, children," he said, "class has begun."

They all looked at him.

"I might as well start with that, and get it out of the way. We now have the school building at Frankford and Castor. We have it because the Board of Education no longer wants it, and the reason they no longer want it—confirmed by Malone and Payne who were over there this morning—is because it's falling down. The up side of that is that as part of the ACT Grant there is money for capital improvements. So as soon as possible, say day after tomorrow, we're going to start making it habitable—"

Malone had noticed that Captain Sabara had raised his hand—like a kid wanting the teacher's attention.

"Yes, Mike?" Wohl asked, interrupting himself.

"Figuratively speaking, you mean, Inspector?"

"No."

"Inspector, we're going to have to let the City put out specifications, get bids, open bids, all that stuff."

"No. Matt read the small print and showed me where it says we don't have to go through that for 'emergency repairs.' 'Emergency repairs' was not more precisely defined. I have decided that it means anything but beautification and additions. Fixing broken windows, plumbing, getting a new furnace— that's emergency repairs because we can't use the building with no heat, or no plumbing, or broken windows. Okay?"

"Department of Public Buildings isn't going to like it. They have their list of friendly folks who do work like that."

"I can't help that. We have to get out of here. And Commissioner Czernich—not Public Buildings—has the authority to spend the ACT Grant money."

"And he knows what you're going to do?"

"He will when he gets the bills."

"Inspector, you're asking for trouble," Sabara said.

"The bottom line is that we have to get out of here, Mike. If it goes before the mayor, and I suppose it eventually will, I'm betting he'll decide that I did the right thing and will tell Public Buildings to shut up."

"And if he doesn't decide that?"

"Then the new commanding officer of Special Operations will have a heated and air-conditioned office in a building he would not have had if his predecessor hadn't screwed up."

"It's liable to cost you your promotion, Peter," Sabara said.

"I appreciate your concern, Mike. But (a) I'm not sure if I'm in line for promotion and (b) I've made this decision. Okay?"

"Yes, sir."

"Item two," Wohl said. "Last night, Chief Inspector Lowenstein called one of our people—all right, Jason Washington—and asked him to do something he thought had to be done. Jason agreed to do it, then tried to find me to tell me, ask me, and couldn't—my fault, he should have been able to find me—and then went ahead and did it."

"What did Lowenstein want?" Pekach asked.

Wohl ignored the question and went on: "Okay. This is now official policy. As soon as Matt has the chance, he'll write it up, and I want it circulated to all supervisors. But I want this word passed immediately. Only three people, besides me, are authorized to take action when the assistance of Special Operations or Highway is asked for by anyone else. They are Captain Sabara for Special Operations, Captain Pekach for Highway, and Sergeant Washington for Special Investigations."

"Special Investigations?" Pekach asked, and then, "*Sergeant* Washington? When did that happen?"

"Washington made sergeant yesterday," Wohl said. "Special Investigations is a little younger. I thought it up about five minutes ago."

"Well, my God, Jason," Pekach said. "Congratulations. I didn't know you even took the examination."

He stood up and gave Washington his hand. The others followed suit.

"The word to be passed is that our supervisors don't—no matter who makes the request—do anything for anybody else unless, in your areas of responsibility, you know about it and approve. That means we have to be available twenty-four hours a day, seven days a week, to make the decision. And if you're not going to be available, you have to make sure I am. Okay?''

"Don't misunderstand me, Inspector," Captain Pekach said. "But there's a reason for this, right?"

"Yes, of course there is," Wohl said impatiently. "I don't want Matt Lowenstein, or anyone else, thinking they can just call up here and give our people things to do."

"It's hard to tell Matt Lowenstein no, Inspector," Jason Washington said.

"Especially if you hope to go back and work for him, right?" Wohl responded.

Washington's face tightened.

"I thought it was important, Inspector," Washington said.

"Just don't forget where you work, Jason. For whom you work."

"I suppose that means I won't be going back to Homicide?"

"The question came up as soon as the commissioner got the exam results. He called me and said he thought Lowenstein and Quaire would like to have you back in Homicide and how did I feel about that? I told him over my dead body. He said, joking of course, that Chief Lowenstein could probably arrange that, and I replied, joking of course, that if he did, the funeral procession would make a detour through the mayor's office, where the corpse would make a final protest."

Sabara chuckled.

"I'm glad you're amused, Mike," Wohl said.

"What I was thinking was, you really don't want to get promoted, do you?"

"I would like to be commissioner, all right? And I think the way to get myself promoted is to do a good job here."

"Hey, take it easy. I'm on your side. I'm one of the good guys."

"If you say so," Wohl said, and then he went on, "Item three: the Islamic Liberation Army."

"Don't tell me they gave us that too?" Pekach asked.

"No. Right now, it's a Homicide job. And properly so. What Lowenstein wanted Jason to do, and what, for the record, Jason quite properly agreed to do, was get in touch with Arthur X to ask him, so to speak, if when the Islamic Liberation Army is picked up, the arresting officers will face the Fruit of Islam, screaming religious and/or racial persecution."

"So they know who they are?" Pekach said.

"Yes, they do. What Chief Lowenstein told the district attorney was going to happen was that Highway would pick all these people up first thing tomorrow morning. They will be run through a lineup, lineups, so that they can be positively identified by the one good witness Homicide has. By then, the DA will have made sure that the municipal court judge doesn't turn these thugs loose on their own recognizance. He will then arrange to get them before the Grand Jury for indictment, and then on the docket. The district attorney has assigned Assistant District Attorney Farnsworth Stillwell to the case."

"What did Arthur X say?" Sabara asked.

"I don't think he considers the gentlemen in question to be bona fide coreligionists," Washington said. "The phrase he used was 'punk niggers.'"

There was a moment's silence.

"Inspector," Pekach said thoughtfully, "I get the feeling that there's something about this that bothers you. I guess I'm just dense—"

"As I was saying to Officer Payne just a few minutes ago, Captain Pekach, listening carefully to what I say may be the thing to do."

Jesus, Wohl can be a sarcastic prick! Jack Malone thought. Then, *Why am I surprised? He's no older than I am, and a staff inspector, a division commander. You don't get to be either as Mr. Nice Guy.*

This was followed by: *If he finds out that I'm still after Bob Holland, which now seems even more likely, with Payne and McFadden being pals, Christ only knows what he'll do.*

"Chief Lowenstein also told the district attorney," Wohl went on, "that Highway will conspicuously protect his one witness, with the idea being that the other witnesses, perhaps counseled by Sergeant Washington, may suddenly have their memories unfogged by coming to realize that the only way they can really cover their asses is to help put the Islamic Liberation Army away, by testifying."

"But Chief Lowenstein did not, I gather, confer with you before he decided what Highway was going to do, right?" Jason Washington asked.

"Sergeant Washington has just won the Careful Listener of the Week Award," Wohl said.

"But he's like that, you know that," Sabara said.

"He may be like that with other people, but he's not going to be like that with me," Wohl said.

"That puts me in the same boat with Dave. I'm lost."

"Special Operations is going to make the arrests," Wohl said. "And Special Operations is going to protect Homicide's one witness. Not Highway."

"And if Special Operations blows it?" Sabara asked.

"We have here an armed robbery, during which a murder occurred. We know who the doers are. The suspects are under surveillance at this moment by Homicide detectives. At five o'clock tomorrow morning, they will tell Sergeant Washington where these people are. At that point, police officers, with warrants, will be sent to assist the Homicide detectives in arresting them. If the police officers in question cannot accomplish this without difficulty, then perhaps they shouldn't be cops, and their supervisors, by whom I mean you and me, Mike, shouldn't be supervisors."

Sabara didn't reply.

"Two things," Wohl said. "I don't want anybody in Highway, or anywhere else, hearing about this before it happens. And I don't want a big deal made of it. I'm not putting Highway down or Special Operations up. I'm treating the robbery and shooting at Goldblatt's like any other robbery where things got out of hand and somebody got killed. The Homicide Bureau found out who did it, and uniformed officers are going to help them make the arrests. I don't want to dignify a bunch of thugs by calling them an army."

"What about the press?"

"We owe Mickey O'Hara one. Actually, we owe Mickey O'Hara a couple of dozen. When you decide where this thing will start, Mike, call Mickey and suggest he might find it interesting to be there."

"Just Mickey?"

"Just Mickey."

"Do we know where these guys are? I mean are they all in one area, or all over the city?" Sabara asked.

"Mostly in Frankford, the Whitehall area," Jason Washington said. "One of them is in West Philadelphia."

"Where'd you get that?" Wohl asked.

Washington met his eyes and then said, "I talked to Joe D'Amata."

"One of Sergeant Washington's responsibilities as head of

the Special Investigations Section will be to keep in touch with the Detective Division, and especially Homicide," Wohl said. "Matt, make sure you put that in when you write the job description."

"Yes, sir. Sir, can I say something?"

"At your peril, Officer Payne."

"There's a parking lot, actually a playground, behind the school building. You could use that as a place to meet."

"We're going to need—" Sabara said, pausing to do the mental arithmetic, "—space to park fifteen, sixteen cars, plus what, four wagons and a couple of stakeout trucks. That big?"

"Yes, sir."

"I don't want stakeout acting like the 2nd Armored Division invading Germany," Wohl said. "They should be available, but—"

"I understand," Sabara said.

"Matt, on your way to the FBI," Wohl said, "swing past the school building and make sure the parking lot will be big enough. And then call Captain Sabara and tell him."

"Yes, sir."

"Jesus," Wohl said angrily. "I haven't looked at this stuff yet."

He flipped through the photocopied documents for the FBI quickly and then looked up at Payne.

"You'd better leave now," Wohl said. "I wouldn't want the FBI to think I had forgotten them. And we won't need you in on this. Get the building dimensions, and whatever other information about that place you think we can use, and be here at eight in the morning." He paused and looked at the others. "By that time, we should have eight thugs, more or less, on their way, without fuss, to the Roundhouse. Then we can turn to important things, like making our new home habitable."

"Yes, sir," Matt said, and got up and started to leave.

"Matt!" Wohl called after him.

"Yes, sir?"

"Don't you think it would be a good idea to take this stuff with you?" Wohl asked innocently, pointing at the stack of copies of the Jerome Nelson job.

"Yes, sir," Matt said. His face flushed. He took the documents from Wohl's desk and walked out.

As he closed the door, he heard Wohl say, "If I didn't know better, I might suspect Young Matt's in love."

"How about 'in rut'?" Sabara said.

Matt closed the door on their laughter.

"May I help you, sir?" Miss Lenore Gray, who was twenty-six, tall, slim, auburn-haired, and the receptionist at the FBI office, asked, smiling a bit more brightly than was her custom at what she judged to be a very well-dressed, nice-looking young man.

"My name is Payne," Matt said. "I'm a police officer. I have some documents for Mr. Davis."

Lenore had been told to be on the lookout for a Philadelphia cop named Payne, and to call SAC Davis (or, if he was out of the office, A-SAC [Criminal Affairs] Frank F. Young, or if he was out too, one of the other A-SACs) when he showed up.

She had expected a cop in uniform, not a good-looking young man like this in a very nice blue blazer.

"I'm sorry, but Mr. Davis is not in the office," she said. "Just a moment, please."

She pushed buttons on her new, state-of-the-art telephone system that caused one of the telephones on the desk of A-SAC (Criminal Affairs) Frank F. Young to ring. She did not want to go through the hassle of telling A-SAC Young's secretary why she wanted to talk to him.

"Frank Young."

"This is Miss Gray at reception, Mr. Young. Officer Payne of the police is here."

"Tell him I'll be right out," Young said.

"Mr. Young will be out in a moment," Lenore said with a smile. "Mr. Young is our A-SAC, Criminal Affairs."

"As opposed to romantic?" Matt asked.

He was obviously making a joke, but it took Lenore a moment to search for and find the point.

"Oh, aren't you terrible!" she said.

"You *do* have an A-SAC, Romantic Affairs?"

"No," Lenore said. "But it sounds like a marvelous idea."

"I'm Frank Young," Young announced, coming into the reception area with his hand out. "The chief had to leave, I'm afraid, and you're stuck with me. Come on in."

Matt was surprised. He had considered himself an errand boy, delivering a package, and errand boys are not normally greeted with a smile and a handshake.

"Thank you," Matt said.

Young led him into the brightly lit, spacious interior, and then into his own well-furnished office, through the windows of which he could see Billy Penn atop City Hall. He could not help but make the comparison between this and Inspector Wohl's crowded office, and then between it and the new home of Special Operations at Frankford and Castor.

In the icy cold, dark recesses of which, I will now spend the next three or four hours, with my little tape measure.

"I'm sure this is just what we asked for," Young said, "but I think it would be a good idea if I took a quick look at it. Can I have my girl get you a cup of coffee?"

"Thank you," Matt said. "Black, please."

The coffee was served in cups and saucers, with a cream pitcher and a bowl of sugar cubes on the side, which was certainly more elegant, Matt thought, than the collection of chipped china mugs, can of condensed milk, and coffee can full of little sugar packets reading *McDonald's* and *Roy Rogers* and *Peking Palace* in Peter Wohl's office coffee service.

There were more surprises. Assistant Special Agent in Charge Young was more than complimentary about the completeness of the Nelson files Matt had brought him. They would be very helpful, he said, and the FBI was grateful.

Then, with great tact, he asked Matt all sorts of questions about himself, why he had joined the cops, how he liked it, whether he liked law enforcement in general—*"I don't really know why I asked that. You seem to have proven that you take to law enforcement like a duck to water. I think everybody with a badge in Philadelphia was delighted when you terminated Mr. Warren K. Fletcher's criminal career."*—and what his long-term career plans were.

"I intend to work myself up through the ranks," Matt said solemnly, "to police commissioner. And then I will seek an appropriate political office."

Young laughed heartily. "Jerry Carlucci's going to be a tough act to follow. But why not? You've got the potential."

If I didn't know better, Matt thought, *I'd think he was about to offer me a job.*

Then came the question: *I am being charmed. Why should they bother to charm me? All I am is an errand-boy-by-another-name to Wohl.*

Young then offered to give him a tour of the office, which Matt, after a moment's indecision, accepted. For one thing, he was curious to see what the inside of an FBI office looked like. And maybe they would actually ask him for something. In any event, the school building could wait.

He was introduced to another A-SAC, whose name he promptly forgot, and to a dozen FBI agents, some singly and some in groups. Every time, A-SAC Young used the same words, "This is the Philadelphia plainclothesman who terminated Mr. Warren K. Fletcher's criminal career."

And everyone seemed pleased to have the opportunity to shake the hand that held the gun that terminated the criminal career of Mr. Warren K. Fletcher.

I really don't know what the hell is going on here, but there is some reason I'm being given the grand tour. It may be that Young is being nice to Wohl through his errand boy; or that he is genuinely impressed with the guy who shot Fletcher—if he knew the circumstances, of course, he would be far less impressed—or, really, that they are going to offer me a job. But it's damned sure they don't give the grand tour to every cop from the Department who shows up here with a pile of records.

The subject of employment with the FBI did not come up. A-SAC Young walked him to the elevator, shook his hand, and said that he was sure he would see Matt again and looked forward to it.

When he was on the street again, Matt saw that the skies were dark. It was probably going to snow.

Not only is it going to be bitter cold in that goddamn building, it's going to be dark.

Shit!

He drove back to Bustleton and Bowler, and turned in the Department car. He couldn't keep it overnight without permission, and he didn't want to ask Wohl for permission, so it was either turn it in now or when he was finished with the measuring job, and now seemed to be better than later.

On the way to the Frankford and Castor building, he remembered thinking that it was going to be dark, as well as cold, inside the building. He would need more than a flashlight. He could go back and draw a battery-powered floodlight from supply, but he didn't want to go back.

He drove down Frankford Avenue until he found a hardware store, and went in and bought the largest battery-powered floodlight they had, plus a spare battery. Then he bought a fifty-foot tape measure.

It then occurred to him that he would need something that provided more space than his pocket notebook. He found a stationery store and bought a clipboard, two mechanical pencils, and a pad of graph paper.

He was carrying all this back to his car when a Highway car suddenly pulled to the curb, in the process spraying his trousers and overcoat with a mixture of snow, soot, grime, and slush.

The driver's door opened and the head and shoulders of Officer Charles McFadden appeared.

"I thought those were your wheels," McFadden said, nodding up the street toward where Matt had parked his Porsche. "What the hell are you doing?"

"I'm on a scavenger hunt. The next thing on my list is the severed head of an Irishman."

McFadden laughed.

"No shit, Matt, what are you doing?"

"Would you believe I am going to measure the school building at Frankford and Castor?"

"I heard we were getting that," McFadden said. "And Inspector Wohl's making you measure it?"

"Right."

"All by yourself?"

"Right."

"Have fun," McFadden said, and got behind the wheel again.

Matt could see in the car. Officer McFadden was explaining to Officer Quinn why Officer Payne was wading through the slush with a floodlight, a tape measure, and a clipboard. To judge by the look on Officer Quinn's face, he found this rather amusing.

Officer McFadden put the Highway RPC in gear and stepped on the accelerator. The rear wheels spun in the dirty slush, spraying same on Officer Payne.

TWELVE

There was a telephone in Lieutenant Jack Malone's suite in the St. Charles Hotel, through which, by the miracle of modern telecommunications, he could converse with anyone in the whole wide world, with perhaps a few minor exceptions like Ulan Bator or Leningrad.

He had learned, however, to his horror, when he paid his first bill for two weeks residency, that local calls, which had been free on his home phone, and which cost a dime at any pay station, were billed by the hotel at fifty cents each.

Thereafter, whenever possible, Lieutenant Malone made his outgoing calls from a pay station in the lobby.

When he dropped the dime in the slot this time, he knew the number from memory. It was the fourth time he'd called since returning to the hotel shortly before six.

"Hello?"

"Officer McFadden, please?"

"You're the one who's been calling, right?"

"Yes, ma'am."

"Well, he hasn't come home," Mrs. Agnes McFadden said.

"I don't really have any idea where he is. You want to give me a number, I'll have him call back the minute he walks in the door."

"I'll be moving around, I'm afraid," Malone said. "I'll try again. Thank you very much."

"What did you say your name was?"

Malone broke the connection with his finger.

"My name is Asshole, madam," he said softly, bitterly. "Lieutenant J. Asshole Malone."

He put the handset back and pushed open the door.

He was not going to get to talk to Officer McFadden tonight, and he would not try again. He had carefully avoided giving McFadden's mother his name—she had volunteered her identity on the first call.

When Officer McFadden finally returns home, his mother will tell him that some guy who had not given his name had called four times for him, but had not said what he wanted or where he could be reached.

McFadden will be naturally curious, but there will be no way for him to connect the calls with me.

On the other hand, if I did call back, and finally got through to him, he would know not only who I am, but whatever I had in mind was important enough that I would try five times to get through to him.

Under those circumstances, there would be no way I could casually, nonchalantly, let it be known that I would be grateful if he didn't tell his pal Payne that I was staking out Holland's body shop. I already know he has an active curiosity, and if I said please don't tell Payne, that's exactly what he will do. And Payne would lose no time in telling Wohl.

That triggered thoughts of Payne in a different area: *The poor bastard's probably still over there in that falling-down building, stumbling around in the dark, measuring it.*

That was chickenshit of Wohl, making him do that. He sent me over there to look it over. I should not have let myself be talked out of doing what I was sent to do by a rookie cop, even if the rookie works for Wohl. I'm a lieutenant, although there seems to be some questions at all levels about just how good a lieutenant. But he's taking the heat for what I did, and that's not right.

If I were a good guy, I'd get in the car and go over there and help him. But Wohl might not like that. He sent the kid over there to rap his knuckles and Wohl might not like it if I held his hand.

Fuck Wohl! A man is responsible for his actions, and other people should not take the heat for them.

He walked out of the lobby of the St. Charles Hotel and found his car and started out for the school building at Frankford and Castor.

Halfway there, he had another thought, which almost made him change his mind: *Am I really being a nice guy about this? A supervisor doing the right thing? Or am I trying to show Payne what a nice guy I am, so that if I get the chance to ask him not to tell Wohl that I am watching Holland, he will go along?*

You can be a conniving prick, Jack Malone, always working the angles, he finally decided, *but this is not one of those times. You are going there because Payne wouldn't be there if you hadn't been a jackass.*

When he reached the building, he at first thought that he was too late, that Payne had done what he had to do and left, because the building was dark. But then he saw, on the second floor, lights. Moving around.

A flashlight. No. A floodlight. Too much light for a flashlight. That's Payne.

Stupid, you know the lights aren't turned on!

He had another *stupid* thought a moment later, when he turned off Frankford Avenue onto Castor Avenue. There was a Porsche 911, what looked like a new one, parked against the curb, lightly dusted by the snow that had begun to fall as he had driven out here.

If there is a more stupid place to park a car like that, I don't know where the hell it would be. When the jackass who owns that car comes back for it, he'll be lucky to find the door handles.

He pulled his Mustang to the curb behind a battered Volkswagen, and added to his previous judgment: *Because of the generosity of the Porsche owner, the Bug is probably safe. Why bother to strip a Bug when you can strip a Porsche?*

It occurred to him, finally, as he got out of the car that possibly the Porsche was stolen. Not stolen-stolen, never to show up again, but stolen for a joy ride by some kids who had found it with the keys in the ignition.

Maybe I should find a phone and call it in.

Fuck it, it's none of my business. A district RPC will roll by here eventually and he'll see it.

Fuck it, it is my business. I'm a cop, and what cops do is protect the citizenry, even from their own stupidity. As soon as I have a word with Payne, I will call it in.

There was now a layer of snow covering the thawed and then refrozen snow on the steps to the building, and he slipped and almost went down, catching himself at the last moment.

When he straightened up, he could see Payne's light, now on the first floor. He stopped just outside the outer door. The light grew brighter, and then Payne appeared. Except it wasn't Payne. It was a Highway cop.

McFadden!

Payne appeared a moment later.

I should have guessed he might be over here helping out his buddy.

All of a sudden, he was blinded by the light from one of the lamps.

"Who are you?" McFadden demanded firmly, but before Malone could speak, McFadden recognized him, and the light went back on the ground. "Hello, Lieutenant. Sorry."

"How's it going?" Malone asked, far more cheerfully than he felt.

"Aside from terminal frostbite, you mean?" Payne said. "Did Wo—Inspector Wohl send you to check on me?"

"No. I just thought you might be able to use some help. You're finished, I guess?"

"Yes, sir. McFadden's been helping me. Do you know McFadden, Lieutenant?"

"Yeah, sure. Whaddaya say, McFadden?"

"Lieutenant."

"Well, at least let me buy you fellas a hamburger, or a cheese-steak, something, and a cup of coffee," Malone said, adding mentally, *said the last of the big spenders.*

"Well, that's very kind, Lieutenant," Payne said. "But not necessary. We're going over to my place and, presuming our fingers thaw, make a nice drawing, drawings, for Inspector Wohl. I thought we'd pick up some ribs on the way."

"It'd be my pleasure," Malone said. "Where do you live?"

"Downtown. Rittenhouse Square."

"I live at 19th and Arch," Malone said. "We're all headed

in the same direction. And I haven't had my dinner. Why don't you let me buy the ribs?''

He looked at Payne and saw suspicion in his eyes.

''Why don't we all go to my place for ribs?'' Payne said, finally.

''Where's your car?'' Malone asked.

''We're parked over there,'' McFadden said, and pointed to where Malone had parked behind the Volkswagen.

''I want to find a phone,'' Malone said. ''And call that Porsche in.''

''Why?'' Payne asked, obviously surprised.

''I have a gut feeling it's wrong,'' Malone said. ''A Porsche like that shouldn't be parked in this neighborhood.''

''That's Payne's car, Lieutenant,'' McFadden said. ''Nice, huh?''

Malone thought he saw amusement in McFadden's eyes.

''Very nice,'' Malone said.

''Lieutenant,'' Payne said. ''You're sure welcome to come with us. I appreciate your coming out here.''

''I haven't had my dinner.''

''You'd better follow me, otherwise there will be a hassle getting you into the garage,'' Payne said.

''I'm sorry?'' Malone asked.

''The parking lot in my building,'' Payne said. ''There's a rent-a-cop—it would be easier if we stuck together.''

''Okay. Sure,'' Malone said.

The little convoy stopped twice on the way to Payne's apartment, first in a gas station on Frankford Avenue, where Payne made a telephone call from a pay booth, and then on Chestnut Street in downtown Philadelphia. There Payne walked quickly around the nose of his Porsche and into Ribs Unlimited, an eatery Jack Malone remembered from happier days as a place to which husbands took wives on their birthdays for arguably the best ribs in Philadelphia, and which were priced accordingly.

In a moment Payne came back out, trailed by the manager and two costumed rib-cookers in red chef's hats and white jackets and aprons, bearing large foil-wrapped packages and what looked like a half case of beer.

Payne opened the nose of his Porsche, and everything was loaded inside. Payne reached in his pocket and handed bills to the manager and the two guys in cook's suits. They beamed at him.

Payne closed the nose of his Porsche, got behind the wheel, and the three-car convoy rolled off again.

I didn't know Ribs Unlimited offered takeouts, Malone thought, and then, *Jesus Christ, me and my big mouth: When I offer to pay for the ribs, as I have to, I will have to give him a check, because I have maybe nineteen dollars in my pocket. A check that will be drawn against insufficient funds and will bounce, unless I can get to the bank and beg that four-eyed asshole of an assistant manager to hold it until payday.*

Five minutes later they were unloading the nose of the Porsche in a basement garage.

Payne's apartment, which they reached after riding an elevator and then walking up a narrow flight of stairs, was something of a disappointment.

It was nicely furnished, but it was very small. Somehow, after the Porsche, and because it was on Rittenhouse Square, he had expected something far more luxurious.

McFadden carried the case of beer into the kitchen, and Malone heard bottles being opened.

"Here you are, Lieutenant," he said. "You ever had any of this? Tuborg. Comes from Holland."

"Denmark," Payne corrected him, tolerantly.

Malone took out his wallet.

"This is my treat, you will recall," he said. "What's the tab?"

"This is my apartment," Payne said with a smile. "You owe us a cheese-steak."

"I insist."

"So do I," Payne said, and put the neck of the Tuborg bottle to his lips.

"Well, okay," Malone said, putting his wallet back in his pocket.

Did he do that because he is a nice guy? Or because he is the last of the big spenders? Or was I just lucky? Or has Wohl had a confidential chat with him about The New Lieutenant, and his problems, financial and otherwise?

"You two eat in the living room," McFadden ordered, "so I can have the table in here."

"Among Officer McFadden's many, many other talents," Payne said cheerfully, "he assures me that he is the product of four years of mechanical drawing in high school. He is going to prepare drawings of that goddamn old building that will absolutely dazzle Inspector Wohl."

McFadden smiled. "My father works for UGI," he said. "My mother wanted me to go to work there as a draftsman." (United Gas Industries, the Philadelphia gas company.)

"My father's a fireman," Malone said. "I was supposed to be a fireman."

"Let's eat, before they get cold," Payne said. "Or do you think I should stick them into the oven on general principles?"

McFadden laid a hand on the aluminum. "They're still hot. Or warm, anyway."

He opened one of the packages. Payne took plates, knives and forks, and a large package of dinner-sized paper napkins from a closet.

"You going to need any help?" he asked McFadden.

"No," McFadden said flatly. "Just leave me something to eat and leave me alone."

"You'd better put an apron on, or you'll get rib goo all over your uniform," Payne said.

"They call that barbecue sauce," McFadden said. " 'Rib goo'! Jesus H. Christ!"

Payne handed him an apron with MASTER CHEF painted on it. Then he began to pass out the ribs, cole slaw, baked beans, salad, rolls, and other contents of the aluminum-wrapped packages.

A piece of paper fluttered to the floor. Malone picked it up. It was the cash register tape from Ribs Unlimited. Three complete Rib Feasts at $11.95 came to $35.85. They had charged Payne retail price for the BEER, IMPORT, which, at $2.25 a bottle, came to $27.00. With the tax, the bill was nearly seventy dollars.

And Payne had tipped the manager and both cooks. Christ, that's my food budget for two weeks.

"Fuck it," McFadden said. "Eat first, work later. McFadden's Law."

He sat down and picked up a rib and started to gnaw on it.

"That makes sense," Payne said. "Sit down, Lieutenant. They do make a good rib."

"I know. I used to take my wife there," Malone said without thinking.

McFadden silently ate one piece of rib, and then another.

He picked up his beer bottle, drank deeply, burped, and then delicately wiped his mouth with a paper napkin.

"Are you going to tell me, Lieutenant, what's going on at half past four tomorrow morning at that school building?" McFadden suddenly asked. "*He* won't tell me."

"What makes you think something's going on?"

"The word is out that something is," McFadden said.

"Can I tell you without it getting all over Highway before half past four tomorrow morning?" Malone replied, after a moment's hesitation.

"Then you'd better not tell me, Lieutenant," McFadden said. "Not that I would say anything to anybody—just between you, me, and the lamppost, Lieutenant, the only thing Highway has going for me is that it keeps me from doing school crossing duty in a district—but Highway is going to find out, and I wouldn't want you to think I was the one who told them."

"He's right, Lieutenant," Payne said. "If Charley knows something's going to happen, so does everybody in Highway, and they will snoop around until they find out what."

"As Lieutenant Malone, I can't tell you," Malone said. "But we're off duty, right? And you're Charley, and I'm Jack, and this won't go any further?"

He saw Payne's eyes appraising him.

Is he going to go to Wohl first thing in the morning? "Inspector, I think I should tell you that that new lieutenant can't keep his mouth shut."

Fuck it, I sense an opening here to get to McFadden. If I can get McFadden to agree not to tell Wohl about finding me at Holland's, Payne will probably, or at least possibly, fall in line. And if he doesn't, if I blow this, things can't get any worse than they are now.

"Okay, Jack," McFadden said. "Out of school, what's going in the morning?"

Malone saw Payne's eyes flash between him and McFadden and back again.

Shit! He's suspicious as hell.

"If I did, Payne, would you feel you had to tell Inspector Wohl I told him?"

Payne met his eyes. Then he picked up his bottle of beer and took a pull at it.

"Lieutenant," Payne said. "I don't really know what the hell is going on here."

"I beg your pardon?"

"We're out of school, right?"

"Absolutely."

"No, then. I would *not* tell the Inspector you told Charley about what's going on at half past four in the morning. I was going to tell him anyway. I was just pulling his chain, not telling him before. That's not what's bothering me."

"What is, then?"

"You showed up at the school tonight, for one thing. 'Call me Jack,' and 'Let me buy you fellas a cheese-steak,' for some more."

Christ, I'm losing control. Am I just bad at this? Or are these two a lot smarter than I gave them credit for being?

"I went out to the school because I thought you were taking heat for something that was my responsibility."

"What do you want from us, Lieutenant?" Payne asked, both his tone of voice and the look in his eyes making it clear he hadn't bought that at all. "Has it got something to do with Charley finding you snooping around Holland's body shop?"

Christ, he already knows! What did I expect? Well, fuck it, I blew it.

"Are you going to tell Inspector Wohl about that?" Malone asked.

"Unless you can come up with a good reason I shouldn't," Payne said.

Malone glanced at McFadden. He recognized the look in McFadden's eyes. He had seen it a hundred times. A cop who knew that the suspect had been lying all along had just told him he knew he had been lying all along, and was waiting to see what reaction that would cause.

And I am the guy they caught lying.

When all else fails, tell the truth.

"Holland is dirty," Malone said.

"How do you know?" McFadden asked, picking up another rib.

"You've been on the street," Malone said, meeting McFadden's eyes. "You *know* when you know someone's dirty."

"Yeah," McFadden said. "But sometimes when you know, you're wrong."

Charley McFadden's response surprised Matt Payne.

What the hell are they talking about? Some kind of mystical intuition?

"I *know*, McFadden," Malone said.

McFadden seemed to be willing to give Malone the benefit of the doubt.

Because he's a lieutenant? Or because Charley was on the street? Is there something to this intuition business that these two, real cops as opposed to me, understand and I don't?

And then Officer Matthew M. Payne had a literally chilling additional thought.

I knew. Jesus H. Christ, I knew. When I saw Fletcher's van, I knew it was wrong. I told myself, consciously, that all it was, was a van, but I knew it was dirty. If I hadn't subconsciously known it was dirty, hadn't really been careful, Warren K. Fletcher would have run over me. The only reason I'm alive and he's dead is because, intuitively, I knew the van was dirty.

"You want to tell us about it?" McFadden asked.

"You know Tom Lenihan?" Malone asked.

McFadden shook his head no.

"He's Chief Coughlin's driver," Matt offered, and corrected himself. "*Was*. He made lieutenant."

"Right," Malone said. "Now he's in Organized Crime."

"What about him?"

"We go back a ways together. When he made lieutenant, he bought a new car. For him new. Actually a year-old one with low mileage. I went out to Holland Pontiac-GMC to help him get it."

"And?"

"He got a Pontiac Bonneville. They gave him a real deal, he said."

"That doesn't make Holland a thief," Matt Payne said.

"Holland himself came out. Very charming. A lot of bull-shit."

"What's wrong with that?" Charley asked.

"Holland has six, seven dealerships. Why should he kiss the ass of a new police lieutenant who just bought a lousy used Bonneville?"

"Maybe because he knew he worked for Denny Coughlin," Matt thought out loud.

"Same thought. Why should a big-shot car dealer kiss the ass of even Denny Coughlin?"

"That's all you have?" McFadden asked.

"Two reasons," Matt said. "One he likes cops, which I

doubt, or because he's getting his rocks off knowing he's making a fool of the cops.''

"What the fuck are *you* talking about?" Charley challenged.

"That's the gut feeling I had," Malone said.

"I don't know what the fuck either one of you is talking about," McFadden said.

"Tell me some more," Matt said. "What do you think? How's he doing it? Why?"

"I don't know *exactly* how he's doing it," Malone said. "But I have an idea why, how it started. A lot of car dealers are dirty. I mean, Christ, you know, they make their living cheating people. The only reason they don't cheat more, which is stealing, is because they don't want to get arrested.''

"Okay," McFadden said. "So what?"

"So they all know how to steal something, cheating on a finance contract, swapping radios and tires around, buying hot parts for repair work," Malone said. "Now let's say Holland, maybe early on, maybe that's the reason he's so successful, figured out a way to steal cars. He's so successful, the thievery is like business, so the thrill is gone.''

"Jesus, Lieutenant," McFadden said, his tone suggesting that Malone had just asked him to believe the cardinal archbishop was a secret compulsive gambler.

"Let him talk, Charley," Matt said, on the edge of sharpness.

"I also read somewhere that some thieves really want to get caught," Malone said. "And I read someplace else that some thieves really do it for the thrill, not the money.''

"So you see Bob Holland as a successful thief who gets his thrills, his sense of superiority, by being a friend of the cops?"

"No wonder they think you're crazy," McFadden said, and then, realizing that he had spoken his thought, looked horrified.

"I don't think—" Matt said. "I'm not willing to join them.''

"Who's them?" McFadden asked.

"Those who suggest Lieutenant Malone is crazy to think Bob Holland could be a thief," Payne said.

McFadden looked at Payne, first in disbelief, and then, when he saw that Payne was serious, with curiosity.

"Based on what, you think he's stealing and selling whole cars?" McFadden asked.

"I know how," Malone said. "I just haven't figured out how to get Holland yet."

"Great!" McFadden said. "Then you *don't* know, Lieutenant."

"I do know," Malone said. "Tom Lenihan is driving a stolen car."

"How do you know that?" McFadden asked, on the edge of scornfully.

"Because the VIN tag and the secret mark on his Bonneville are different," Malone said. "I looked."

The VIN tag is a small metal plate stamped with the *V*ehicle *I*dentification *N*umber and other data, which is riveted, usually where it can be seen through the windshield, to the vehicle frame.

"No shit?" McFadden asked.

"What's the secret mark?" Matt asked, curiosity having overwhelmed his reluctance to admit his ignorance.

"The manufacturer's stamp," Malone said, "in some place where it can't be seen, unless you know where to look, either all the numbers, or some of the numbers, on the VIN tag. So that if the thief swaps VIN tags, you can tell."

If he knows that, Matt wondered, *why doesn't he just go arrest Holland?*

"Does Lieutenant Lenihan know?" Charley asked.

"No," Malone said.

"Why?"

"Because I didn't tell him. If I told him, he would go to the Auto Squad, and they would get a warrant and go out there. I don't want some body shop mechanic, or even the guy that runs the body shop, taking the rap for this, I want Holland."

"Holland probably hasn't been in the body shop for years, and can prove it," McFadden said. "You're sure they're doing this in the body shop?"

"Where else?"

"Well, let's figure out how he's stealing cars, and then we can figure out how to catch him," Charley said.

"Stealing and selling," Matt corrected him.

"Hypo-something," McFadden said. "What is that you're always saying, Matt?"

"Hypothetically speaking," Matt furnished.

"Right," McFadden said. "Okay. From the thief's angle. You steal a car, and you can do what with it?"

"Strip it or chop it," Malone said.

"What's the difference?" Matt asked.

"A quick strip job means you take the tires and wheels, the radio, the air-conditioner compressor, the battery, anything you can unbolt in a hurry. A chop job is when you take maybe the front clip—you know what that is?"

"The fenders and grill," Matt answered.

"Sometimes the whole front end, less the engine," Malone said. "Engines have serial numbers. Or the rear end, or the rear quarter panels. Then you just dump what's left. Clip job or strip job."

"Or you get the whole car on a boat and send it to South America or Africa, or someplace," McFadden said. "You don't think that's what Holland is doing, do you, Lieutenant?"

"Holland is selling whole cars."

"With legitimate VIN tags," McFadden said. "Where's he get those?"

"From wrecks," Malone said. "There's no other place. He goes—*he* doesn't go, he sends one of his people—to an insurance company auction—"

"A what?" Matt interrupted.

"You run your car into a tree," Malone explained. "The insurance company decides it would cost too much to fix. They give you a check and take your car. Once a week, once every other week, they—not just one insurance company, a bunch of them—have an auction. The wrecks are bought by salvage yards, body shops, people like that."

"And Holland just takes the VIN off the wreck and puts it on the stolen car, right, and says it's been repaired, and puts it on one of his lots?" Matt asked.

"That's how I see it," Malone said.

"Well, if we know that," Matt asked, "what's the problem? All we have to do is—"

"Let me tell you, Payne, all we have to do," Malone said, more than a little contempt in his tone. "Let me give you a for example. For example, we take Tom Lenihan's car. We go back to Holland with it and say it's stolen, and where did you get it? They say, *'Gee, whiz, we didn't know it was stolen. We carefully checked the VIN tag when we bought it at the insurance auction. See, here's the bill of sale.'* So then we go to the insurance auction, and they say, *'That's right, we auctioned that car off for ABC Insurance, and sure, we checked the VIN tag. No, we didn't check for the secret stamping, there's no law says we have to, all the law says we have to do is check the VIN tag and fill out the forms for the Motor Vehicle Bureau. We did that. Besides, we are respectable businessmen, and we resent you hinting we're a bunch of thieves.' "*

"Oh," Matt said, chagrined.

"If we went out there tomorrow morning, with Tom Lenihan's Pontiac, which we *know* is stolen, you know what would happen? First of all, nobody would get arrested. Lenihan would have to give the car up, because it's stolen. The original owner would get it back, but would have trouble with Motor Vehicles because the VIN tag doesn't match the stamped ID on the frame somewhere. Holland would piss his pants, he was so sorry that this happened to an honest man like himself and an honest man like Lenihan. He would give Lenihan another car, maybe even a better one, to show what a good guy he is. Holland would then have his lawyer sue the auction for selling him a hot car. It would take years to get on the docket. There would be delays after delays after delays. Finally it either would die a natural death or the auction would settle out of court, and as part of the deal, both parties would agree never to divulge the amount of the settlement. You getting the picture, Payne?"

"Yes, sir."

"And then he wouldn't steal any more cars until he figured we didn't have the time to watch him anymore," Malone said.

"Then how do you plan to catch Holland, Lieutenant?" McFadden asked.

"I've got a couple of ideas."

"That's what I'm asking," McFadden said.

"If Inspector Wohl finds out I haven't listened to all the good advice I've been given to forget Holland, in other words, if you tell him you saw me at the body shop, or Payne tells him about tonight, what's the difference?"

"The only people I told about you being outside the body shop is Matt and Hay-zus."

Jesus, he has told somebody!

"Who's—what did you say?"

"Hay-zus, Jesus in English, Martinez. He was my partner when we was undercover in Narcotics."

"And how many people do you think he's told, since you told him?"

"Nobody. I told him to keep it under his hat until I had a chance to ask Payne."

"So what about you, Payne?" Malone asked. "Are you going to get on the phone to Wohl the minute I leave here, or wait until tomorrow morning, or what?"

"It's an interesting ethical question," Matt said. "On one hand, for reasons I don't quite understand. I would *really* like to see Holland caught. On the other, so far as Wohl is concerned, my primary loyalty is to him—"

"Your primary loyalty should be to the Police Department," Malone interrupted. "You're a cop. It's your duty to catch crooks."

Matt met Malone's eyes, but didn't respond.

"That's the reason you would really like to see Holland caught. You're a cop," Malone went on.

"And on the other hand, Inspector Wohl trusts me," Matt said. "I like that. I admire him. I don't want to betray whatever confidence he has in me."

"So you are going to tell him?"

"I don't do very well deciding ethical questions when I've had four bottles of beer," Matt said. "I think I'd better sleep on this."

"I see."

"I won't, if I decide I have to tell him, tell him about tonight. If I tell him anything, it will be just that Charley saw you staking out Holland's body shop. Maybe that can slip my mind too. I don't want to decide that, either way, tonight. But if I decide to tell him, I'll tell you before I do."

"Fair enough," Malone said.

He stood up and offered Matt his hand.

"Thank you."

"For the ribs, you mean," Matt said.

"Yeah, for the ribs," Malone said. Then he leaned over and shook McFadden's hand. Charley nodded at him, but said nothing.

Malone found his coat and walked out of the apartment.

"I wonder if he really has some ideas about catching Holland, or whether that was just bullshit," McFadden said.

"Why couldn't he tell—who did he work for in Auto Squad?"

"That's part of Major Crimes. Major Crimes is commanded by a captain. I forget his name."

"Why couldn't he tell him what he told us?"

"You really don't understand, do you?" McFadden said. "Sometimes, you're smart, Matt, and sometimes you're dumber than dog shit."

"I prefer to think of it as 'inexperienced,' " Matt said. "Answer the question."

"Okay. Don't Make Waves."

"Meaning what?"

"Meaning the Auto Squad and Major Crimes has enough, more than enough, already to do without getting involved in something that might turn against them. It's not as if people are going to die because Holland is stealing cars. Who the hell is really hurt except the insurance company?"

"I could debate that: *You* are. Your premiums are so high because cars are stolen and have to be paid for."

"And sometimes," Charley said, smiling at him, "you sound like the monks in school. Absolute logic. You're absolutely right. But it don't mean a fucking thing in the real world. Whoever runs Major Crimes decided he didn't want to go after Bob Holland because there are other car thieves out there he *knows* he can catch, car thieves who *will* go to jail, and who don't call the mayor by his first name. You understand?"

"Yeah, I guess so."

"Don't get me wrong, Matt. For the record, I hope, when you settle your *ethical problem*, that you decide you don't have to tell Wohl. I'd like to go after Holland."

"Help Malone, you mean?"

"Yeah. Don't you?"

"Yeah. I would. But I think it would be stupid. And probably dangerous."

"To your job, you mean? I don't think you'd be likely to get shot or anything trying to catch Holland."

"Yeah, to my job. I like my job."

"Right. You get your rocks off stumbling around fall-down buildings in the dark with a tape measure, right?"

"You'd better finish those drawings while you can still draw a reasonably straight line."

"Yeah. Jesus, it's getting late, isn't it?"

He sat down at the table. Matt went around picking up the remnants of the meal and the empty beer bottles. When he opened the cabinet under the sink, to put rib bones in the garbage can, he saw the martini glass. It had Helene's lipstick on it. It had somehow gotten broken when they had been thrashing around on the couch.

As the memories of that filled his mind's eye, he felt a sudden surge of desire.

My God, I'd like to be with her again!

"You going to tell me what's happening at half past four tomorrow morning?" Charley asked.

"They know who the doers are on that Goldblatt furniture job—"

"The Islamic Liberation Army?"

"—and they're going to pick them up all at once."

"Highway, you mean?"

"No. Special Operations. ACT."

"Jesus, that's interesting. How come not Highway?"

"A couple of reasons. I think Wohl wants Special Operations—the ACT guys—to do something on their own. And I think he's concerned that this Islamic Liberation Army thing could get out of hand."

"What do you mean, 'out of hand'?"

"He doesn't want a gang of armed robbers to get away with it, or get special treatment, because they're calling themselves a liberation army."

"That liberation army business is bullshit, huh?"

"Yeah. And finally, Chief Lowenstein told Wohl he wanted Highway to pick up these guys. I think Wohl wants to make the point that he will take requests, or suggestions, from Lowenstein, but not orders. In other words, if Lowenstein had said he wanted ACT to make the arrests, Wohl would have sent Highway."

"If the ACT guys blow it, Wohl'll have egg on his face."

"Yeah," Matt said, "and if you should happen to be around Castor and Frankford at that time of the morning, Wohl would figure out where you heard what was happening and I would have egg, or worse, on mine."

"Yeah, I suppose. Shit! Okay. I won't be there."

Matt finished cleaning up and then stood and looked over Charley's shoulder as he worked. It became quickly apparent that Charley was a quite competent draftsman.

I didn't learn a damned thing in high school, for that matter in college, that has any practical value.

"I wish I could do that," Matt said.

"So do I," McFadden said. "Then I could get the fuck out of here."

THIRTEEN

At 3:45 the next morning Officer Matthew M. Payne, in his bathrobe, was watching the timer on his combination washer-drier. It had twenty-five minutes to run.

At approximately 3:25 Officer Matthew M. Payne had experienced what the Rev. H. Wadsworth Coyle of Episcopal Academy had, in a euphemistically titled course (Personal Hygiene I), euphemistically termed a "nocturnal emission." The Reverend Coyle had assured the boys that it was a natural biological phenomenon, and nothing to be shamed about.

It had provoked in Officer Payne a mixed reaction. On one hand, it had been a really first-class experience, with splendid mental imagery of Helene, right down to the slightly salty taste of her mouth on his, and on the other, a real first-class pain in the ass, having to get out of goddamn bed in the middle of the goddamn night to take a goddamn shower and then wash the goddamn sheets so the maid would not find the goddamn tell-tale spots on the goddamn sheets.

"Fuck it!" Officer Payne said, aloud and somewhat angrily. He draped his bathrobe carefully on the stove, went into his bedroom, and dressed. The last item of his wardrobe was his revolver and his ankle holster, which he had deposited for the night on the mantelpiece over the fireplace.

Picking up the revolver triggered another mental image of the superbly bosomed Helene, but a nonerotic, indeed somewhat disturbing, one: the way she had handled the gun, and even the cartridges. That had been weird.

He went down the stairs, and then rode the elevator to the basement. When he drove out of the garage onto Manning Street, he saw that not only was it snowing, but that it had apparently been snowing for some time. Small flakes, which were not melting, and which suggested it was going to continue to snow for at least some time.

He made his way to North Broad Street, and drove out North Broad to Spring Garden, and then right on Spring Garden to Delaware Avenue, and then north on Delaware to Frankford Avenue and then out on Frankford toward Castor.

Except for a few all-night gas stations and fast-food emporia, the City of Philadelphia seemed to be asleep. The snow had not yet had time to become soot-soiled. It was, Matt thought, rather pretty.

On the other hand, there was ice beneath the nice white snow, and twice he felt the wheels of the Porsche slipping out of control.

And there is a very good chance that when I get out there, Inspector Wohl will remind me that he said he would see me at eight o'clock in the office, not here at four-fifteen, remind me that he has suggested it would well behoove me to listen carefully to what he says, and send me home.

There was a white glow, of headlights and parking lights reflecting off the fallen and falling snow in the school building parking lot. And just as he saw an ACT cop open the door of an RPC standing at the curb to wave a flashlight to stop him, Matt saw Inspector Wohl, Captain Sabara, and Lieutenant Malone standing in the light coming through the windshield of a stakeout van.

Malone and Sabara were in uniform. Wohl was wearing a fur-collared overcoat and a tweed cap. He looked, Matt thought, like a stockbroker waiting for the 8:05 commuter train at Wallingford, not like the sort of man who would be in charge of all this police activity.

Matt pushed the button and the window of the Porsche whooshed down.

"I'm a Three Six Nine," he said to the ACT cop. "I work for Inspector Wohl."

The cop waved him through, and Matt turned into the parking lot and found a place to park the car.

As he walked across the snow, which crunched under his shoes, toward them, he was aware that they were looking at him. He decided that there was a good chance that Wohl would be sore he had come here.

"Good morning," Matt said.

Wohl looked at him a good thirty seconds before speaking, then said, "There's a thermos of coffee in the stakeout van, if you'd like some."

"Thank you," Matt said.

When he came back out of the van, Mickey O'Hara was standing with the others.

"You know Officer Payne of the Building Measuring Detail, don't you, Mickey?" Wohl asked, straight-faced.

"Whaddaya say, Payne?" Mickey said. "Relax, I'm not going to play straight man to your boss."

A lieutenant whose name Matt could not recall walked up and with surprising formality saluted.

"Everything's in place, Inspector," he said.

Matt was pleased to see that Wohl was somewhat discomfited by the lieutenant's salute, visibly torn between returning it, like an officer returning a soldier's salute, or not.

"You check with West Philly?" Wohl asked after a moment, making a vague gesture toward his tweed cap that could have been a salute, but did not have to be.

"Yes, sir. Two cars, a sergeant, a stakeout truck, and a van."

"Can you make it over there in thirty"—looking at his watch—"seven minutes?"

"Yes, sir."

"Well, you—" Wohl interrupted himself. Captain Pekach, in full Highway uniform, walked up. The lieutenant saluted again. Pekach, although he looked a little surprised, returned it.

"Good morning," Pekach said.

Wohl ignored him.

"Lieutenant, when did you get out of the Army?" he asked.

"I've been back about four months, sir."

"What were you?"

"I had a platoon in the First Cavalry, sir."

"That worries me," Wohl said. "Let me tell you why. We are policemen, not soldiers. We are going to arrest some small-time robbers, not assault a Vietcong village. I'm a little worried that you don't understand that. I don't want any shooting, unless lives are in danger. I would rather that one or two of these scumbags get away—we can get them later—than to have anybody start shooting the place up. Did Captain Sabara make sure you understood that?"

"Yes, sir. I understand."

"I am about to promulgate a new edict," Wohl said. "Henceforth, no one will salute the commanding officer of Special Operations unless he happens to be in a uniform."

"Yes, sir," the lieutenant said. "I'm sorry, Inspector. I didn't know the ground rules."

"Go and sin no more," Wohl said with a smile, touching his arm. "Take over in West Philly. Get going at five o'clock, presuming you think they're ready."

"Yes, sir," the lieutenant said.

He walked away.

"Good morning, David," Wohl said to Pekach. "Captain Sabara and myself are touched that you would get out of your warm bed to be with us here."

"I figured maybe I could help," Pekach said.

"You and Officer Payne," Wohl said dryly. He looked at his watch. "H-hour in thirty-five minutes, men," he added in a credible mimicry of John Wayne.

"What happens at H-hour, General?" Mickey O'Hara asked.

"We know the whereabouts, as of fifteen minutes ago, of all eight of the people who stuck up Goldblatt's and murdered the maintenance man—"

"Ah, the Islamic Liberation Army," Mickey interrupted, "I thought that's what this probably was."

"The eight suspects in the felonies committed at Goldblatt's is what I said, Mr. O'Hara," Wohl said. "I didn't say anything about any army, liberation or otherwise."

"Pardon me all to death, Inspector, sir, I should have picked up on that."

"As I was saying," Wohl went on. "Shortly after five, the

officers you see gathered here will assist detectives of the Homicide Bureau in serving warrants and taking the suspects into custody. Simultaneously. Or as nearly simultaneously as we can manage.''

"I would have expected Highway," Mickey said.

"You are getting the ACT officers of Special Operations," Wohl said.

"How exactly are you going to do the arrests?" Mickey asked. "It looks like an army around here."

"Seven of the eight suspects are known to be in this area, in other words, around Frankford Avenue. One of them is in West Philly. Two ACT cars, each carrying two officers, will go to the various addresses. There will be a sergeant at each address, plus, of course, the Homicide detective who has been keeping the suspects under surveillance. We anticipate no difficulty in making the arrests. But, just to be sure, there are, under the control of a lieutenant, stakeout vans available. One per two sergeants, plus one more in West Philly. Plus four wagons, three here and one in West Philly.''

"Okay," Mickey said.

"At Captain Sabara's suggestion," Wohl went on, "when the arrests have been made, the suspect will be taken out the back of his residence, rather than out the front door. There he will be loaded into a van and taken to Homicide.''

"Instead of out the front door, where there might be angry citizens enraged that these devout Muslims are being dragged out of their beds by honky infidels?''

"You got it, Mickey," Wohl said. "What do you think?''

"I think Lowenstein thinks you were going to use Highway," Mickey said.

"Chief Lowenstein does not run Special Operations," Wohl replied.

"May I quote you?''

"I wish you wouldn't," Wohl said. "If you need a quote, how about quoting me as saying these suspects have no connection with the fine, law-abiding Islamic community of Philadelphia.''

Mickey O'Hara snorted.

"Where do you think I might find something interesting?'' O'Hara asked.

"One of the suspects is a fellow named Charles D. Stevens," Wohl said. "Word has reached me that he sometimes uses the alias Abu Ben Mohammed. Rumor has it that he fancies himself to be the Robin Hood of this merry band of bandits. Perhaps you might find that a photograph of Mr. Stevens, in handcuffs and under arrest, would be of interest to your readers."

"Okay, Peter," Mickey chuckled. "Thank you. Who do I go with?"

"Officer Payne," Wohl. said, "please take Mr. O'Hara to Lieutenant Suffern. Tell him that I have given permission for you and Mr. O'Hara to accompany his team during the arrest of Mr. Stevens."

"Yes, sir," Matt said.

"You will insure that Mr. O'Hara in no way endangers his own life. In other words, he is not, repeat not, to enter the building in which we believe Mr. Stevens to be until Mr. Stevens is under arrest."

"Ah, for Christ's sake, Peter!" O'Hara protested.

"You listened carefully, didn't you, Officer Payne, to what I just said?"

"Yes, sir."

"If necessary, you will sit on Mr. O'Hara. Clear?"

"Yes, sir."

Lieutenant Ed Suffern, a very large, just short of fat, ruddy-faced man, pushed himself off the fender of his car when he saw Mickey O'Hara and Matt Payne walking up.

"How are you, Mickey?" he said, smiling, offering his hand, obviously pleased to see him. "I'm a little surprised to see you."

"Officially, I just happened to be in the neighborhood."

"Yeah," Suffern said, chuckling. "Sure."

"Got a small problem, Ed," O'Hara said. "How am I going to get to see you catching—whatsisname?—*Abu Ben Mohammed* with Matt Payne sitting on my shoulders?"

"What?"

"Wohl says I can't go in the building until you have this guy in cuffs, and he sent Payne along with orders to sit on me if necessary."

"I wondered what he was doing here," Suffern said. "No problem. Here, let me show you."

He opened the door of his RPC and took a clipboard from the seat.

"Somebody give me a light here," he ordered, and one of

the ACT cops took his flashlight from its holster and shined it on the clipboard. It held a map.

"This is Hawthorne Street," he said, pointing. "Mr. Abu Whatsisname—his real name is Charles D. Stevens, Wohl tell you that?"

O'Hara nodded.

"—lives here, just about in the middle of the block." He pointed. "There's a Homicide detective, he has the warrant, sitting here, right now. This is the way we're going to do this: One ACT car, with two cops and the Homicide guy, will go to the front door. Another ACT car, with two ACT guys and the sergeant, will go around to the back, via the alley here." He pointed again. "When they're in place, the sergeant will give the word. The Homicide guy will knock or ring the bell or whatever. We'll give him thirty seconds to open the door. Then they'll take both doors. When they have him in cuffs, they'll take him out the back. There's a wagon, here." He pointed again, this time to a point a block away. "The van will start for the alley the moment he hears they're going in. They'll put Abu Whatsisname in the van, with one cop from each of the ACT cars, and get out of the neighborhood. The same thing, the same sort of thing, will be going on here in the 5000 block of Saul Street. Two ACT cars, a sergeant, and a Homicide detective will pick up Kenneth H. Dorne, also known as 'King' Dorne, also known as Hussein Something. When they have *him*, the sergeant will call for the wagon. When both of these guys are in the van, they'll be taken to Homicide. Got it?"

"Yeah," Mickey said thoughtfully.

"So there's no problem, Mickey," Lieutenant Suffern finished. "I'll put you and Payne in my car. We'll go into the alley behind Stevens's house, from the other direction. I'll let you two out, and I'll go in with the sergeant when he takes the back door. When you see us coming out, you can make your pictures. Okay?"

"Can you give me a list of the names?" O'Hara asked. "I really hate to spell people's names wrong. And point them out to me, so I know who's who?"

"Absolutely," Suffern said.

Lieutenant Suffern, Officer Payne thought, *is entertaining hopes that the next issue of the* Bulletin *will carry a photograph of Lieutenant Ed Suffern with the just arrested felon in his firm personal grip.*

"Payne," Lieutenant Suffern said, "if answering this puts you on a spot, don't answer it. Are we really going to move in here?" He waved in the general direction of the school building.

"I think so," Matt said. "I think the Board of Education wants to get rid of it."

"My mother went to school in there," Suffern said. "I thought they were going to tear it down."

"Okay," Inspector Peter Wohl's voice suddenly came over, with remarkable clarity, all the loudspeakers in all the vehicles in the playground. "Let's go do it."

There was the sound of starters grinding, and then an angry voice.

"I'm going to need a jump start here!"

Headlights came on, their beams reflecting off the still falling snow.

Suffern opened the rear door of his car and waved Mickey O'Hara and Matt in. The hem of Matt's topcoat got caught in the door, and the door had to be reopened and then closed again.

The cars and vans began to roll out of the playground, onto Frankford Avenue. Most turned left, but some turned right. Matt looked at his watch. It was twenty minutes to five.

At ten minutes to five, they drove down Hawthorne Street. There were a number of cars, their roofs and windshields now coated with snow, parked on the street.

If this snow keeps up, Matt thought, *these cars are going to be buried.*

The headlights of a rusty and battered Chrysler flicked on and off quickly.

"That's the Homicide guy," Lieutenant Suffern said, and then added, "That wasn't too smart."

"Maybe he's just glad to see you," Mickey O'Hara said. "How long has he been there?"

"Probably since midnight," Suffern said. "When he tries to get out of the car, he'll probably be frozen stiff."

Suffern made the next right, turned his headlights off, and then turned right again into the alley and stopped.

Matt started to open the door.

"We got a couple of minutes," Suffern said, stopping him. "Better to stay in the car."

"Right," Matt said.

Said Officer Payne, the rookie, who don't know no better.

"I want to get out," O'Hara said. "If I just jump out of the car, my lens is likely to fog over."

"Okay, Mick," Suffern said obligingly. "But stick close to the walls, huh?"

O'Hara got out and Matt followed him, carefully closing the car's door. Suffern put the car in gear and inched away from them, stopping fifty yards farther down the alley.

It took Matt's eyes a minute to adjust to the darkness, but gradually the alley took shape. They were standing between two brick walls, but thirty feet away, the alley was lined with wooden fences. There was what looked like a derelict car parked against one wall, between them and Suffern's car. Matt wondered how Suffern had managed to get past it in the dark.

And then, as he looked at Mickey O'Hara, who was wiping the lens of his 35-mm camera with a handkerchief, the hair on the back of Matt's neck began to curl.

What the hell is the matter with me? Abu Ben Whatsisname is sound asleep in his bed. He won't know what hit him when those guys come crashing into his house. And I am a good hundred yards from where the action is going to be anyway.

But he pulled off his right glove, stuffed it into the pocket of his topcoat, and then quickly knelt and took his revolver from the ankle holster on the inside of his left leg. Hoping that Mickey O'Hara hadn't seen him, he quickly put it, and the hand that held it, into his topcoat pocket.

And then there was first a creaking, tearing noise, like a board being split, somewhere down the alley, and then the sound of crunching snow.

A moment later he saw something moving.

It has to be a cat, or a dog, or something—

Then he realized that what was coming down the alley toward them was too large to be a dog.

Everything shifted into slow motion.

"Stop!" Matt heard himself say. He had trouble finding his voice. "Police officer—"

"Out of my way, motherfucker!" an intensely angry voice called.

There followed a series of orange flashes, accompanied by sharp cracks.

"Jesus, Mary, and Joseph!" Mickey O'Hara said softly.

Matt was slapped in the face and then, a half second later,

with terrifying force, in his right calf. He felt himself falling hard against the brick wall to his side.

As a voice from the recesses of his brain told him, *Hold it in both hands,* he pulled his revolver from his topcoat pocket. He got it free and up as he slid to the ground.

There was no way to hold the pistol with both hands. He fired instinctively. And then again. And a third time.

There was a grunt from the vague figure coming down the alley, and then the figure stood erect. Matt fired again. The figure took two more steps, and then fell forward.

Matt tried to get on his feet by pushing himself up the wall, but his hands slipped and his leg seemed unstable. He got on all fours, and somehow, that way, managed to get on his feet.

Now holding the pistol in both hands, Matt moved unsteadily toward the fallen figure.

You only have one cartridge left! Don't fuck this up!

The man on the ground was writhing in pain. Matt saw his pistol—*a semiautomatic, probably a Colt .45*—on the ground, half buried in snow. The man made no move for it. Matt hobbled to it and put his foot on it and nearly fell down.

There was a white flash, and he turned quickly toward it, pistol extended.

It was Mickey O'Hara's goddamn camera!

"Easy, kid!" Mickey said, fear in his voice.

Matt aimed the pistol at the man on the ground.

A moment later the camera flash went off again.

"Fuck you, O'Hara!" Matt heard himself shout furiously.

Now there were lights, all kinds of lights, headlights, flashing red and blue lights, portable floodlights.

He looked down the alley and saw an RPC squeeze past Lieutenant Suffern's car, and then, in his headlights, Suffern, his pistol drawn, running down the alley.

Suffern hoisted the skirt of his coat and holstered his pistol and came out with handcuffs. He put his knee in the back of the man on the ground and grabbed his arm to handcuff him.

The man screamed in pain.

The Special Operations car slid to a stop and two cops jumped out.

Suffern came to Matt, said, "Jesus!" and touched his face.

"You can put your pistol away, Payne," Suffern said, and then raised his hand and gently forced Matt's arm down.

Matt looked at him. He saw something sticky on Suffern's

fingers, and then touched his face. His fingers, too, came away bloody.

He squatted to feel his calf, and fell down.

Suffern ran to the RPC, slid behind the wheel, and found the microphone.

"This is Suffern, get the van here, now!" he called, then: "This is Team A Supervisor. We have had a shooting. We have an officer down. We have a suspect down."

Matt, at the moment he was aware he was lying facedown in the snow, felt hands on his shoulders. He felt himself being first rolled over, and then being held up in a slumping position.

He put his hands to his eyes, and wiped away the bloody slush over them. He could see one of the Special Operations cops looking down at him with concern in his eyes.

"You all right?"

"Shit!"

He heard the wail of a siren in the distance, and then other sirens.

"Suffern, where are you?" Wohl's voice came over the radio.

"In the alley behind the scene."

"Who's down?"

"Payne and the suspect."

"On my way."

Matt saw Suffern's face now, close to his.

"Just take it easy, the van's on the way. We'll have you in a hospital in two minutes."

Mickey O'Hara's flashgun went off again.

"Get that fucking camera out of here, Mickey!" Suffern said angrily.

"You all right, Matt?" O'Hara asked.

"I'm shot, for Christ's sake!"

There was the sound of squealing brakes, of clashing gears, and tires slipping on the ice and snow.

Matt looked over his shoulder and saw a van backing into the alley.

"Here's the van," Suffern said, quite unnecessarily.

Matt felt something scrubbing at his face. When his vision cleared, he saw the cop who had rolled him over throwing a bloody handkerchief away and being handed another. He put the fresh handkerchief to Matt's forehead.

"Can you hold that?" he asked.

Matt put his hand to it.

Two more cops appeared, carrying a stretcher.

"Get me to my feet," Matt said. "I don't need that."

They ignored him. He felt himself being unceremoniously picked up and then dumped onto the stretcher. Then he was lifted up and carried to the van. The feet of the stretcher screeched as it was pushed inside.

"Where do you think you're going, Mickey?" someone asked.

"Where does it look like?" O'Hara replied, and then he was sitting on the floor of the van beside Matt.

And then something else was thrown in the van. Matt looked and saw that it was the man he had shot. He was unconscious.

Two uniformed cops, neither of whom Matt recognized, scrambled inside. The van's rear doors slammed closed, and then a moment later, there was the sound of the front doors slamming. The engine raced and the siren began to wail again.

"Is he dead?" Matt asked.

"I don't know," Mickey replied, and then matter-of-factly turned and put his fingers to the unconscious man's jugular. "Not yet, anyway," he added.

"Look at my leg," Matt said.

"What's wrong with your leg?"

"You tell me."

He propped himself up, awkwardly, and watched as Mickey pulled his trouser leg up.

"Looks like you got it there too," Mickey said. "Not much blood. It hurt?"

"No, not much," Matt said. "It feels like I got hit with a rock or something."

"There's only one hole," Mickey said. "The bullet's probably still in there. I don't think anything is broken."

When Matt let himself fall back on the stretcher, he saw that the man he had shot was bleeding from the nose and mouth. There was a froth of bloody bubbles on his lips. Matt looked away, wondering if he was going to be sick to his stomach.

Matt suddenly started to shiver. Mickey looked around the interior of the van.

"Hand me one of those blankets," he ordered.

A gray, dirt-spotted blanket appeared, and O'Hara draped it over him.

"Throw one on him too," Matt Payne ordered.

Two minutes or so later the van leaned on its springs as it made a turn, then bounced over a curb. It stopped and the doors were jerked open.

Three men in hospital whites and a nurse with a purple, sequin-decorated sweater thrown over the shoulders of her whites peered into the van. One of the men grabbed the handles of the stretcher and Matt felt himself sliding down the van's floor.

Once the stretcher was out of the van, he felt himself being moved, and then he realized he had been transferred to a gurney; he could feel the cold plastic beneath the thin sheet on his stomach.

"Get the handcuffs off him!" he heard his nurse order angrily. "He's unconscious, for Christ's sake!"

Matt's gurney began to move into the hospital. There were two sets of doors. The gurney slammed into the outer set, and then the inner set.

"Out of the way!" the nurse's voice called, and Matt's gurney was moved to the wall, where it stopped. He saw a second gurney being pushed, at a trot, by two of the attendants, down the corridor.

And then Staff Inspector Peter Wohl's face appeared next to his.

"How are you doing?"

"I'm all right," Matt said.

Why the hell did I say that?

"They'll take care of you in a minute."

"Why not now?"

"Because the guy you shot is in a lot worse shape than you are," Wohl said matter-of-factly.

"Is he going to live?"

"I don't think they know yet."

"Shit, my car!"

"What about your car?"

"It's in the playground. With the keys in it."

"I'll take care of it," Wohl said. "Don't worry about it."

"I think I'm going to be sick to my stomach."

All of a sudden, Matt found himself looking at Peter Wohl's stomach.

He must have had to squat to get down to me.

"Get me a towel or a bucket or something," Wohl ordered.

Matt rolled on his side, and then completely over, onto his back.

That's better. Now I won't have to throw up.

He propped himself up on his elbows, and then the nausea

came so quickly he barely had time to get his head over the edge of the gurney.

He now felt faint, and his leg began to throb.

The gurney began to move. He looked up and back and saw that he was being towed by a very tall, six feet six or better, very thin black man in hospital greens.

He was pulled into a cubicle walled by white plastic curtains.

A new face appeared in his. Another black one.

"I'm Dr. Hampton. How you doing?"

"Just fine, thank you."

Dr. Hampton removed the handkerchief, jerking it quickly off, and painfully prodded Matt's forehead.

"Nothing serious," he said. "It will have to be sutured, but that can wait."

"What about my leg?"

"I'll have a look," Dr. Hampton said, and then ordered: "Get an IV in him."

Somebody got him into a sitting position and he felt his topcoat and jacket being removed, and then his shirt.

"I'm cold."

He was ignored.

He felt a blood pressure apparatus being strapped around his left arm, and then his right arm was held firmly immobile as a nurse searched for and found a vein.

"Nothing broken. There's no exit wound. There's a bullet in there somewhere. Prep him and send him up to Sixteen."

"Yes, Doctor," the nurse said.

Peter Wohl watched as the gurney with Matt on it was wheeled out of the Emergency treatment cubicle, and then ran after the doctor he had seen go into the cubicle.

"Tell me about the man you just had in there," he said.

"Who are you?" Dr. Hampton asked.

"I'm Inspector Wohl."

"You don't look much like a cop, Inspector."

"What do you want to do, see my badge?"

"No. Take it easy. I suppose I said that because I was just thinking he doesn't either. Look like a cop, I mean."

"Actually," Wohl said. "He's a pretty good cop. How badly is he injured?"

"A good deal less seriously than most people I see who have

been shot with a large caliber weapon,'' Dr. Hampton said, and then went on to explain his diagnosis and prognosis.

Wohl thanked him, and then went to one of the pay phones mounted on the wall between the outer and inner doors of the Emergency entrance and took first a dime from his pocket and then his wallet. Inside the wallet was a typewritten list of telephone numbers, on both sides of a sheet of paper cut to the size of a credit card, and then coated with Scotch tape to preserve it.

He dropped a dime in the slot and then dialed one of the numbers. There was an answer, surprisingly wide awake, on the third ring: ''Coughlin.''

''Chief, this is Peter Wohl.''

''What's up, Peter?''

''Matt Payne has been shot.''

There was a just perceptible pause.

''Bad?''

''He's got a .45 bullet in his calf. It apparently was a ricochet off a brick wall. And his face was hit, the forehead, probably by a piece of bullet jacket. It slit the skin. Not serious, take a couple of stitches.''

''But the bullet in the leg *is* serious?''

''There's not much damage. I don't know for sure what I'm talking about, but what I think happened was that the bullet hit the wall, a brick wall, and lost most of its momentum, and then hit him. It's still in him. They just took him into the operating room.''

''Where is he?''

''Frankford Hospital.''

''What the hell happened, Peter?''

I have just become the guy who is responsible for getting Denny Coughlin's godson, the son he never had, shot.

''At five o'clock this morning, we picked up the doers of the Goldblatt job.''

'' 'We' presumably meaning Highway,'' Coughlin said coldly. ''I didn't know that Matt was in Highway. When did that happen?''

''ACT Teams from Special Operations, working with Homicide, made the arrests. Simultaneously—''

''Not Highway?''

''No, sir. Not Highway.''

''Go on, Peter.''

''Mickey O'Hara was there. I invited him. I sent Matt with him to make sure Mickey didn't get in the way, get himself hurt.

One of the doers, a scumbag named Charles D. Stevens, apparently saw either the cars, or more likely the Homicide guy sitting on him, and then the cars. As the ACT cars were getting in place, he—this is conjecture Chief, but I think this is it—made his way to either the next house, or the house next to that, and tried to get away through the alley. O'Hara and Matt were at the head of the alley. He—Stevens—started shooting. And got Matt.''

''Did you get Stevens?''

''Matt got Stevens. He shot at him four times and hit him twice. Once in the arm, and once in the liver. Stevens was brought here. I have the feeling he's not going to live.''

''But Matt is in no danger?''

''No, sir. I don't even think there is going to be much muscle damage. As I said, I think the bullet lost much of its momentum—''

''That's nice,'' Coughlin said.

''He's more worried about his car than anything else, Chief.''

''What about his car?''

''We formed up in the playground of the school at Castor and Frankford. Matt went to the scene with Lieutenant Suffern. And left his car, with the keys in it in the playground.''

''You're taking care of it, I suppose?''

''Yes, sir.''

''Have you called the commissioner?''

''No, sir. Chief Lowenstein is doing that.''

''Lowenstein was there?''

''No, sir. But he heard about it, and told me he would take care of calling the commissioner.''

''Is the Department going to look bad in this, Peter?''

''No, sir. I don't see how. The other seven arrests went very smoothly. They're all down at 8th and Race already. As soon as I get off the phone, I'm going down there.''

''Have you notified Matt's family?''

''No, sir. I thought I should call you before I did that.''

''Well, at least your brain wasn't entirely disengaged,'' Coughlin said. And then, immediately, ''Sorry, Peter. I shouldn't have said that.''

''Forget it, Chief. I don't think I have to tell you how bad I feel about this. And I know how you feel about Matt.''

''I've been on the job twenty-seven years and I've never been hurt,'' Coughlin said. ''Matt's father gets killed. His Uncle Dutch gets killed, and now he damned near does.''

"I thought about that too, Chief."

"I'll take care of notifying his family," Coughlin said. "You make sure nobody else gets carried away with procedure and tries to."

"I've already done that, Chief."

"You're sure he's going to be all right?"

"Yes, sir."

"Keep yourself available, Peter. You say you're going to be at Homicide?"

"Yes, sir. Mr. Stillwell asked me to be there."

"Farnsworth Stillwell?"

"Yes, sir."

"When you can break loose, it might be a good idea to go back to the hospital; to have a word with Matt's family."

"Yes, sir, I'd planned to do that."

"Well, don't blame yourself for this, Peter. These things happen."

"Yes, sir."

Coughlin, without another word, hung up. He swung his feet out of bed, pulled open the drawer of a bedside table, and took out a telephone book. He dialed a number.

"Police Department."

"Let me speak to the senior officer on duty."

"Maybe I can help you."

"This is Chief Inspector Dennis V. Coughlin. Get the senior police officer present on the telephone!"

"This is Lieutenant Swann. Can I help you?"

"This is Chief Inspector Dennis V. Coughlin—"

"Oh, sure. How are you, Chief?"

"I need a favor."

"Name it."

"You know where the Payne house is on Providence Road in Wallingford?"

"Sure."

"Their son is a police officer. He has just been shot in the line of duty. He is in Frankford Hospital. I am about to notify them. I would consider it a personal favor if you would provide an escort for them from their home to the Philadelphia city line. I'll have a car meet you there."

"Chief, when the Paynes come out of their driveway, a car will be sitting there."

"Thank you."

"He hurt bad?"

"We don't think so."

"Thank God."

"Thank God," Denny Coughlin repeated, and, unable to trust his voice any further, hung up.

He walked into the kitchen, poured an inch and a half of John Jameson's Irish whiskey in a plastic cup, drank it down, and then reached for the telephone on the wall. He dialed a number from memory. It took a long time to answer.

Please, God, don't let Patty answer.

"Hello?"

"Brewster, this is Denny Coughlin."

"Is something wrong, Denny?" Brewster Cortland Payne, suddenly wide awake, asked.

"What is it?" a familiar female voice came faintly over the telephone.

"Matt's got himself shot," Denny Coughlin said very quickly. "Not seriously. He's in Frankford Hospital. By the time you get dressed, there will be a police car waiting in your driveway to escort you to the hospital. I'll meet you there."

"All right."

"My God, I'm sorry, Brewster."

"Yes, I know. We'll see you there, Denny."

The phone went dead.

Coughlin broke the connection with his finger and then dialed another number from memory.

"Highway."

"This is Chief Coughlin."

"Yes, sir."

"I have cleared this with Inspector Wohl. A Media police car is about to escort a car to the city line. I want a Highway car to meet it and take it the rest of the way to Frankford Hospital. Got that?"

"Yes, sir."

"Thank you," Coughlin said, and hung up. Then he went into his bedroom and started to get dressed. As he was tying his shoes, he suddenly looked up, at the crucifix hanging over his bed.

"It could be worse. Thank you," he said.

FOURTEEN

Shortly after Mr. Michael J. O'Hara appeared in the city room of the Philadelphia *Bulletin* at a little after six A.M., the *Bulletin*'s city and managing editors decided that since they had an exclusive (the term ''scoop'' is considered déclassé by modern journalists) in Mr. O'Hara's coverage of the shooting during the arrest of the Islamic Liberation Army, together with some really great pictures, it clearly behooved them to run with it.

The front pages of Sections A and B were redone. On Page 1A, a photograph of the President of the United States shaking hands with some foreign dignitary in flowing robes was replaced with a photograph of the cop bleeding all over himself as he held his gun on the guy who had shot him. Under it was the caption:

> Special Operations Officer Matthew M. Payne, blood streaming from his wounds, holds his pistol on Charles D.

Stevens, whom he had just bested in an early morning gun battle in Frankford. Stevens was one of eight men, alleged to be participants in the murder-robbery of Goldblatt's furniture store, whom police rounded up at dawn. Payne collapsed moments after this photo was taken. Full details on Page 1B. [Bulletin Photograph by Michael J. O'Hara.]

Most of Page 1B was redone. When finished it had three photographs lining the top, and a headline reading, EXCLUSIVE BULLETIN COVERAGE OF EARLY MORNING SHOOTOUT.

Below the photographs—which showed Matt Payne being held up by the ACT cop; Charles D. Stevens being rolled into Frankford Hospital on a gurney; and Matt Payne, his face caked with blood, on his gurney in the corridor at Frankford Hospital—was the story:

By Michael J. O'Hara
Bulletin Staff Writer

Blood stained the freshly fallen snow in an alley in Frankford early this morning after Charles D. Stevens chose to shoot it out with the cops rather than submit to arrest and picked the wrong cop for his deadly duel.

Stevens, who sometimes calls himself Abu Ben Mohammed, is one of eight suspects in the murder-robbery of Goldblatt's Furniture earlier this week. It was the intention of Staff Inspector Peter Wohl, commanding the Special Operations Division, to arrest all eight suspects at once, and in the wee hours, to minimize risks to both the public and his officers.

Seven of the eight carefully orchestrated arrests went smoothly. But, as this reporter and Officer Matthew M. Payne, administrative assistant to Inspector Wohl, waited in a dark alley behind Stevens's house in the 4700 block of Hawthorne Street for the meticulously planned arrest procedure to begin, Stevens suddenly appeared in the alley, a blazing .45 automatic in his hand.

As this reporter dove for cover, two of Stevens's bullets struck Payne, who had been assigned to escort this reporter during Stevens's arrest. Payne went down, but he was not out. Somehow, Payne managed to get his own pistol into action. When the shooting was over, Stevens was critically, possibly fatally, wounded, and the young cop he had tried to gun down without warning was standing over him, blood dripping from his own wounds.

This was not the first battle for his life fought by Payne, who is twenty-two and a bachelor. Three months ago, while attempting to arrest Warren K. Fletcher, the Northwest Philadelphia serial rapist, Fletcher, who had his latest victim in his van, tried to

run over the young policeman. Moments later he was
dead of a bullet in the brain
fired by the then six-months-
on-the-police-force rookie.

Payne, who collapsed mo-
ments after making sure
Stevens posed no further
threat, was taken to Frankford Hospital, where he un-
derwent surgery for the
removal of the bullet in his
leg. His condition is de-
scribed as "good."

Stevens, who was also
rushed to Frankford Hospital by police, is in intensive
care, his condition described
as "critical" by hospital authorities.

Chief Inspector Matt
Lowenstein, who commands
the Detective Division, under whose overall command
the mass arrest took place,
said that Stevens, if he lives,
will have assault with a
deadly weapon and resisting
arrest added to the other
charges, which include first-
degree murder, already
lodged against him.

"I regret that force was
necessary," Chief Lowen-
stein said. "Inspector Wohl
and his men took every step
they could think of to avoid
it. But I cannot conceal my
admiration for this young officer (Payne) who bravely
stood up to this vicious
criminal."

* * *

By 6:45 A.M., the appropriate plates had been replaced on the presses, and with a deep growl, they began to roll again.

It was the opinion of the managing editor that they could probably sell an additional thirty-five or forty thousand copies of the paper. Blood and shooting always sold.

How that goddamn O'Hara manages to always be in on things like this is a mystery, but giving the sonofabitch his due, he always is, and he probably is worth all the money we have to pay him.

Hector Carlos Estivez was in the first of the vans carrying the prisoners to arrive at the Police Administration Building at 8th and Race Streets in downtown Philadelphia. The others arrived over the next fifteen minutes.

The van carrying Mr. Estivez entered the parking lot at the rear of the Roundhouse, and immediately backed up down the ramp leading to the Central Cell Room.

The driver and his partner got out and went to the rear of the van. They found Homicide detective Joe D'Amata, who had driven in his own car from Frankford, waiting for them. The driver opened the rear door of the van and Mr. Estivez, who had been handcuffed, was helped out of the van.

Detective D'Amata took one of Mr. Estivez's arms, and one of the officers who had been in the back of the van with him took the other.

Mr. Estivez was then led through the Cell Room to an elevator, and taken in it to the Homicide Bureau on the third floor.

There were several people standing just outside the office of Captain Henry Q. Quaire, commanding officer of the Homicide Bureau. Mr. Estivez recognized only one of them, Sergeant Jason Washington. The others were Farnsworth Stillwell, an assistant district attorney of Philadelphia County; Staff Inspector Peter Wohl; and Captain Quaire himself.

Mr. Estivez was taken to a small room furnished with an Early American-style chair and a small table. There was a window with one-way glass in one wall of the room. The chair was made of steel and was bolted to the floor. One end of a pair of handcuffs was looped through a hole in the chair seat.

Mr. Estivez's handcuffs were removed. Detective D'Amata

told him to sit down and, when he had done so, put Mr. Estivez's left wrist in the handcuff cuffed to the chair.

Mr. Estivez was then left alone.

He looked with a mixture of contempt and uneasiness at the one-way glass window. There was no way of telling if someone was on the other side, looking in at him.

A minute or so later the door to the room opened, and Detective D'Amata returned. On his heels came Sergeant Jason Washington, Staff Inspector Wohl, and Assistant District Attorney Stillwell.

"Which one is this one?" Sergeant Washington inquired.

"This is Mr. Hector Carlos Estivez," Detective D'Amata replied.

Sergeant Washington, a carefully calculated (and in fact, once practiced before a mirror) look of contempt, scorn, and dislike on his face, then took two steps toward Mr. Estivez. Mr. Estivez, who was sitting, had to look up at him. There was no way that Mr. Estivez could not be aware of Washington's considerable bulk.

Sergeant Washington then squatted down, so that his face was on a level with Mr. Estivez, and examined him carefully for twenty seconds or so.

He then grunted, stood erect, said, "Okay, Hector Carlos *Estivez*. Fine," and scribbled something in his notebook.

This was a little psychological warfare, Jason Washington having long ago come to believe that the greatest fear is the fear of the unknown.

Washington knew he enjoyed a certain fame (perhaps notoriety) in the criminal community. There was a perhaps fifty-fifty chance that Estivez knew who he was. And even if he didn't, Washington was sure that the sight of a very large, very well-dressed black man in an obvious position of police authority would be unnerving.

Jason Washington then covered his mouth with his hand and said softly, so that Mr. Estivez could not understand him, "Obviously a pillar of his community, wouldn't you say?"

The remark caused Wohl to smile, which was Washington's intention. He had long ago also come to believe that knowing that one is the source of amusement, but not knowing specifically how, is also psychologically disturbing, particularly if the person amused holds great—if undefined—power over you.

At that point, Inspector Wohl, Assistant District Attorney

Stillwell, and Sergeant Washington left the interview room, closing the door behind them and leaving Detective D'Amata alone with Mr. Estivez.

"Mr. Estivez," Detective D'Amata said, "you have been arrested on warrants charging you with murder and armed robbery. Before I say anything else, I want to make sure that you are aware of your rights under the Constitution."

He then took a small card from his jacket pocket and read Mr. Estivez his rights under the Miranda Decision. Mr. Estivez had seen them enough on television to know them by heart, but he listened attentively anyway.

"Do you understand the rights I have pointed out to you?" Detective D'Amata said.

"Yeah," Mr. Estivez said. "I'm not going to say one fucking word without my lawyer."

"That is your right, sir," Detective D'Amata said.

He then left Mr. Estivez alone in the interview room again.

"Mr. Estivez," Detective D'Amata said dryly to Mssrs. Washington, Wohl, and Stillwell, "has elected to exercise his rights under the Miranda Decision."

"Really?" Wohl replied with a smile.

"So what happens now?" Farnsworth Stillwell asked. "We're not going to run into trouble with the Six-Hour Rule are we?"

The Pennsylvania Supreme Court had issued another ruling designed to protect the innocent from the police. It had decreed that unless an accused was brought before an arraignment judge within six hours of his arrest, any statement he had made could not be used against him.

"Correct me if I'm wrong, Counselor," Jason Washington said with more than a hint of sarcasm in his voice, "but as I understand the Six-Hour-Rule, it does not prohibit the use of a statement inadmissable against the individual who made it being used against other participants in the offense."

"Yes, of course, you're right." Stillwell said. It was obvious he did not like being lectured on the law.

"We'll take him back downstairs, process him, and send him over to the House of Detention," D'Amata replied.

"What I'm going to do, Inspector, unless you have something else in mind," Jason Washington announced, "is give them all day to thoughtfully consider their situation, and maybe get a little sound advice from the legal profession. Then, after they have had their supper, and are convinced that nothing further is going to happen to them today, starting at six-fifteen, I'm going to run them all through the lineup, for a positive identification by Mr. Monahan. Then I will give them the rest of the night to consider their situation, now that they know we have a witness, and then starting at eight tomorrow morning, I will interview them.''

''Have at it, Jason,'' Wohl said.

''By then, I think we can count on somebody going to Mr. Stillwell to make a deal,'' Washington said. ''There's seven of them. I think the odds are pretty good that at least one of them will try to save his skin.''

Farnsworth Stillwell, whose wordless role in the little playlet had been orchestrated by Sergeant Washington, had played along for several reasons. For one thing, he had never seen how something like this was actually carried out, and he was curious. For another, when he had worked with Wohl during the investigation and prosecution of Judge Findermann, he had come to understand that Wohl was anything but a fool, and it logically followed from that that if Wohl was willing to play along with Washington, there was probably a good reason for it.

Secondly, the one bit of specific advice he had been given by District Attorney Thomas J. Callis had concerned Jason Washington.

''Not only does he know how to deal with, in other words, read, this kind of scum, but he has forgotten more about criminal law than you know. So don't make the mistake of trying to tell him how to do his job. I can't imagine Washington doing anything dumb, but if he does, Wohl will catch him at it, and he will take 'suggestions' from Wohl. Understand?''

The idea of getting one or more of the seven to testify against the others to save himself had a positive appeal. The State had only Monahan as a witness, which was rather frightening to consider. If this case went down the toilet, he would have egg all over his face. People with egg on their faces only rarely ever get to become the governor.

Kenneth H. Dorne, aka ''King,'' aka Hussein El Baruca, in handcuffs, a uniformed police officer on each arm, was led into Homicide and taken into a second, identical interview room and cuffed to the steel chair.

''Here we go again,'' D'Amata said. ''Anyone want to bet

that this one will announce that he has been thinking of his aged mother and wants to make a clean breast of the whole thing?''

D'Amata, Wohl, and Washington waited until Mr. Estivez had been uncuffed from his steel chair, cuffed behind his back, and led out of Homicide before going into the second interview room. Stillwell followed them.

The only thing that bothered him was how long this process was taking. He had scheduled a press conference to announce the arrest of these people, and the determination of Assistant District Attorney Farnsworth Stillwell to prosecute them to the full extent of the law, for nine o'clock, and two things bothered him about that: Should he take Wohl and Washington with him, or, more accurately, *ask* them, one of them, or both, to come along?

Having Washington in the picture—literally the picture, there were sure to be photographers—might be valuable, vis-à-vis the Afro-American voters, somewhere down the pike. Wohl, however, was a little too attractive, well dressed, well spoken, and with a reputation. The goddamn press was likely to be as interested, even more interested, in what he had to say than they would be in Farnsworth Stillwell.

And finally, is there going to be time to get from here to my office in time to meet the press?

The little playlet was run again, and a few minutes later, Wohl, Washington, and Stillwell were standing outside Captain Quaire's office again.

''I don't want to bubble over with enthusiasm,'' Washington said. ''But I have a feeling that Mr. Dorne may decide that being a religious martyr is not really his bag.''

Detective D'Amata came out of the interview room, and announced, surprising no one, that Kenneth H. Dorne, aka ''King,'' aka Hussein El Baruca, had also elected to avail himself of his right to legal counsel before deciding whether or not he would answer any questions.

''What about him, Joe?'' Washington said.

''You picked up on that too, huh, Jason?'' D'Amata replied. ''Yeah. Maybe. Maybe after the lineup. I wouldn't bet on it.''

''I'm tempted to,'' Stillwell said. ''Sergeant Washington's insight into things like that is legendary.''

The flattery, he decided, after looking at Washington's face, *had not gone wide of the mark.*

"If you and Inspector Wohl could find the time," he went on, having made that decision, "I'd like you to come help me deal with the press. I asked the ladies and gentlemen of the press to be at the office at nine."

"I'll beg off, thank you just the same," Washington said. "I want a good look at the others."

"Peter?"

"No, thank you. I live by the rule never to talk to the press unless I have to. And anyway, I want to go back to Frankford Hospital. The officer who was shot works for me."

"I'm going up there too," Washington said. "When I'm finished here."

"Tragic, tragic," Stillwell said. "Thank God, he's alive."

"Yes," Washington said.

"Would you call my office, Sergeant, when you're finished? I'd really like to hear your assessment of these people."

"Certainly."

Farnsworth Stillwell offered Wohl and Washington his hand.

"Thank you very much for letting me share this with you," he said. "It's been a—an *education.* I've never been in here before."

"This is where it happens, Mr. Stillwell," Washington said.

Stillwell rode the elevator down to the main lobby and started for the parking lot, but as he reached the door, he had a second thought, one he immediately recognized to be a first-rate idea.

He turned and went to the desk, asked permission of the sergeant to use the telephone, and dialed his office number.

"When the press arrives," he ordered. "Give them my apologies, and tell them I have gone to Frankford Hospital to visit the police officer who was shot this morning. I feel I have that duty. Tell them that too. And tell them if they come to the hospital, I'll meet with them there."

When he hung up, he had another idea, even better, and pulled the telephone to him again and dialed his home.

"Darling," he said when his wife answered, "I'm glad I caught you. Something has come up. I'm going to Frankford Hospital, to visit with the cop who got himself shot this morning—"

"What are you talking about?"

"—I'll tell you all about it in the car. I want you there with me. The press will be there."

There was twenty seconds of silence.

"Darling, this is important to me," he said firmly. "I'll be waiting outside for you in fifteen minutes."

He hung up thinking, somewhat petulantly, *If she really wants to be the governor's wife, she damned well had better learn that there is no free lunch, that certain things are going to be required of her.*

"Mother," Officer Matt Payne said, "why don't you get out of here? I'm all right, and there's nothing you can do for me here."

Patricia and Brewster C. Payne had been in the Recovery Room when Matt was taken there from the surgical suite. It was strictly against hospital policy, but the chairman of the board of trustees of Frankford Hospital entrusted his legal affairs to Mawson, Payne, Stockton, McAdoo & Lester. A telephone call to him had resulted not only in a telephone call to the senior staff physician, but the physical presence of that gentleman himself, three minutes later, to make sure that whatever Brewster Payne thought the hospital should do for his son was being done.

Aside from access to the Recovery Room, the only request Brewster Payne had made was that Matt be given a private room, something the senior staff physician had already decided to provide to spare some other patient from the horde of people who had come to the hospital to see Matt Payne.

The mayor, the police commissioner, two chief inspectors, and their respective entourages, plus a number of less senior police officers, plus representatives of the print and electronic media had begun to descend on the hospital at about the same time screaming sirens on two Highway Patrol cars had announced the arrival of the Payne family.

While the press could be required to wait in the main lobby, the others immediately made it plain they would wait right where they were, overflowing the small waiting room on the surgical floor, until Officer Payne was out of surgery and his condition known.

And when that had come to pass—the removal of a bullet from the calf musculature was a fairly simple procedure, routinely handled by surgical residents half a dozen times on any given weekend—and Young Payne was taken to the Recovery Room, the Hospital Security Staff was unable to deter the mayor's driver from carrying out his assigned mission—"Go down and bring the press up here. They'll want a picture of me with Payne when he wakes up."

The senior staff physician was able to delay the picture taking until the staff had put Young Payne in a private room, and after the mayor had taken the necessary steps to keep the public aware that their mayor, in his never-ceasing efforts to rid the streets of Philadelphia of crime, was never far from the action, he left, and so did perhaps half of the people who had arrived at about the time he had.

"You'll need pajamas," Patricia Payne said to her son. "And your toilet things—"

"I won't be in here long," Matt said.

"You don't know that," Patricia Payne said, and looked at her daughter, Amelia.

"I don't know how long they're going to keep him, Mother," she replied. "But I'll find out. I'll call you at home and let you know. And I'll go by his apartment and get him what he needs. I have to come back out here anyway. You and Dad go on home."

"I suppose he should rest," Patricia Payne gave in. She leaned over her son and kissed him. "Do what they tell you to do, for once."

"Yes, ma'am," Matt said.

"If you need anything, Matt," Brewster Payne said, "I'm as close as that phone."

"Thank you, Dad. I don't think I'll need anything."

"I'll call as soon as I have a chance to go home, change, and get to the office."

"Go on, you two, get out of here," Amelia Payne said.

They left.

"Thank you," Matt said when the door had closed.

"Don't look so pleased with yourself, you sonofabitch," Amy Payne snapped. "I did that for them, not you."

"Wow!"

"You *bastard*! Are you trying to drive Mother crazy, or what?" She dipped into an extra large purse, came out with a copy of the *Bulletin* and threw it at him. "I hope she doesn't see that!"

The front page showed Matt, bloody-faced, holding his gun on Charles D. Stevens.

"Hey, I didn't do this on purpose. That bastard was shooting at me."

"That bastard died thirty minutes ago. You can carve another notch on your gun, Jesse James."

"He died?" Matt asked, wanting confirmation.

"I didn't think Mother needed to know that."

She looked at him. Their eyes met.

"How do you feel about that?" she asked.

"I'm not about to wallow in remorse, if that's what you're hoping. He was trying to kill me."

"And almost did. Do you have any idea how lucky you are? Have you ever seen what a .45-caliber bullet does to tissue?"

"I just found out."

"No, you didn't. The bullet that hit you had lost most of its energy bouncing off a wall."

"Amy, I wasn't trying to be hero. This just happened. I can't understand why you're sore at me."

"Because, you *ass*, of what you're doing to Mother. When are you going to come to your senses, for her sake, if nothing else?"

Matt was not given time to form a reply. The door opened, and a nurse put her head in.

"Are you a family member?"

"I'm Dr. Payne," Amy replied, not at all pleasantly. "What do you want?"

"Mr. Payne's grandmother and aunt are here, Doctor. They'd like to see him."

"Let them come in, I'm leaving."

The nurse pushed the door open. A stout, somewhat florid-faced woman in her sixties, her gray hair done up in a bun, followed by a blond woman in her late thirties came into he room.

"Hello, Mother Moffitt," Amy Payne said. "Jeannie."

"Hello, Amy," the younger woman replied.

The older woman flashed Amy a cold look, nodded, and said, "Miss Payne."

"It's *Dr.* Payne, Mrs. Moffitt," Amy said, and walked out of the room.

"Hello, Grandma," Matt said.

"Your grandfather, your father, and your Uncle Richard would be proud of you, darling," Gertrude Moffitt said emotionally, walking to the bed and grasping his hand.

"Hello, Aunt Jeannie," Matt said.

"I'm just sorry you didn't kill the man who did this to you," Mother Moffitt said.

"I apparently did," Matt said. "They told me he died half an hour ago."

"Then I hope he burns in hell."

"Mother Moffitt!" Jeannie Moffitt protested. "For God's sake."

"I have lost two sons to the scum of this city. I have no compassion in my heart for them, and neither should you."

"I'm just grateful Matt's not more seriously injured," Jeannie said.

"Chief Coughlin called and told me," Mother Moffitt said. "Your mother apparently couldn't be bothered."

"She was upset, for God's sake!" Jeannie Moffitt protested. "You, of all people, should understand that."

"No matter what trials and pain God has sent me, I take pride in always having done my duty."

Jeannie Moffitt shook her head, and she and Matt exchanged a smile.

"So, how are you, Matty?" she asked.

"Aside from that, Mrs. Lincoln, how was the play?"

Jeannie Moffitt laughed.

"What was that? I don't understand that," Mother Moffitt said.

"A little joke, Grandma," Matt said.

The nurse stuck her head through the door again.

"I'm afraid you'll have to leave now," she said.

"I just got here," Mother Moffitt said indignantly.

"Doctor's orders," the nurse said, and walked to the side of Matt's bed. "Mr. Payne needs rest."

"*Officer Payne*, thank you," Mother Moffitt said.

"Do you need anything, Matty?" Jeannie asked.

"Not a thing, thank you."

"I'll come back, of course, if Jeannie can find the time to bring me," Mother Moffitt said.

"Of course, I will. You know that."

"It's a terrible thing when the only time I get to see him is in a hospital bed with a bullet in him," Mother Moffitt said.

She bent and kissed his cheek and marched out of the room. The nurse went to the door and turned and smiled.

"Dr. Payne said to tell you, you owe her one," she said.

"Thank both of you," Matt said.

"There's some other people out here to see you. You feel up to it?"

"Who?"

"A Highway Patrolman, some kind of a big-shot cop named Coughlin, and a man from the district attorney's office. And his wife."

"The district attorney?"

"I think he said *assistant*. And his wife. I can run them off."

"No. I'm all right. Isn't this thing supposed to hurt?"

"It will. When it starts to hurt, ring for a nurse."

"I'm also hungry. Can I get something to eat?"

"I can probably arrange for something," she said. "So you want to see them?"

"Please."

Chief Inspector Dennis V. Coughlin, Officer Charles Mc-Fadden, and Assistant District Attorney and Mrs. Farnsworth Stillwell filed into the room.

"Hey, Charley," Matt said. "Uncle Denny."

"I'm Farnsworth Stillwell, Officer Payne," the assistant district attorney said, walking up to the bed with his hand extended, "and this is Mrs. Stillwell."

"How do you do?" Matt said politely. He had previously had the pleasure of making Mrs. Stillwell's acquaintance. He not only knew her Christian name, but a number of other intimate details about her.

Her name was Helene, and the last time he had seen her, she was putting her clothing back on in his apartment, whence they had gone from the Delaware Valley Cancer Society's cocktail party.

"Hello," Helene said. "I'm a little vague about the protocol here. Is it permitted to say I'm so sorry you've been shot?"

"This is my first time too," Matt said. "I'm a little fuzzy about the protocol myself."

She walked to the bed and offered him her hand.

"I'm sorry you've been shot."

"Thank you. So am I," Matt said.

"Are you all right?"

"Just fine."

"We're all sorry you've—this has happened," Farnsworth Stillwell said. "And I must tell you, I feel to some degree responsible."

"Nonsense," Denny Coughlin said. "No one is responsible except the man who pulled the trigger."

"I'm sorry we didn't bring you anything," Helene Stillwell said. "But I didn't know who you were, what you would be like, and at this time of the morning—"

"It was good of you to come," Matt said.

Helene finally took her hand back.

"We wanted you to know that we were concerned," Stillwell said, "concerned and grateful."

"I think we should let Officer Payne get some rest, darling," Helene said.

"There are some members of the press outside who would like to have our picture together," Farnsworth Stillwell said. "Would you feel up to that?"

Matt looked at Denny Coughlin, who shrugged and then nodded his head.

"Sure," Matt said.

A photographer came into the room. He asked if the bed could be cranked up, and when it had, he suggested that Mr. Stillwell get on one side of him, and Mrs. Stillwell on the other. When they had done so, he suggested that they get closer to Matt. "It feels a little awkward, but the picture comes out better."

When they had moved into the desired positions, they had to swap sides, so that Assistant District Attorney Stillwell and Officer Payne could shake hands. Mrs. Stillwell, in order to get closer, put her arm behind Officer Payne's shoulders, a position that pressed her breast against his arm, and for a moment allowed her fingers to caress the back of his neck.

And then the flashbulb went off, Farnsworth Stillwell told Officer Payne that if he needed anything, anything at all, all he had to do was let him know, and they were gone.

"I don't like that sonofabitch," Denny Coughlin said, "but I wouldn't be surprised if he really does get to be governor."

"Really?" Matt asked.

"So how are you, Matty?" Denny Coughlin asked.

"Worried about my car," Matt said, looking at Charley.

"I got it downstairs," Charley said. "Aside from no radio, doors, or seats, it's okay."

"You'd better be kidding."

"I got it downstairs, all in one piece. Inspector Wohl asked me to ask you where you want it."

"In the garage under the apartment, please."

"You got it. You need anything else?"

"Can't think of anything."

"I'll come see you when I get off. But I'd better get going now. Quinn's sitting in the car about to shit a brick."

"Thanks, Charley," Matt said.

Dennis V. Coughlin closed the door after McFadden, and then exhaled audibly. He walked to the bed and sat down on it.

"Jesus, Matty, you gave us a scare. What the hell happened?"

This is more than a godfather, more than my blood father's buddy, doing his duty, Matt suddenly realized. *This man loves me.*

He remembered that his father, the other father, the only one he had ever known, Brewster C. Payne, had told him that he believed Dennis V. Coughlin had always been in love with his mother.

"Lieutenant Suffern let us out of his car in the alley behind Stevens's house—"

"You and O'Hara?"

"Yeah. We were waiting for the ACT team and the sergeant to bring Stevens down so Mickey could get a picture. Then I heard a noise, a creaking noise, like wood breaking. I think now it was Stevens coming over a fence. Anyway, all of a sudden, there he was shooting at us."

"He shot first?"

"He shot first."

"That makes it justifiable homicide. You're absolutely sure he shot first?"

"Hey, I thought you were here to comfort me on my bed of pain, not interview me?"

"Are you in pain?" Coughlin asked, concern and possibly even a hint of pity—or maybe shame—in his voice.

"No, Uncle Denny, I'm not," Matt said, and touched the older man's shoulder. After a moment, Coughlin's hand came up and covered his.

"It'll probably start to hurt later, Matty," he said. "But they'll give you something for it. I'm sure."

Their eyes met.

Coughlin stood up.

"I got to go. You need anything, you know how to reach me."

FIFTEEN

A motherly, very large black woman wearing a badge identifying her as a licensed practical nurse delivered a fried egg on limp toast sandwich, a container of milk, and a Styrofoam cup of coffee.

"Lunch is at eleven-thirty," she announced. "Unless you like beans and franks you won't be thrilled."

"Thank you."

"You know how to work the TV clicker?"

She showed him, walked to the door to leave, and then turned.

"I heard what happened," she said. "Good for you. Animals like that bum you shot are taking over the city."

Matt found the controls for the bed, adjusted the back to his satisfaction, and turned on the television. Not surprising him at all, there was nothing on that he would watch if he were not in a hospital bed feeling lousy and with his leg wrapped up like that of an Egyptian mummy.

If it were Saturday morning, he thought, *at least I could watch the teenagers flopping their boobs around on that dance show on WCAU-TV.*

He settled for a quiz show, quickly deciding that the participants had been chosen not for their potential ability to call forth trivia but rather on their ability to jump up and down, shrieking with joy, when they were awarded a lifetime supply of acne medication.

His calf began to feel prickly, as if it had fallen asleep, and it seemed to him he could feel blood pumping through it.

The door opened and a handsome young man with long blond hair entered, bearing a floral display.

"Where do you want this, buddy?"

"On that dresser, I suppose."

The handsome young man jerked the card free from the display and tossed it onto the bed and left.

The card read, "Best Wishes for a Speedy Recovery. Fraternal Order of Police."

Officer Payne was surprised at how much the gesture touched him.

There was no question about it now, he *could* feel the beating of his heart in his calf.

The moron on television, even though he had eagerly pushed the I-know-the-answer button, erroneously located Casablanca in Tunisia, the you-goofed fog horn sounded, and the moron's face registered as much sorrow as if his mother had just been run over by a truck.

The door opened again, to another florist's delivery man, this one bearing two floral displays. One of the cards read, "Mother, Dad, & House Apes." The second, "Charley & Margaret."

He was aware that he had audibly let his breath out, and then that it was more than that; he had moaned. Every time his heart made his leg throb, it hurt.

Well, why am I surprised? They told me it would start to hurt.

With some effort, (the device, at the end of an electrical cord, had fallen off the back of the bed when he had raised it) he found the button to summon the nurse.

A minute or so later, the door opened, but it was not an angel of mercy with the wherewithal to deaden his pain, but another delivery person, this one female, fat, and bearing an expensively wrapped package.

"You're the one who got shot, aren't you?" she greeted him. "I seen it in the newspaper."

Whoopee! Ring the you-got-it-right! siren. You have just won a year's supply of Acne Free!

"I guess I am."

The package contained a pound of Barricini assorted chocolates and a copy of Art Buchwald's latest book. The card read, "Ask the nurse to explain the big words to you. Amy."

Jesus Christ, I hurt! Where the hell is that goddamn nurse?

The nurse's head appeared in the partially opened door. A new one. This one was blond, and had intelligent hazel eyes in a very attractive face.

"Is there a problem?" she asked.

Nice voice. Deep. Soft. I wonder what the rest of her looks like?

"Actually, there are two."

"Oh?"

"I hurt."

"And?"

"Nature calls."

"Bowels or bladder?"

"Bladder," he said, and then reconsidered. "Probably both."

God, what a perfectly wonderful way to begin a romantic conversation.

The head withdrew from the door, and the door closed.

"I give you my personal guarantee," Mr. Robert Holland announced sincerely from the television screen, "that you'll never get a better deal anywhere in the Delaware Valley than you'll get from me. Step into any one of our locations today, and one of our sales counselors of integrity will prove it to you."

"You hypocritical fucking thief!" Officer Payne responded indignantly.

The nurse returned, more quickly than Matt had expected, carrying a tray with a tiny paper cup on it, and two stainless-steel devices, one under her arm, which reminded Matt of the phrase "form follows function."

The rest of her was as attractive as her face. She was tall, and lithe, and moved with grace.

Scandinavian, he thought. *Or maybe one of those Baltic countries, Latvia, Estonia. Maybe Polish? Jesus, she's attractive!*

She put the functional utensils on the bed beside him, and then half filled a plastic glass with water from a carafe. Then she handed him the tiny paper cup. There was one very small pill, half the size of an aspirin in it.

"What's this?"

"Demerol."

"Will it work?"

"The doctor apparently thinks so."

Matt shrugged, then reached into the cup for the pill. He lost it between the cup and his lip.

The nurse shook her head, and then when Matt was unable to find it in the folds of his sheets found it for him.

"Watch," she said. She picked up the cup, stuck out her tongue, and then mimed upending the pill cup onto her tongue.

"Think you can manage that?"

"I'll give it a good shot."

She dropped the pill into the paper cup and handed it to him.

"How do I know you don't have some loathsome disease?" Matt asked.

"She said you'd probably be trouble," the nurse said.

"Who's she?"

"Margaret McCarthy," the nurse said. "Trust me. Take your pill."

He succeeded in getting the pill into his mouth and then swallowing it.

"How do you know Margaret?"

"We're going for our BSs at Temple together," the nurse said.

"Are you going to tell me what to call you, or am I going to have to ask Margaret?"

"You can call me Nurse," she said.

"Here I am, in pain, and you won't even tell me your name?"

"Lari," she said. "Lari Matsi."

"What is that, Estonian?

"*Estonian?* No. Finnish."

"I never met a Finn before."

"Now you have."

"How come Margaret mentioned me?"

"She knew I worked here, and she called me and said you and Prince Charming were buddies."

"How long is that little pill going to take to work?"

"A couple of minutes. You do know how to work those?" She nodded at the bedpans. "You won't need a demonstration?"

"No."

"Ring when you're through," she said. "They'll come take them away for you."

"They'll?"

"I'm a surgical nurse," Lari said. "I've graduated from bedpan handling."

"I see. Then we're just ships passing in the night?"

"I'll be back when the doctor, doctors, come to see you."

She walked out of the room. The rear view was as attractive as the front.

Matt picked up one of the bedpans.

I don't really want to use that goddamn thing, and I really don't want to use the other flat one.

He looked around the room. There were two doors. One of them had to be a bathroom.

He tried moving his wounded leg. It hurt like hell, but he could raise it.

I can stagger over there, hopping on one leg. I don't have to stand on it.

It proved possible, but considerably more painful than he thought it would be. By the time he had arranged himself on the commode, he was covered with a clammy sweat.

The telephone began to ring.

Goddammit! That's probably Dad. He said he would call when he finally got to the office. Well, I'll just have to call him back.

After a long time, it stopped ringing.

Three minutes later, he pushed open the bathroom door, which took considerably more effort than he thought it would.

Lari was standing there.

"I thought you would probably try something stupid like that," she said. "Put your arm around my shoulders."

Using Lari as a crutch, he made his way back to the bed. She watched him get in and then rearranged the thin sheet over him.

"Does this mean I don't get a gold star to take home to Mommy?"

"I'd have gotten you a crutch if you had asked for one," she said. "If that was uncomfortable, it's your own fault."

"Uncomfortable, certainly, but far more dignified."

Finally, he got her to smile. He liked her smile.

"You should start feeling a little drowsy about now," she said. "That should help the pain."

"I don't suppose I could interest you in waltzing around the room with me again?"

"Not right now, thank you," she said, and smiled again, and left, taking the bedpans with her.

He lowered the head of the bed, and then shut the television off. He was feeling drowsy, but the leg still hurt.

The telephone rang again. He picked it up.

"Dad?"

"No, not Dad," Helene's voice said.

"Oh. Hi!"

"That went far more smoothly than one would have thought, didn't it?"

"I guess."

"It's a good thing I didn't know who he was taking me to see. I just ten minutes ago saw the *Bulletin*."

"I've seen it," he said. "It's not a very good likeness."

"Oh, I think it is. I thought it rather exciting, as a matter of fact. Not as exciting as being in the room with you like that, but exciting."

"Jesus!"

"If I thought there was any way in the world to get away with it, I'd come back. Would you like that?"

"Under the circumstances, it might not be the smartest thing to do."

" 'Faint heart ne'er won fair maiden,' " she quoted.

Matt was trying to find a reply to that when he realized that she had hung up.

"Jesus H. Christ!" he said, and put the phone back in its cradle.

He recalled the pressure of her breast against his arm, and

her fingers at the back of his neck. And other things about Helene.

He looked down at his middle.

"Well," he said aloud. "At least that's not broken."

Martha Washington was sitting on the narrow end of the grand piano in the living room looking out the window when she heard the key in the door and knew her husband had come home.

She looked at her watch, saw that it was a few minutes after three, and then turned to look toward the door. She didn't get off the piano.

"Hi!" she called.

Jason came into the living room pulling off his overcoat. He threw it onto the couch. When it was wet, as it was now, that tended to stain the cream-colored leather, but Martha decided this was not the time to mention that for the five hundredth time.

"How come I get hell when I set a glass on there, and you can sit on it?" he greeted her en route to the whiskey cabinet.

"Because *I* don't drip on the wood and make stains," she said.

He turned from the whiskey cabinet and smiled. That pleased her.

"How's Matt?" she asked.

"Apparently he was lucky; he's not seriously hurt. I haven't seen him."

"Why not?"

"Because when I went to the hospital this morning it looked like Suburban station at half past five. Even Farnsworth Stillwell—*and* his wife—were there. I thought I'd have a chance to go back, but I haven't."

"Are you going to tell me what happened? That picture of Matt in the paper was horrifying!"

"From what I have been able to piece together, he wasn't even supposed to be there, but he showed up when they were getting ready to go, and Wohl sent him with Mickey O'Hara. They were in an alley behind the bastard's house, waiting for the detectives and the cops to go in, when the sonofabitch showed up in the alley, shooting. He was a lousy shot, fortunately—''

"He got Matt!"

"With a ricochet, it hit a brick wall first. If it had hit Matt first, he'd be—a lot worse off.''

"He was covered with blood in the newspaper.''

"Minor wound, scratch, really, in the forehead. The head tends to bleed a lot.''

"The radio said the man died," Martha said. "Poor Matt.''

" 'Poor Matt' ?"

"It will bother him, having taken someone's life.''

"The last one he shot didn't bother him that I could see.''

"That you could see.''

Jason's face wrinkled as he considered that.

"Touché," he said, finally.

"I got him a box of candy. I didn't know what else to get him.''

"You could have given him the picture of the naked lady. I know he'd like that.''

She looked at him a minute, smiled, and said, "Okay. I will.''

"Really?"

"Why not?" she asked.

"You're not thinking of taking it to the hospital?''

"Are we going to the hospital?''

"Yeah. Well, I thought maybe if you took off early and were here when I came home, you might want to go up there with me.''

"I was about to go without you," she said. "You didn't call all day.''

"I was busy," he said, and then added, "I found Tony.''

"Oh?"

"In a bar in Roxborough. Specifically, in the back of a bar in Roxborough.''

"Oh, honey!"

"I was right on the edge of taking him to a hospital. God, he looked awful. But I managed to get him to go home. I put him to bed. I just hope he stays there.''

"Does Inspector Wohl know?''

He shook his head no.

"Well, maybe with all this—''

"He won't find out? You underestimate Peter Wohl.''

"What's going to happen?"

"Drunks don't really reform until they hit bottom. Tony's pretty close to the bottom. Maybe I should have left him there and let him face Wohl. Maybe that would straighten him out."

"You know you couldn't do that."

"No," he agreed.

"The picture's in the spare bedroom."

"You really want to take it to the hospital?"

"If it will make him feel better, why not?"

When Jason and Martha Washington got off the elevator carrying the oil painting of the naked voluptuous lady, Jason found that Officer Matthew M. Payne had, in addition to the two uniformed cops guarding his door, other visitors, none of whom he was, in the circumstances, pleased to see.

Chief Inspector Matt Lowenstein and Staff Inspector Peter Wohl were standing in the corridor outside Matt's room, in conversation with a tall, angular man wearing a tweed jacket, a trench coat, gray flannel slacks, loafers, and the reserved collar affected by members of the clergy.

Lowenstein had seen them; there was no option of getting back on the elevator.

"Chief," Jason said.

"I'm glad you're here. I was about to suggest to Inspector Wohl that we try to find you," Lowenstein said, then changed his tone of voice from business to social: "Hello, Martha. It's been a long time."

"How are you, Chief Lowenstein?" Martha asked, giving him her hand.

"Reverend Coyle, may I introduce some other friends of Matt Payne's? Detective and Mrs. Jason Washington."

"That's *Sergeant* Washington, Chief," Wohl corrected him. "How are you, Martha?"

"Christ," Lowenstein said. "That's right, I forgot. Well, let me then be among the last to congratulate you, Jason."

"I'm very pleased to meet you," the Reverend H. Wadsworth Coyle said, enthusiastically pumping their hands in turn.

"Reverend Coyle," Lowenstein said, "has been telling us that he was Matt's spiritual adviser at Episcopal Academy—"

"Yes, indeed," Coyle interrupted him. "And just as soon as I heard of this terrible, terrible accident, I—"

"—so perhaps you had better explain what that picture is you're carrying," Lowenstein concluded.

Wohl looked amused.

"Inspector Wohl has one very much like this, Reverend." Martha Washington replied, "which Matt admires. He asked me to see if I could find him one as much like it as possible, and I have. I thought it might cheer him up."

Wohl no longer looked amused, but Lowenstein did.

"Very nice," the Reverend Coyle said, not very convincingly.

"They gave him something, for the pain, I suppose," Wohl said. "He's sleeping. We're waiting for him to wake up. But I think you could stick your head in, maybe he's just dozing."

"Martha," Lowenstein said, "your husband is not the silent gumshoe of legend. Why don't you stick your head in? That way, if Matt's asleep, he'll stay that way."

"Perhaps the both of us?" the Reverend Coyle said.

"Go on, Reverend," Lowenstein said. There was something in his eyes that kept Jason from challenging the "suggestion" not to go in.

As Mrs. Washington, trailed by Reverend Coyle, disappeared into Matt's room, Lowenstein took a paper from his pocket and handed it to Washington.

ISLAMIC LIBERATION ARMY

There Is No God But God,
And Allah Is His Name

PRESS RELEASE:

Allah has taken our Beloved Brother Abu Ben Mohammed into his arms in Heaven. Blessed be the Name of Allah!

But the cold-blooded murder of our Beloved Brother Abu Ben Mohammed by the infidel lackeys of the infidel sons of Zion, who call themselves police, shall not go unpunished!

Death to the murderers of our Brother!

Death to those who bear false witness against the Brothers of the Islamic Liberation Army in their Holy War against the infidel sons of Zion, who for too long have victimized the African Brothers (Islamic and other) and other minorities of Philadelphia.

Death to the Zionist oppressors of our people and the murderers who call themselves police!

Freedom Now!

Abdullah el Sikkim
Chief of Staff
Islamic Liberation Army

Washington read it, and then looked at Lowenstein.

"Sent by messenger to Mickey O'Hara at the *Bulletin*," Lowenstein said. "And to the other papers, and the TV and radio stations."

"The question, obviously, is, who sent this?" Washington said. "And the immediate next question is, is it for real, or are we dealing with kooks?"

"I think we have to work on the presumption that there's something to it," Wohl said.

"What's something?"

"The first question that occurred to me was who did we miss, maybe how many, when we picked up those people this morning?" Wohl went on.

"There were eight people in the store; eight people Mr. Monahan identified from photographs; the eight people we had warrants for."

"There was probably, almost certainly," Lowenstein said, "a ninth man. Who drove the van."

"*Muhammed* el Sikkim is a guy named Randolph George Dawes," Washington said. "Little guy." He held up his hand at shoulder level. "Who is this *Abdullah* el Sikkim? His brother?"

"Dawes has two brothers," Lowenstein said. "One of them is nine years old. The other one's in Lewisburg."

"He could be the one guy we missed, the one driving the van," Wohl said. "Or he could be any one of any number of people we don't know about."

"Well, whoever he is, he's guilty of plagiarism," Washington said. "A lot of this," he dropped his eyes to the sheet of paper and read, " 'infidel sons of Zion, who for too long have victimized the African Brothers (Islamic and other) and other minorities of Philadelphia,' and some more of it too, I think, is right out of the first press release."

"He also used the phrase 'death to' more than once," Lowenstein said.

"He says 'murderers,' not 'murderer,' " Wohl injected. "Does that mean he doesn't know Matt shot Dawes?"

"It was all over the papers, and TV too," Washington said. "I can't see how he can't know. Are we taking this as a bona fide threat to Matt?"

"It seems to me the first thing we have to do is find this *Abdullah* el Sikkim," Lowenstein said. "Did you get anything out of the ones we arrested about more people being involved?"

"I'm letting them stew until after supper," Washington replied. "I'm going to start running them through lineups at half past six."

"Why haven't you done that already?" Lowenstein demanded.

"Because I think I will get more out of them after they have been locked up, all alone, all day," Washington explained. "The adrenaline will have worn off. They may even be a little worried about their futures by half past six. That's the way I called it, but I could go down there right now, Chief, if you or Inspector Wohl think I should."

"You're a sergeant now, Jason, a supervisor, but since you don't have anybody but Tony Harris to supervise, I guess it's your job." Wohl said. "I won't tell you how to do it."

Washington met his eyes.

"Are you going to tell Matt about this?" he asked.

"The question we wanted to ask you," Wohl said, "for quotation, I think I should tell you, at a five o'clock meeting with the commissioner, was, do we take this thing seriously? Are they really going to try to kill Matt, and/or the witnesses, which right now is Monahan, period?"

"So you asked *us* if we thought it should be taken seriously," Lowenstein said. "Why the hell are we letting these scumbags get to us, the three of us, this way?"

"And the next question was going to be," Wohl went on, "did Monahan go ahead and make a positive ID of these people after the threat was made? Obviously, since you're not going to run the lineup until half past six, that can't be answered.''

"The reason the three of us are upset by this," Washington said thoughtfully, "is that as much as we don't want to believe it, as incredible as this whole Islamic Liberation Army thing sounds, we have a gut feeling that these people are perfectly serious. They *are* just crazy enough, or dumb enough, to try to kill Matt and Monahan.''

Lowenstein took a fresh cigar, as thick as his thumb and six inches long, from his pocket. He bit off the end, and then took a long time lighting it properly.

"Harry will be back in a minute," he said finally. "I sent him to have a talk with Hospital Security. He's a retired Internal Affairs sergeant. I want whatever he can give us to keep this under control.''

Detective Harry McElroy was Chief Inspector Lowenstein's driver.

"I want to get plainclothes people to guard Matt," Wohl said. "A lot of uniforms are going to signal these idiots—and the public—that we're taking them seriously.''

"You mean you don't want us to look scared," Lowenstein said. "OK. Good point. But protecting Monahan is something else. You did intend, Peter, to put Highway on him and his wife twenty-four hours a day?''

"Special Operations will continue to provide two police officers to guard Mr. Monahan and his wife around the clock," Wohl said, and then when he saw the look on Lowenstein's face went on: "To take the ACT people off that job—they *are* police officers, Chief—as a result of this 'press release' would both signal the Liberation Army that we're afraid of them, and send the message to the ACT cops that I don't have any faith in them.''

"I hope your touching faith is justified, Peter," Lowenstein said. "If they get to Monahan, either kill him, or scare him so that he won't testify, this whole thing goes down the tube, the scumbags go free, and the whole police department, not just you, will have egg all over its face.''

"I intend to protect Mr. Monahan," Wohl said, a little sharply. "I'm even thinking about shotguns.''

"You have enough ex–Stakeout people who are shotgun qualified?" Lowenstein asked.

Unlike most major city police departments, which routinely

equip police officers with shotguns, Philadelphia does not. Only the specially armed Stakeout unit is issued shotguns.

"I've got people finding out," Wohl said.

"I'll call the range at the Police Academy, Peter," Lowenstein said. "Have ten of your people there in an hour. The Range Training Officers will be set up to train and certify them in no more than two hours."

"Thank you," Wohl said, simply.

"I hope Harry gets something from hospital security," Washington said. "How long is Matt going to be in here, anyway?"

"Not long," Wohl said. "They'll probably let him go tomorrow."

"That soon?" Washington asked, surprised.

"The new theory is that the more he moves around, the quicker he'll heal," Lowenstein said.

The door to Matt's room opened.

"Matt's awake," Martha Washington announced.

"Jason," Lowenstein said quickly, softly, "when somebody asks, as somebody surely will, how you're coming with the ones we have locked up, could I say that I don't know, the last I heard you were off to see Arthur X?"

"You're reading my mind again, Chief," Washington said.

"And there's one more thing you could do that would help, Jason," Wohl said.

"What's that?"

"Find Tony Harris and sober him up. I'd like him in on this."

Washington's face registered momentary surprise, then he met Wohl's eyes.

"I've found him. I'm working on sobering him up."

"Are you going to come in here or not?" Martha asked.

The three men filed into Matt's room. He was sitting up in bed.

"I'll be running along now," the Reverend Coyle said. "The hospital doesn't like to have a patient have too many visitors at once."

"Thank you for coming to see me," Matt said politely.

"Don't be silly," the Reverend Coyle said. "You feel free to call me, Matt, whenever you want to talk this over."

"I will, thank you very much," Matt said.

Jason Washington caught Martha's eye and made a barely perceptible gesture.

"I'll be outside," she said.

Matt looked from one to the other.

Lowenstein finally broke the silence.

"How much dope are you on?"

"One tiny little pill of Demerol whenever they feel I should have one."

"Could you do without it?"

"Why?"

"Your judgment is impaired when you're on Demerol."

"Am I going to need my judgment in here?"

Lowenstein handed him the press release.

Matt read it, and looked at Lowenstein.

"Jesus, are they serious?" he asked.

Lowenstein shrugged.

"I think we should err on the side of caution," Wohl said. "In this case meaning having a pistol in your bedside table might be a good idea."

Matt felt a cramp in his stomach.

Jesus, is that fear?

"The sergeant from the Mobile Crime Lab took my pistol," Matt said, desperately hoping his voice did not betray him, that he sounded like a matter-of-fact cop explaining something.

Simultaneously, Chief Inspector Lowenstein and Staff Inspector Wohl reached into the pockets of their topcoats and came out with identical Smith & Wesson Chief's Special snub-nosed .38 Special caliber revolvers.

Matt took the one Wohl had extended to him, butt first. He laid it on the sheet and covered it with his hand.

"One should be enough, don't you think?" he said. "You just happened to have spares with you, right?"

He's frightened, Wohl thought. *He's cracking wise, but he's frightened.* Then he grew angry. *Those dirty sonsofbitches!*

"Harry McElroy is arranging with hospital security to make sure nobody even knows where you are in here, much less gets close to you," Lowenstein said. "I think that threat is pure bullshit. But better safe than sorry."

"Yes, of course," Matt said.

"Just make sure no one knows you have a weapon," Wohl said. "The hospital would throw a fit."

"You'll be out of here tomorrow, or the day after," Washington said. "Even if this is not fantasy on the part of these people, they won't look for you in Wallingford. You are going to Wallingford, right?"

"I was, but not now," Matt said. "Christ, I don't want my family to hear about this!"

"It'll be in the papers," Wohl said. "They'll hear about it."

"I'll go to my apartment," Matt said, "not Wallingford."

"You in the phone book?" Lowenstein asked.

"No, sir."

"What I think this is intended to do, Payne," Lowenstein went on, "is frighten Mr. Monahan. I think they're trying to get him to think that if they can threaten a cop—You take my meaning?"

"Yes, sir."

"I can't believe they'd come after you. If they were serious about revenge, they wouldn't have given a warning."

"Yes, sir."

On the other hand, Matt thought, *if they did kill me, that would really send Mr. Monahan a message.*

The pain in his stomach had gone as quickly as it had come.

Jesus, that Demerol must be working. I'm not even afraid anymore. This is more like watching a cops-and-robbers show on TV. You know it's not real.

And then he had a sudden, very clear image of the orange muzzle blasts in the alley, and heard again the crack of Abu Ben Mohammed's pistol, and felt again getting slammed in the calf and forehead, and the fear, and the cramp in his stomach, came back.

"I'll have a talk with your father, Matt," Wohl said. "And put this in perspective. If you'd like me to."

"Please," Matt said.

"I'm sure McElroy has arranged with the switchboard to put through only calls from your family and friends," Lowenstein said. "But some calls may get through—"

"Calls from whom?" Matt interrupted.

"I was thinking of the press, those bastards are not above saying they're somebody's brother, but now that I think of it, these people may try to call you too."

"In either case, hang up," Wohl said. "No matter what you would say, it would be the wrong thing."

"Yes, sir."

"And above all," Wohl said, "as the hangman said as he led the condemned man up the scaffold steps, try not to worry about this."

"Oh, God!" Washington groaned, and then they all laughed.

A little too heartily, Matt thought. *That wasn't that funny.*

SIXTEEN

The Honorable Jerry Carlucci, mayor of the City of Philadelphia, sat in the commissioner's chair at the head of the commissioner's conference table in the commissioner's conference room on the third floor of the Roundhouse rolling one of Chief Inspector Matt Lowenstein's big black cigars in his fingers. His Honor was visibly not in a good mood.

One indication of this was the manner in which he had come by the cigar.

"Matt, I don't suppose you have a spare cigar you could let me have, do you?" the mayor had politely asked.

Lowenstein knew from long experience that when The Dago was carefully watching his manners, it was a sure sign that he was no more than a millimeter or two away from throwing a fit.

"Thank you very much, Matt," the mayor said very politely.

Police Commissioner Taddeus Czernich, a large, florid-faced man sitting to the mayor's immediate left, next to Chief Inspector Dennis V. Coughlin, produced a gas-flame cigarette lighter, turned it on, and offered it to the mayor.

"No, thank you, Commissioner," the mayor said, very politely, "I'm sure Matt will offer me a match."

He turned to Lowenstein, sitting beside Peter Wohl on the other side of the table. Lowenstein handed him a large kitchen match and the mayor then took a good thirty seconds to get the cigar going. Finally, exhaling cigar smoke as he approvingly examined the coal on the cigar, he said, very politely, "Well, since we are all here, do you think we should get going? Why don't you just rough me in on this, Commissioner, and then I can ask specific questions of the others, if there's something I don't quite understand."

"Yes, sir," Commissioner Czernich said. "Should I start, sir, with the Goldblatt robbery and murder?"

"No, start with what happened at five o'clock this morning. I know what happened at Goldblatt's."

"Chief Lowenstein asked the assistance of Inspector Wohl, that is, Special Operations, in arresting eight men identified by a witness as the doers of the Goldblatt job. They obtained warrants through the district attorney. The idea was to make the arrests simultaneously, and at a time when there would be the least risk to the public and the officers involved, that is at five o'clock in the morning."

"And the operation presumably had your blessing, Commissioner?"

"I didn't know about it until it was over, Mr. Mayor."

"You and Lowenstein had a falling out?" Carlucci demanded, looking from one to the other. "You're not talking to each other? What?"

"It was a routine arrest, arrests, Jerry," Lowenstein said. "There was no reason to bring the commissioner in on it."

"Just for the record, Matt, correct me if I'm wrong, this is the first time we've arrested the Islamic Liberation Army, right? Or any other kind of army, right? So how is that routine?"

"Just because eight *schwartzers* call themselves an army doesn't make them an army," Lowenstein said. "So far as I'm concerned, these guys are thieves and murderers, period."

"Yeah, well, tell that to the newspapers," Carlucci said. "The newspapers think they're an army."

"Then the newspapers are wrong," Lowenstein said.

"And it never entered your mind, Peter," Carlucci asked,

turning to Wohl, "to run this past the commissioner and get his approval?"

"Mr. Mayor, I thought of it like Chief Lowenstein did. It was a routine arrest."

"If it was a routine arrest—don't hand me any of your bull-shit, Peter, I was commanding Highway when you were in high school—Homicide detectives backed up by district cops would have picked these people up, one at a time. Did you see what the *Daily News* said?"

"No, sir."

The mayor jammed his cigar in his mouth, opened his brief-case, took out a sheet of Xerox paper, and read, "They said, 'A small army of heavily armed police had their first battle with the Islamic Liberation Army early this morning. When it was over, Abu Ben Mohammed was fatally wounded and Po-lice Officer Matthew M. Payne, who two months ago shot to death the Northwest Philadelphia serial rapist, was in Frank-ford Hospital suffering from multiple gunshot wounds. The po-lice took seven members of the ILA prisoner.'"

He looked at Wohl.

"I didn't see that," Wohl said.

"Maybe you should start reading the newspapers, Peter."

"Yes, sir."

"Just don't give me any more bullshit about a routine arrest. If this thing had been handled like a routine arrest none of this would have happened."

"You're right," Lowenstein said angrily. "Absolutely right. If I had tried to pick up these scumbags one at a time, using district cops, we'd have three, four, a half dozen cops in Frank-ford Hospital, or maybe the morgue. And probably that many civilians."

"Yeah?"

"Yeah. We took a goddamn arsenal full of guns away from these people. The only reason they didn't get to use them was because we hit them all at once. If we had taken them one at a time, by the time we got to the second or third one, they would either have been long gone, in Kansas City or some-place, if we were lucky. Or, if we were unlucky, they would have done what this scumbag Stevens did, come out shooting."

There were very few people in the Police Department, for that matter in city government, who would have dared to tell the mayor in scornful sarcasm that he was right, absolutely right, and then explain in detail to him why he was wrong. Matt Lowenstein was one of them. But there was doubt in the minds of everyone else in the conference room that he was going to get away with it this time.

He and the mayor glared at each other for a full fifteen seconds.

"Is that his name? Stevens? The dead one?" the mayor finally asked, almost conversationally.

"Charles David Stevens," Lowenstein furnished.

The mayor turned his attention to Staff Inspector Wohl again: "Presumably you were aware of this 'arsenal of weapons'? That being the case, how come you didn't use Highway?"

"I didn't want the *Ledger* complaining about excessive force by 'Carlucci's Jackbooted Gestapo,' " Wohl replied evenly. "Highway was alerted, in case they would be needed, and there were also stakeout units available. Neither was needed, which was fine with me; I didn't want an early morning gun battle."

Carlucci thought that over for a long moment before replying: "I'm not sure I would have taken that kind of a chance, Peter."

"We also have to submit quarterly reports to the Justice Department on how we're spending the ACT Grant funds. I thought that reporting that ACT-funded cops had assisted Homicide in the arrest of eight individuals charged with murder and armed robbery would look good."

"I still think I would have used Highway," the mayor said. "You *did* have a gun battle."

"I haven't had a chance to figure that out yet," Wohl said. "I don't think Stevens spotted the Homicide detective. Possibilities are that he got up to take a leak, and looked out his window, just as the units were moving into place."

"You said possibilities."

"Or somebody saw all the activity at the school playground, or as they were moving from the playground, and called Stevens."

"Somebody who?"

"Maybe the same somebody who issued the second press release."

"So you don't have all of them?"

"No. What Jason Washington is doing, right now, is trying

to find out how many there are. He hopes Arthur X will tell him.''

''What does Intelligence have to say about these people? Or Organized Crime?'' Carlucci asked.

''Intelligence has nothing on the Islamic Liberation Army, period,'' Lowenstein answered. ''And until they pulled this job, none of these people did anything that would make them of interest to Organized Crime. They had their names, or some of them, but with no ties to anyone serious. They're—or they were—small-time thieves.''

''Czernich,'' the mayor said, ''maybe you'd better have a talk with Intelligence. I find it hard to believe that one day last week, out of the clear blue sky, these bastards said, 'Okay, we're now the Islamic Liberation Army.' Intelligence should have something on them.''

''Yes, sir,'' Commissioner Czernich said.

''But you are,'' the mayor said, looking at Lowenstein, ''taking this second so-called press release seriously?''

''I don't think we should ignore it,'' Lowenstein replied.

''The newspapers aren't going to ignore it, you can bet your ass on that,'' Carlucci said.

''There's almost certainly at least one more of them,'' Wohl said. ''Somebody was driving the van. Washington maybe can get a lead on him after he runs the seven of them through lineups.''

''He hasn't done that yet?'' Carlucci asked incredulously.

''He wanted them to have all day to consider their predicament. He'll start the lineups at half past six.''

''There was an implied threat against Matt Payne in that second press release,'' Chief Inspector Dennis V. Coughlin said. It was the first time he had spoken. ''How are you going to handle that?''

''Not specifically,'' the mayor said. ''What it said was—'' he went into his briefcase again for another photocopy and then read, '' 'Death to the murderers of our Brother.' Murderers, plural, not Payne by name.''

''Maybe that was before he knew Matt shot him,'' Coughlin said.

''Denny, I know how you feel about that boy—'' Carlucci said gently.

''Chief, he's a cop,'' Wohl interrupted, ''and I don't want

to give these people the satisfaction of thinking that they have scared us to the point where we are protecting a cop—''

"He's in a goddamn hospital bed!" Coughlin flared. "I don't give a good goddamn what these scumbags think."

"We had a talk with hospital security," Lowenstein said. "We changed his room. They're screening his phone calls. And Peter loaned him a gun."

"—And," Wohl went on, "and, purely as a routine administrative matter, while he is recovering, I'm going to ask Captain Pekach of Highway to rearrange the duty schedules of Officers McFadden and Martinez so that they can spend some time, off duty, in civilian clothes, with Matt."

Coughlin looked at him, with gratitude in his eyes.

"And I wouldn't be surprised if other friends of his looked in on him from time to time," Wohl said.

"You, for example?" Carlucci asked, chuckling, "and maybe Denny?"

"Yes, sir. And maybe Sergeant Washington."

"Satisfied, Denny?" the mayor asked.

"I never thought I'd see the day in Philadelphia, Jerry," Coughlin said, "when scumbags would not only threaten a cop's life, but send out a press release announcing it."

"I think the press release is bullshit," Lowenstein said. "I think it's intended to scare Monahan."

"He the witness? Will it?" Carlucci asked.

"He's the only one with any balls," Lowenstein said. "And no. I don't think he'll scare."

"But we can forget the others, right? So we'd better hope this one doesn't scare. Or get himself killed."

"I haven't given up on the other witnesses," Lowenstein said. "Washington hasn't talked to them yet. I mean *really* talked to them."

"Don't hold your breath," Carlucci said.

"It seems to me," Commissioner Czernich said, "that our first priority is the protection of Mr. Monahan."

The mayor looked at him and shook his head.

"You figured that out all by yourself, did you?" he asked.

Then he closed his briefcase and stood up.

There is a price, Wohl thought, *for being appointed police commissioner.*

Commissioner Czernich waited until the mayor had left the conference room. Then, his face still showing signs of the flush

that had come to it when Carlucci had humiliated him, he
pointed at Lowenstein and Wohl.

"That's the last time either one of you will pull something
like that harebrained scheme you pulled this morning without
coming to me and getting my permission. The last time. Am
I making myself clear?"

"Yes, sir," Wohl said.

"Whatever you say, Commissioner," Lowenstein said.

"And I want Highway in on the protection of Mr. Monahan,
Wohl. We can't take any chances with him."

"Yes, sir."

Commissioner Czernich looked sternly at each man, and
then marched out of his conference room.

"Remember that, Peter," Coughlin said. "No more harebrained schemes are to be pulled without the commissioner's
permission."

"Jesus," Wohl said, and then laughed, "I thought that's
what he said."

"Well, it made him happy," Lowenstein said. "It gave him
a chance to give an order all by himself."

"*Two* orders," Coughlin replied. "You heard what he told
Peter. He wants Highway in on protecting Monahan."

"That's the exception proving the rule. That makes sense."

"I'm not so sure," Wohl said.

"Now you're not making sense," Lowenstein said.

"The first priority, agreeing with the commissioner, is to
protect the Monahans. The second priority is to make the Monahans feel protected. I decided the best way I could do that,
during the day, when Mr. Monahan's at work, is with two
plainclothes officers in an unmarked car. A blue-and-white sitting in front of Goldblatt's all day would give people the impression we're afraid of the ILA—" He interrupted himself.
"That's dangerous. Did you hear what I said?"

"I heard," Lowenstein said.

"I called these scumbags the ILA. I don't want to get in the
habit of doing that."

"No, we don't," Coughlin agreed.

"There is another car, a blue-and-white, with uniformed
officers, at his house," Wohl went on. "There will be one
there, twenty-four hours a day, from now on. That will reassure Mrs. Monahan, and if an associate of *these felons* should

happen to ride by the Monahan house, they will see the blue-and-white.''

"Okay," Lowenstein said. "I see your reasoning. So what are you going to do?''

"Obey the order he gave me," Wohl said. "Have a Highway car meet Washington and the unmarked car at Goldblatt's and go with them when they bring Mr. Monahan here to the Round-house. Unless I heard the commissioner incorrectly, he only said he wanted 'Highway *in* on protecting Mr. Monahan.' ''

"You're devious, Peter. Maybe you *will* get to be commissioner one day.''

"I'm doing the job the best way I can see to do it," Wohl said.

"I think you're doing it right," Coughlin said.

"We won that encounter in there, Peter," Lowenstein said. "I think Czernich expected both of us to be drawn and quartered. I think Czernich is disappointed. So watch out for him.''

"Yeah," Wohl said.

"I'd appreciate being kept up-to-date on what's happening," Coughlin said.

"I'll have Washington call you after the line-up. Lineups.''

"Lineups. Lineups, for Christ's sake," Lowenstein said, chuckling. He touched Wohl's arm, nodded at Coughlin, and walked out of the room.

"I appreciate your concern for Matt, Peter," Coughlin said.

"Don't be silly.''

"Well, I do," Coughlin said, and then he left.

Wohl started to follow him, but as he passed through the commissioner's office, the commissioner's secretary asked him how Matt was doing, and he stopped to give her a report.

In the elevator on the way to the lobby, he remembered that he had promised Matt to have a word with his father. He stopped at the counter, asked for a phone book, and called Mawson, Payne, Stockton, McAdoo & Lester.

Brewster C. Payne gave him the impression he had expected him to call. He asked where Wohl was, and then suggested they have a drink in the Union League Club.

"Thank you, I can use one," Peter said.

"I think we can both use several," Payne said. "I'll see you there in a few minutes.''

Wohl started to push the telephone back to the corporal on duty, and then changed his mind and dialed Dave Pekach's number and explained why a Highway car was going to have to be at Goldblatt's.

Lari Matsi came into Matt Payne's, carrying a small tray with a tiny paper cup on it.

"How's it going?" she asked.

"I'm watching *The Dating Game* on the boob tube. That tell you anything?"

"Maybe you have more culture than I've been giving you credit for," she said. "Anyway, take this and in five minutes you won't care what's on TV."

"I don't need that, thank you."

"It's not a suggestion. It's on orders."

"I still don't want it," he said.

She was standing by the side of the bed. She looked down at it, and grew serious.

"I don't think you're supposed to have that in here."

He followed her eyes, and saw that she was looking at the revolver Wohl had given him, its butt peeking out from a fold in the thin cotton blanket.

He took the revolver and put it inside the box of Kleenex on the bedside table.

"Okay?" he asked.

"No. Not okay. You want to tell me what's going on here?"

"Like what? I'm a cop. Cops have guns."

"They moved you in here, and your name is not Matthews, which is the name on the door."

"I don't suppose you'd believe that I'm really a rock-and-roll star trying to avoid my fans?"

"Do they really think somebody's going to try to—do something to you?"

"No. But better safe than sorry."

"I suppose this is supposed to be exciting," she said. "But what I really feel is that I don't like it at all."

"I'm sorry you saw the gun," he said. "Can we drop it there?"

"You don't want the Demerol because it will make you drowsy, right?"

He met her eyes, but didn't reply.

"This was going to be your last one, anyway," Lari said. "I could get you some aspirin, if you want."

"Please."

"Are you in pain?"

"No."

"If anybody asks, you took it, okay?" she asked. "It would be easier that way."

She went to the bathroom, and in a moment, with a mighty roar, the toilet flushed.

"Thank you," he said when she came out.

"I'll get the aspirin," she said, and went out.

She came back in a minute with a small tin of Bayer aspirin.

"These are mine," she said. "You didn't get them from me. Okay?"

"Thank you."

"There's a security guard at the nurse's station, I guess you know. He's giving everybody who gets off the elevator the once-over."

"No, I didn't."

"In the morning, they're going to send you a physical therapist, to show you how to use crutches," she said. "When she tells you the more you use your leg, the more quickly it will feel better, trust her."

"Okay."

"I'll see you around, maybe, sometime."

"Not in the morning?"

"No. I won't be coming back here. I'm only filling in."

"I'd really like to see you around, no maybe, sometime. Could I call you?"

"There's a rule against that."

"You don't know what I have in mind, so how can there be a rule against that?"

"I mean, giving your phone number to a patient."

"I'm not just any old patient. I'm Margaret's Prince Charming's buddy. And, anyway, don't you ever do something you're not supposed to?"

"Not very often," she said, "and something tells me this is one of the times I should follow the rules."

She walked out of the room.

Matt watched the door close slowly after her.

"Damn!" he said aloud.

The door swung open again.

"My father is the only Henry Matsi in the phone book," Lari announced, "but I should tell you I'm hardly ever home."

Then she was gone again.

"Henry Matsi, Henry Matsi, Henry Matsi, Henry Matsi," Matt said aloud, to engrave it in his memory.

A minute or so later the door opened again, but it was not Lari. A chubby, determinedly cheerful woman bearing a tray announced, "Here's our supper."

"What are we having?"

"A *nice* piece of chicken," she said. "Primarily."

She took the gray cover off a plate with a flourish.

"And steamed veggies."

"Wow!" Matt said enthusiastically. "And what do you suppose that gray stuff in the cup is?"

"Custard."

"I was afraid of that."

Five minutes later, as he was trying to scrape the custard off his teeth and the roof of his mouth with his tongue, the door opened again.

A familiar face, to which Matt could not instantly attach a name, appeared.

"Feel up to a couple of visitors?"

"Sure, come on in."

Walter Davis, special agent in charge, Philadelphia Office, FBI, came into the room, trailed by A-SAC (Criminal Affairs) Frank Young.

"We won't stay long, but we wanted to come by and see if there was anything we could do for you," Davis said as Matt finally realized who they were.

You could tell me you just arrested the guy who wants to get me for shooting Charles D. Stevens. That would be nice.

What the hell are they doing here? What do they want?

Mr. Albert J. Monahan was talking with Mr. Phil Katz when Sergeant Jason Washington came through the door of Goldblatt & Sons Credit Furniture & Appliances, Inc., on South Street. Mr. Monahan smiled and seemed pleased to see Sergeant Washington. Mr. Katz did not.

"Good evening," Washington said.

"How are you, Detective Washington?" Mr. Monahan replied, pumping his hand.

Mr. Katz nodded.

"I guess you heard—" Washington began.

"We heard," Katz said.

"—we have the people who were here locked up," Washington continued. "And I hope Detective Pelosi called to tell you I was coming by?"

"Yes, he did," Monahan said.

"What I thought you meant," Katz said, "was, had we heard about what the Islamic Liberation Army had to say about people 'bearing false witness.' "

"We really don't think they're an army, Mr. Katz."

Katz snorted.

"Do what you think you have to, Albert," Mr. Katz said, and walked away.

"He's a married man, with kids," Al Monahan said, "I understand how he feels."

"Are you about ready, Mr. Monahan?" Washington asked.

"I've just got to get my coat and hat," Monahan replied. "And then I'll be with you."

Washington watched him walk across the floor toward the rear of the store, and then went to the door and looked out.

Things were exactly as he had set them up. He questioned whether it was really necessary, but Peter Wohl had told him to 'err on the side of caution' and Washington was willing to go along with his concern, not only because, obviously, Wohl was his commanding officer, but also because of all the police brass Washington knew well, Peter Wohl was among the least excitable. He did not, in other words, as Washington thought of it, run around in circles chasing his tail, in the manner of other supervisors of his acquaintance when they were faced with an out-of-the-ordinary situation.

There were three cars parked in front of Goldblatt's. First was the Highway car, then Washington's unmarked car, and finally the unmarked car that carried the two plainclothes officers.

Both Highway cops, one of the plainclothesmen, and the 6th District beat cop were standing by the fender of Washington's car.

"Okay," Mr. Monahan said in Washington's ear, startling him a little.

Washington smiled at him, and led him to the door.

When they stepped outside, one of the Highway cops and the plainclothesmen stepped beside Mr. Monahan. As Washington got behind the wheel of his car, they walked Monahan between the Highway car and Washington's, and installed him in the front seat.

The beat cop, as the Highway cop and the plainclothesmen got in their cars, stepped into the middle of the street and held up his hand, blocking traffic coming east on South Street, so that the three cars could pull away from the curb together.

The Highway car in front of Washington had almost reached South 8th Street and had already turned on his turn signal when Washington saw something dropping out of the sky.

He had just time to recognize it as a bottle, whiskey or ginger ale, that big, then as a bottle on fire, at the neck, when it hit the roof of the Highway car and then bounced off, unbroken, onto South Street, where it shattered.

The Highway car slammed on his brakes, and Washington almost ran into him. As he jammed his hand on the horn, the unmarked car behind him slammed into his bumper.

Washington signaled furiously for the Highway car to get moving. It began to move again the instant there was a sound like a blown-up paper bag being ruptured, and then a puff of orange flame.

Those dirty rotten sonsofbitches!

"Jesus, Mary, and Joseph!" Mr. Monahan said.

Washington's hand found his microphone.

"Keep moving!" he ordered. "The beat cop'll call it in. Go to the Roundhouse."

Washington looked in his mirror. The unmarked car behind him was still moving, already through the puddle of burning gasoline.

"What the hell was it, a fucking Molotov cocktail?" an incredulous voice, probably, Washington thought, one of the Highway guys, came over the radio.

"Can you see, Mr. Monahan, if the car behind us is all right?" he asked.

"It looks okay."

Washington picked up the microphone again.

"Okay. Everything's under control," he said.

In a porcine rectum, he thought, *everything's under control. What the* hell *is going on here? This is* Philadelphia, *not Saigon!*

SEVENTEEN

The tall, trim, simply dressed woman who looked a good deal younger than her years stood for a moment in the door to the lounge of the Union League Club, running her eyes over the people in the room, now crowded with the after-work-before-catching-the-train crowd.

Finally, with a small, triumphant smile, she pointed her finger at a table across the room against the wall.

"There," she announced to her companion.

"I see them," he replied.

She walked to the table, with her companion trailing behind her, and announced her presence by reaching down and picking a squat whiskey glass up from the table.

"I really hope this is not one of those times when you're drinking something chic," she said, taking a healthy swallow.

Mr. Brewster Cortland Payne, who had just set the drink (his third) down after taking a first sip, looked up at his wife and, smiling, got to his feet.

Patricia Payne sat down in one of the heavy wooden chairs.

"I needed that," she said. "Denny has been trying to convince me, with not much success, that we don't have anything to worry about. Has Inspector Wohl been more successful than he has?''

"I hope so," Peter Wohl said. "Good evening, Mrs. Payne. Chief."

"Peter," Chief Inspector Dennis V. Coughlin said. "Brewster."

Brewster C. Payne raised his hand, index finger extended, above his shoulders. The gesture was unnecessary, for a white-jacketed waiter, who provided service based on his own assessment of who really mattered around the place, now that they were letting every Tom, Dick, and Harry in, was already headed for the table.

"Mrs. Payne, what can I get for you?"

"You can get Mr. Payne whatever he was drinking, thank you, Homer," she said. "I just stole his."

"Yes, ma'am," the waiter said with a broad smile. "And you, sir?"

"The same please," Coughlin said.

"To answer your question, Pat," Brewster C. Payne said, "Yes. Peter has been very reassuring."

"Did he reassure you before or after you heard about the Molotov cocktail?" Patricia Payne asked.

"I beg your pardon?"

"I was in the bar of the Bellevue-Stratford, being reassured by Denny," she said, "when Tom Lenihan came running in and said, if I quote him accurately, 'Jesus Christ, Chief, you're not going to believe this. They just threw a Molotov cocktail at the cars guarding Monahan.' "

"My God!" Payne said.

"At that point, I thought I had better get myself reassured by *you*, darling, so I called the office and they said you had come here. So Denny brought me. So how was *your* day?"

Both Wohl and Payne looked at Chief Coughlin, and both shared the same thought, that they had never seen Coughlin looking quite so unhappy.

"Oh, Denny, I'm sorry," Patricia Payne said, laying her hand on his. "That sounded as if I don't trust you, or am I blaming you. I didn't mean that!"

"From what I know now," Coughlin said, "what happened was that when Washington picked up Monahan at Goldblatt's to take him to the Roundhouse, somebody tossed a bottle full of gasoline down from a roof, or out of a window. It bounced off the Highway car, broke when it hit the street, and then caught fire."

"Anyone hurt?" Wohl asked.

"No. The burning gas flowed under a car on South Street and set it on fire."

"Monahan?"

"I got Washington on the radio. He said Monahan was riding with him. They were behind the Highway car, and one of your unmarked cars was behind them. Monahan is all right. He's at the Roundhouse right now. The lineups at the Detention Center will go on as scheduled, as soon as they finish at the Roundhouse."

"What are they doing over there?" Wohl asked.

"I suppose Washington thought that was the best place to go; Central Detectives will want to get some statements, put it all together. And the lab probably wants a look at the Highway car they hit with the bottle. Maybe pick up another car or two to escort them to the Detention Center."

If you were thinking clearly, Peter Wohl, you would not have had to ask that dumb question.

"I think I'd better get over there," Wohl said.

Coughlin nodded.

"Peter, I called Mike Sabara and told him I thought it would be a good idea if he sent a Highway car over to Frankford Hospital. I hope that's all right with you."

"Thank you. That saves me making a phone call," Wohl said. He got to his feet. "Mrs. Payne," he began, and then couldn't think of what to say next.

She looked up at him and smiled.

"Peter—you don't mind if I call you Peter?"

"No, ma'am."

"Peter, as I walked over here with Denny, I thought that I couldn't ask for anyone better than you and Denny to look out for Matt."

"Absolutely," Brewster C. Payne agreed.

"Patty, we'll take care of Matt, don't you worry about that," Denny Coughlin said emotionally.

"Sit down, Peter," Brewster C. Payne said, "and finish your drink. I'm sure that everything that should be done has been done."

"He's right. Sit down, Peter," Chief Coughlin chimed in.

"Right now, both of us would be in the way at the Round-house."

Wohl looked at both of the men, and then at Patricia Payne, and then sat down.

The Police Department records concerning Captain David R. Pekach stated that he was a bachelor, who lived in a Park Drive Manor apartment. Captain Pekach had last spent the night in his apartment approximately five months before, that is to say four days after he had made the acquaintance of Miss Martha Peebles, who resided in a turn-of-the-century mansion set on five acres at 606 Glengarry Lane in Chestnut Hill.

Miss Peebles, who had a certain influence in Philadelphia (according to *Business Week* magazine, her father had owned outright 11.7 percent of the anthracite coal reserves of the United States, among other holdings, all of which he had left to his sole and beloved daughter), had been burglarized several times.

When the police had not only been unable to apprehend the burglar, but also to prevent additional burglaries, she had complained to her legal adviser (and lifelong friend of her father) Brewster Cortland Payne, of Mawson, Payne, Stockton, McAdoo & Lester.

Mr. Payne had had a word with the other founding partner of Mawson, Payne, Stockton, McAdoo & Lester, Colonel J. Dunlop Mawson, who handled the criminal side of their practice. Colonel Mawson had had a word with Police Commissioner Taddeus Czernich about Miss Peebles's problem, and Commissioner Czernich, fully aware that unless Mawson got satisfaction from him, the next call the sonofabitch would make would be to Mayor Carlucci, told him to put the problem from his mind, he personally would take care of it.

Commissioner Czernich had then called Staff Inspector Peter Wohl, commanding officer of the Special Operations Division, and told him he didn't care how he did it, he didn't want to hear of one more incident of any kind at the residence of Miss Martha Peebles, 606 Glengarry Lane, Chestnut Hill.

Staff Inspector Wohl, in turn, turned the problem over to Captain Pekach, using essentially the same phraseology Commissioner Czernich had used when he had called.

Working with Inspector Wohl's deputy, Captain Mike Sabara, Captain Pekach had arranged for Miss Peebles's residence to be placed under surveillance. An unmarked Special Operations car would be parked on Glengarry Lane until the burglar was nabbed, and Highway RPCs would drive past no less than once an hour.

Captain Pekach had then presented himself personally at the Peebles residence, to assure the lady that the Philadelphia Police Department generally and Captain David Pekach personally were doing all that was humanly possible to shield her home from future violations of any kind.

In the course of their conversation, Miss Peebles had said that it wasn't the loss of what already had been stolen, essentially bric-a-brac, that concerned her, but rather the potential theft of her late father's collection of Early American firearms.

Captain Pekach, whose hobby happened to be Early American firearms, asked if he might see the collection. Miss Peebles obliged him.

As she passed him a rather interesting piece, a mint condition U.S. Rifle, model of 1819 with a J.H. Hall action, stamped with the initials of the proving inspector, Zachary Ellsworth Hampden, Captain, Ordnance Corps, later Deputy Chief of Ordnance, their hands touched.

Shortly afterward, Miss Peebles, who was thirty-six, willingly offered her heretofore zealously guarded pearl of great price to Captain Pekach, who was also thirty-six, who took it with what Miss Peebles regarded as exquisite tenderness, and convincing her that she had at last found what had so far eluded her, a true gentleman to share life's joys and sorrows.

And so it was that when Captain David Pekach, after first having personally checked to see that there was a Highway RPC parked outside Goldblatt & Sons Credit Furniture & Appliances, Inc., on South Street, under orders to obey whatever orders Sergeant Jason Washington might issue, left his office at Bustleton and Bowler for the day, he did not head for his official home of record, but rather for 606 Glengarry Lane in Chestnut Hill.

When he approached the house, he reached up to the sun visor and pushed the button that caused the left of the double steel gates to the estate to swing open. Three hundred yards up the cobblestone drive, he stopped his official, unmarked car under the two-car-wide portico to the left of the house and got out. There was a year-old Mercedes roadster, now wearing its steel winter top, in the other lane, pointing down the driveway.

Evans, the elderly, white-haired black butler (who, with his wife had been in the house when Miss Martha had been born, and when both of her parents had died), came out of the house.

"Good evening, Captain," he said. "I believe Miss Martha's upstairs."

"Thank you," Pekach said.

As Pekach went into the house, Evans got behind the wheel of the unmarked car and drove it to the four-car garage, once a stable, a hundred yards from the house.

There was a downstairs sitting room in the house, and an upstairs sitting room. Martha had gotten into the habit of greeting him upstairs with a drink, and some hors d'oeuvres in the upstairs sitting room.

He would have a drink, or sometimes two, and then he would take a shower. Sometimes he would dress after his shower, and they would have another drink and watch the news on television, and then go for dinner, either out or here in the house. And sometimes he would have his shower and he would not get dressed, because Martha had somehow let him know that she would really rather fool around than watch the news on television.

Tonight, obviously, there would be no fooling around. At least not now, if probably later. Martha, when she greeted him with a glass dark with Old Bushmill's and a kiss that was at once decorous and exciting, was dressed to go out. She had on a simple black dress, a double string of pearls, each the size of a pencil eraser, and a diamond and ruby pin in the shape of a pheasant.

"Precious," she said, "I asked Evans to lay out your blazer and gray slacks. I thought you would want to look more or less official, but we're going out for dinner, and I know you don't like to do that in uniform, and the blazer-with-the-police-buttons seemed to be a nice compromise. All right?"

He had called Martha early in the morning, to tell her that Matt Payne, thank God, was not seriously injured. He knew that she would have heard of the shooting, and would be concerned on two levels, first that it was a cop with whom he worked, and second, perhaps more important, that Matt was the son of her lawyer. He told her that he would be a little late getting home; he wanted to put in an appearance at Frankford Hospital.

"I'd like to go too, if that would be all right," she said.

He had hesitated. He could think of no good reason why she should not go to see Payne. After all, Payne's father was her lawyer, and they probably more or less knew each other, but he suspected that Martha was at least as interested in appearing as Dave Pekach's very good lady friend as she was in offering her sympathy to Matt Payne.

He had tried from the beginning, and so far successfully, to keep Martha away from his brother officers. Every sonof-abitch and his brother in the Police Department seemed to think his relationship with the rich old maid from Chestnut Hill was as funny as a rubber crutch.

Martha, he knew, had sensed that he was keeping their personal life very much separate from his professional life. One of the astonishing things about their relationship was that he knew what she was thinking. The flip side of that was that she knew what he was thinking too.

He had hesitated, and lost.

"Precious, if that would in any way be embarrassing to you, just forget it."

"Don't be silly. How could it be embarrassing? I'll come by the house right from work and pick you up."

"All right, if you think it would be all right," Martha had said, her pleased tone of voice telling him he had really had no choice. "And then we'll go out for dinner afterward? Seafood?"

"Seafood sounds fine," he had said.

He had spent a good deal of time during the day considering his relationship with Martha, finally concluding that while the way things were was fine, things could not go along much longer unchanged.

Sometimes, he felt like a gigolo, the way she was always giving him things. It wasn't, he managed to convince himself, that he had fallen for her because she was rich, but that didn't make her just another woman. There was no getting away from the fact that she was a rich woman.

How could he feel like a man when she probably spent more money on fuel oil and having the grass cut at her house than he made?

But when he was with her, like now, he could not imagine life without her.

Jesus, just being around her makes me feel good!

"Was that all right, precious, having Evans lay out your blazer?"

"Fine," Captain David Pekach said, putting his arm around Miss Martha Peebles and kissing her again.

"Precious, behave," she said, when he dropped his hand to her buttock. "We don't have time."

The blazer to which she referred was originally the property of her father.

When Evans and his wife (after an initial three- or four-week period during which their behavior had been more like that of concerned parents rather than servants) had finally decided that Dave Pekach was going to be good for Miss Martha, they had turned to being what they genuinely believed to be helpful and constructive.

Dave Pekach now had an extensive wardrobe, formerly the property of the late Alexander Peebles. No one had asked him if he wanted it, or would even be willing to wear what he had at first thought of as a dead man's clothes. It had been presented as a fait accompli. Evans had taken four suits, half a dozen sports coats, a dozen pairs of trousers, and the measurements Martha had made of the new uniform Dave had given himself as a present for making captain to an Italian custom tailor on Chestnut Street.

Only minor adjustments had been necessary, Evans had happily told him. Mr. Alex had been, fortunately, just slightly larger than Captain Pekach, rather than the other way.

The buttons on the blazer, which bore the label of a London tailor, and which to Dave Pekach's eyes looked unworn, had been replaced with Philadelphia Police Department buttons.

"You have no idea what trouble Evans had to go to for those buttons!" Martha had exclaimed. "But it was, wasn't it, Evans, worth it. Doesn't the captain look nice?"

"The captain looks just fine, Miss Martha," Evans had agreed, beaming with pleasure.

It had not been the time to bring up the subjects of being able to buy his own damned clothing, thank you just the same, or being unable to comfortably wear a dead man's hand-me-downs.

And the trouble, Dave Pekach thought, as he walked into the bedroom carrying his drink in one hand and a bacon-wrapped oyster in the other, and saw the blazer hanging on the mahogany clothes horse, *is that I now think of all these clothes as mine.*

He unbuckled his Sam Browne belt and hung it over the clothes horse, and then stripped out of his uniform, tossing it onto a green leather chaise lounge, secure in the knowledge that in the morning, freshly pressed, it (or another, fresh from the cleaners) would be on the clothes horse.

And that I'm getting pretty used to living like this.

When he came out of the glass-walled shower, Martha was in the bathroom. He was a little confused. Sometimes, when she felt like fooling around, she joined him, but not all dressed up as she was now.

"Captain Sabara called," Martha announced. "He wants you to call. I wrote down the number."

She extended a small piece of paper, but snatched it back when he reached for it.

"Put your robe on, precious," she said. "You'll catch your death!"

He took a heavy terry-cloth robe (also ex-Alexander Peebles, Esq.) from the chrome towel warmer, shrugged into it, took the phone number from Martha, and went into the bedroom, where he sat on the bed and picked up the telephone on the bedside table.

Martha sat on the bed next to him.

"Dave Pekach, Mike," he said. "What's up?"

Martha could hear only Dave's side of the conversation.

"They did *what*? . . .

"Monahan okay? . . .

"Anyone else hurt? . . .

"Where's Wohl? . . .

"Okay. If you do get in touch with him, tell him I'm on my way to the Roundhouse. It should take me twenty minutes, depending on the traffic. Thanks for calling me, Mike."

He put the telephone back in its cradle and stood up.

He saw Martha's eyes, curiosity in them, on him.

She never pries, he thought. *She's pleased when I tell her things, but she never asks.*

"When they started to take Monahan, the witness to the Goldblatt job, from Goldblatt's to the Roundhouse, they were firebombed."

"Firebombed?"

"Somebody threw a whatdoyoucallit? A Molotov cocktail, a bottle full of gas."

"Was anyone hurt?"

He looked at the green leather chaise lounge where he'd tossed his uniform. It had already been removed.

Damn!

He started to put on the clothing Evans had laid out for him, and remembered she had asked a question.

"No. Not as far as Sabara knew. I sent a Highway RPC down there. I can't imagine anybody trying to firebomb a Highway car." He looked at her, and added, "I'll have to go down there, to the Roundhouse."

"Of course," she said, and then, a moment later, "I suppose that means I should make arrangements for my dinner? And about seeing the Payne boy?"

"I don't know how long I'll be," he said. "You'd probably have to wait around—"

"I don't mind," Martha said very evenly.

Pekach suddenly realized that a very great deal depended on his response to that.

"On the other hand, if you came along, it would save me coming all the way back out here to get you. You sure you wouldn't mind waiting?"

"I don't have anything else to do," she said. "Why should I?"

Dave Pekach understood that he had come up with the proper response. He could see it in her eyes, and then confirmation came when she impulsively kissed him.

When they went out under the portico, the Mercedes was there. He looked at the garage. Not only had the Department's car been put away, but a snowplow sat in front of the garage door where it had been put.

He went to the Mercedes and put his hand on the door, and then remembered his manners and went around and held the passenger side door open for Martha.

I have been manipulated, he thought. *Why am I not pissed off?*

As Peter Wohl looked for a place to park at Frankford Hospital, he saw two Highway cars, the first parked by the main entrance, and the second near the Emergency entrance.

Jesus Christ, has something happened?

His concern, which he recognized to contain more than a small element of fear for Matt Payne's well-being, immediately chagrined him.

You're getting paranoid. They have this clever thing called "police radio." You have one. If something had happened, you'd have heard about it.

He had trouble finding a place to park and finally decided he had as much right to park by the main entrance as the Highway RPC did. He wasn't here to visit an ailing aunt.

He walked past the "Visitors Register Here" desk by holding out his leather badge-and-photo-ID case to the rent-a-cop on duty. But when he walked across the lobby toward the bank of elevators he saw that the hospital rent-a-cops had set up another barrier, a guy sitting behind a table you had to get past before you could get on an elevator.

This time, holding out the leather folder and murmuring the magic words "police officer" didn't work.

"Excuse me, sir," the rent-a-cop said, getting to his feet after Wohl had waved the leather folder in front of him. "I don't see your visitor's badge."

Another rent-a-cop he hadn't noticed before stepped between Wohl and the elevator.

"I don't have one," Wohl said. "I'm a police officer." He gave the rent-a-cop a better look at his identification.

"Who are you going to see?"

"Matthew M. Payne," Wohl said. "He's on the surgical floor."

"I'm sorry, sir, there's no patient here by that name," the rent-a-cop said.

He had not, Wohl noticed, checked any kind of a list before making that announcement.

He chuckled. "I'm *Inspector* Wohl," he said. "The police officers keeping an eye on Officer Payne work for me."

"Just a moment, sir," the rent-a-cop said, and sat down at his table and dialed a number. A moment later he said, "You can go up, sir."

"You guys are really doing your job," Wohl said. "Thank you."

The compliment, which was genuine, didn't seem to make much of an impression on either of the rent-a-cops.

When Wohl stepped off the elevator, there was a Highway Patrolman Wohl could not remember having seen before, and

a Highway Sergeant he had seen around and whose name came
to him almost instantly.

"Hello, Sergeant Carter," Wohl said, smiling, extending his
hand. "For a while there, I didn't think they were going to let
me come up here."

"Good evening, sir," Sergeant Carter said. "You know
Hughes, don't you?"

"I've seen him around," Wohl said, offering his hand.
"How are you, Hughes?"

"Inspector."

Then Wohl saw something he didn't like. Behind Hughes,
leaning against the wall, was a short-barreled pump shotgun.

I don't think that's a Remington 870, Wohl thought automatically. *Probably an Ithica.*

"Do you really think we're going to need the shotgun?"
Wohl asked.

"My experience is, Inspector," Carter said, "that if you
have a shotgun, you seldom need one."

Wohl smiled.

*Now, how am I going to tactfully tell him to get it out of
sight without hurting his feelings?*

The first time he had seen Carter, shortly after assuming
command of Highway, Wohl had taken the trouble of reading
his name on the name tag and committing it to memory. First
impressions *did* matter, and he had been favorably impressed
with his first look at Carter. He was a good-looking guy, tall
and lean, about as black as Jason Washington, who wore his
uniform not only with evident pride, but according to the regulations. Highway guys were prone—Sergeant Peter Wohl had
himself been prone—to add little sartorial touches to the prescribed uniform that sometimes crossed the line into ludicrous.

Most commonly this was a crushed brim cap four sizes too
small, shined cartridges (and/or extra cartridges), patent leather
boots, and Sam Browne belt, that sort of thing. Carter looked
like he could pose for a picture with the caption "The Prescribed Uniform for a Highway Patrol Sergeant."

"I understand that the Secret Service guys guarding the
President carry their shotguns in golf bags," Wohl said. "To
keep from frightening the voters. Is there some way you can
think of to get that out of sight, but handy?"

"Not offhand, but I'll come up with something. You said

'handy,' inspector. Does that mean you take this threat seriously?"

"They threw a Molotov cocktail at Sergeant Washington. You would have to be serious, or crazy, to do something like that. Yeah, I take them seriously. These people want two things, I think. To get themselves in the newspapers and to frighten off the witnesses to the Goldblatt job. They're already facing murder one. From their perspective, they have more to gain than to lose from killing a cop."

"Did it scare off the witness?"

"It made him mad," Wohl laughed. "I just talked to Jason Washington. He said Mr. Monahan couldn't wait to get over to the Detention Center and identify these creeps."

"I looked in on Payne," Carter said. "I wondered if he was—if he had a gun. I didn't think I should ask him. I didn't know how much he knows about what the ILA has threatened."

"Do me a favor, Sergeant," Wohl said. "Don't use the term 'ILA.' Don't call these scumbags an army. That's just what they want. They're thieves and murderers, that's all."

"Sorry," Carter said. "I see what you mean."

"And pass that word too," Wohl said. "To answer your question: Yes, he's got one. The Mobile Crime Lab guys took his to the laboratory, so I loaned him one."

"How long is he going to be in here?"

"I'm not sure that I know what I'm talking about, but I think he'll be out of here tomorrow. Apparently, the doctors think the sooner you're moving around, the better it is."

"And then what?"

"It's sort of a delicate question. We don't want these lunatics to think they have frightened us silly. Payne is, after all, a cop. Captain Pekach is working out some kind of an arrangement where Payne's friends can keep an eye on him in plainclothes, maybe on overtime."

"I'd be happy to take a little of that, if you need somebody."

Wohl chuckled. "You'd look a little out of place, Sergeant, but thank you anyway."

"Because I'm black, you mean?"

"No. Because you're what—thirty-five? And because you look like a cop. The three guys who are going to sit on Payne are his age."

"And white?"

I can't let that pass.

"Tiny Lewis is as black as you are," Wohl said coldly. "He's also as old as Payne. He's one of the three. And since we're on this sensitive minority kick, Hay-zus Martinez is the second one. That means only one of the three will be what these scumbags would call a honky."

"No offense, Inspector. I didn't mean that the way it sounded."

"Okay. I hope not. But just for the record, the only color I see in a cop is blue."

"Yes, sir."

Wohl saw that Carter looked genuinely unhappy.

Did I have to jump on his ass that way? Was it because this whole thing has got me more upset than I should let it?

The elevator door whooshed open again. The Highway cop with the shotgun, who had been leaning against the wall, straightened, and then relaxed when he recognized Captain David Pekach.

"Inspector," Pekach said, somewhat stiffly. "Sergeant Carter." He nodded at the Highway cop standing against the wall.

Martha Peebles, smiling a little uneasily, stood behind him.

Nice-looking woman, Wohl thought.

"Hello, Dave."

"Inspector, I don't think you know Miss Peebles," Pekach said, slowly and carefully, as if reciting something polite he had memorized, and then he blurted, "my fiancée."

"No, I don't," Wohl said, and, catching the look on Martha Peebles's face, decided, *I'll bet that's the first time he ever used that word.* Confirmation came when he looked at Pekach, whose face was now red.

"How do you do?" Martha Peebles said, offering Wohl her hand.

Classy, Wohl decided. *Just what Dave needs.*

"I'm very pleased to meet you," Wohl said.

"Honey," Pekach went on, "this is Sergeant Carter and Officer Hughes."

They nodded at one another.

"I hope I'm not intruding, Inspector," Martha Peebles said. "Matt Payne's father is an old family friend."

"We were at the Roundhouse, and they told me I'd just

missed you; that you were coming here," Pekach said. "We were already on our way here when Sabara called and told me what happened."

"I'm sure Matt will be delighted to see you," Wohl said. "Why don't you go on in? I'd like a quick word with Dave."

He pointed toward Matt's door. Martha walked to it, opened it a crack, peered in, and then pushed the door fully open and went in.

Pekach waited until the automatic closing device had closed the door and then looked at Wohl.

"Well, what do you think?"

"About the security arrangements for Matt or Miss Peebles?"

Pekach flushed again, and then smiled.

"Both," he said.

"Frankly, I can't see what a beautiful woman like that sees in an ugly Polack like you, but they say there's no accounting for taste."

"Thanks a lot."

"And so far as the security arrangements are concerned, it looks to me as if Sergeant Carter has things well in hand," Wohl said.

Why am I uneasy saying that?

"What about when Payne leaves the hospital?"

"We're working on that. Question one, to be answered, is when he will be leaving. We can talk about that in the morning."

Why didn't I just say we're going to have Lewis, McFadden, and Martinez sit on him?

Wohl put his hand on Pekach's arm and led him to Matt Payne's door.

EIGHTEEN

"I'm sorry, we have no patient by that name," the hospital operator said.

"But I know he's there," Helene Stillwell said snappishly. "I *visited* him this morning."

"One moment, please," the operator said.

"Damn!" Helene said.

A male voice came on the line: "May I help you, ma'am?"

Helene hung up.

They're monitoring his calls. Obviously. After that threat to—what did it say?

She dropped her eyes to the *Ledger*, which she had laid on the marble top of the bar in the sun room, and found what she was looking for. It was in a front-page story with the headline ISLAMIC LIBERATION ARMY THREATENS REVENGE FOR POLICE SHOOTING.

"Death to the Zionist oppressors of our people and the murderers who call themselves police!" she read aloud. "My God!"

Under the headline was a photograph of Matt and Mayor

Jerry Carlucci, with the caption "Officer M. M. Payne, of Special Operations, apparently the target of the ILA threat, shown with Mayor Jerome Carlucci three months ago, shortly after Payne shot to death Germantown resident Warren K. Fletcher, allegedly the 'North Philadelphia serial rapist.' "

Looking at Matt's face, she had a sudden very clear mental image of his gun, and the slick, menacing cartridges for it, which was then replaced by the memory of his naked body next to hers, and of him and the eruption, the explosion, in her, which had followed.

"Christ!" she said softly, and reached for the cognac snifter on the marble.

There was the clunking noise the garage door always made the moment the mechanism was triggered. When she looked out the glass wall at the end of the sun room, she saw Farny's Lincoln coupe waiting for the garage door to open fully.

I didn't see him come up the drive, she thought, and then: *I wonder what he's doing home so early.*

Helene went behind the bar, intending to give the cognac snifter a quick rinse and to put the bottle away. But then she changed her mind, splashed more Rémy Martin in the glass and drank it all down at a gulp. Then she rinsed the glass and put the Rémy Martin bottle back on the shelf beneath the bar.

Before Farny came into the house, there was time for her to fish in her purse for a spray bottle of breath sweetener, to use it, replace it, and then move purse and newspaper to the glass-topped coffee table. She had seated herself on the couch and found and lit a cigarette by the time she heard the kitchen door open and then slam.

He always slams that goddamn door!

"I'm in here," she called.

He didn't respond. She heard the sound of his opening the cloak closet under the stairs, the rattling of hangers, and then the clunk of the door closing.

He appeared in the entrance to the sun room.

"Hello," he said.

"Hi," Helene said. "I didn't expect you until later."

"I've got to go way the hell across town to the Detention Center," he said. "I thought it made more sense to get dressed now. I may have to call you and ask you to meet me at the Thompsons'. All right?"

She nodded. "I've been thinking about having a drink. Specifically, a straight cognac. Does that sound appealing?"

"Very tempting, but I'd better not. I don't want someone sniffing my breath over there."

"You don't mind if I do? I think I'm fighting a cold."

"Don't fight too hard. You heard what I said about you maybe having to drive yourself to the Thompsons'?"

"Why don't I just skip the Thompsons'?"

"We've been over this before. Thompson is important in the party."

"You make him, you make the both of you sound like apparatchiks in the Supreme Soviet," Helene said.

"That's the second, maybe the third, time you made that little joke. I don't find it funny this time, either."

"You're certainly in a lousy mood. Has it to do with—what did you say? 'The Detention Center'? What is that, anyway?"

She got up and walked to the bar, retrieved her glass and the bottle of Rémy Martin, and poured a half inch into the snifter.

"The Detention Center is where they lock people up before they're indicted, or if they can't make bail. Essentially, it's a prison in everything but name."

"What are you going to be doing there?"

"The one witness we have to the robbery and murder at Goldblatt's is going to try to pick the guilty parties out in line-ups. Washington—that great big Negro detective?—has scheduled it for half past six. Christ only knows how long it will take."

"I think you're supposed to say 'black,' not 'Negro,' " Helene said.

"Whatever."

"Have you seen the paper?"

"I wasn't in it, my secretary said."

"I meant about the Islamic Liberation Army threatening reprisal, revenge, whatever."

"I heard about it," he said, and then followed her pointing finger and went and picked up the *Ledger*.

She waited until he had read the newspaper story, and then asked, "Do they mean it?"

"Who the hell knows?" he said, and then had a thought. "Going over to see that kid was a good idea. I don't know if

I knew or not, but I didn't make the connection. You do know who his father is?''

"Tell me."

"Brewster Cortland Payne, of Mawson, Payne, Stockton, McAdoo & Lester."

"He's important in the party too, I suppose?"

"Helene, you're being a bitch, and I'm really not in the mood for it."

"Sorry."

"But to answer your question, yes. He is important in the party. And if this political thing doesn't work out, Mawson, Payne, Stockton, McAdoo & Lester is the sort of firm with which I would like to be associated."

"Then maybe we should have gotten him a box of candy or something."

He looked at her and took a moment to consider whether she was being sarcastic again.

"It's not too late, I suppose," Helene said.

He considered that a moment.

"I think that's a lost opportunity," he said.

Damn, it would have given me an excuse to go see him.

"Well, maybe we could have him for drinks or dinner or something," Helen said. "If it's important."

"We'll see," Farnsworth Stillwell said. "I'm going to get dressed."

He had just started up the stairs when the telephone rang. Helene answered it.

"Mr. Farnsworth Stillwell, please," a female voice said. "Mr. Armando Giacomo is calling."

"Just a moment, please," Helene said, and covered the mouthpiece with her hand.

"Are you home for a Mr. Giacomo?" she called.

"*Armando* Giacomo?" Stillwell asked, already coming back into the room.

She nodded. "His secretary, I think."

Stillwell took the phone from her.

"This is Farnsworth Stillwell," he said, and then, a moment later, "How are you, Armando? What can I do for you?"

The charm is on, Helene thought, *Armando Whatsisname must be somebody else important in the party.*

"Well, I must say I'm surprised," Stillwell said to the telephone. "If I may say so, Armando, hiring you is tantamount to saying 'I'm guilty as sin and need a genius to get me off.' "

There was a reply that Helene could not hear.

He's wearing one of his patently insincere smiles. Whatever this was about, he doesn't like it.

"Well, I'll see you there, then, Armando," Stillwell said. "I'm going to change my clothes and go over there. Helene and I are having dinner with Jack Thompson, and I have no idea how long the business at the Detention Center will take. I appreciate your courtesy in calling me."

He absentmindedly handed her the handset.

"What was that all about?" Helene asked.

"That was Armando C. Giacomo," he said.

"So the girl said. Who *is* Armando C. Giawhatever?"

A look of annoyance crossed his face, but he almost visibly made the decision to answer her.

"The top two criminal lawyers in Philadelphia, in my judgment, and practically everyone else's, are Colonel J. Dunlop Mawson of the aforementioned Mawson, Payne, Stockton, McAdoo & Lester and Armando C. Giacomo. Giacomo telephoned to tell me he has been retained to represent the people the police arrested this morning."

"That's bad news, I gather."

"Frankly, I would rather face some public defender six months out of law school, or one of the less expensive members of the criminal bar," Stillwell said. "I don't want to walk out of the courtroom with egg all over my face. I'll have to give this development some thought."

He turned and left the room and went to their bedroom on the second floor.

Farnsworth Stillwell had several disturbing thoughts. Armando C. Giacomo was very good, and consequently very expensive. Like Colonel J. Dunlop Mawson, he had a well-earned reputation for defending, most often successfully and invariably with great skill, people charged with violation of the whole gamut of criminal offenses.

But, like Mawson, Giacomo seldom represented ordinary criminals, for, in Stillwell's mind, the very good reason that ordinary criminals seldom had any money. They both drew their clientele from the well heeled, excluding only members of the Mob.

If he was representing the Islamic Liberation Army, he certainly wasn't doing it *pro bono publico*; he was being paid, well paid. By whom? Certainly not by the accused themselves. If there was money around to hire Armando C. Giacomo, it challenged Matt Lowenstein's (and Peter Wohl's) theory that the Islamic Liberation Army was nothing more than a group of thugs with a bizarre imagination.

Farnsworth Stillwell had a good deal of respect for Armando C. Giacomo, not all of it based on his professional reputation. On a personal basis, he regarded Giacomo as a brother in the fraternity of naval aviators. They hadn't flown together—Giacomo had flown in the Korean War, Stillwell in Vietnam—but they shared the common experience of Pensacola training, landing high-performance aircraft on the decks of aircraft carriers, flying in Harm's Way, and the proud self-assurance that comes with golden wings pinned to a blue Navy uniform.

Stillwell did not really understand why a man who had been a naval aviator would choose to become a criminal lawyer, except for the obvious reason that, at the upper echelons of the speciality, it paid very well indeed.

He was forced now to consider the unpleasant possibilities, starting with the least pleasant to consider, that Armando C. Giacomo was a better, more experienced lawyer than he was.

I will have absolutely no room for error in the courtroom.

Or, for that matter, in all the administrative garbage that has to be plowed through before we get into court.

Christ, why didn't I keep my mouth shut when Tony Callis brought this up? When am I going to learn that whenever something looks as if the gods are smiling on me, the exact opposite is true?

Farnsworth Stillwell had been told by Sergeant Jason Washington that the lineups were going to start at the Detention Center at half past six.

Stillwell often joked that his only virtue was punctuality. The truth was that he believed punctuality to be not only good manners, but good business practice. He made a genuine effort to be where he was supposed to be when he was supposed to be there. He expected reciprocity on the part of people with whom he was professionally associated, and demanded it from both his subordinates and those who ranked lower in the government hierarchy than he did.

He had never been to the Detention Center before, so in

order to be on time, he had taken the trouble to locate it precisely on a map, and to leave his house in sufficient time to arrive on time.

When he pulled into one of the Official Visitor parking spots at the Detention Center, it was 6:28.

He entered the building, and went to the uniformed corrections officer sitting behind a plate-glass window.

"Assistant District Attorney Stillwell," he announced. "To meet Sergeant Washington."

"He's not here yet," the corrections officer, a small black woman, said. "You can take a seat and wait, if you like."

He smiled at her and said, "Thank you."

He sat down on a battered bench against the wall, more than a little annoyed.

He and Helene were due at Jack Thompson's at eight, and he intensively disliked the idea of arriving there late. He had told Helene that if he wasn't back, or hadn't called, by half past seven, she was to drive to the Thompsons'.

He now regretted that decision. The way she was throwing the cognac down, the possibility existed that the headlines in tomorrow's *Bulletin* and *Ledger* and *Daily News* would not concern the ILA, but rather something they knew their readers would really like to read, "Assistant District Attorney Stillwell's Wife Charged in Drunken Driving Episode."

If the lineups were to begin at half past six, Stillwell fumed, *obviously some preparatory steps had to be taken, and therefore Washington should have arrived, with the witness in tow, at whatever time before half past six was necessary in order for him to do what he had to do so that they could begin on schedule.*

Stillwell was aware that one of his faults was a tendency to become angry over circumstances over which he had no control. This seemed to be one of them. He told himself that Washington was not late on purpose, that things, for example delays in traffic because of the snow, sometimes happened.

Washington will be along any moment, with an explanation, and probably an apology, for being tardy, Stillwell thought, taking just a little satisfaction in knowing that he was being reasonable.

At quarter to seven, however, when Sergeant Washington had still not shown up, or even had the simple courtesy to send word that he would be delayed, Farnsworth Stillwell decided that he had been patient enough.

While he thought it was highly unlikely that Staff Inspector Peter Wohl would know where Sergeant Washington was and/or why he wasn't at the Detention Center when he was supposed to be, calling Wohl would at least serve to tell him (a) that his super detective was unreliable, time-wise, and (b) that Farnsworth Stillwell did not like to be kept waiting.

He asked the female corrections officer behind the plate-glass window if he could use the telephone.

"It's for official business only, sir."

Farnsworth Stillwell had a fresh, unpleasant thought. There was no one else here. Armando C. Giacomo was supposed to be here, and certainly there would be others besides Washington and the witness.

Had the whole damned thing been called off for some reason, and he had not been told?

"Are you sure Sergeant Washington isn't here? Could he be here and you not be aware of it?"

"Everybody has to come past me," she said. "If he were here, I'd know it."

"May I have the telephone, please?"

"It's for official business only, like I told you before."

"I'm Assistant District Attorney Stillwell. This is official business."

She gave him a look that suggested she doubted him, but gave in.

"I'll have the operator get the number for you, sir."

"I don't know the number. I want to talk to Inspector Wohl of Special Operations."

The corrections officer obligingly searched for the number on her list of official telephones. It was not listed, and she so informed Farnsworth Stillwell.

"Check with information."

Information had the number.

"Special Operations, may I help you?"

"This is Assistant District Attorney Stillwell. Inspector Wohl, please."

"I'm sorry, sir. Inspector Wohl has gone for the day."

"Do you have a number where he can be reached?"

"Just one moment, sir."

"This is Lieutenant Kelsey. May I help you, sir?"

"This is Assistant District Attorney Stillwell. It's important that I get in touch with Inspector Wohl."

"I'm sorry, the inspector's gone for the day. Is there something I can do for you, Mr. Stillwell?"

"Do you have a number where he can be reached?"

"No, sir."

"You mean you have no idea where he is?"

"The inspector is on his way to Frankford Hospital, sir. But until he calls in, I won't have a number there for him."

"What about Sergeant Washington?"

"Are you referring to Detective Washington, sir?"

"I understood he was promoted."

"Well, what do you know? I hadn't heard that."

"Do you know where he is?"

"He's at the Detention Center, sir. I can give you that number."

"I'm at the Detention Center. He's not here. That's what I'm calling about."

"Hold one, sir," Lieutenant Kelsey said.

The pause was twenty seconds, but seemed much longer, before Kelsey came back on the line.

"They're at Cottman and State Road, Mr. Stillwell. They should be there any second now."

"Thank you."

"Should I ask Inspector Wohl to get in touch with you when he calls in, sir?"

"That won't be necessary, thank you very much," Farnsworth Stillwell said.

He put the telephone back in its cradle, and slid it back through the opening in the plate glass window. He walked to the door as the first of the cars in what had become a five car convoy rolled up.

Heading the procession was a Highway Patrol Sergeant's car. A second Highway Patrol RPC with two Highway cops followed him. The third car was Jason Washington's nearly new Ford. Stillwell saw a man in the front seat beside him, and decided that he must be Monahan The Witness. There was another unmarked car, with two men in civilian clothing in it behind Washington's Ford and bringing up the rear was another Highway RPC.

The sergeant leading the procession stopped his car in a position that placed Washington's car closest to the entrance of the Detention Center. Everyone except Monahan The Witness got quickly out of their cars. The Highway Patrolmen stood on the sidewalk as the plainclothes went to the passenger side of Washington's car and took him from the car. Washington and the Highway Sergeant moved to the entrance door of the building and held it open.

Sergeant Jason Washington saw Farnsworth Stillwell and nodded.

"Good evening, Mr. Stillwell," he said.

"You told me this was going to take place at half past six. It's now"—He checked his watch—"four past seven."

"We were delayed," Washington said.

"Were you, indeed?"

"We were Molotov-cocktailed, is what happened," the man Stillwell was sure was Monahan The Witness said.

"I beg your pardon?"

"Mr. Stillwell," Washington said, "this is Mr. Albert J. Monahan."

Stillwell smiled at Monahan and offered his hand.

"I'm Farnsworth Stillwell, Mr. Monahan. I'm very pleased to meet you."

"Can you believe that?" Monahan said. "A Molotov cocktail? Right on South Street? What the hell is the world coming to?"

What is this man babbling about? A Molotov cocktail is what the Russians used against German tanks, a bottle of gasoline with a flaming wick.

"I'm afraid I don't quite understand," Stillwell said.

"As we drove away from Goldblatt's," Washington explained, "party or parties unknown threw a bottle filled with gasoline down—more than likely from the roof—onto a Highway car that was escorting us here."

"I will be *damned!*" Farnsworth Stillwell said.

My God, wait until the newspapers get hold of that!

"The bottle bounced off the Highway car, broke when it hit the street, and then caught fire," Washington went on.

"Was anyone hurt?"

"I understand a car parked on South Street caught fire," Washington said. "But no one was hurt. We went to the Roundhouse. I knew Central Detectives and the laboratory people would want a look at the Highway car."

"You could have called," Stillwell said, and immediately regretted it.

Washington looked at him coldly, but did not directly respond.

"I'm going to explain to Mr. Monahan how we run the lineup, lineups," Washington said. "And show him the layout. Perhaps you'd like to come along?"

"Yes, thank you, Sergeant, I'd appreciate that," Stillwell said. He smiled at Washington. Washington did not return it.

"The way this works, Mr. Monahan," he said, "is that the defense counsel will try to question your identification. One of the ways they'll try to do that is to attempt to prove that we rigged the lineup, set it up so that you would have an idea who we think the individual is. Lead you, so to speak. You follow me?"

"Yeah, sure."

"So we will lean over backward to make sure that the lineups are absolutely fair."

"Where do you get the other people?" Monahan said, "the innocent ones?"

"They're all volunteers."

"Off the street? People in jail?"

"Neither. People being held here. This is the Detention Center. Nobody being held here has been found guilty of anything. They're awaiting trial. The other people in the lineup will be chosen from them, from those that have volunteered."

"Why do they volunteer?"

"Well, I suppose I could stick my tongue in my cheek and say they're all public spirited citizens, anxious to make whatever small contribution they can to the criminal justice system, but the truth is I don't know. If they had me in here for something, I don't think I'd be running around looking for some way I could help, particularly if all I got out of it was an extra ice cream chit or movie pass. And, of course, most of the people being held here don't volunteer. As for the ones that do, I can only guess they do it because they're bored, or figure they can screw the system up."

"How do you mean?"

"Let's say there's a guy here who has a perfect alibi for the Goldblatt job; he was here. So he figures if he can get in the lineup, and somehow look nervous or guilty and have you point him out, the guy who did the Goldblatt job walks away, and so does he; he has a perfect alibi.''

"I'll be goddamned," Monahan said.

"So it's very important to the good guys, Mr. Monahan," Washington said, "that before you pick somebody out you be absolutely sure it's the guy. It would be much better for you not to be able to recognize somebody in the lineup than for you to make a mistake. If you did that, it would come out in court and put in serious question every other identification you made. You understand, of course."

"Yeah," Monahan said thoughtfully, then added: "I'll be damned."

Washington pushed open a door and held it open as Monahan and Stillwell walked through it.

Stillwell found himself in a windowless, harshly lit room forty feet long and twenty-five wide. Against one of the long walls was a narrow platform, two feet off the floor and about six feet wide. Behind it the wall had been painted. The numbers 1 through 8 were painted near the ceiling, marking where the men in the lineup were to stand. Horizontal lines marked off in feet and inches ran under the numbers. Mounted on the ceiling were half a dozen floodlights aimed at the platform. There was a step down from the platform to the floor at the right.

Facing the platform were a row of folding metal chairs and two tables. A microphone was on one table and a telephone on the other.

There were a dozen people in the room, four of them in corrections officer's uniforms. A lieutenant from Major Crimes Division had a 35-mm camera with a flash attachment hanging around his neck. There were two women, both holding stenographer's notebooks.

I wonder how it is that I was left sitting outside on that bench when everyone else with a connection with this was in here?

Stillwell recognized Detectives D'Amata and Pelosi and then a familiar face. "The proceedings can now begin," Armando C. Giacomo announced sonorously, "the Right Honorable Assistant District Attorney having finally made an appearance."

Giacomo, a slight, lithe, dapper man who wore what was left of his hair plastered to the sides of his tanned skull, walked quickly to Stillwell and offered his hand.

"Armando, how are you?" Stillwell said.

"Armando C. Giacomo is, as always, ready to defend the rights of the unjustly accused against all the abusive powers of the state."

"Presuming they can write a nonrubber check, of course," Jason Washington said. "How are you, Manny?"

"Ah, my favorite gumshoe. How are you, Jason?"

Giacomo enthusiastically pumped Washington's hand.

They were friends, Stillwell saw, the proof being not only their smiles, but that Washington had called him "Manny." He remembered hearing that Giacomo was well thought of by the cops because he devoted the *pro bono publico* side of his practice to defending cops charged with violating the civil rights of individuals.

"Aside from almost getting myself fried on the way over here, I'm fine. How about you?"

"Whatever are you talking about, Detective Washington?" Giacomo asked.

"Detective Washington is now Sergeant Washington," Stillwell said.

"And you stopped to celebrate? Shame on you!"

"We was Molotov-cocktailed, is what happened," Albert J. Monahan explained.

"You must be Mr. Monahan," Giacomo said. "I'm Armando C. Giacomo. I'm very happy to meet you."

"Likewise," Monahan said.

"What was that you were saying about a Molotov cocktail?"

"They threw one at us. Off a roof by Goldblatt's."

Giacomo looked at Washington for confirmation. Washington nodded.

"Well, I'm very glad to see that you came through that all right," Giacomo said.

"I came through it pissed, is the way I came through it. That's fucking outrageous."

"I absolutely agree with you. Terrible. Outrageous. Did the police manage to apprehend the culprits?"

"Not yet," Washington said.

"Mr. Giacomo, Mr. Monahan," Washington said, "is here to represent the people we think were at Goldblatt's."

"And you're friends with him?"

"Yes, we're friends," Giacomo said solemnly. "We have the same basic interest. Justice."

Jason Washington laughed deep in his stomach.

"Manny, you're really something," he said.

"It is not nice to mock small Italian gentlemen," Giacomo said. "You ought to be ashamed of yourself."

Washington laughed louder, then turned to Joe D'Amato: "Are we about ready to do this?"

"Yeah. We have seven different groups of people." He pointed toward the door at the end of the platform.

Washington turned to Monahan: "If you'll just have a chair, Mr. Monahan—"

Detective Pelosi smiled at Monahan and put his hands on the back of one of the folding chairs. Monahan walked to it and sat down.

Washington waved Giacomo ahead of him and headed for the door. Stillwell followed them.

There were two corrections officers and eight other people in a small room. The eight people were all Hispanic, all of about the same age and height and weight. One of them was Hector Carlos Estivez.

"Okay with you, Manny?" Washington asked.

Armando C. Giacomo looked at the eight men very carefully before he finally nodded his head.

"That should be all right, Jason," he said, and turned and walked out of the room. Washington and Stillwell followed him.

Giacomo sat down in a folding chair next to Monahan. Washington sat on the other side of him, and Stillwell sat next to Washington.

"Okay, Joe," Washington said.

"Lights," D'Amato ordered.

One of the corrections officers flicked switches that killed all the lights in the room except the floodlights shining on the platform. The people in the room would be only barely visible to the men on the platform.

"Okay," D'Amata ordered. "Bring them in."

The door to the room at the end of the platform opened, and eight men came into the room and took the two steps up to the platform.

"Stand directly under the number, look forward," D'Amato ordered. The men complied.

The Major Crimes lieutenant with the 35-mm camera walked in front of the men sitting in the chairs. He took three flash photographs, one from the left, one from the center, and one from the right.

"You didn't have to do that, Jason," Giacomo said.

"Oh, yes, I did, Manny." Washington said. "I only get burned once."

I wonder what the hell that's all about, Stillwell thought, and then the answer came to him: *I will get copies of those photographs. If Giacomo suggests during the trial that Monahan was able to pick out Estivez because the other people in the lineup were conspicuously different in age, or size, or complexion, or whatever, I can introduce the pictures he's taking.*

He remembered what Tony Callis had said about Washington having forgotten more about criminal law than he knew.

"Number one, step forward," D'Amato ordered when the photographer had stepped out of the way.

"Number three," Albert J. Monahan said positively.

"Just a moment, please, Mr. Monahan," Washington said.

"Number three is one of them. I recognize the bastard when I see him."

"Mr. Monahan," Washington said, "I ask you now if you recognize any of the men on the platform."

"Number three," Monahan said impatiently. "I told you already."

"Can you tell us where you have seen the man standing under the number three on the platform?" Washington asked.

"He's one of the bastards who came into the store and robbed it and shot it up."

"You are referring to January third of this year, and the robbery and murder that occurred at Goldblatt's furniture store on South Street?"

"Yes, I am."

"There is no question in your mind that the man standing under number three is one of the participants in that robbery and murder?"

"None whatever. That's one of them. That's him. Number three."

"Mr. Giacomo?" Washington asked.

Armando G. Giacomo shook his head, signifying that he had nothing to say.

"Jason?" Joe D'Amato asked.

"We're through with this bunch," Washington said.

"Take them out," D'Amata ordered.

A corrections officer opened the door at the end of the platform and gestured for the men on the platform to get off it.

That man didn't show any sign of anything at all when Monahan picked him out, Stillwell thought. *What kind of people are we dealing with here?*

"Mr. Monahan," Giacomo said. "I see that you're wearing glasses."

"That's right."

"Before this is all over, I'd be grateful if you would give me the name of your eye doctor."

"You're not going to try to tell me I couldn't see that bastard? Recognize him?"

"I'm just trying to do the best job I can, Mr. Monahan," Giacomo said. "I'm sure you understand."

"No, I don't," Monahan said. "I don't understand at all."

NINETEEN

Lieutenant Jack Malone had just carefully rewrapped the aluminum foil around the remnants of his dinner—two egg rolls and beef-and-pepper—and was about to shoot it, basketball-like, into the wastebasket under the writing desk in his room in the St. Charles Hotel when his telephone rang.

He glanced at his watch as he reached for the telephone. Quarter past seven. Sometimes Little Jack would telephone him around this hour. His first reaction was pleasure, which was almost immediately replaced with something close to pain:

If it is Little Jack, he's liable to ask again why I'm not coming home.

"Peter Wohl, Jack," his caller said. "Am I interrupting anything?"

"No, sir."

"Sorry to bother you at home, but I want to talk to you about something."

"Yes, sir?"

"Have you had dinner?"

"Yes, sir."

"Would you mind watching me eat? I've got to get something in my stomach."

"Not at all."

"You know Ribs Unlimited on Chestnut Street?"

"Yes, sir."

"Can you meet me there in—thirty, thirty-five minutes?"

"Yes, sir, I'll be there."

"At the bar, Jack. Thank you," Wohl said, and hung up.

What the fuck does Wohl want? Is this going to be one of those heart-to-heart talks better held in an informal atmosphere? Has word finally got to him that I was watching Holland's body shop?

"Malone, you disappoint me. A word to the wise should have been sufficient. Get Bob Holland out of your mind. In other words, get off his case."

Malone pushed himself out of bed and started to dress. He really hated to wear anything but blue jeans and a sweater and a nylon jacket, *because sure as Christ made little apples, if I put on a suit and shirt, I will get something—slush or barbecue sauce, something—on them and have to take them to the cleaners.*

"But on the other hand," he said aloud as he took a tweed sports coat and a pair of cavalry twill trousers from the closet, "one must look one's best when one is about to socialize with one's superior officer. Clothes indeed do make the man."

When he got outside the hotel, he saw that the temperature had dropped, and frozen the slush. He decided to walk. It wasn't really that close, but if he drove, he might not be able to find a place to park when he came back, and he had plenty of time. Wohl had said thirty, thirty-five minutes.

Now I won't soil my clothes, I'll slip on the goddamn ice and break my fucking leg.

Ribs Unlimited, despite the lousy weather, was crowded. There was a line of people waiting for the nod of the headwaiter in the narrow entrance foyer.

Malone stood in the line for a minute or two, and then remembered Wohl had said "in the bar."

The headwaiter tried to stop him.

"I'm meeting someone," Malone said, and kept walking.

He found an empty stool next to a woman who was desperately trying to appear younger than the calendar made her, and whose perfume filled his nostrils with a scent that reminded him of something else he hadn't been getting much—any—of lately.

When the bartender appeared, he almost automatically said "Ortleib's" but at the last moment changed his mind.

"John Jameson, easy on the ice," he said.

Fuck it, I've been a good boy lately. One little shooter will be good for me. And one I can afford.

Wohl appeared as the bartender served the drink.

"Been waiting long?"

"No, sir, I just got here."

"What is that?"

"Irish."

"I feel Irish," Wohl said to the bartender. "Same way, please. Not too much ice."

A heavyset man appeared, beaming.

"How are you, Inspector?"

"How are you, Charley?" Wohl replied. "Charley, this is Lieutenant Jack Malone. Jack, Charley Meader, our host."

"You work with the inspector, Lieutenant?" Meader said, pumping Malone's hand.

"Yes, sir," Malone said.

"I've got you a table in the back anytime you're ready, Inspector," Meader said.

"I guess we could carry our drinks, right?" Wohl said. "When I get mine, that is."

"Whatever you'd prefer," Meader said, and waited until the bartender served Wohl.

"House account that, Jerry," he said.

"Very kind, thank you," Wohl said.

"My pleasure, Inspector. And anytime, you know that."

He patted Wohl on the shoulder and shook hands with both of them.

"Whenever you're ready, Inspector, your table's available," Meader said. "Good to see you. And to meet you, Lieutenant."

Wohl waited until he was gone, then said, "There was once a Department of Health inspector who led Charley Meader to believe that he would have far less trouble passing his inspections if he handed him an envelope once a week when he came in for a free meal."

"Oh," Malone said.

"Charley belongs to the Jaguar Club," Wohl went on. "You know I have a Jaguar?"

"I've seen it."

"1950 SK-120 Drophead Coupe," Wohl said. "So he came to me after a meeting one night and said he had heard I was a cop, and that he didn't want to put me on the spot, but did I know an honest sergeant, or maybe even an honest lieutenant. He would go to him, without mentioning my name, and tell him his problem."

"A long time ago?"

"Just before they gave me Special Operations," Wohl said.

"He didn't know you were a staff inspector?"

"No. Not until I testified in court."

"So what happened?"

"The next time the Health Department sleaze-ball came in, I was tending bar and I had a photographer up there." He gestured toward a balcony overlooking the bar and smiled. "I put a microphone in the pretzel bowl. Hanging Harriet gave the Health Department guy three to five," Wohl said.

Hanging Harriet was the Hon. Harriet M. McCandless, a formidable black jurist who passionately believed that civilized society was based upon a civil service whose honesty was above question.

"No wonder he buys you drinks."

"The sad part of the story, Jack, is that Charley really was afraid to go to the cops until he found one he thought *might* be honest."

Wohl took a swallow of his drink, and then said, "Let's carry these to the table. I've got to get something to eat."

The headwaiter left his padded rope and showed them to a table at the rear of the room. A waiter immediately appeared.

"The El Rancho Special," Wohl ordered. "Hold the beans. French fries."

"What's that?"

"Barbecued beef. Great sauce. You really ought to try it."

"I think I will," Malone said.

"Yes, sir. And can I get you gentlemen a drink?"

"Please. The same thing. Jameson's, isn't it?"

"Jameson's," Malone offered.

"And I don't care what Mr. Meader says, I want the check for this," Wohl said.

The waiter looked uncomfortable.

"You're going to have to talk to Mr. Meader about that, sir."

"All right," Wohl said. He waited until the waiter left, and then said, "Well, you can't say I didn't try to pay for this, can you?"

Malone chuckled.

Wohl reached in the breast pocket of his jacket and came out with several sheets of blue-lined paper and handed them to Malone.

"I'd like to know what you think about that, Jack. I don't have much—practically no—experience in this sort of thing."

"What is it?"

"How to protect Monahan, the witness in the Goldblatt job, and Matt Payne. Monahan positively identified everybody we arrested, by the way. Washington called me just after I called you."

The protection plan was detailed and precise, even including drawings of Monahan's house, Matt's apartment, and the areas around them. That didn't surprise Malone, for he expected as much from Wohl. His brief association with him had convinced him that he really was as smart as his reputation held him to be.

But he was surprised at the handwriting. He had read somewhere, years before, and come to accept, that a very good clue to a man's character was his handwriting. From what he had seen of Wohl, what he knew about him, there was a certain flamboyance to his character, which, according to the handwriting theory, should have manifested itself in flamboyant, perhaps even careless, writing. But the writing on the sheets of lined paper was quite the opposite. Wohl's characters were small, carefully formed, with dots over the *i*'s, and neatly crossed *t*'s. Even his abbreviations were followed by periods.

Maybe that's what he's really like, Malone thought. *Beneath the fashionable clothing and the anti-establishment public attitude, there really beats the heart of a very careful man, one who doesn't really like to take the chance of being wrong.*

"You have three officers at Monahan's house when he's there," Malone said, but it was meant as a question, and Wohl answered it.

"Two two-man Special Operations RPCs," Wohl said. "Four cops. One car and three cops at Monahan's. The fourth officer will be the guy wearing the rent-a-cop uniform in the garage on Rittenhouse Square.''

"He'll have the second car with him at Payne's place?" Malone asked.

Wohl nodded, and went on. "I think Monahan's at the greatest risk. There is a real chance that they will try to kill him. And I don't want everybody there just sitting in a car. I want one man, all the time, walking around. It's cold as hell now, so they can split it up any way they want.''

"I understand.''

"Payne's apartment is really easy to protect. After five-thirty, the main door is locked. There's a pretty good burglar alarm not only on the door, but on the first-, second-, and third-floor windows. There's a key for the elevator from the basement. They haven't been using it, but starting tomorrow, they'll have to.''

"Payne gets out of the hospital tomorrow?''

"Right. Before lunch. He'll go to the Roundhouse for the Homicide interviews—Chief Coughlin got Chief Lowenstein to hold off on that, kept them out of Frankford Hospital, but it has to be done—and then he'll go to his apartment. We'll give the officer in the rent-a-cop uniform a shotgun; he can stay inside that little cubicle with it. And, of course, we'll have one of the three guys with Payne around the clock. I don't think that's going to be a problem. Monahan might be.''

"And district and Highway cars will make passes by both places all night, right?''

"District, Highway, and Special Operations," Wohl said. "There should be at least one of them going by both places at least once an hour, maybe more often. And if Monahan keeps insisting on going to work, by Goldblatt's during the day.''

"I don't want to sound like I'm polishing the apple, Inspector, but I can't think of a thing I'd do differently.''

"Good," Wohl said. "Because, until further notice, you're in charge. I told Captain Sabara and Captain Pekach that they are to give you whatever you think you need.''

"Yes, sir," Malone said. "I met McFadden, and I've seen Martinez, but I don't know this man Lewis.''

"Great big black kid," Wohl said. "He just came on the job, sort of.''

"Sort of?''

"He worked Police Radio for four, five years before he came

on the job, while he was in college. His father is a cop. He
made lieutenant on the list before yours. He used to be a sergeant in the 18th District.''

"Great big guy? Mean as hell, and goes strictly by the
book?''

"That's him.''

"And the young one's in Highway?''

"No. He's been working as a gofer for Detective Harris.
Frankly—don't misunderstand this, he's a nice kid and he'll
probably make a very good cop—he's in Special Operations
because the mayor made a speech at some black church saying
Czernich had assigned him to Special Operations. The same
sort of thing that Carlucci did with Payne. Carlucci told the
newspapers Payne was my administrative assistant, so I named
Payne my administrative assistant. Carlucci told the people at
the church that Czernich had assigned this well-educated,
highly motivated young black officer to Special Operations, so
Czernich assigned him to us—''

The waiter delivered two plates heaped high with food. The
smell made Malone's mouth water.

"I'll get your drinks, gentlemen,'' the waiter said.

"—so not knowing what to do with him,'' Wohl went on,
"I gave him to Harris. He needed a gofer. We still don't have
a fucking clue about who shot that young Italian cop, Magnella. That's what Harris is working.''

Malone, who had heard the gossip about Detective Tony
Harris being on a monumental bender, wondered if Wohl knew.

Wohl started eating.

"The idea, if I didn't make this clear,'' he said a moment
later, "is that with three young cops, in plainclothes, one of
whom is actually Payne's buddy, it will look, I hope, that
they're just hanging around with him.''

"I got that. Instead of a protection detail, you mean?''

"Right. I don't want these scumbags to get the idea that
they're worrying us as much as they are.''

"How long is this going to go on?''

"So far as Monahan is concerned, I don't know. At least
until the end of the trail, and probably a little longer. Stillwell
is going to go before the Grand Jury as soon as he can, probably in the next couple of days, and then they're going to put
it on the docket as soon as that can be arranged. Giacomo will
do his damnedest to get continuances, of course, but with a

little bit of luck, we'll have a judge who won't indulge him. As far as Payne is concerned: He's a cop. As soon as he's back for duty, we'll call off official protection. Encourage him to do his drinking and wenching in the FOP.''

Malone nodded and chuckled.

"There is also a chance that we'll be able to get our hands on the people who are issuing the press releases. I want the people on Monahan's house to take license numbers, that sort of thing."

"That wasn't in here," Malone said, tapping the lined paper Wohl had given him, "but I thought about it."

"There is also a chance, a very slim one, that we can get some of the other witnesses to agree to testify. Washington's going to talk to them. And I'm sure that Stillwell will probably try too. If we can get more people to come forward—"

"Which is exactly what these scumbags are worried about, what they're trying to prevent," Malone said, and then, really surprising Wohl, said bitterly, "Shit!"

Then, having heard what he said, and seeing the look on Wohl's face, he explained.

"Second table from the headwaiter's table. My wife. Ex-wife."

Wohl looked, saw a not-especially-attractive woman, facing in their direction, across a table from a man with long, silver-gray hair, and then turned to Malone.

"That the lawyer?"

"That's him."

"What I think you should do, Jack," Wohl said, "is smile and act as if you're having a great time. I'm only sorry that I'm not a long-legged blonde with spectacular breastworks."

Malone looked at him for a moment, and then picked up his glass.

"Whoopee!" he said, waving it around. "Ain't we having fun!"

"What do you say, kiddo?" Mickey O'Hara asked as he stuck his head into Matt Payne's room. "Feel up to a couple of visitors?"

"Come on in, Mickey," Matt said. He had been watching an especially dull program on public television hoping that it would put him to sleep; it hadn't. He now knew more of the water problems of Los Angeles than he really wanted to know.

Mickey O'Hara and Eleanor Neal came into the room. O'Hara had a brown bag in his hand, and Eleanor carried a potted plant.

"I hope we're not intruding," Eleanor said, "but Mickey said it would be all right if I came, and I wanted to thank you for saving his life."

"Matt, say hello to Eleanor Neal," Mickey said.

"How do you do?" Matt said, a reflex response, and then: "I didn't save his life."

"Yeah, you did," Mickey said. "But for a moment, in the alley, I thought you had changed your mind."

Matt had a sudden, very clear mental picture of the fear on Mickey's face and in his eyes, right after it had happened, when he had, startled by the flash from Mickey's camera, turned from the man he had shot and pointed his revolver at Mickey O'Hara.

"What does that mean?"

"Not important," Mickey said. He pulled a bottle of John Jameson Irish whiskey from the brown paper bag. "Down payment on what I owe you, Matt."

"Hey, I didn't save your life, okay? You don't owe me a damned thing."

Mickey ignored him. He bent over and took two plastic cups from the bedside table, opened the bottle, poured whiskey in each cup, and then looked at Matt.

"You want it straight, or should I pour some water in it?"

"I'm not sure you should be giving him that," Eleanor said.

"He's an Irishman," Mickey said. "It'll do him more good than whatever else they've been giving him in here."

"Put a little water in it, please, Mickey," Matt said.

Mickey poured water from the insulated water carafe into the paper cup and handed it to Matt.

"Here's to you, Matt," he said, raising his glass.

"Cheers," Matt said, and took a swallow.

Maybe the booze will make me sleepy, or at least take the edge off the pain in the goddamn leg.

And then: *Does he really think I saved his life, or is that bullshit? Blarney.*

"How do you feel, Matt?" Mickey asked.

"I'm all right," Matt said. "I get out of here tomorrow."

"So soon?" Eleanor asked, surprised.

"Current medical wisdom is that the sooner they get you moving around, the better," Matt said.

"You going home?" Mickey said.

"If by 'home,' you mean my apartment, yes, of course."

"I was thinking of—where do your parents live, Wallingford?"

"My apartment."

"You know getting in to see you is like getting to see the gold at Fort Knox?" Mickey asked. Matt nodded. "So you know what these people have been up to?"

Matt nodded again.

"The Molotov cocktail, the press release, the second one? All of it?"

Matt nodded again.

"What do you think, Mickey?" he asked.

"I know a lot of black guys, and a lot of Muslims," Mickey said. "Ordinarily, I can get what I want to know out of at least a couple of them. So far, all I get is shrugs when I ask about the Islamic Liberation Army. That could mean they really don't know, or it could mean that they think I'm just one more goddamn honky. I'd watch myself, if I were you."

"I was thinking—with what they have on television, there's been a lot of time for that—about what the hell they're after."

"And?"

"In the thirties, during the Depression, when Dillinger and Bonnie and Clyde were running around robbing banks, killing people, there was supposed to be some support for them; people thought they were Robin Hood."

"From what I've heard about Bonnie, she was no Maid Marion," Mickey said.

"What does that mean?" Eleanor asked.

"Not important," Mickey said. "For that matter, Clyde wasn't exactly Errol Flynn, either. What is it you're saying, Matty, that they're after public support?"

Matt nodded.

"A political agenda?"

"Why else the press releases?"

"That's pretty sophisticated thinking for a bunch of stickup guys who have to have somebody read the Exit sign to them."

"Somebody wrote those press releases," Matt argued. "For their purpose—getting themselves in the newspapers and on

TV—they were, by definition, effective. At least one of them can write. And plan things, like the gasoline bomb.''

"What do you mean, 'plan the gasoline bomb'? Anybody knows how to make one of those. *That* I would expect from these people.''

"When and where to throw it," Matt said. "They had to be watching Goldbatt's. One man, just standing around, would have been suspicious. So they had a half a dozen of them, plus of course the guy on the roof who threw it.''

O'Hara grunted.

"Unless, of course, Matty, they have somebody inside the cops, inside Special Operations, who just called them and told them when Washington was going to pick up Monahan. *That* suggests an operation run by people who know what they're doing.''

"You really think that's possible?" Matt asked, genuinely shocked. "That they have somebody inside?''

O'Hara never got the chance to reply. The door opened again and Mr. and Mrs. Brewster C. Payne walked in.

"Hi!" Matt said.

"How are you, honey?" Patricia Payne asked.

"Just fine," Matt said. "Mother, you didn't have to come back. I'm getting out of here tomorrow.''

She held up her arm, around which was folded a hang-up bag.

"In your underwear?''

"It's the cocktail hour, I see," Brewster C. Payne said.

"Dad, do you know Mickey O'Hara?''

"Only by reputation. How are you, Mr. O'Hara?''

"Are you allowed to have that?" Patricia Payne asked.

"Probably not, but I can't see where it will do any harm," Brewster Payne said. He smiled at Eleanor. "I'm Brewster Payne, and this is my wife.''

"I'm Eleanor Neal.''

"How do you do?" Patricia Payne said.

"Can I offer you a little taste, Mr. Payne?" Mickey asked.

"Is there a glass?''

"How do you know they aren't giving you some medicine that will react with that?" Patricia Payne asked.

"All I'm taking is aspirin," Matt replied.

Mickey made drinks for the Paynes.

Patricia Payne nodded her thanks, sipped hers, and said, "I

have this terrible premonition that some two-hundred-pound nurse is going to storm in here, find the party in progress, yell for the guards, and I will win the Terrible Mother of the Year award.''

"I thought bringing Matt a little taste was the least I could do for what he did, saving my life, for me.''

Thank you, Mickey O'Hara.

"It was very kind of you, Mr. O'Hara," Brewster Payne said.

And thank you, Dad, for cutting off the colorful story of my courage in the face of death.

"Call me Mickey, please."

"Mickey."

"Mickey, we should be going," Eleanor said. "We've been here long enough."

"You're right," Mickey said. He tossed his drink down, shook hands all around, and opened the door for Eleanor.

"Interesting man," Brewster Payne said as the door closed after them.

"He's supposed to be the best police reporter on the Eastern Seaboard."

"He has a Pulitzer, I believe," Brewster Payne said, and then changed the subject. "Denny Coughlin tells me you insist on going to your apartment when they turn you loose?"

"Yes, sir."

"How much do you know of what else has happened?"

"I know about the threats, and the firebomb. Is there something else?"

"No. I just didn't know how much you knew. Just before we came here, Dick Detweiler phoned. They wanted to come see you—he called earlier, as soon as he heard what had happened—but I told him you were getting out in the morning."

"Thank you."

"He also volunteered to send out to Wallingford as many of the Nesfoods plant security people as would be necessary for as long as would be necessary. The point of this is that if the reason you don't want to come home is because of your concern for your mother and me, that won't be a problem. Dick would really like to help."

"I'm a cop," Matt said. "I'm not about to let these scumbags run me out of town."

"I told you that's what he would say," Patricia Payne said.

"And I'll have people with me," Matt said.

"That was explained to us in great detail by Denny Coughlin. Having said that, I think Denny would be more comfortable if you were in Wallingford."

"I'm going to the apartment, Dad," Matt said.

"The police are taking these threats seriously, honey," Patricia Payne said. "Getting in to see you is like trying to walk into the White House."

"I suspect Uncle Denny had a lot to do with whatever security there is here," Matt said. "In his godfather, as opposed to chief inspector of police, role."

"I think that probably has a lot to do with it," Brewster Payne agreed, smiling. "Okay. You change your mind—I suspect you'll get claustrophobia in your apartment—and we'll get you out to the house."

The door opened again, and a nurse came in. She was well under one hundred pounds, but she was every bit as formidable and outraged as the two-hundred-pounder Patricia Payne had imagined.

"Liquor is absolutely forbidden," she announced. "I should think you would have known that."

"I tried to tell my wife that," Brewster C. Payne said, straight-faced, "but she wouldn't listen to me."

Matt laughed heartily, and even more heartily when he saw the look on his mother's face. Each time his stomach contracted in laughter his leg hurt.

Jason Washington was waiting for Peter Wohl when he walked into the building at Bustleton and Bowler at five minutes to eight the next morning.

"Morning, Jason."

"Can I have a minute, Inspector?"

"Sure. Come on in the office. With a little bit of luck, there will be hot coffee."

"How about here? This will only take a yes or a no."

"Okay. What's on your mind?"

"Captain Sabara told me he wants Tiny Lewis—you know who I mean?"

"Sure."

"—on the security detail for Matt Payne. I'd rather he got somebody else."

"You have something for Lewis to do?"

Washington nodded.

"You got him. You discuss this with Sabara?"

"No."

"I'm sure he would have let you have Lewis."

"He would have asked why."

"You're losing me."

"I didn't know if he knew Tony Harris has been at the bottle."

"What's that got to do with Lewis?"

"Harris is sober. If we can keep him that way for the next seventy-two hours, I think we can keep him that way more or less indefinitely. Lewis will be with Harris all day, with orders to call me if Tony even looks at a liquor store."

"And at night?"

"Martha likes him. We have room at the apartment. He can stay with us for a while."

"Martha is a saint," Wohl said.

"No," Washington said, "it's just—"

"*Yeah,*" Wohl interrupted coldly. "Only a saint or a fool can stand a dedicated drunk, and Martha's not a fool."

"He's a good cop, Inspector."

"That's what I've been thinking, with one part of my mind, for the last three or four days. The *other* part of my mind keeps repeating, 'He's a drunk, he's a drunk, he's a drunk.' "

"I think it's under control," Washington said.

"It better be, Jason."

"Thanks, Inspector," Washington said.

"You got something going now? I'd like you to sit in on what Malone has set up for Matt and Monahan. They're supposed to be waiting for me in my office."

"I can make time for that," Washington said.

Wohl led the way to his office. Sabara was standing by his desk, a telephone to his ear.

"He just walked in, Commissioner," Sabara said. He covered the mouthpiece with his hand. "This is the third time he called."

Wohl nodded and took the telephone from him.

"Good morning, Commissioner. Sorry you had to call back."

The others in the room could hear only Wohl's end of the conversation:

"I'm sure Mr. Stillwell has his reasons. . . ."

"I checked with the hospital fifteen minutes ago. We're planning on taking him out of there at about half past ten. . . .

"Yes, sir. . . .

"I can stop by your office as soon as the interview is over, Commissioner. . . .

"I'm sure everyone else—No. I don't know about O'Hara, come to think of it. But every one involved but O'Hara has given a statement, sir. I'll check on O'Hara right away and let you know, sir. . . .

"Yes, sir. I'll see you in your office as soon as they've finished with Payne. Good-bye, sir."

He put the telephone in its cradle, but, deep in thought, did not take his hand off it.

He finally shrugged and looked at the others.

"Stillwell wants to run Matt Payne, the shooting, past the Grand Jury. It probably makes sense, if you think about it—"

He paused, thinking, *I wonder why that sonofabitch didn't tell me—*

"—they will decline to indict, and then Giacomo can't start making noise about a police cover-up."

"It was a good shooting," Sabara said. "Stevens—what does he call himself?"

"Abu Ben Mohammed," Wohl furnished.

"—came out shooting. It wasn't even justifiable force, it was self-defense."

"I guess that's what Stillwell figures," Wohl said, and then changed the subject. "Jack has polished my rough plan to protect Matt and Monahan. I'd like to hear what you think of it. Jack?"

Malone took the protection plan, which he had just had typed up and duplicated, from his jacket pocket.

Is he trying to give me credit for this to be a nice guy, Malone wondered, *or trying to lay the responsibility on me in case something goes wrong?*

TWENTY

Matt had been told "The Doctor" would be in to see him before he would be discharged, and therefore not to get dressed.

"The Doctor" turned out to be three doctors, accompanied, to Matt's pleasant surprise, by Lari Matsi, R.N.

No one acted as if there was a live human being in the bed. He was nothing more than a specimen.

"Remove the dressing on the leg, please," a plump doctor with a pencil-line mustache Matt could not remember ever having seen before ordered, "let's have a look at it."

Lari folded the sheet and blanket back, put her fingers to the adhesive tape, and gave a quick jerk.

"Shit!" Matt yelped, and then, a moment later, added, "Sorry."

Lari didn't seem to notice either the expletive or the apology.

The three doctors solemnly bent over and peered at the leg. Matt looked. His entire calf was a massive bruise, the purple-black of the bruise color coordinated with the circus orange antiseptic with which the area had apparently been painted.

There was a three-inch slash, closed with eight or ten black sutures. A bloody goo seemed to be leaking out.

"Healing nicely," one doctor opined.

"Not much suppuration," the second observed.

Pencil-line mustache asked, "What do I have him on?"

Lari checked an aluminum clipboard, announced something ending in "—mycin, one hundred thousand, every four hours," and handed Pencil-line mustache the clipboard. He took a gold pen from his white jacket and wrote something on it.

"Have that filled before he leaves the hospital," he ordered.

"Yes, Doctor," Lari said.

Pencil-line mustache pointed at Matt.

Lari reached over and snatched the bandage on Matt's forehead off.

He didn't utter an expletive this time, but it took a good deal of effort.

Pencil-line mustache grunted.

"Nice job," Doctor Two opined. "Who did it?"

"Who else?" Doctor One answered, just a trifle smugly.

Pencil-line mustache looked from one to the other. Both shook their heads no.

Pencil-line mustache finally acknowledged that a human being was in the bed.

"You will be given a medication before leaving—"

" 'Medication'?" Matt interrupted. "Is that something like medicine?"

"—which should take care of the possibility of infection," Pencil-line went on. "The dressing should be changed daily. Your personal physician can handle that. Your only problem that I can see is your personal hygiene, in other words, bathing. Until that suppuration, in other words that oozing, stops, I don't think you should immerse that leg, in other words, get it wet."

"I see," Matt said solemnly.

"The best way to handle the problem, in my experience, is with Saran Wrap. In other words, you wrap the leg with Saran Wrap, holding it in place with Scotch tape, and when you get in the bathtub, you keep the leg out of the water."

"Do I take the bandage off, or do I wrap the Saran Wrap over the bandage?"

"Leave the dressing—that's a *dressing*, not a bandage—on."

"Yes, sir."

"In a week or so, in his good judgment, whatever he thinks is appropriate, your personal physician will remove the sutures, in other words those stitches."

"In other words, whatever he decides, right?"

"Right," Pencil-line said. A suspicion that he was being mocked had just been born.

"Got it," Matt said.

"Nurse, you may replace the dressing," Pencil-line said.

"Yes, Doctor," Lari said.

Pencil-line nodded at Matt. His lips bent in what could have been a smile, and he marched out of the room. Doctors One and Two followed him.

"You're a wise guy, aren't you?" Lari said, when they were alone.

"No. I'm a cop. A wise-guy is a gangster. Who was *that* guy, in other words, Pencil-line, anyway?"

"Chief of Surgery. He's a very good surgeon."

"In other words, he cuts good, right?"

She looked at him and smiled.

"You told me you weren't coming back," Matt said.

"I go where the money is. They were shorthanded, probably because of the lousy weather, so they called me."

"I'm delighted," Matt said. "But we're going to have to stop meeting this way. People will start talking."

"How's the pain?" she asked, pushing a rolling cart with bandaging material on it up to the bed.

"It's all right now. It hurt like hell last night."

"It's bruised," she said. "But I think you were very lucky."

"Yeah, look at the nurse I got."

"Have you ever used a crutch before?"

"No. Do I really need one?"

"For a couple of days. Then you can either use a cane, or take your chances without one. When I finish bandaging this, I'll get one and show you how to use it."

"That's not a bandage, that's a dressing."

"I'm bandaging it with a dressing," Lari said, and smiled at him again.

It was, he decided when she had finished, a professional dressing. And she hadn't hurt him.

"What happens now?"

"I get your prescription to the pharmacy, get your crutch,

show you how to use it, and presuming you don't break your leg, then—I don't know. I'll see if I can find out."

Charley McFadden, in civilian clothes, blue jeans and a quilted nylon jacket, came in the room as Matt was practicing with the crutch.

"Hi ya, Lari," he said, obviously pleased to see her.

"Hello, Charley," she said. "What are you doing here?"

"I'm going to carry Gimpy here to the Roundhouse. Can he operate on that crutch?"

"Why don't you ask me?" Matt asked.

"You wouldn't know," Charley said.

"He'll be all right," Lari said.

"Are you here officially?" Matt asked.

"Oh, yeah. Unmarked car—Hay-zus is downstairs in it—whatever overtime we turn in, the works. Even a shotgun. And on the way here, I heard them send a Highway RPC here to meet the lieutenant. You get a goddamn—sorry, Lari—convoy."

"When?"

"Whenever you're ready."

"When is that going to be, Lari?" Matt asked.

"As soon as you get dressed," she said. "I'll go get a wheelchair."

Matt was amused and touched by the gentleness with which Charley McFadden helped him pull his trouser leg over his injured calf, tied his shoes, and even offered to tie his necktie, if he didn't feel like standing in front of the mirror.

Lari returned with the wheelchair, saw him installed in it, put his crutch between his legs, and then insisted on pushing it herself.

"Hospital rules," she said when McFadden stepped behind it.

"I like it," Matt said. "In China, they make the females walk three paces behind their men. This is even better."

"You're not my man," Lari said.

"We could talk about that."

What the hell am I doing? Making a pass at her when two minutes ago I was wondering how I could get Helene back in the sack?

Both Highway cops on duty at the nurse's station by the elevator greeted Matt by name, and then got on the elevator with them.

Lieutenant Malone was waiting in the main lobby when the door opened.

"There's a couple of press guys," he said to the Highway cops, nodding toward the door. "Don't let them get in the way."

Matt saw two men, one of them wearing earmuffs and both holding cameras, just outside the hospital door.

Lari rolled him up the side of the circular door.

"End of the line," she said.

Chief Inspector Dennis V. Coughlin came through the revolving door, trailed by a very large, neatly dressed young man whom Matt correctly guessed was Coughlin's new driver.

"Morning, Matt," he said.

"Good morning."

"You two make a hand seat," Coughlin ordered. "Put him in back of my car. There's more room."

Coughlin's official car was an Oldsmobile Ninety-Eight.

"I can walk."

"It's icy out there, and you're no crutch expert," Coughlin said.

"Thanks for everything," Matt said to Lari. "I'll see you around."

She crossed her arms under her breasts and nodded.

Charley and Coughlin's driver made a seat with their crossed hands. Matt lowered himself into it, Coughlin pushed open a glass door and they carried him out of the lobby.

"How do you feel, Payne?" one of the reporters called to him, in the act of taking his picture.

"I'm feeling fine."

"Any regrets about shooting Charles Stevens?"

"What kind of a question is that? What the hell is the matter with you people?" Denny Coughlin flared.

The interruption served to give Matt time to reconsider the answer—"Not a one"—that had come to his lips.

"I'm sorry it was necessary," he said.

Matt saw that he was indeed being transported in a convoy. There was a Highway Patrol RPC, an unmarked car (*probably Malone's*, he thought), Coughlin's Oldsmobile, and behind that another unmarked car with Jesus Martinez behind the wheel.

They set him on his feet beside the Oldsmobile. Coughlin's driver opened the door, and Matt got in.

"Let him sit sideward with his leg on the seat," Coughlin ordered. "McFadden, you ride in your car."

"There's plenty of room back here," Matt protested. "Get in, Charley."

Charley looked at Coughlin for a decision.

"Okay, get in," Coughlin said.

By the time Coughlin had gotten into the front seat, his driver had gotten behind the wheel and started the engine.

Coughlin turned in his seat and put his arm on the back of it.

"You haven't met Sergeant Holloran, have you, Matt?"

"What do you say, Payne?" the driver said.

"Thanks for the ride," Matt said.

"You're McFadden, right?" Holloran asked, turning his head to look at McFadden. "The guy who ran down the guy who shot Dutch Moffitt?"

"Yeah. How are you, Sergeant?"

"While we're doing this, Matty," Coughlin said, "and before I forget it, Tom Lenihan called and asked if it would be all right if he went to the hospital, and I told him you had enough visitors, but he said to tell you hello."

"Thank you."

"There's been another development, one I just heard about, which is the reason I came to the hospital myself," Coughlin said.

Bullshit, Uncle Denny. You wanted to be here.

"What?"

"Stillwell is going to run you past the Grand Jury."

"I don't know what that means."

"Once they take a case before the Grand Jury, and the Grand Jury declines to issue a true bill, that's it."

"I don't know what that means, either."

"It means the facts of the case will be presented to a Grand Jury, who will decide that there is no grounds to take you to trial."

"That doesn't always happen?"

"Normally, in a case like this, the district attorney will just make the decision, and that would be the end of it. But with Armando C. Giacomo the defense counsel—"

"Who's—what was that name?"

"Armando C. Giacomo. Very good criminal lawyer. Half a dozen one way, six the other if he or Colonel Mawson is the best there is in Philadelphia."

"You never heard of him?" Charley McFadden asked, genuinely surprised, which earned him a no from Matt and a dirty, keep-out-of-this look from Coughlin.

"The assistant DA, Stillwell, or maybe Tom Callis, the DA himself, is probably worried that Giacomo will start hollering 'police whitewash' or 'cover-up.' Giacomo couldn't do that if you had been before the Grand Jury and they hadn't returned a true bill. You understand all this?"

"I think so."

"It gets a little more complicated," Coughlin said. "I called your father as soon as I heard about this, and he said Colonel Mawson would be in the Roundhouse for your interview."

"Good."

Whatever the hell this Grand Jury business is all about—it never came up when I shot Fletcher—I am very unlikely to get screwed with J. Dunlop Mawson hovering protectively over me.

"Maybe good and maybe not," Coughlin said. "If you had done something wrong, then having Mawson there to protect your rights would be fine. So let me ask you again, Matty, you already told me, but let me ask you again: You didn't shoot at Stevens until he had shot at you, right?"

"Right."

"Did you shoot at him before or after you got hit?"

"After."

"You're absolutely sure about that?"

"Absolutely."

"And that's what Mickey O'Hara will say?"

"He was there. He saw what happened."

"That being the case, you have done absolutely nothing wrong," Coughlin said.

"I already had that figured out," Matt said, which earned him a pained look.

"Let me tell you how this works, Matty," Coughlin said. "You have civil rights, even if you are a cop—"

Well, that's nice to know.

"—in other words, when you are interviewed by Homicide, you don't have to say anything at all, and you have the right to have an attorney present. Miranda. You understand?"

Matt nodded.

"Some cops, if they're worried, will want a lawyer. The FOP will provide one. If you figure you need one, you could have an FOP lawyer. Or Colonel Mawson—"

What the hell is he leading up to?

"—but on the other hand, you don't have to have a lawyer. Just answer the questions in the interview as honestly as you can."

"Are you telling me I shouldn't ask for a lawyer?"

"I'm telling you that Armando C. Giacomo, if you have a lawyer, especially if you have Colonel Mawson, is probably going to try to twist that around so it looks as if you were reluctant to tell the Homicide people what really happened, to make it look as if the only reason you didn't get indicted by the Grand Jury is because Mawson was there when you were interviewed."

"You *are* telling me I should tell Colonel Mawson 'thanks, but no thanks'?"

"I'm telling you that you have to make up your mind what's best for you and the Police Department."

Jesus H. Christ!

STATEMENT OF: P/O Matthew Mark Payne, Badge 7701

DATE AND TIME: 1105 A.M. Jan. 5, 1973

PLACE: Homicide Bureau, Police Admin. Bldg.

CONCERNING: Death by Shooting of Charles David Stevens, aka Abu Ben Mohammed

IN PRESENCE OF: Captain Henry C. Quaire; Detective Kenneth J. Summers, Badge 4505

INTERROGATED BY: Det. Alonzo Kramer, Badge 1967

RECORDED BY: Mrs. Jo-Ellen Garcia-Romez

I am Detective Kramer of the Homicide Bureau

We are questioning you concerning your involvement in the fatal shooting of Charles David

Stevens, also known as Abu Ben Mohammed. We have a duty to explain to you and to warn you that you have the following legal rights:

A. You have the right to remain silent and do not have to say anything at all.

B. Anything you say can and will be used against you in court.

C. You have a right to talk to a lawyer of your own choice before we ask you any questions, and also to have a lawyer here with you while we ask questions.

D. If you cannot afford to hire a lawyer, and you want one, we will see that you have a lawyer provided to you, free of charge, before we ask you any questions.

E. If you are willing to give us a statement, you have a right to stop anytime you wish.

---

1. Q. Do you understand that you have a right to keep quiet and do not have to say anything at all?
   A. Yes, I do.

2. Q. Do you understand that anything you say can and will be used against you?
   A. Yes, I do.

3. Q. Do you want to remain silent?
   A. I'll tell you anything you want to know.

4. Q. Do you understand you have a right to talk to a lawyer before we ask you any questions?
   A. Yes, I do.

5. Q. Do you understand that if you cannot afford

to hire a lawyer, and you want one, we will not ask you any questions until a lawyer is appointed for you free of charge?

A. Yes, I do.

6. Q. Do you want to talk to a lawyer at this time, or to have a lawyer with you while we ask you questions?

A. I don't want a lawyer, thank you.

7. Q. Are you willing to answer questions of your own free will, without force or fear, and without any threats and promises having been made to you?

A. Yes, I am.

---

8. Q. State your name, city of residence, and employment?

A. Matthew M. Payne, I live in Philadelphia, and I am a police officer.

9. Q. State your badge number and duty assignment?

A. Badge Number 7701. Special Operations Division.

10. Q. What is your specific assignment?

A. I am administrative assistant to Inspector Wohl.

11. Q. That is Staff Inspector Peter Wohl, commanding officer of the Special Operations Division?

A. That's right.

12. Q. Were you on duty at approximately five A.M. January 4 of this year?

A. Yes, I was.

13. Q. What was the nature of your duty at that time and place?

A. Inspector Wohl ordered me to accompany Mr. Mickey O'Hara of the Bulletin during an arrest that was taking place.

14. Q. That is Mr. Michael J. O'Hara, a police reporter employed by the Philadelphia Bulletin?

A. That's correct.

15. Q. Were you in uniform and armed at this time?

A. I was in civilian clothing. I was armed.

16. Q. Why were you in civilian clothing?

A. I am in a plainclothes assignment.

17. Q. You do not then normally wear a uniform on duty?

A. No, sir.

18. Q. With what type weapon were you armed?

A. A Smith & Wesson Undercover revolver.

19. Q. That is a five-shot .38 Special caliber short-nosed revolver?

A. Correct.

20. Q. Was that weapon issued to you by the Police Department for use in your official duties?

A. No.

21. Q. Where did you get that revolver?

A. Colosimo's Gun Store.

22. Q. That revolver is your personal property?

A. Yes.

23. Q. Have you been issued a revolver or other weapon by the Police Department for use in your duties?
A. Yes.

24. Q. Since you were on duty, why were you not carrying that weapon?
A. I have permission to carry the Undercover.

25. Q. From whom?
A. From Inspector Wohl.

26. Q. For what purpose?
A. It's easier to conceal, more concealable, than the Police Special.

27. Q. The Police Special being the .38 Special Caliber Smith & Wesson Military and Police revolver with four-inch barrel issued to you by the Police Department?
A. Yes.

28. Q. Have you undergone any official instruction, testing, and/or qualification involving the Smith & Wesson Undercover revolver with which you were armed on January 3 of this year?
A. I went through the prescribed course at the Police Firearms Range before I was authorized to carry the Undercover revolver.

29. Q. With what type of cartridge was your Undercover revolver loaded at the time and date we're talking about?
A. Standard Remington .38 Special cartridges, with a 158-grain round nose lead bullet.

30. Q. Where did you get that ammunition?
A. It was issued to me.

31. Q. It is the standard ammunition prescribed by regulation for the Undercover revolver?

A. So far as I know, for both of them. The Military and Police and the Undercover.

32. Q. What were your specific orders in regard to Mr. O'Hara?

A. Inspector Wohl told me to take Mr. O'Hara to Lieutenant Suffern.

33. Q. That is Lieutenant Edward J. Suffern, who is assigned to Special Operations?

A. Yes, sir.

34. Q. Go on.

A. Inspector Wohl told me to take Mr. O'Hara to Lieutenant Suffern, and to tell him that he had authorized Mr. O'Hara to accompany Lieutenant Suffern during the arrest, but that Mr. O'Hara was not to enter the building where Stevens was until he had been arrested.

35. Q. Who is Stevens?

A. Charles David Stevens. Also known as Abu Ben Mohammed. A warrant had been issued for his arrest in connection with an armed robbery and murder at Goldblatt's furniture store.

36. Q. Were you charged with serving this warrant?

A. No. It was to be served by a Homicide detective, backed up by men under Lieutenant Suffern.

37. Q. You took Mr. O'Hara to Lieutenant Suffern?

A. Yes, I did.

38. Q. And then what happened?

A. Lieutenant Suffern said that Mr. O'Hara and myself should accompany him. When the time came, we got in his car and went with him.

39. Q. Where did you go with Lieutenant Suffern in his car?

A. To the alley behind Stevens's house.

40. Q. I now show you a map of the Frankford area of Philadelphia. Would you please mark on the map where you were taken by Lieutenant Suffern?

A. All right.

(See Map marked as Attachment 1.)

41. Q. And then what happened?

A. Mr. O'Hara got out of the car.

42. Q. Why, if you know, did Mr. O'Hara get out of the car?

A. He said he didn't want his camera lens to become fogged as he was afraid it might if he jumped out of the car when the arrest was made.

43. Q. Go on.

A. I got out of the car too.

44. Q. Did you have Lieutenant Suffern's permission to do so?

A. My orders were to accompany Mr. O'Hara. So I got out of the car too.

45. Q. What comment, if any, did Lieutenant Suffern have about either of you getting out of the car?

A. I seem to recall he told Mickey, Mr. O'Hara, to stick close to the wall.

46. Q. What, if anything, did you or Mr. O'Hara do at this time?

A. Mr. O'Hara wiped the lens of his camera with his handkerchief.

47. Q. And what, if anything, happened next?

A. I heard noise, what sounded like wood breaking, in the alley in the direction of Stevens's house. After a moment, I detected movement in the alley.

48. Q. Had you, at that time, drawn your weapon?

A. Not drawn it. I had taken it from my ankle holster and put it in my overcoat pocket.

49. Q. Your weapon, was it in sight or not?
A. No. It was not.

50. Q. Why did you take your weapon from its holster and put it in your pocket?

A. Because I thought I could get at it easier that way if I needed it.

51. Q. Then you anticipated having need of your weapon?

A. No. I was just being careful.

(Chief Inspectors Lowenstein and Coughlin became additional witnesses to the interrogation at this point.)

52. Q. Did Mr. O'Hara see you take your weapon from your ankle holster?

A. I don't know if he did or not.

53. Q. How about Lieutenant Suffern?
A. I don't know. I don't believe so.

54. Q. Go on.
A. Where were we?

55. Q. You and Mr. O'Hara were in the alley, you said. You said you detected movement.

A. Okay. I realized that what I was seeing was a man coming in my direction. So I called to him to stop.

56. Q. Did you identify yourself as a police officer?

A. I said, Stop. Police officer.

57. Q. At this time, did you recognize the person in the alley as Mr. Charles D. Stevens?

A. No.

58. Q. Had you, previous to this occasion, ever seen Mr. Charles D. Stevens?

A. No.

59. Q. Had you ever seen a photograph of Mr. Stevens and/or were you familiar with his description?

A. No.

60. Q. Then you did not recognize the individual coming toward you as Mr. Stevens?

A. No. But it didn't matter. It was too dark. All I saw was somebody coming down the alley.

61. Q. But you shot at him. Why did you shoot at him?

A. Because he had shot at me, because he had shot me. Jesus Christ!

62. Q. (Captain Quaire) Take it easy, Payne.

A. Yes, sir. Sorry.

63. Q. (Detective Kramer) Did you see any weapon in Mr. Stevens's hand?

A. Not until he was down.

64. Q. How did you know he, Stevens, was

shooting at you?

A. He was the only one in the alley. I didn't know who it was until later. I saw flashes. I was hit.

65. Q. What was the response of the individual you now know to be Charles David Stevens to your order, Stop. Police officer?

A. He screamed, Get out of my way, motherfucker.

66. Q. Those precise words?

A. That's a direct quote. For some reason, I remember it very clearly.

67. Q. (Captain Quaire) Payne, spare us the sarcasm.

A. Yes, sir.

68. Q. (Detective Kramer) You said, screamed. That suggests pain.

A. Strike, screamed. Insert, shouted angrily.

69. Q. He angrily shouted, Get out of my way, motherfucker, or words to that effect. Is that what you mean to say?

A. He angrily shouted, Get out of my way, motherfucker. Those exact words.

70. Q. And then what happened?

A. Then he started shooting.

71. Q. You're sure it was Charles D. Stevens who started shooting?

A. I am sure the man in the alley started shooting. He was subsequently identified as Charles D. Stevens.

72. Q. And?

A. He hit me. I got my gun out and started shooting back at him.

73. Q. Until he shot at you, your pistol was out of sight, in your overcoat pocket. Is that what you're telling me?
   A. Right.

74. Q. How many times did you fire your weapon?
   A. Four times.

75. Q. You're sure?
   A. I'm sure.

76. Q. Was there any indication that any of your bullets struck Mr. Stevens?
   A. Yes. He went down. Somebody, I don't remember who, subsequently told me I had hit him twice.

77. Q. By, went down, do you mean he fell down in the alley?
   A. Yes.

78. Q. What, if anything, did you then do?
   A. I went to him to make sure he was down.

79. Q. You have stated you were wounded. Where were you wounded?
   A. In the forehead and left calf.

80. Q. Since you were wounded, how did you manage, as you said you did, to go to Mr. Stevens?
   A. I don't know. Hobbled over, I suppose.

81. Q. Hobbled? What do you mean by, hobbled?
   A. When I was shot, I fell down, fell against a wall, and then fell down. I had trouble getting to my feet. I was, sort of, on all fours.

82. Q. Sort of on all fours?

A. Yes, sort of on all fours. I finally got to my feet and went to the man I had shot.

83. Q. What did you do when you reached Mr. Stevens?

A. I stepped on his gun.

84. Q. What type of weapon was this? Could you identify it?

A. It looked to me like an Army Colt .45 automatic, the Army service pistol.

85. Q. But you're not sure?

A. I didn't closely examine it.

86. Q. Why not?

A. I was otherwise occupied, for Christ's sake.

87. Q. (Captain Quaire) Watch it, Payne.

88. Q. (Detective Kramer) Was Stevens holding the weapon when you stepped on it?

A. No. He had dropped it, and it was half buried in the snow. I stepped on it to make sure he couldn't pick it up.

89. Q. Did you see him drop it?

A. No.

90. Q. Then how do you know the pistol you stepped on was dropped by Mr. Stevens?

A. Didn't you say I could stop answering questions whenever I wanted? Okay. I want to stop answering questions.

91. Q. (Captain Quaire) Is something bothering you, Payne?

A. Yes, sir. This guy's stupid questions are bothering me. How do I know it was dropped by Mr. Stevens? Who else could have dropped it, the good fairy?

92. Q. (Detective Kramer) We're just trying to clear this up as best we can, Payne.
A. I'm sorry I lost my temper.

93. Q. (Chief Inspector Coughlin) How long have you been discharged from the hospital, Officer Payne? I think that should be made note of in this interview.
A. I came here directly from the hospital. I don't know how long. Maybe an hour.

94. Q. (Detective Kramer) The first time you saw the .45 automatic pistol you stepped on was when you found it in the snow. Is that correct?
A. Yes.

95. Q. You saw a pistol in the hand of the man subsequently identified to you as Charles D. Stevens, is that correct?
A. Correct.

96. Q. But you cannot positively identify the pistol you stepped on near Mr. Stevens after you shot him as the same pistol you saw earlier in his hand, is that correct?
A. Yes, that's correct.

97. Q. Did you see Mr. Stevens fire the pistol you saw him holding in his hand?
A. Yes. He shot me with the pistol he held in his hand.

98. Q. Did Mr. Stevens say anything to you when you went to him in the alley after you shot him?
A. No.

99. Q. What happened after you stepped on the pistol?

A. Mickey O'Hara was there. He took a couple of pictures, and then Lieutenant Suffern showed up and handcuffed Mr. Stevens.

100. Q. Was Mr. Stevens conscious?

A. Yes.

101. Q. Could you tell anything of the nature of his wounds?

A. No.

102. Q. Did you attempt to render first aid to Mr. Stevens?

A. No.

103. Q. What happened to you then?

A. I was put onto a stretcher, loaded in a van, and taken to Frankford Hospital.

104. Q. Do you know what happened to Mr. Stevens at that time?

A. He was in the same van as I was. He was taken to Frankford Hospital with me.

105. Q. (Chief Inspector Coughlin) Considering your weakened physical condition, Officer Payne, do you feel up to answering any more questions at this time?

A. I would rather not answer any more questions at this time.

106. Q. (Detective Kramer) You understand, Officer Payne, that we will be asking you more questions when your physical condition permits?

A. Yeah.

107. Q. Thank you, Payne.

TWENTY-ONE

There was a Mercury station wagon with a Rose Tree Hunt Club decal in the rear window parked beside Matt Payne's silver Porsche in the underground parking lot of the building on Rittenhouse Square when the convoy rolled in.

"My mother's here," Matt said.

"I thought she might be," Chief Inspector Dennis V. Coughlin said matter-of-factly, and then added, to Sergeant Holloran, "Francis, we can get him upstairs. You take the car around and park it in front."

"Yes, sir. You want me to come up, Chief?"

Coughlin hesitated just perceptibly.

"Yeah. You might as well see the layout."

The Highway Patrol RPC had dropped out, but otherwise, the convoy was the same as the one that had carried Matt to the Roundhouse. Malone's car had led the way from the Roundhouse, followed by Coughlin's Oldsmobile, and Jesus Martinez in a second unmarked Special Operations Ford.

Holloran stopped the car as near as he could get to the elevator. Charley McFadden got out and then turned to help Matt get out and onto his feet.

Coughlin got out of the front seat.

"You and me lock wrists, McFadden," Coughlin ordered. "I don't think Martinez could handle Matt."

"Hey. I'm not a cripple. I can manage," Matt said, standing on his good leg and waving the crutch. "I've got to learn to use this thing anyway."

Coughlin looked doubtful, but finally walked to Martinez.

"Park that wherever you can find a place," he ordered.

Matt, with Charley McFadden hovering around him, made his way to the elevator door, where Malone was waiting. He pushed the button to open the door, waited for Matt and McFadden to get in, and then joined them. When the door started to close, Matt leaned against the elevator wall, and then stuck his crutch into the opening, holding the door open.

Coughlin walked quickly to the door and then stopped.

"You got room for one more?" he asked.

"The more the merrier," Matt said.

Coughlin got in. The door closed.

Sergeant Carter was on the third-floor landing when the door opened.

He saluted Coughlin.

"Good morning, Chief," he said, and then nodded at Malone. "Lieutenant."

"Carter, isn't it?" Coughlin said, offering his hand.

"Yes, sir. I was here, checking the arrangements, and Mrs. Payne—she and your father are in your apartment, Payne—said you would be coming. So I thought I had better wait."

"Everything seems to be all right. The rent-a-cop in the garage is one of ours, isn't he?"

"Yes, sir. And we have a man in the lobby, downstairs, in a Holmes uniform."

"I see a problem," Matt said. "Getting up those stairs."

They all turned to look at the flight of stairs leading up to the attic apartment. They were steep and narrow.

"We could put a rope around your neck and haul you up," McFadden said cheerfully. "Or you could get on my back and I could carry you up piggyback."

"Or," Matt said, handing McFadden the crutch, "I can do this."

He sat down on the stairs, and then, using his arms and one good leg, started pushing himself up the stairs.

Thirty seconds later, he turned to see how far he had to go and found himself looking at the hem of a woman's slip and skirt. He craned his neck and identified the woman.

"I didn't know shrinks made house calls," he said.

"Only when the patient is an unquestioned danger to himself," Amelia Payne, M.D., said without missing a beat. "To judge by the way you did that, you've had some practice scuttling along like a crab." She turned and called, "Sound the trumpet. Our hero is home."

"Amy!" Patricia Payne said.

Matt got to his feet, and leaned against the wall at the head of the stairs.

"Where's your crutch?" Patricia Payne asked.

"Here," McFadden said, coming up the stairs and handing it to him. He stuck it under his arm and made it to the couch. His mother leaned over and kissed him.

"You all right?"

"I'm fine," he said. "Hi, Dad."

"How are you doing?" Brewster C. Payne said.

"If Amy didn't guzzle it down, there was a bottle of Scotch here."

"And I brought one," Brewster Payne said. "And a drink seems like a fine idea."

"That would depend on what they're giving him," Amy said.

"The Mayo Clinic has been heard from," Matt said.

"Let me see it, Matt," Amy said firmly.

He fished in his pocket and handed her the bottle of capsules from the hospital pharmacy.

Denny Coughlin and Jack Malone were now standing at the head of the stairs. Patricia Payne went and kissed Coughlin on the cheek, and then Coughlin introduced Malone.

"What is that stuff they gave him, Amy?" Coughlin asked.

"Just an antibiotic, Uncle Denny," Amy said. "I'm very sorry to report that alcohol is not contraindicated."

Brewster Payne laughed. "You and Lieutenant Malone will have a little taste, Denny?"

"Not for me, thank you," Malone said.

"I will, thank you."

"I still have the bottle of Jameson's you gave me, Uncle Denny," Matt said.

"I'll have a little of that, then, please," Coughlin said.

"So will I," Patricia Payne said. "In fact, I'll even make them."

Sergeant Carter and Jesus Martinez appeared at the head of the stairs. Martinez was wearing an electric blue suit, a shirt with very long collar points, and a yellow necktie. But what caught everyone's attention was that he held a pump shotgun in each hand.

"Hay-zus," Matt said. "Why don't you put those in that closet?" He pointed. "I guess everybody's met Sergeant Carter. Does everybody know Hay-zus Martinez?"

Patricia Payne made a valiant, but failed, effort to conceal her surprise at Officer Martinez.

"Matt's spoken of you often, Mr. Martinez," she said when he turned from putting the shotguns in a tiny closet at the head of the stairs. "I'm glad you'll be looking out for him."

"Yes, ma'am," Martinez said.

"We're about to have a drink. Can we offer you something?"

"No, ma'am, thank you."

"Officer Martinez, Amy," Coughlin said, "was with Charley McFadden when they caught the man who was responsible for what happened to Dutch Moffitt."

"I know who he is," Amy said, not very pleasantly. "Are those shotguns really necessary?"

"Probably not, Miss Payne," Malone said. "It's one of those cases where it's better to take the extra precaution."

"It's *Doctor* Payne," Amy said.

"Sorry."

"Ease off, Amy," Matt said sharply.

Patricia Payne came out of the kitchen with two glasses. She handed one to Denny Coughlin and the other to Matt.

"Thank you," Matt said, and took a sip, and then turned and set the glass on the chair at the end of the couch.

The red light on his telephone answering machine was blinking. He shifted on the couch and stretched to push the button that would play his messages.

"Matt—" Brewster Payne said, stopping him.

"Dad?"

"There's some pretty unpleasant stuff on there," Brewster C. Payne said. "The only reason I didn't erase them was because I thought they would be of interest to Denny. Maybe you'd better wait until your mother and Amy have gone."

"Don't be silly, Brewster," Patricia Payne called from the kitchen. "I'm not a child, and I've already heard them."

"What are you talking about, Dad?" Amy asked.

Holloran appeared at the head of the stairs.

"Sorry, Chief, I had trouble finding a place to park."

"Push the button, Matt," Patricia Payne ordered. "Get it over with."

There were, it was later calculated when the tape was transcribed, forty-one messages on the tape, all that the thirty-minute tape would hold. Four of the messages were from people known to Matt Payne. One was a recorded offer to install vinyl siding at a special price good this week only. One was a cryptic message, a female voice saying, "You know who this is, call me after nine in the morning." Matt recognized the voice to be Helene Stillwell's, but had the presence of mind in the circumstances to shrug and shake his head and smile, indicating he had no idea who it might be.

The other thirty-five messages recorded on his machine were from persons unknown to him.

The voices were different (later voice analysis by police experts indicated that four individuals, three males and one female, had telephoned several times each) but the gist of the messages was that Matt Payne, variously described as a motherfucker, a honky, a pig, and a cocksucker (each noun coming with various adjectival prefixes, most commonly "fucking," "goddamn," and "motherfucking"), was going to be killed for having murdered Abu Ben Mohammed.

Patricia Payne, except to pass drinks around, stayed in the kitchen while the tape played. Amy, after the first thirty seconds or so, came and sat beside Matt on the couch, took a notebook from her purse, and made notes.

The policemen in the apartment looked either at the floor or the ceiling, and seemed quite uncomfortable. Sergeant Holloran's and Officer McFadden's faces quickly turned red with embarrassment and stayed that way, even after the tape suddenly cut off in midsentence and began to rewind.

"Nice friends you have, Matthew," Amy Payne broke the

silence. "You ever hear what happens to people who roll around with the pigs in the mud?"

"I wonder how they got the number?" Matt asked. "I'm not in the book."

"There are ways to get unlisted numbers," Denny Coughlin said absently. "I'll want to take that tape with me, Matt, and see what the lab boys can make of it."

"Well, the thing to do is have Matt's number changed," Brewster C. Payne said.

"Some of that was spontaneous," Amy said thoughtfully. "But some, maybe most, seemed to me to be rehearsed, perhaps even read."

"What did you say, Amy?" Coughlin asked.

"If you know what to listen for, Uncle Denny," Amy said, "you sometimes can hear things in people's voices. I said, I think that some of those people called and said whatever came into their minds, but others, I think, seemed to be reading what they said, or at least had a good idea of what they were going to say before they said it. Oddly enough, those are the ones who sounded awkward or hesitant."

"Interesting," Coughlin said, not very convincingly. "I'd rather not have that number changed, Brewster. Maybe we can get Matt another line—that will take a day or two, probably—"

"No, it won't," Payne said.

"What won't?"

"Getting Matt another line. I think I know who to call."

"What I was saying, Brewster, is that I would like to leave that line as it is, and record what calls come in."

"Oh, I see what you mean."

"Have you got a spare tape for the machine, Matty?"

Matt considered that a minute, then replied, "No. I don't think so."

"Let's take it apart and see what we need," Coughlin said.

Matt opened the telephone recorder and removed the tape cassette and handed it to Coughlin.

Brewster C. Payne reached for the telephone and dialed a number.

"Mr. Arnold, please," he said. "Brewster Payne calling." There was a brief pause, and then he went on: "Jack, for reasons I would rather not get into, I need another telephone line installed in my son's apartment, in the Delaware

Valley Cancer Society Building on Rittenhouse Square, right away." There was another pause. "No, I don't mean first thing tomorrow. In the next hour or so is what I had in mind."

Matt saw Denny Coughlin smiling.

"No, I am not kidding," Brewster Payne went on. "You told me, Jack, to call you if I ever needed something. This is that call." There was one last pause. "Two hours would be fine, Jack. His name is Matthew M. Payne and it's the apartment in the attic. Thank you very much."

He turned somewhat triumphantly from the telephone.

"Two hours, Denny."

"You are an amazing man," Coughlin said.

"How kind of you to recognize that," Payne said smugly.

Patricia Payne groaned.

"I wonder where we can get one of these?" Coughlin said, examining the tape cassette.

"I bought that in the electronics store on Walnut and 15th," Matt said.

"Okay. We'll take Officer Martinez with us when we go, and he can bring it back. Until we get another tape in there, just don't answer the phone. Better yet, take it off the hook."

He picked up his drink and drained it.

"Patty, Brewster," he said. "Matt's in good hands. You have nothing to worry about."

"Good try, Denny," Patricia Payne said. "But not a very successful one."

"Let's go," Coughlin said. He looked at Matt Payne. "I'll check in with you later, Matty."

"Thank you, Uncle Denny."

"Have you got any special orders for me, Chief?" Sergeant Carter said.

"No. You know what to do. Do it."

"Carter, why don't you and I take a run past Mr. Monahan's house?" Malone said.

"He's at Goldblatt's, sir. I checked."

"I want to check the arrangements at his house," Malone said tartly. "I know where he is."

"Yes, sir."

"It was nice to meet you, Mrs. Payne," Malone said. "Mr. Payne."

"It was nice to meet you, Lieutenant," Patricia Payne said, "and you too, Sergeant Carter. Thank you."

"Yes, ma'am," Carter said.

In a few moments everyone but the Paynes and Charley McFadden had gone down the steep stairway.

"Are you hungry, Matt?"

"I think there's some ribs in the refrigerator," Matt said.

"There's more ribs in the refrigerator than you know," she said. "I stopped off at Ribs Unlimited—I know how you like their ribs—on my way here and got you some."

"Then take yours home with you or give them to Amy."

"Why don't I heat them all up, and we can have lunch? I haven't had anything to eat, either."

"I've got to get back to the office," Brewster Payne said.

"Can you drop me at Hahnemann, Dad?" Amy asked.

He nodded.

At the head of the stairs, Amy turned and pointed her finger at Matt.

"For once in your life, Matt, do what people tell you."

"Yes, ma'am."

"Well, then, the three of us can eat the ribs," Patricia Payne said with forced cheerfulness.

"Four," Charley McFadden said. "Hay-zus will be back in a couple of minutes."

"The four of us, then," she agreed.

The telephone rang. Matt reached to pick it up, then stopped. They all watched it wordlessly until, after seven rings, it stopped.

I have the strangest feeling that was Helene, Matt thought.

Charley McFadden suddenly got up from his chair and started down the stairs.

"Where are you going?"

"From now on," Charley called, "I think we should keep that door locked."

Matt glanced at his mother. She looked very sad. When she sensed his eyes on her, she smiled.

"He really is large, isn't he?"

Jesus Martinez came back to the apartment almost an hour later, as Matt's mother was cleaning up the kitchen.

"They don't make that model anymore," he said. "I have

been in every electronics store in Center City trying to find these.''

He held up three tape cassettes.

The telephone had rung twice more while they had been eating. They hadn't answered it.

It rang again almost immediately after Matt had installed a new tape.

"What are we supposed to do?" McFadden asked. "Answer it? Or let the machine answer it?"

"Let the machine do it," Martinez said. "I think the chief wants the recording."

With the machine reconnected, it was possible to hear the caller's message.

It was a variation of the previous calls, no more scatologically obscene than the others, but enough, because of Patricia Payne—whom McFadden thought of as Matt's Mother—to cause McFadden to blush with embarrassment and his face to tighten in anger.

"I can rig that thing so we don't have to listen to that crap—sorry, Mrs. Payne," he said.

"That might be a good idea," she said. "But I'm leaving anyway, if that's what's bothering you."

"I'd like to get my hands on that guy," McFadden said.

"So would I," she said. "But don't you see, Charley, that's what they're trying to do, make us angry?"

"They're succeeding," Charley said.

She put her hat and coat on, and then went and stood before Matt, who was sprawled in an overstuffed leather armchair, his bad leg resting on a pillow sitting on the matching ottoman.

"After I leave, maybe you can get Charley to hang your art work," she said.

"What?" Matt asked, and then understood. "Oh, that. How did it get here?"

"Your dad and I brought it from the hospital," she said.

"Thank you."

"Now, there's plenty of food there for breakfast and sandwiches, and I'll bring more when I come tomorrow. But for dinner, your father called the Rittenhouse Club, and they'll bring you anything you want to eat."

"I don't like Rittenhouse Club food in the Rittenhouse Club," Matt said. "Why should I have them haul it over here?"

He saw the hurt look in her eyes and added, "I'm in a lousy mood, sorry, Mother."

"Are you in pain?"

He shook his head no.

"They do a very nice mixed grill, and you like their London broil, I know you do, and besides, beggars can't be choosers." She leaned over and kissed him.

"Ignore him," Patricia Payne said to Charley and Jesus. "Make him feed you."

"Yes, ma'am," Charley said. "I will."

When he came back up the stairs after locking the door after her, McFadden asked, "What art work is she talking about?"

"There's a great big picture of a naked woman in his bedroom," Jesus said.

"No shit?"

"It was a gift from Mrs. Washington," Matt said. "Mrs. Washington and I think of it as a splendid example of Victorian art."

"I gotta see this," Charley said, and went into the bedroom.

He returned carrying the oil painting.

"Over the fireplace, right?"

"Why not?" Charley said.

McFadden went to the fireplace, leaned the picture against it, and then took something from the mantelpiece. He walked to Matt with a snub-nosed revolver in the palm of each hand.

"Maybe you'd better keep these—one of them, anyway—with you. What are you doing with two?"

"One of them belongs to Wohl. He loaned it to me in the hospital. The shooting team took mine away from me. I just got it back."

McFadden sniffed the barrel of one of the revolvers and then the other.

"This must be yours," he said. "I'll clean it for you, if you have the stuff. Otherwise, you'll fuck up the barrel."

"There's cleaning stuff in one of the drawers in the kitchen," Matt said.

"You got any bullets? There's none in this."

"*Cartridges*, Charley. *Bullets* are the little lead things that come out the end. There's a box with the cleaning stuff."

"Fuck you, clean your own pistol," Charley said, laid both pistols beside the answering machine, and returned to the oil painting. He picked it up and held it in place over the fireplace, turning his head for approval.

"Great," Matt said.

"What are you going to do when your mother comes back?"

"Mother will modestly avert her eyes," Matt said.

"You got a brick nail?"

"What's a brick nail?"

"A nail you can drive in bricks. You can't do that with regular nails, asshole, they bend."

"No."

There was a knock at the door at the foot of the stairs.

Jesus erupted from his chair and went to the closet and took the shotgun from it.

"It's probably Wohl or Washington," Matt said.

"Who's there?" Jesus called.

"Telephone company."

Jesus went down the stairs. In a moment, he returned, followed by two telephone company technicians, one of whom was visibly curious and made more than a little uncomfortable by Jesus's shotgun.

"Where do you want your phone?" one of them asked.

"One here and one in the bedroom, please," Matt said.

"Is something going on around here?" the other one asked, curiosity having overwhelmed him.

"Like what?" Charley asked.

"Hey, you're the cop who shot the Liberation Army guy, aren't you?" the first one asked.

"Just put the goddamn phone in," Jesus snapped.

"What the hell is wrong with you? I just asked, is all."

It took forty-five minutes to install the two telephones. The installers refused a drink, but accepted Matt's offer of coffee.

"It's cold as a bitch out there," one said.

When they were gone, Martinez said, "That's not going to work."

"What's not going to work?"

"Having people knock on the door, and we ask who is it, and then go down and open the door."

"Why not?" Charley asked.

"What we need is an intercom," Jesus said. "They ring the bell, we ask the intercom who's there. I saw one in the store where I bought the tapes."

"Who would put it in?" Charley asked.

"I would."

"Do you really think it's necessary?" Matt said. "More to the point, do you think that anybody's really going to try to come up here?"

"They threw the firebomb at Monahan," Charley said.

"Jesus," Matt said.

"Save your money, if you want to," Jesus said. "They cost twenty-four ninety-five."

"You can install it?" Matt asked.

"You got a screwdriver, a drill, and a staple machine, I can install it."

"I think I've got a screwdriver, but I don't have a drill or a staple machine."

"You don't have a drill?" McFadden asked, surprised.

"No."

"How about a hammer? You're going to need a hammer for the brick nails."

"No hammer, either."

"Hay-zus can get a hammer and the brick nails and the drill and the staple machine when he gets the intercom," Charley said.

"Don't forget the screwdriver," Matt said, and shifted on the couch and took out his wallet.

"What the fuck, Payne, if they don't kill you, it'll come in handy later," Jesus said as he took three twenties. "If you've got some broad up here, and some other broad comes to see you, you could tell her you're busy on the intercom."

"I could also just not answer her knock," Matt said.

"You want the intercom or not? You're not doing me any favors."

"I want the intercom, Hay-zus, thank you."

Martinez returned in a little over half an hour, his arms full of kraft paper bags.

"Goddamn sidewalks are all ice," he said. "I almost busted my ass, twice."

"How would you like to be walking a foot beat in this weather?" McFadden asked.

"How about standing at Broad and Vine in a white cap, directing traffic?" Martinez said as he put the packages on the coffee table.

In one of the bags was a Philadelphia *Daily News*. He tossed it on Matt's lap.

"In case you don't know where you are," he said. "This is an 'undisclosed location.' "

"What?"

"You're on the front page," Jesus said.

Matt unfolded the newspaper. There was a photograph of him being carried to Coughlin's car at Frankford Hospital. Beneath it was the caption:

> COP UNDER DEATH THREAT—As heavily armed police stand by, Officer Matthew M. Payne, whose life has been threatened by the Islamic Liberation Army is carried from Frankford Hospital to a police car that took him to an undisclosed location. Payne was wounded in the gun battle in which he shot to death ILA member Abu Ben Mohammed. (See ILA, Page 5)

Charley leaned over Matt's shoulder and read the caption.

"Well, the bastards got what they wanted, didn't they?" he asked. "The front page of the *News*, and we sure look like we're scared of them."

"I don't know about *you* being scared, white boy," Matt heard himself say, "but *we* are."

McFadden looked at him curiously, and after a moment said seriously, "You'll be all right, buddy. You can take that to the bank."

There was a moment's awkward silence, which Jesus finally broke.

"The first thing you have to decide is where you want this end of the intercom."

"How about on the kitchen wall?"

"Why not?"

Matt was impressed with the skill with which Jesus installed the intercom. He seemed to know exactly what he was doing. It reminded him of Charley's mechanical drawing skill, and that made him consider his own practical ineptitude.

Matthew Mark Payne, B.A., Cum Laude, University of Pennsylvania, you don't have one salable skill, something you could find a paying job doing, except being a cop, and, truth to tell, you ain't too good at that.

By half past five, the intercom was installed and tested.

"Anybody else getting hungry?" Matt asked as Jesus—workmanlike, Matt thought—neatly coiled the leftover wire and put the tools back in their boxes.

"I could eat something," Jesus said.

"I'm going to finish hanging your naked lady picture," Charley said, "and then leave. I'm going to have supper with Margaret. I'll be back at midnight and relieve Hayzus."

"Bring her back here, and her friend Lari too, and we'll send out for food."

"No," Charley said. "For one thing, I wouldn't bring a nice girl like her anyplace where there's a naked lady hanging on the wall."

"You're kidding!"

"Her uncle and aunt are feeding us," Charley said. "We have to go there."

"Don't break your ass on the way to the subway," Jesus said.

"You don't have your car, do you?" Matt asked, and, when Charley shook his head, asked, "where is it, Bustleton and Bowler?"

"Yeah."

"Why don't you leave it there and take the Porsche?"

"I don't know, Matt. I'd hate to tear it up."

"You can't leave a Porsche sit," Matt said. "And I damned sure can't drive it. Where'd you put the keys?"

"Jesus, I forgot!" Charley said, and pulled them from his trouser pocket.

"Take the car. Just try to keep it under a hundred and ten."

"Well, okay," Charley said, trying and failing to give the impression he would drive the Porsche only as a favor to Matt.

Five minutes after Charley left, the intercom was first put to use.

"Let me in, Hay-zus," Charley's voice announced mechanically from the speaker in the kitchen. "It's me."

Jesus went down and unlocked the door and Charley followed him back up the stairs.

"Wouldn't start?" Matt asked.

"The front tires are slashed," McFadden announced. "And they got the hood and doors with a knife or something."

"Jesus H. Christ!" Matt exploded.

"Did you look at the car when we came here?" Charley asked.

"No. Except to see that it was there. My mother's car was there. You couldn't see it clearly."

"Shit!"

The bell rang.

Martinez went into the kitchen.

"Who's there?"

"Peter Wohl."

"Just a minute, Inspector."

Wohl appeared at the head of the stairs carrying a large paper bag.

"I thought the patient might like a beer," he said, and then, when he saw the look on Matt's face, asked, "What's going on?"

"Those fuckers slashed my tires and did a scratch job on my hood and doors," Matt said. "Charley just found it that way."

Wohl walked into the kitchen and started putting the beer into the refrigerator.

"You just found this out, McFadden?"

"Yes, sir. I went down to get the car, and I saw it was down in front."

"And you didn't see any damage to it when they brought Matt here?"

"No, sir."

"We didn't look," Matt said.

"I just walked past it myself," Wohl said, "and didn't see anything out of the ordinary."

Wohl came into the living room and picked up the telephone beside Matt. He dialed a number from memory.

"This is Inspector Wohl," he announced. "Let me speak to the senior supervisor present."

I wonder who he's calling? Matt thought.

"Inspector Wohl, Lieutenant. We have a case of vehicular vandalism. The vehicle in question belongs to Officer Payne. I rather doubt we'll be able to find the vandals, but I want a complete investigation, especially photographs. Even dust the damned car for fingerprints. We may get lucky. It's in the parking lot under the Delaware Valley Cancer Society Building on Rittenhouse Square. Payne lives in the top-floor apartment. I'll be here with him."

He put the telephone down.

"Inspector, I'm supposed to meet my girl," Charley said uncomfortably.

"Well, I guess that will have to wait, won't it?" Wohl snapped. "Central Detectives are on their way. Obviously, they'll want to talk to you."

"Yes, sir."

"No. Wait a minute," Wohl said, exhaling audibly. "What exactly did you see, Charley, when you went down to the garage?"

"When I started to unlock the door, I saw the nose was down. So I looked at the tires. And then I saw what they did to the hood and doors with a knife or something."

"You're coming on at midnight, right?"

"Yes, sir."

"I'll tell the detectives what you told me," Wohl said. "Go ahead, Charley. I didn't mean to snap at you like that."

"That's okay, sir."

He hurried down the stairwell as if he was afraid Wohl would change his mind.

Wohl lost his temper, Matt thought. *He was nearly as mad as I am about the car. No. That's impossible. Nobody can be nearly as fucking outraged as I am.*

"Inspector, I was about to send out for supper for Hay-zus and me," Matt said. "Will you have something with us?"

"No pizza."

"Actually, I was thinking of either a London broil or a mixed grill. My father fixed it with the Rittenhouse Club."

"In that case, Officer Payne, I gratefully accept your kind invitation."

TWENTY-TWO

Lieutenant Foster H. Lewis, Sr., was of two minds concerning Officer Foster H. Lewis, Jr. On one hand, it was impossible to feel like anything but a proud father to see one's son and namesake drive up to the house in an unmarked car, wearing a very nice looking blazer, gray flannel slacks, a starched white shirt and a regimentally striped necktie and know that Tiny had a more responsible job after having been on the job less than a year than he had had in his first five years on the job.

But there were two problems with that. The first being that he had hoped—and for a long time believed—that Tiny would spend his life as Foster H. Lewis, M.D. But that hadn't come to pass. Tiny had been placed on Academic Probation by the Temple University Medical School and reacted to that by joining the cops.

And then the Honorable Jerry Carlucci had put his two cents in, in what Foster H. Lewis, Sr., believed to be an understandable, but no less contemptible, ploy to pick up a few more Afro-American voters. The mayor had told a large gathering at the Second Abyssinian Baptist Church that, as one more proof that he was determined to see that the Police Department afforded Afro-Americans equal opportunities within the Department, that he had recommended to Commissioner Czernich that Officer Foster H. Lewis, Jr., son of that outstanding Afro-American police Lieutenant, Foster H. Lewis, Sr., be assigned to Special Operations.

It was said that if The Mayor looked as if he might be about to fart, Commissioner Czernich instantly began to look for a dog to blame, and, in case he couldn't find one, pursed his lips to apologize for breaking wind.

Lieutenant Lewis thought that Special Operations was a good idea, and he would have been proud and delighted to see Tiny assigned there *after* he'd done a couple of years in a district, working a van, walking a foot beat, riding around in an RPC, learning what being a cop was all about. Sending Tiny over there before he'd found all the little inspection stickers on his new uniform was really—unless, of course, you were interested in Afro-American votes—a lousy idea.

And then Staff Inspector Peter Wohl, for whom Lieutenant Lewis had previously had a great deal of respect, had compounded the idiocy. Instead of sending Tiny out to work with experienced Special Operations uniformed officers, from whom he could have learned at least some of what he would have to know, he had put him in plain clothes and given him to Detective Tony Harris for use as a go-fer.

At the time, Harris had been working on two important jobs, the Northwest Philadelphia Serial Rapist, and the murder of Officer Magnella near Temple University. It could be argued that Harris needed someone to run errands, and to relieve him of time-consuming chores, thus freeing his time for investigation. And certainly, working under a really first class homicide detective would give Tiny experience he could get nowhere else.

But only as a temporary thing. It now looked as if it was becoming permanent. The serial rapist had been shot to death by another young, college-educated, Special Operations plainclothesman. Harris was now devoting his full time to the Officer Magnella job.

And in Lieutenant Lewis's judgment, that was becoming a dead end. In his opinion, if those responsible for Magnella's murder were ever apprehended, it would not be because of brilliant police work, or even dull and plodding police work, but either because of the reward offered, or simple dumb luck: Someone would come forward and point a finger.

Tiny Lewis rang the door buzzer, as he had been doing to his father's undiminished annoyance since he was fourteen, to the rhythm of *Shave-And-A-Haircut-Two Bits*, and Lieutenant Lewis walked from the window to the door to let him in.

"Hi ya, Pop."

"Come in."

"Hi ya, Mom?" Tony said, considerably louder.

The men shook hands.

"I'm in the kitchen, honey."

"Nice blazer," Lieutenant Lewis said. "New?"

"Yeah. It is nice, isn't it?"

Tiny walked past his father into the kitchen, put his arms around his mother, who weighed almost exactly one-half as much as he did, and lifted her off the floor.

"Put me down!" she said, and turned to face him. "Don't you look nice!"

"Thank you, ma'am," he said. "It's new."

She fingered the material. "*Very* nice."

"What are we eating?"

"Roast pork."

"Pork goes nicely, he said, apropos of nothing whatever, with beer."

"Help yourself," she laughed. "You know where it is."

"You're driving a department car," Lieutenant Lewis said.

"Yes, I am."

"You know what it would do to your record if you had an accident and had been drinking," Lieutenant Lewis said, and immediately regretted it.

"Well, then, I guess I better not have an accident. You want a beer, Dad?"

"Yes, please."

"I saw your boss earlier this evening," Lieutenant Lewis said.

"Sergeant Washington?"

"I meant Inspector Wohl," Lieutenant Lewis said. "Do you consider Jason Washington your boss?"

"They formed a Special Investigations Section. He's in charge. I'm in it."

"Doing what?"

"Baby-sitting honkies," Tiny said, with a smile.

"And what does that mean?" Lieutenant Lewis snapped.

"You know a Highway sergeant named Carter?"

Lieutenant Lewis nodded.

"That's what he said, that I was 'baby-sitting honkies.' "

"Foster, I have no idea what you're talking about."

"You heard about these screwballs calling themselves the Islamic Liberation Army threatening to get Matt Payne for blowing away one of them?"

Lewis nodded.

"Well, Wohl's got some people sitting on him—"

"You might well form the habit, Foster, of referring to Inspector Wohl as Inspector Wohl," Lewis said.

He received a look of tolerance from his son, who went on, "—and I was supposed to be one of them. But then *Sergeant* Washington went to *Inspector* Wohl and said he'd rather I stick with *Detective* Harris, and *Inspector* Wohl said okay, he'd get somebody else, and *Sergeant* Carter—"

"Your sarcasm is becoming offensive."

"—heard about it, apparently. Anyway, he struck up a conversation with me, said he'd heard I was going to be one of the guys—the other two are McFadden and Martinez, the ex-Narcs who ran down the junkie who shot Captain Moffitt?"

He waited to see understanding on his father's face, and then went on:

"—sitting on Payne, and then that I wasn't, and how come? And I said, mine not reason why, mine but to do what the Great Black Buddha orders—"

"Is that what you call Jason Washington?" Mrs. Lewis interrupted. "That's terrible! You ought to be ashamed of yourself!"

"Think about it, Mom," Tiny said, unrepentant.

She did, and laughed, but repeated, "That's terrible."

"And?" Lieutenant Lewis prompted.

"And Carter said, 'I don't suppose it matters, in either case, what you're doing is baby-sitting a honky.' "

"Which means what?"

"How the hell do I know, Pop?"

"Watch your tone of voice, please."

"Sorry, Dad."

"I don't ordinarily listen to gossip—"

"Watch your father's nose grow, honey."

"—but the word is that Harris is having a problem with liquor. Is that what Carter meant about baby-sitting?"

"I guess so. He's been on a bender. Washington's taking care of him."

"How, taking care of him?"

"I keep him out of bars during the day, and at night he's staying with the Washingtons."

"Martha must love that," Mrs. Lewis said.

"Jason and Tony Harris have been close for years," Lieutenant Foster said, thoughtfully. "Is that how you feel about it, Foster? That you're baby-sitting a honky?"

"Hey, Pop. Tony Harris has been good to me. And Matt Payne is sort of a friend of mine."

" 'Sort of a friend'?" Mrs. Lewis asked.

"Well, I haven't been invited to the Rose Tree Hunt Club yet, but yeah. We're friends. We get along well. If Harris wasn't sick, I would have liked to be one of the guys sitting on him."

"I don't like the idea of one police officer using the word 'honky' to describe another," Lieutenant Lewis said.

"Pop, I didn't use it. Carter did."

"You repeated it."

"My mistake," Tiny said, a hint of anger in his voice. "Where did you see Wohl—*Inspector* Wohl?"

"You know that your friend Payne is being protected in his apartment?"

Tiny nodded.

"I was supposed to have the midnight to eight tour before—*my boss*—got me out of it."

"I was driving by and saw some activity in the garage. A lab van, specifically. So I stopped. Someone, presumably the low-lifes who are calling themselves a Liberation Army, did a job on his car."

"What kind of a job?"

"Slashed the tires. Scraped the paint."

"That's going too far!" Tiny said. "That's absolutely sacrilegious! That's not an automobile, it's a work of art!"

"Now it's a work of art with flat tires and a scratched paint job," Lieutenant Lewis said.

"And Wohl was there?"

"*Inspector* Wohl was there. And nearly as offended by the desecration of the work of art as you are."

"What kind of a car are you talking about?" Mrs. Lewis asked.

"A Porsche 911."

"Very expensive," Lieutenant Lewis said. "Only rich people can afford them—lawyers, *doctors*, people like that—"

"Stop, Foster!" Mrs. Lewis said. "Not one more word!"

"What's the matter with you?"

"You know damned well what's the matter. You are not going to needle him the rest of his life about not being a doctor! He wants to be a cop. What's wrong with that? I'm married to a cop. You should be proud that he wants to do what you do!"

Lieutenant Lewis looked at Officer Lewis.

"The lady used profane language, Officer Lewis. Did you pick up on that?"

"Yes, sir. I heard her."

"I guess that means she's serious, huh?"

"Yes, sir, I guess it does."

"Then maybe you and I better get another beer and go in the living room until she calms down, what do you think?"

"I think that's a fine idea, sir."

"Don't try to make a joke of it, Foster. I meant every word I said!"

"I somehow had the feeling you did," Lieutenant Foster said.

When Chief Inspectors Dennis V. Coughlin and Matthew Lowenstein and Staff Inspector Peter Wohl filed into the Commissioner's Conference room at eight-ten the next morning, The Honorable Jerry Carlucci, Mayor of the City of Brotherly Love, was already there, his back to them, looking out the window, supporting himself on both hands.

Commissioner Taddeus Czernich, holding a cup of coffee in his hands, stood by the open door to his office. Coughlin, Lowenstein and Wohl stood behind chairs at the table, waiting for the Mayor to turn around.

He took his time in doing so, prompting each of them, privately, to conclude that the first psychological warfare salvo had been fired.

Finally, he turned around.

"Good morning," he said. "I'm aware that all of you have busy schedules, and that in theory, I should be able to get from

Commissioner Czernich all the details of whatever I would like to know. But since there seems to be some breakdown in communications, I thought it best to ask you to spare me a few minutes of your valuable time.''

"Good morning, Mr. Mayor," Lowenstein said. "I'm sure I speak for all of us when I say I'm sorry you fell out of the wrong side of the bed this morning."

Carlucci glared at him for a moment.

"Oh, for Christ's sake, sit down, all of you," he said. "I know you're doing your best." He looked at Czernich. "Can we get some coffee in here, Tad?"

"Yes, sir. There's a fresh pot."

"I was reading the overnights," the Mayor said. "Did you notice that some wiseass painted *'Free The Goldblatt's Six'* on a wall at the University?"

"Those villains we have," Coughlin said.

"No kidding?"

"The railroad cops caught three of them doing it again on the Pennsy Main Line right of way. You know those great big granite blocks where the tracks go behind the stadium? They had lowered themselves on ropes. Two they caught hanging there. They squealed on the third one."

"Who were they?"

"College kids. Wiseasses."

"The judge ought to make them clean it off with a toothbrush," Carlucci said. "But that's wishful thinking."

"Mike Sabara told me when I called him just before I came here that there's 'ILA' painted all over North Philadelphia," Wohl said. "I don't think that's college kids, and I would like to know who did that."

"What do you mean?"

"How much of it is spontaneous, and how much was painted by the people who issued those press releases."

"Let's talk about the ILA," Carlucci said. "Now that it just happened to come up. What do we know today about them that we didn't know yesterday?"

"Not a goddamn thing," Coughlin said. "I was over at Intelligence yesterday. They don't have a damned thing, and it's not for want of trying."

"They're harassing Monahan. And for that matter, Payne, too. Telephone calls to Goldblatt's from the time they open the doors until they close."

"What about at his house?" Carlucci asked.

"Telephone calls. The same kind they're making to Matt Payne's apartment."

"Driving by Monahan's house? Anything like that?"

"Nothing that we've been able to get a handle on. Nobody hanging around, driving by more than once."

"What have you got on Monahan, at his house?"

"Three uniformed officers in an unmarked car. One of the three is always walking around."

"Supervised by who?"

"A lieutenant named Jack Malone. He came to Special Operations from Major Crimes."

"Where he got the nutty idea that Bob Holland is a car thief," the mayor said. "I know all about Malone. Is he the man for the job, Peter? This whole thing would go down the toilet if we lose Monahan as a witness, or lose him, period. Christ, what that bastard Nelson and his *Ledger* would do to me if that happened."

"Malone strikes me, Mr. Mayor, as a pretty good cop who unfortunately has had some personal problems."

The mayor looked at Wohl for a moment and then said. "Okay. If you say so. You say they're harassing Payne? How? What's going on with him?"

"He has an apartment on the top floor of the Delaware Valley Cancer Society Building on Rittenhouse Square. There's an underground garage with a Holmes rent-a-cop at the entrance, and, during the day, there's a Holmes rent-a-cop in the lobby. There's a pretty good burglar alarm system. We have an officer wearing a Holmes uniform, replacing the Holmes guy, in the garage at night."

"That's all?"

"And we have somebody with Payne all the time."

"Two of them are those kids from Narcotics who ran down the punk who shot Dutch Moffitt," Chief Inspector Coughlin said. "McFadden and Martinez. They're friends, and in regular clothes. We don't want to give the impression that we're—"

"Baby-sitting a cop, huh?" the mayor interrupted. "I get the point."

"They call him, these sleaze-bags," Wohl said, "every fifteen minutes or so. Say something dirty, and hang up. No time to trace the call."

He took a tape cassette from his pocket and held it up.

"What's that?"

"A recording of the calls," Wohl said. "I'm going to take it to the lab."

"That sounds as if we're chasing our tails," the mayor said. "What do they hope to find?"

"We're trying everything we can think of, Mr. Mayor," Wohl said.

"Sometime yesterday afternoon, they got to his car," Coughlin said. "Slashed the tires, and did a job with a knife or a key, or something on the paint job."

"And nobody saw anything?" the mayor said, unpleasantly.

"All we can do is guess," Wohl said.

"So guess."

"Somebody came in the front door during business hours, rode the elevator down to the garage, slashed the tires, etcetera—the car is parked right by the elevator, it wouldn't have taken more than thirty seconds, a minute, tops—got back on the elevator, rode back to the lobby floor and walked out."

"The rent-a-cop in the garage didn't see anything?"

"He can't see where the car is parked."

"I don't suppose anybody bothered to check the car for prints, call the lab people?"

"I did, Mr. Mayor," Wohl said. "They took some pictures, too. Should I have them send you a set?"

"No, Peter, thank you. They would just make me sick to my stomach. I don't like these people thumbing their noses at the cops."

They all knew Jerry Carlucci well enough to recognize the signals of an impending eruption, and they all waited for it to come. It was less violent, however, than any of them expected.

"Okay. Now I'll tell you what's going to happen," he said, and pointed his finger at Dennis V. Coughlin. "You, Denny—and this should in no way be construed as a suggestion that Wohl isn't doing the job right, but he's a Staff Inspector and you're a Chief—are going to go to Intelligence and Organized Crime and light a fire under them. I said before and I'm saying now that these clowns didn't wake up one morning and say, 'Okay, today we're the Islamic Liberation Army, we're going to go out and make fools of the police and incidentally stick up a furniture store.' They came from somewhere, and I want to know where, and I want to know who the other ones of them are, the ones issuing these goddamned press releases.''

''Yes, sir,'' Coughlin said.

The mayor turned to Matt Lowenstein. ''You're the Chief Inspector of Detectives. Get out there and detect. Whatever you're doing now isn't working.''

Lowenstein's face flushed, but he didn't reply.

''And you, Peter: I won't start telling you how to run Special Operations. If you're comfortable having a guy who beats up on his wife and has paranoid ideas about Bob Holland in charge of protecting the only goddamned witness we have, okay. I'm sure you're smart enough to understand that it's your ass if this goes wrong.''

''Yes, sir, I understand.''

''And you will, all three of you, keep Commissioner Czernich up to date on what's going on. I'm sick and tired of calling him up and having him tell me, 'I don't know, Jerry. I haven't talked to Wohl, or Lowenstein or Coughlin today.' ''

''Yes, sir,'' the three of them replied almost in unison.

The mayor ground out his cigar in the ashtray in front of him, stood up, and walked out of the room without another word.

''When the police department looks bad,'' Commissioner Czernich said, ''it makes all of us, but especially the mayor, look bad. I think we should all keep that in mind.''

''You're right, Tad,'' Matt Lowenstein said. ''You're absolutely right.''

He turned his face so Czernich couldn't see him and winked at Coughlin and Wohl.

At just about the same time, Officer Charles McFadden looked over Officer Matthew Payne's shoulder at what was being stirred in a small stainless steel pot and offered:

''I always wondered how they made that shit.''

''I gather that creamed beef is not a regular part of your diet?''

''I eat in restaurants all the time, but I never had it in a house before.''

''But then, until you met me, you never knew that people had indoor toilets, did you?''

''Fuck you.''

''What's his name?'' Matt asked, softly, nodding toward the

living room, where a large, muscular young man with a crew cut sat facing the television.

"Hartzog," Charley furnished quietly.

"You sure you don't want some of this, Hartzog?" Matt called, raising his voice. "There's more than enough."

"It's okay. I ate just before I came over," Hartzog replied.

Matt began to swirl the boiling water in another stainless steel pot.

"What the hell are you doing now?"

"I am about to poach eggs. Eggs are these unborn chickens in the obloid white containers you see in my hand."

"In there?" Charley asked, genuinely surprised as Matt skillfully cracked eggs with one hand into the swirling water.

"As you see," Matt said.

"My mother uses a little pan. It's got little cups you put the eggs in."

"Is that so?"

"I'll be damned," Charley said, peering into the pan. "That works, don't it?"

"Just about every time," Matt said. "Now, if you will be so good as to take the English muffins from the toaster—"

Matt split the English muffins, laid a half on each of two plates, ladled creamed beef on top of them, and then added, using a pierced spoon, two poached eggs on top.

"Maybe you are good for something," Charley said, taking the plates and carrying them into the living room.

Matt, using a cane, hobbled after him. He lowered himself into the arm chair and Charley handed him his plate.

"Oh, good!" Matt said. "We're in time for today's episode of Mary Trueheart, Girl Nymphomaniac."

Officer Hartzog looked at him without comprehension.

"I got the Today Show on there. Is that all right?"

"Fine," Matt said.

"Is there really such a thing?" Charley asked.

"As what?"

"As a nymphomaniac."

"Yeah, sure."

"How come I never met one?"

"They only go after men whose dicks are longer than two inches," Matt said.

"Then I guess you never met one, either, huh?"

In point of fact, I have. Or at least it could be argued that

Helene's peculiar sexual appetites might, using the term loosely, qualify her as a nymphomaniac. But somehow, Charley, I don't think you would approve if I told you about her.

"One works downstairs," Matt said. "Brunette. Name of Jasmine."

"No shit?" Charley asked, fascinated, and then saw the look on Matt's face. "Bullshit."

"There was one when I was in junior high school," Officer Hartzog said. "They caught her fucking the janitor. They arrested him and sent her off to a girl's home someplace."

The door buzzer sounded.

"Who the hell can that be?" Charley wondered aloud.

Hartzog got up and went to get his shotgun, which he had leaned against the wall at the head of the stairs. Charley went to the intercom in the kitchen.

"Who's there?"

"My name is Young."

"What can we do for you?"

"I'd like to see Matt Payne."

"What for?"

"Am I speaking with a police officer?"

"What kind of a question is that?"

"This is Special Agent Frank F. Young of the FBI. Would you let us in please?"

"I know him, Charley," Matt called. "Let him in."

Hartzog went down the stairs, two at a time, carrying his shotgun.

There was the sound of multiple footsteps on the stairs, and then Young appeared, followed by another neatly dressed, hat wearing, clean-cut man who didn't look any older than Matt or Charley.

"Hello, Matt," Young said with a smile. "I see you're in good hands."

"How are you, Mr. Young?"

What the fuck do you want?

"I apologize for the hour, but we had to be in this neck of the woods, and I thought we'd take the opportunity to drop by."

"Can we offer you coffee?"

"Love a cup. It's bitter cold out there. This is Special Agent Matthews."

Matthews walked up to Matt, offered his hand, and said, "Jack Matthews. I've wanted to meet you."

"How are you?" Matt said. "The large one is Officer Charley McFadden. The other's Officer Hartzog."

They shook hands. Hartzog put the shotgun back and sat down where he had been sitting watching television.

"Charley, will you get the FBI some coffee?"

"Yeah, sure."

"You've wanted to meet him, too, Jack," Young said. "Officer McFadden is the man who located, and ran to earth, the individual who shot Captain Moffitt."

"Yes, I have," Matthews said. "I'm one of your fans, McFadden. That was good work."

Charley looked uncomfortable.

"You want something in your coffee, or black?" he responded.

"Black for me, please."

"A little sugar for me, if you have it, please," Young said.

"You want some more, Matt? Hartzog?"

"Please," Matt said.

"Not now, thanks," Hartzog said.

"How do you feel, Matt?" Young asked.

"I feel all right."

"No pain in the leg?"

"Only when I forget and step on it."

"It'll take a while," Young said. "It could have been a lot worse. .45, wasn't it?"

"Apparently a ricochet," Matt said.

Charley passed out the coffee.

"They must be taking this ILA threat pretty seriously," Young said. "Judging by the fact that you have two men on you."

"I'm off duty," McFadden said. "Hartzog came on at eight. Just one."

"Matt, is there somewhere we could have a word?" Young asked.

What the hell is this all about?

"We can go in my bedroom."

"Please," Young said, smiling. "You need any help?"

"No. I just move a little slowly."

He pushed himself out of the chair and, using a cane, made his way to his bedroom.

Young followed and closed the door after them.

"Nice apartment."

"It gets a little crowded with more than me in it."

Young smiled dutifully, then said, seriously, "Matt, I won't ask you if I can trust your discretion, but you didn't get this from me, all right?"

"All right."

"I heard yesterday that a charge has been brought that you have violated the civil rights of Charles David Stevens, and that Justice will ask us to conduct an investigation."

"*What?*" Matt asked, incredulously.

"It's becoming a fairly standard tactic. All it does as far as we're concerned—in cases like yours—is waste manpower. From their standpoint, the only thing I can imagine is that they hope the very charge will sow a seed of doubt in some potential juror's mind. If the FBI is investigating, the police, the police officer, must have done something wrong."

"Who brought the charges?" Matt asked, angrily.

"One of the civil rights groups, I don't remember which one. But it's more than safe to say that Armando C. Giacomo is behind it."

"What, exactly, am I being charged with?"

"Violating the civil rights of Stevens by taking his life unlawfully, or excessive force, something like that."

"That sonofabitch was trying to kill me when I shot him!"

"Don't get all excited. The investigation will bring all that out. There's also a story that they're going to take you before the Grand Jury. Is that right?"

Why don't I want to tell him?

"I've heard they are."

"Well, that may—more than likely *will*—take the wind out of their sails. I can't imagine a Grand Jury returning a true bill under the circumstances. As I say, what I really think they're after is sowing that seed of doubt. Where there's smoke, there must be fire, so to speak."

"I will be Goddamned!"

"As well as I can, there's an ethical question here, of course, I will keep you advised. More specifically, when I hear something I think you ought to know, I'll have Matthews pass the word to you. He's one of the good guys."

"Jesus!" Matt said. "That's absolute bullshit! He tries to

kill me. I defend myself, and *I'm* accused of violating *his* civil rights."

"It's a crazy world. But don't worry too much about it. Remember, you didn't do anything wrong."

"Yeah."

"Do you play chess?"

What the hell has that got to do with anything?

"Yes, I play chess."

"So does Matthews. That would give him an excuse to come here."

Why is he doing this?

"I very much appreciate your telling me this, Mr. Young."

"Frank, please. What the hell, we have different badges, but we're both cops, right?"

I really would like to believe that. I wonder why I don't?

Young looked at his watch.

"Gotta get moving," he said, and offered Matt his hand.

When Matt followed him back into the living room, Matthews was holding the Queen of a set of green jade chess pieces Matt had been given for his fifteenth birthday.

"Interesting set," Matthews said. "Do you play much?"

"Some."

"We'll have to have a game sometime."

"Anytime. I'll be here."

"I might surprise you, and just come knocking some night."

"I wish you would."

TWENTY-THREE

"How are you, Inspector?" Lieutenant Warren Lomax greeted Peter Wohl cheerfully, offering his hand. "What can we do for you?"

Lomax was a tall, quite skinny man in his early forties. He had been seriously injured years before in a high-speed chase accident as a Highway Patrol sergeant, and pensioned off.

After two years of retirement, he had (it was generally acknowledged with the help of then Commissioner Carlucci) managed to get back on the job on limited duty. He'd gone to work in the Forensics Laboratory as sort of the chief clerk. There, he had become fascinated with what he saw and what the lab did, actually gone back to school at night to study chemistry and electronics and whatever else he thought would be useful, and gradually become an expert in what was called "scientific crime detection."

Three years before he had managed to get himself off limited duty, taken and passed the lieutenant's exam, and now the Forensics Lab was his.

Wohl thought, as he always did, that Lomax looked like a

ick man (he remembered him as a robust Highway sergeant),
elt sorry for him, and then wondered why: Lomax obviously
lidn't feel sorry for himself, and was obviously as happy as a
ig in mud doing what he was doing.

"How are you, Warren?" Wohl said, and handed him the
assette tape from Matt Payne's answering machine with his
ree hand.

"What's this?" Lomax asked.

"The tape from Officer Matt Payne's answering machine.
Payne told me that Chief Coughlin wanted to run them through
ere. And as I had to come here to face an irate mayor anyhow,
brought it along."

"Christ, Carlucci even called me, wanting to know if I had
leard anything about the—what is it—the Islamic Liberation
Army."

"Had you?"

"The first I ever heard of them was in the newspapers. Who
he hell are they, anyway?"

"I wish I knew," Wohl said. "You come up with anything
on Payne's car?"

Lomax turned and walked stiffly, reminding Wohl that the
accident had crushed his hip, to a desk and came back with a
manila folder.

"My vast experience in forensics leads me to believe a. that
the same instrument was used to slice his tires and fuck up his
paint job, and b. that said instrument was a pretty high quality
collapsible knife, probably with a six-inch blade."

"How did you reach these conclusions, Dr. Lomax? And
what is a collapsible knife?"

"A *switchblade*," Lomax said, "is like a regular penknife,
the blade folds into the handle, except that it's spring loaded,
so that when you push the button, it springs open. A *collapsible*
knife is one where the blade slides in and out of the handle.
Some are spring loaded, and some you have to push. You follow me?"

Wohl nodded.

"Okay. Switchblades aren't much good for stabbing tires,
particularly high-quality tires like the Pirelli's on Payne's car.
They're slashing instruments. The blades are thin. You try to
stab something, like the walls of tires, the blade tends to snap.
Payne's tires were stabbed, more than slashed. The contour of
the penetration, the holes, shows that the blade was pretty thick

on the dull side. A lot of switchblades are just thin pieces of
steel sharpened on *both* sides. Hence, a collapsible knife of
pretty good quality. Six inches long or so because there's generally a proportion between blade width and length. The same
instrument because we found particles of tire rubber in the
scratches in the paint. And, for the hell of it, the size and depth
of the scratches indicates a blade shape, the point shape, con-
firming what I said before.''

"I am dazzled," Wohl said.

"Now all you street cops have to do is find the knife, and
there's your doer. There can't be more than eight or ten thousand knives like that in Philadelphia. Forensics is happy to
have been able to be of service."

Wohl slid photographs out of the folder and looked at them.

"I hate to think what it's going to cost to have that car re-
painted," he said.

"Well, I have a nice heel print of who I suspect is the doer,"
Lomax said. "Heel and three clear fingers, right hand. Maybe
you can get him to pay to have it painted."

Wohl looked at him curiously.

"It's in a position suggesting that he laid his hand on the
hood, left side, when he bent over to stick the knife in the
ninety-dollar tire," Lomax said, and then pointed to one of
the photographs. "There."

"Well, when we have a suspect in custody," Wohl said,
"I'm sure that will be very valuable."

Lomax laughed. Both knew that while the positive identification of an individual by his fingerprints has long been established as nearly infallible—fingerprints are truly unique—it is
not true that all you have to do to find an individual is have his
fingerprint or fingerprints. Trying to match a fingerprint without a name to go with it, with fingerprints on file in either a
police department or in the FBI's miles of cabinets in Washington, and thus come up with a name, is for all practical
purposes impossible.

"What's on here?" Lomax asked, picking up the cassette
tape.

"I don't know. I didn't hear it. I don't think anybody has.
They're calling there every fifteen minutes or so, so Mc-
Fadden—one of the guys sitting on Payne—fixed it so that the
machine worked silently."

"You want to hear it?"

"Not particularly," Wohl said, and then reconsidered. He looked at his watch. "Maybe I'd better," he said. "Let me have the phone, will you, please, Warren?"

Lomax pushed a telephone to him, and Wohl dialed a number.

"This is Inspector Wohl. Have Detective Harris call me at 555-3445."

When he had put the phone down, Lomax asked, "He getting anywhere with the Magnella job?"

"Not so far."

"How's he doing?"

"If you mean, Warren, 'is he still on a bender?' he better not be. Christ, is that all over the Department?"

"People talk, Peter."

"The word is gossip, and cops do it more than women," Wohl said.

"I was having my own troubles with good ol' Jack Daniel's for a while," Lomax said. "I'm sympathetic."

"I sometimes wonder if people weren't so sympathetic if the people they feel sorry for would straighten themselves out."

"He's a good cop, Peter."

"So I keep telling myself," Wohl said. "But then I keep hearing stories about him waving his gun around and getting thrown in a holding cell to sober up."

"You heard that, huh?"

"Let's play the tape."

Lieutenant Lomax had methodically made notes on seventeen recorded messages when his telephone rang. He answered it, then handed it to Wohl. "Tony Harris."

"Where are you working, Harris?" Wohl asked. There was a pause while Harris told him. Wohl thought a moment, then said, "Okay. Meet me at the Waikiki Diner on Roosevelt Boulevard at noon. If you get there before I do, get us a booth."

He hung up without waiting for a reply.

"Would you think me a racist if I told you I suspect all of these calls were from those of the Afro-American persuasion?" he asked.

"What did you expect?" Lomax replied. "Two kinds, though, I think. Some of these sleaze-balls have gone past the sixth grade."

"Yeah, I sort of noticed that. A little affectation in the diction."

"And not all of them are black, I don't think."

"No?"

"At least not on the first tape. There was a very sexy lady on tape one. 'You know who this is,' she said, in a very sultry voice indeed, 'call me in the morning,' or 'after nine in the morning.' Something like that."

"Now you're a racist. How do you know the sexy lady isn't black?"

"I doubt it. This was a pure Bala Cynwyd, Rose Tree Hunt Club accent. She talked with her teeth clenched."

Wohl chuckled. "I think one might reasonably presume that if one is young, good-looking, rich, and drives a Porsche, one might reasonably expect to get one's wick dipped."

"Even a Porsche with slashed tires?" Lomax quipped, and then started the tape again.

The fifth message next played was, "Darling, he's gone out again, thank *God*, and I'm sitting here with a *martini*—and you *know* what *they* do to me—thinking of all the things I'd like to do to you. So if you get this before eight-thirty, call me, and we can at least *talk*. Otherwise, call me after nineish in the morning."

Wohl could see the lady, teeth clenched, talking. He even had a good idea of what she looked like. Blond hair, long, parted in the middle and hanging to her shoulders. She was wearing a sweater and a pleated skirt. From Strawbridge & Clothier in Jenkintown.

"I wonder what she has in *mind* to *do* to Officer Payne?" Lomax asked, teeth clenched. "Something frightfully *naughty*, wouldn't you say?"

"We gonna stick a .45 down your throat, motherfucker, and blow your fucking brains out your ass!"

"On the whole, I think I prefer the lady's offer," Wohl said.

"Yeah," Lomax said.

"Her voice," Wohl thought aloud, "sounds vaguely familiar."

"If he who has gone out again, thank *God*," Lomax said, in a credible mimicry, "finds out, Payne is going to have a bullet in both legs."

"We gonna cut your cock off and shove it down your throat, motherfucker!"

"I think that's more or less what the lady has in mind,"

Wohl said. "Except that she wants to bite it off and shove it down her own throat."

"Peter, you're a dirty old man."

"Shut it off, I've heard enough," Wohl said. "I'm on my way to 'counsel' Detective Harris. I shouldn't have a mind full of lewd images."

"I don't think you missed anything. I'll play the whole thing to be sure. But that's about what the first one had on it."

"Why do you think they're doing this, Warren?"

"I don't know," Lomax said thoughtfully. "Just to be a pain in the ass, maybe. Or they get their jollies talking nasty to a cop."

"Wouldn't that get dull after a while? How many times can you say 'fuck you'?"

"I had the feeling too, that it's organized. Some of them sound like they're reading it."

"That brings us back to why?"

"It could be, playing a psychiatrist, that they're getting a little worried, and calling Payne and Goldblatt's makes them think they're doing something useful for the revolution."

"You think they're really revolutionaries?"

"They don't sound like bomb throwers. Christ, I've listened to enough of them. *They* sound either really bananas, or very calm, as if they're going about God's work. These clowns don't even sound particularly angry."

"Yeah," Wohl said. "Well, thanks, Warren. It was good to see you."

"I got some really dirty tapes back there, Peter," Lomax said, gesturing toward a row of file tapes, "and some blue movies, now that we know you react to them. Come back anytime."

Martha Peebles woke thinking that she was—to her joyous surprise; four months before she would have given eight to five that she would end her life as a virginal spinster—not only a woman in love, but a *betrothed* woman.

David—sweet, shy David—had never actually proposed, of course, getting down on his knees and asking her to be his bride, giving her an engagement ring. But that didn't matter. He knew in his heart as she knew in hers that they were meant for each other, that it was ordained, perhaps by God, that they share life's joys and pains together, that they be man and wife.

Getting down on his knees wasn't David's style. She could not, now that she had time to think about it, imagine her father getting down on his knees either. And she already had an engagement ring. It had been her mother's. *And it looked so good on her finger!*

She got out of bed and put on a robe and went into the bath and watched David shave and then get dressed, and, hanging on his arm, her head against his shoulder, walked with him downstairs for breakfast.

Evans gave her, she thought, a knowing look.

Well, have I got a surprise for you! It's not what you think at all.

Evans disappeared into the kitchen, and then returned a moment later with the coffee service.

"Good morning, Miss Martha, Captain," he said. "It's cold out, but nice and clear. I hope you slept well?"

"Splendidly, thank you," Martha said. "Evans, Captain Pekach and I have a little announcement."

David looked uncomfortable.

"I saw the ring when you came in, Miss Martha," Evans said. "Your mother and dad would be happy for you."

He held out his hand to David.

"May I offer my congratulations, Captain?"

"Thank you," David said, getting to his feet, visibly torn between embarrassment and pleasure.

Harriet Evans came through the swinging door to the kitchen and wrapped her arms around Martha.

"Oh, honey baby, I'm so happy for you," she said, tears running down her cheeks. "I knew the first time I saw you with the captain that he'd be the one."

"I knew the first time I saw him that he was the one," Martha said.

Harriet touched Martha's face and then went to Pekach and hugged him.

David's embarrassment passed. He was now smiling broadly.

I will never be as happy ever again as I am at this moment, Martha thought.

She waited until Evans and Harriet had gone to fetch the rest of breakfast, and then asked, "Precious, would you do something for me?"

"Name it," he said, after a just perceptible hesitation.

"I know how you feel about people and parties, precious.
But I do want to share this with *someone*."

"Who?" David asked suspiciously.

"I was thinking we could have a very few people, Peter
Wohl, for example, in for cocktails and dinner. Nothing elaborate—"

"*Wohl?*"

"Well, he is your boss, and he was the first one who knew."

"Yeah, I guess he was."

"And he's not married, and I suspect that he's under terrible
pressure—"

"You can say that again."

"Well?"

"Well, what?"

"Would you ask him?"

"For when?"

"For tonight."

"I'll ask him."

"And maybe Captain and Mrs. Sabara?"

"I can ask."

*And I will think of one more couple. Somebody who can do
David some good. I would like to ask Brewster and Patricia
Payne, but with their boy in the condition he is, that probably
isn't a good idea. I'll think of someone. Since my husband-to-
be wants to be a policeman, it is clearly the duty of his wife-
to-be to do everything in her power to see that he becomes
commissioner.*

"You ask the minute you get to work, and call me and tell
me what they said."

"That sounds like a wifely order."

"Yes, I guess it does. Do you want to change your mind
about anything?"

Smiling broadly, he shook his head no.

She got up and went to his end of the table and stood behind
his chair and put her arms around him.

And so it was that when Assistant District Attorney Farnsworth Stillwell finally managed to get Staff Inspector Peter Wohl
on the telephone at half past one that afternoon, Wohl was able
to make the absolutely truthful statement, "Well, that's very
kind of you, Farnsworth, but I have previous plans."

He was to take cocktails and dinner with Miss Martha Peebles and her fiancé at Miss Peebles's residence, primarily be-

cause when Dave Pekach asked him, Pekach took him by surprise, and he could think of no excuse not to accept that would not hurt Pekach's feelings.

Until Stillwell had called, he had taken some consolation by thinking that the food would probably be good, and even if that didn't happen, he would be able to satisfy his curiosity about what the inside of the mansion behind the walls at 606 Glengarry Lane looked like.

Now he was extremely grateful to have been the recipient of Miss Peebles's kind invitation.

I may even carry her flowers.

"Can't you get out of it?" Stillwell insisted. "Peter, this is important. Possibly to both of us."

You for sure, and me possibly. Fuck you, Stillwell.

"I just can't. One of my men is having a little party to celebrate his engagement. I have to be there. You understand."

"Which one of your men?"

You are a persistent bastard, aren't you?

"Captain David Pekach, as a matter of fact."

Farnsworth Stillwell laughed, which surprised Wohl.

"I wondered what the hell that was all about. I'll see you there, Peter," he said, and hung up.

What the hell does he mean by that?

Farnsworth Stillwell broke the connection with his finger and dialed his home. "Helene, call the Peebles woman back, tell her that I was able to rearrange my schedule and that we'll be able to come after all."

Margaret McCarthy, trailed by Lari Matsi, came up the narrow staircase into Matt Payne's apartment. Both of them were wearing heavy quilted three-quarter length jackets and earmuffs.

"I could have come and picked you up," Charley McFadden said.

"Next time, take him up on it," Lari said. "It's *cold* out there."

Jesus Martinez came up the stairs.

"Hay-zus, you don't know Lari, do you?" Margaret said. "Hay-zus Martinez, Lari Matsi."

"How are you?" Martinez said.

"I didn't catch the name?" Lari replied.

"It's 'Jesus' in Spanish," Charley offered.

"Oh," Lari said, and smiled.

"I don't think we've met," Margaret said, smiling, to the third young man in the room. "And Charley's not too good about introducing people."

He was wearing a mixed sweat suit, gray trousers and a yellow sweatshirt, on which was painted, STOLEN FROM THE SING SING PRISON ATHLETIC DEPARTMENT. There was little doubt in her mind that he was a cop; a shoulder holster with a large revolver in it was hanging from the chair that he was straddling backward. He stood up and put out his hand.

"Jack Matthews," he said.

"Where's Matt?"

"In his bedroom with a woman," Charley said.

"He thought you'd never ask," Jack Matthews said.

"What are you talking about?" Margaret said, not quite sure her leg was being pulled.

"You asked where Matt was, and I told you. He's in his bedroom with a woman."

"I don't believe you."

"Probably with his pants off," Charley added, exchanging a pleased smile with Jack Matthews. Jesus Martinez shook his head in disgust.

Amy Payne came out of Matt's bedroom, saw the women in the living room, and smiled.

"Hi! I'm Amy," she said. "Matt'll be out in a minute, presuming he can get his pants on by himself."

Officer McFadden and Special Agent Matthews for reasons that baffled all three women found this announcement convulsively hilarious. Even Jesus smiled.

"Just what's going on around here, Charley?" Margaret demanded.

"Let me take it from the beginning," Amy said. "I'm Amy Payne. Matt's sister. I happen to be a doctor. And knowing my idiot brother as I do, I felt reasonably sure that he would not change his dressings, and that's what I've been doing."

"Not very funny at all, Charley," Margaret said, but she could not keep herself from smiling.

Lari dipped into an enormous purse and held up a plastic bag full of bandages and antiseptic.

"I don't know him as well as you do, Doctor," she said. "But that's why I'm here too. He is that category of patient best described as a pain-in-the-you-know-what. I was filling in on the surgical floor at Frankford when they brought him in."

"Well, that was certainly nice of you," Amy said. "Apparently, you don't know my brother very well. If you did, you would encourage gangrene."

"No," Lari said. "That would put him back in the hospital. Anything to prevent that."

They smiled at each other.

Matt came into the room, supporting himself on a cane.

"Oh, good!" he said. "Everybody's here. Choir practice can begin."

"I promised Mother I would see that you were eating," Amy said. "What are your plans for that?"

"We're going out for the worst food in Philadelphia," Matt said. "You're welcome to join us, Amy."

"I know I shouldn't ask, but curiosity overwhelms me. Where are you going to get the worst food in Philadelphia?"

"At the FOP," Matt replied. "As a special dispensation, because I have been a very good boy, I have permission to go there, providing I don't drink too much and I come directly home afterward."

"Actually, I'm looking forward to it," Jack Matthews said. "I've never been there."

"I think I'll pass, thank you just the same," Amy said.

"You're a cop, and you've never been to the FOP?" Lari Matsi asked.

"Oh, come on, Amy," Matt said. "I'll even buy you a chili dog."

"I haven't had supper," Amy said. "For some perverse reason, a chili dog has a certain appeal to me."

"How is it," Lari pursued, "that you've never been to the FOP?"

"He's not a *real* cop," Charley said. "More like a Junior G-man."

"In deference to the ladies, Officer McFadden," Jack Matthews said. "I will not suggest that you attempt a physiologically impossible act of self-impregnation."

Matt laughed. After a moment, Amy did too, and then Lari.

"Then what's the gun for?" Lari asked.

"I work for the Justice Department," Jack replied.

"He's an FBI agent, Lari," Matt said.

"Oh, really?"

Matt saw the way Lari was looking at Jack Matthews, and knew that whatever chance there might have been for him to know Lari Matsi in the biblical sense had just gone up in smoke.

"Are you here *officially*?" Amy asked. "I mean, are you part of Matt's bodyguard, or whatever it's called?"

"Actually, I came to play chess," Jack said. "But these evil people pressed intoxicants on me. Have I shattered your faith in the FBI?"

"Yeah," Amy said, smiling.

Yeah, you are here officially, Matt thought, *or at least quasi-officially. You came here, under cover of playing chess, to tell me that yes, indeed, the rumors are true. I am to be investigated by the FBI regarding formal charges made that I violated the civil rights of Charles David Stevens, Esq., by shooting the murderous sonofabitch.*

"Has any thought been given to how we're going to get Matt—I guess I mean all of us—from here to the FOP?" Amy asked. "I don't have my car."

"No problem," Charley said. "We—Hay-zus and me—have an unmarked car downstairs. We'll take Matt in that. The rest of you can ride with Jack in his G-man wagon."

"That should work," Lari Matsi said.

And I will bet twenty dollars to a doughnut that when the convoy gets under way, Lari will be in the front seat of same with J. Edgar Hoover, Junior, both of them wondering how they can get rid of Amy and Margaret.

Oh, what the hell. There's always Helene.

Staff Inspector Peter F. Wohl left his office at Bustleton and Bowler Streets a few minutes after half past five.

On the way to his apartment in the 800 block of Norwood Street in Chestnut Hill, Wohl decided that tonight was a good opportunity to give the Jag a little exercise. He hadn't had it out of the garage since the lousy weather had started.

Among its many not-so-charming idiosyncrasies, the Jag frequently expressed its annoyance at being ignored for more than forty-eight hours at a time by absolutely refusing to start when the person privileged to have the responsibility for its care and feeding finally came to take it out.

Driving it back and forth to Martha Peebles's house—plus maybe a run past Monahan's house on the way home, just to check—would be just long enough a trip to give it a good warm-up, get the oil circulating, and get the flat spots out of the tires.

He thought again that if there was only room to *safely* park a car like the Jag at Bustleton and Bowler, he could drive it to work every other day or so. He made a mental note to tell Payne, when he came back on duty, and could devote some attention to the "new" school building at Frankford and Castor, to make sure that, as a prerogative of his exalted rank and position, the commanding officer of Special Operations have reserved for him a parking place that was at once convenient and would provide a certain protection against getting its fenders dinged.

When he reached the garages behind the mansion he put his city-owned car in the garage, and then took a shovel and started to clear the ice and snow away from the doors of the Jag's garage. He finally got the doors open, but it was even more difficult than he thought it would be. The snow had melted and frozen into ice and thawed and refrozen. He had, he thought, actually *chiseled* his way through the ice into the garage, rather than *shoveled* his way through the snow.

He got behind the wheel and put the key in the ignition. To his delighted surprise, the engine caught immediately. It ran a little roughly, but it ran. It would not, as he had worst-scenario predicted, refuse to start until he had run the battery down and then recharged it.

"Good girl," he said.

He sat there, running the engine just above idle until the engine temperature gauge needle finally moved off the peg. He shut the engine off, opened the hood and checked the oil and brake fluid, looked at the tires, and then closed the doors, locked them, and went up the stairs at the end of the building to his apartment.

He showered and shaved, put on a glen plaid suit, and wondered—he had little experience in this sort of thing—if he was expected to bring a gift to the affair, and if so, what?

To hell with it.

He put on his overcoat, which had a collar of some unidentified fur, and a green felt snap-brim hat.

There were no messages on his answering machine, which surprised him. He called Special Operations and told the lieutenant on duty that he would be at the residence of Miss Martha

Peebles in Chestnut Hill from fifteen minutes from now until he advised differently.

Then he went down and got back in the Jaguar. It started immediately. All was right with the world, he told himself, until he glanced at his watch and saw that he was not due at Glengarry Lane for almost an hour.

What the hell, I'll check on the people sitting on Monahan now, instead of later.

When he reached the neighborhood, he drove slowly east on Bridge Street, looking up Sylvester Street at the intersection. There was an unmarked car parked at the curb. He could see the heads of two men in the car, one of them wearing a regular uniform cap, the other what he thought of as a Renfrew of the Royal Canadian Mounted Police cap.

He turned left into the alley behind the row of houses of which, he now remembered. Mr. and Mrs. Albert J. Monahan occupied the sixth from this corner.

He had gone perhaps fifty yards into the alley when a uniformed officer stepped into it and, somewhat warily, Wohl thought approvingly, motioned for him to stop.

Wohl braked and rolled down the window.

"Good evening, sir," the cop began, and then recognized him. "Oh, it's you, Inspector."

"This way to the North Pole, right?" Wohl said, and offered his hand through the window. The cop laughed dutifully.

"Aside from frostbite, how's things going?" Wohl asked with a smile.

"Quiet as a tomb, Inspector."

An unfortunate choice of words, but I take your point.

"I guess everybody but cops are smart enough to stay inside, huh?"

"Sure looks that way. Anything I can do for you, Inspector?"

"No. I just thought I'd better check on what was going on. Mr. Monahan is very important."

"Well, we're sitting on him good. There's either a Highway or a district RPC by here every fifteen to twenty minutes. Or a supervisor, or both. Sergeant Carter drove through the alley just a couple of minutes ago."

"But nothing out of the ordinary?"

"Not a thing."

"Well, then, I guess I can go. Good to see you. I'm sorry

you have to march around in the snow and ice, but I think it's necessary.''

"I've been telling myself the guys in Traffic do this for twenty years," the cop said. "Good evening, sir.''

Wohl smiled, rolled up the window, and drove the rest of the way down the alley, looking at the rear of the Monahan house as he went past.

He turned left from the alley onto Sanger Street, and then left again onto Sylvester Street. He would stop and say hello to the two cops in the car.

Now there were two unmarked cars on Rosehill Street.

That's probably Sergeant Carter.

The cop with the Renfrew of the Royal Canadian Mounted Police cap got—surprisingly quickly, Wohl thought—from behind the wheel and stepped into the street, signaling him to stop.

Christ, I hope they're not stopping every car that comes down the street!

This time there was no recognition in the cop's eyes when Wohl rolled the window down and looked up at him.

"Sir," the cop said, "you're going the wrong way down a one-way street. May I see your driver's license please?''

Wohl took his leather ID folder from his pocket and passed it out the window.

"Maybe you could give me another chance, Officer," he said. "I'm usually not this stupid.''

"Oh, Jesus, Inspector!''

"I honest to God didn't see the one-way sign," Wohl said. "Who's that in the back of the RPC? Sergeant Carter?''

"Lieutenant Malone, sir.''

"Let me pull this over—turn it around, I guess—I'd like a word with him.''

"Yes, sir.''

Wohl turned the car around and parked it, and then went and got in the back of the unmarked car.

"We all feel a little foolish, Inspector," Malone said when Wohl got in the backseat of the RPC. "We should have recognized you.''

Wohl saw that Malone was in civilian clothing.

"You don't feel half as foolish as I do," Wohl said. "If I had been doing ninety in a thirty-mile zone, that I would understand. But going the wrong way down a one-way street—''

"I'll let you go with a warning this time, Inspector," the cop who had stopped him said, "but the next time, right into Lewisburg!"

Everyone laughed.

"Something on your mind, Inspector?" Malone asked.

"Just wanted to check on Monahan, that's all."

"He's been home about an hour and a half," the cop who had stopped Wohl said. "I don't think he'll be going out again tonight in this weather."

"How are you working this?" Wohl asked, and touched Malone's knee to silence him when it looked like Malone was going to answer.

"Simple rotation," the second cop answered. "One of us walks for thirty minutes—when the wind's really blowing, only fifteen minutes—and then one of us takes his place. We do a four-hour tour, and then go on our regular patrols."

"Your reliefs showing up all right?"

"Yes, sir."

"Does the man walking the beat have a radio?"

"We all have radios."

"Can you think of any way to improve what we're trying to do? Even a wild hair?"

"How about a heated snowmobile?"

"I'll ask Commissioner Czernich in the morning about a snowmobile. Don't hold your breath. But I meant it, anybody got any ideas about something we should, or should not, be doing?"

Both cops shook their heads.

"Well, I can see that I'm not needed here," Wohl said. "I guess everybody understands how important Monahan is as a witness?"

"Yes, sir," they said, nearly in unison.

"Can I have a word with you, Lieutenant?"

"Yes, sir, certainly."

Wohl shook hands with both cops and got out of the car. Malone followed him to the Jaguar.

"Yes, sir."

"You have anything else to do here?"

"No, sir."

"Any hot plans for tonight? For dinner, to start with?"

"No, sir."

"Okay, Jack. Get in your car and follow me."

"Where are we going?"

"Somewhere where it's warm, and where, I suspect, there will be a more than adequate supply of free antifreeze."

TWENTY-FOUR

Miss Martha Peebles had decided that it would be better to receive her and Captain Pekach's guests in the family (as opposed to the formal) dining room of her home. For one thing, it had been her father's favorite room. She had good memories of her father and his friends getting up from the dinner table and moving to the overstuffed chairs and couches at the far end of the room for cognac and cigars and coffee.

Tonight, she would more or less reverse that. She had had Evans and his nephew Nathaniel set up a little bar near the overstuffed furniture. Nathaniel would serve drinks first, before they moved to the dining table for the meal. Then, after they had eaten, they could move back.

Besides, she reasoned, the formal dining room was just too large for the few people who would be coming. When she was a little girl, for her eleventh birthday party, it had been converted into a roller-skating rink.

But her father had preferred the family dining room, and it seemed appropriate for tonight. And she thought that her father would appreciate the arrangements she had made. She was convinced that her father would have liked David, and vice versa. They were men. And if he liked David, her father would also like David's friends, Inspector Wohl and Captain Sabara.

Daddy probably wouldn't like Farnsworth Stillwell any more than I do, she thought, but she could clearly hear his voice telling her, *"Like it or not, kitten, you are who you are, and from time to time, you have to go through the motions and put up with people of your own background."*

And, besides, now that Stillwell had entered politics, he might turn out to be useful to David.

Captain and Mrs. Michael J. Sabara were the first to arrive. As Evans led them into the family dining room, Martha had the thought—which she instantly recognized as unkind and regretted—that Mrs. Sabara was a trifle overdressed. Captain Sabara was dressed almost exactly as David was, that is to say in a blazer and gray slacks, and that pleased her.

"I'm Martha Peebles," she said, offering her hand to Mrs. Sabara. "I'm so glad you could come on such short notice."

"Your home is beautiful!" Mrs. Sabara said.

"David calls it the fortress," Martha said. "But I grew up here, and I guess I'm used to it."

Sabara and Pekach shook hands, although they had seen each other only two hours before.

"Why don't you have Nathaniel make Captain and Mrs. Sabara something to chase the chill, David?"

As they approached the bar, Captain Sabara said, "I told you I didn't need a tie. Dave's not wearing one."

"When you come to a house like this," Mrs. Sabara said firmly. "You wear a necktie." Then she turned to Pekach. "She's beautiful, David."

"Yeah," Pekach said. "Look, Lois, don't say anything about us being engaged. I think she wants to make an announcement."

Lois Sabara put her index finger before her lips.

"You name it, we got it," Dave said as they reached the bar.

"What are you drinking?" Mike Sabara asked.

"Scotch. Some kind her father liked. He bought it by the truckload."

"I'll have what Captain Pekach is drinking," Sabara said. "Lois?"

"Wine, I think. Have you any red wine?"

''There's a California Cabernet Sauvignon, madam, and a very nice Moroccan burgundy that Miss Martha likes,'' Nathaniel said.

''I'll have the burgundy, please.''

Staff Inspector Peter Wohl and Lieutenant John J. Malone entered the family dining room next.

''Who's he?'' Lois asked softly, as they walked toward the bar.

''Jack Malone. New lieutenant,'' her husband told her.

''He's the one with the wife trouble, right?''

''Jesus Christ, Lois!''

''Where's the lady of the house?'' Wohl asked.

''I guess she's checking on the food,'' Pekach said. ''Thank you for coming, Inspector. And welcome, Jack.''

''The inspector said it would be all right,'' Malone said.

''Absolutely.''

''You don't know Mike's wife, do you, Jack?'' Wohl said. ''Lois, this is Jack Malone.''

''How do you do?'' Lois Sabara said.

Madam Sabara, Wohl thought, *has obviously heard the gossip vis-à-vis Mrs. Malone. Her tone of voice would freeze a penguin.*

''We just ran past Monahan's house,'' Wohl offered. ''Things seem well in hand.''

''And Payne?'' Sabara asked.

''Officer Payne is dining at the FOP,'' Wohl said.

''Can he get around well enough for that?'' Lois asked. ''I thought he was shot in the leg?''

''He will not be the first young police officer to crawl into the FOP,'' Wohl said. ''For that matter, I've seen some pretty old ones crawl in there.''

''May I get you gentlemen a cocktail?'' Nathaniel asked.

''I'll have Scotch, light on the ice and water, please,'' Wohl said.

He saw the hesitancy in Malone's eyes, and made the quick decision that when Lois, as she certainly would, recounted her encounter with Lieutenant-Jack-Malone-the-Wife-Beater to her peers, it would be better if she could not crow, ''Well, at least he wasn't drinking,'' from a position of moral superiority.

''Try the Scotch, Jack,'' he said. ''David's been bragging about it.''

''Same for me, then,'' Malone said.

Martha came through a door Wohl hadn't noticed. He approved of what he saw, both sartorially—Martha was wearing a simple black dress with a double string of pearls—and on her face: She was a happy woman.

A wholesome one too, he thought. *Dave's going to have a hard time adjusting to life in the palace, and she's going to have a hard time being a cop's wife, but Dave is a decent human being, and I think he's just what this poor little rich girl really needs.*

"Good evening, Inspector," she said. "I'm so glad you could come."

"Thank you for asking me," Wohl said. "And David said, when I told him I didn't have a lady to bring, to bring somebody. This is somebody, Lieutenant Jack Malone."

"David's told me about you, Lieutenant," Martha said, shaking his hand.

I wonder how much? Wohl thought.

Farnsworth and Helene Stillwell appeared in the room.

"I don't know him well," Martha said, quickly and softly to Wohl, "but my father knew her father. And I thought that since you're working together, having them would be appropriate."

"Absolutely," Wohl said.

What she's doing—good for her—is trying to foster Dave's career. If she's as smart as I think she is, I will be working for Dave in a couple of years.

He next had a somewhat less upbeat thought when he took a good look at Helene Stillwell.

That one has had a couple of little nips to give her courage to face the party.

"Small world, Peter, eh?" Stillwell greeted him.

"It looks that way, doesn't it?"

"You remember my wife, of course?"

"Yes, of course. Nice to see you, Mrs. Stillwell."

"Oh, please call me Helene."

Helene Stillwell was wearing a black dress, almost an exact duplicate of Martha's, and a similar string of pearls.

The necessary introductions were made and drinks offered and comments about the foul weather exchanged.

I wonder why Martha Peebles doesn't talk that way, using the teeth-clenched diction Stillwell's wife does? Peter Wohl wondered.

According to Matt Payne, Martha has more money than God, and this house makes it rather obvious that she didn't make it last week. Ergo, she too should talk through her nose and as if she has lockjaw.

But she doesn't. Martha sounds, if not like Lois Sabara, at least like my mother, and Stillwell's wife sounds exactly like the horny married lady from Bala Cynwyd on Matt's answering machine.

"And how, Inspector Wohl, is Officer Payne?" Helene asked.

Jesus H. Christ! Don't let your dirty imagination run away with you!

"It's quarter to eight, Helene. By now I'd say he's on the third pitcher of beer and convinced, given the chance, he could solve all the problems of the Police Department."

"I don't quite follow you?"

"He's on the town, more or less."

"I thought he was—that you had him under protection in some mysterious place. And he's on the town?"

"No mysterious place. He's in his apartment. And tonight he's at the FOP—the Fraternal Order of Police building, on Spring Garden Street. Jack Malone, who is in charge of his security, decided that if there was any place more secure than Matt's apartment, it would be downstairs in the FOP, where there are generally at least a hundred armed cops."

"Yes, of course," Helene said through clenched teeth and sounding exactly like the horny lady from Bala Cynwyd on Matt's answering machine.

Except, of course, we don't know that she's from Bala Cynwyd. Warren Lomax said she sounded like she was from Bala Cynwyd.

"I'm going to drop in on him tomorrow morning," Wohl said. "I'll tell him you were asking about him."

"Yes, please. He's such a nice young man."

And such a comfort to a bored teeth clencher to boot? And that is a martini you're drinking, Helene, isn't it?

"Peter," Farnsworth Stillwell said, walking up. "I really do have to have a word with you."

"Certainly."

"Martha, I need a few minutes alone with Inspector Wohl. Is there somewhere?"

"David, darling, would you take them into the library?"

"Sure," Pekach said.

"Thank you, David darling," Wohl said softly as he followed Pekach out of the room.

Pekach glared at him, and then smiled and shook his head.

"Do I detect a certain element of jealousy, Inspector?"

"Absolutely, David."

Do I really think that Matt is fucking Stillwell's wife? And presuming for the sake of argument that I do, am I annoyed because that's a pretty fucking dumb thing for him to be doing? Or because he's getting in where Peter Wohl ain't?

"I hope, Farnsworth," Wohl said as he followed Pekach into the library, "that this won't take long. My glass seems to have a hole in it."

"No problem," Pekach said. "Martha's father never liked to get far from the sauce."

He heaved on what looked like a chest. It unfolded upward into a bar.

"There's even a refrigerator and running water in this thing," Pekach said, demonstrating.

"How nice," Stillwell said.

And thank you, Farnsworth Stillwell. I was just about to say, "It must be nice to be rich," and that would have been a dumb thing to say.

"I think Martha's about to serve dinner," Pekach said.

"This won't take long," Stillwell said.

Wohl went to the bar, poured more Scotch into his glass, and added a little water. By then Pekach had left the library and closed the door after himself.

"Now there's a man who knows what to do with an opportunity," Stillwell said, nodding toward the door through which Pekach had left.

"How do you mean?"

"Unless she is smart enough to get an airtight premarital agreement, and floating on the wings of love as she is at the moment, I rather doubt if she will be, your man Pekach is shortly going to be co-owner of half the anthracite coal in Northeast Pennsylvania."

I will be on my good behavior. I will not get into it with this cynical wiseass sonofabitch.

"It couldn't happen to a nicer guy."

"Don't misunderstand me, Peter," Stillwell said. "I like

Dave Pekach, and I admire people who take advantage of opportunities that come their way.''

Wohl smiled and nodded.

What is this sonofabitch up to?

"Tomorrow morning, Peter, the governor will hold a press conference at which he will appoint a new deputy attorney general for corporate crime. Nice ring to that, isn't there? *'Corporate crime.'* Everybody knows that the men in corporate boardrooms are robbing the poor people blind. I thought it was one of the governor's brighter moves recently, figuring out for himself that there are more poor people voting than people in corporate boardrooms. I told him so.''

"I'm missing something here?"

"A brilliant gumshoe like you? I just can't believe that, Peter.''

"I'm not much good at games, either, Farnsworth.''

"Okay. The facts and nothing but the facts, right, Sergeant Friday? I am going to be the deputy attorney general for corporate crime.''

"Well, in that case, congratulations," Peter said, and put out his hand.

"And you are going to be the new chief investigator for the deputy attorney general for corporate crime," Stillwell went on.

"I am?"

"Starting at a salary that's ten, maybe twelve thousand more than you're making now.''

He means this! He's absolutely goddamn serious! And he's looking at me as if he expects me to get down on one knee and kiss his ring.

"Farnsworth, why would you want me to work for you?''

"Very simple answer. I don't know the first goddamn thing about corporate crime. And you do. There doesn't seem to be much question that you are the best white-collar crime investigator in Philadelphia. Your record proves that. If you can do that in Philadelphia, you certainly can do it elsewhere in Pennsylvania. I want the best, and you're it.''

There is a certain element of truth in that, he understands, with overwhelming immodesty.

"When did all this come up?''

"Yesterday and today. What absolutely perfect timing, wouldn't you say?''

"Perfect timing for what?"

"This Islamic Liberation Army thing is just about to blow up in our faces."

"Is it? I'm a little dense. The doers are in jail. We have a witness. And you're going to prosecute."

"I would hate to think you were being sarcastic, Peter."

"Like I said, sometimes I'm dense. You tell me. Why is it going to blow up in our faces?"

"Armando C. Giacomo, for one thing. More important, whatever shadowy faces in the background have come up with the money to engage Mr. Giacomo's professional services."

"I don't think you're saying that anytime a sleaze-ball, or a group of sleaze-balls, comes up with the money to hire Giacomo, the DA's office should roll over and apologize for having them arrested in the first place."

He saw in Stillwell's eyes that he was becoming annoyed, at what he perceived to be his naiveté.

Fuck you, Farnsworth!

"I heard—I have some contacts in the FBI, the Justice Department—that the Coalition for Equitable Law Enforcement has filed a petition demanding an investigation of Officer Payne, alleging that he violated the civil rights of Charles David Stevens."

"The what?"

"The Coalition for Equitable Law Enforcement. It's one of those lunatic bleeding heart groups. One of the more articulate ones, unfortunately."

"That shooting was not only justifiable use of force, it was self-defense."

"The allegation will be investigated. It will get in the papers. Arthur Nelson—in both the *Ledger* and over WGHA-TV—will be overjoyed with the opportunity to paint Officer Payne as a trigger-happy killer murdering the innocent. He will gleefully point out that Mr. Stevens's unfortunate demise was the second notch on Payne's gun."

"The bottom line will be—if it gets as far as a Grand Jury—"

"It will," Stillwell interrupted.

"—that the shooting was justified."

"I am surprised that I have to remind you, of all people, Peter, that all it will take is *one* juror—during the ILA trial I mean—to come to the conclusion that since the police were so willing to murder in cold blood one of the alleged robbers, they are entirely capable of coming up with manufactured evidence and a perjuring witness, that they have not, in the immortal words of Perry Mason, proved their case beyond a reasonable doubt.''

Wohl took a long pull on his drink, but didn't reply.

"I would rate the chances of a conviction in the ILA case as no better than fifty percent,'' Stillworth said. "And that is if we can get Monahan into court. I don't like those odds, Peter. I don't want to be thought of as the assistant district attorney who was unable to get a conviction of the niggers who robbed Goldblatt's and killed the watchman or whatever he was.''

"You want to be governor, right?''

"Is there something wrong with that? Wouldn't you like to be police commissioner?'' Wohl met his eyes. "The police commissioner is an appointive post. I don't think it's impossible, some years down the pike, that the mayor of Philadelphia would want to appoint to that position someone who both had earned a reputation state-wide as a highly successful investigator of corporate crime, and who also had been a respected police officer in Philadelphia for many years.''

The odds are that no matter what you say now, you will later regret it.

"Such a hypothetical person might even have a high recommendation from a hypothetical governor, right?''

Stillwell laughed.

"Farnsworth, frankly, you've taken me be surprise.''

"I've noticed.''

"I'll need some time to think this over.''

"There isn't much time, Peter. I've scheduled a press conference for ten tomorrow morning, at which I will announce my acceptance of the governor's appointment. I'd like to be able to say, at that time, who my chief investigator will be.''

"Let me sleep on this,'' Wohl said. "I'll get back to you first thing in the morning.''

"Deal,'' Stillwell said, offering his hand. "I admire, within reason of course, people who look before they leap. Now let us go back in there and share the joy of Romeo and Juliet.''

Officer Charles McFadden, who, on his fifth cup of black coffee, was watching an Edward G. Robinson/Jimmy Cagney gangster movie on the *Late, Late Show*, was startled when the telephone rang. It was, according to the clock on the mantelpiece, a few minutes before three A.M.

He got quickly out of the chair and went to the telephone.

"Hello?"

"Who is this?"

"Who's this?"

"This is Inspector Wohl. Who's that, McFadden?"

"Yes, sir."

"Everything under control, McFadden?"

"Yes, sir."

"Is Officer Payne there?"

"Yes, sir."

"Put him on, please."

"He's asleep, Inspector."

"Then I suppose it will be necessary to wake him up, won't it?"

"Yes, sir. Sir, is anything wrong?"

"No. Not at all. The world, Officer McFadden, is getting, day by day, in every way, better and better. You might keep that in mind."

"Yes, sir. Hold on, Inspector. I'll go wake Payne up."

Officer McFadden had some difficulty in waking Officer Payne. Officer Payne had consumed pitchers of FOP beer like a sponge earlier on. He now smelled like a brewery.

"Jesus Christ, Matt, wake up! Wohl's on the phone!"

Officer Payne managed to get into a semireclining position in his bed.

"What the hell is going on?" he demanded. He looked up at the time projected on the ceiling by the clock Amy had given him. "It's three o'clock in the morning, for Christ's sake!" he protested.

"Wohl's on the phone."

"What the hell does he want?"

"I don't know. He sounds crocked."

"Jesus!"

Officer Payne, with some difficulty, finally managed to make it from a semireclining to a fully sitting-up position. Officer McFadden then removed the handset of the newly installed telephone and handed it to him.

"Yes, sir?" Matt said.

"Sorry to trouble you at this late hour, Officer Payne," Inspector Wohl said, his syllables sufficiently slurred to remind Officer Payne that Officer McFadden had said, "He sounds crocked."

"No problem, sir."

"But I have to have an answer to a certain question that has come up."

"Yes, sir."

"Allegations have reached me, Officer Payne, that you have had, on one or more occasions, carnal knowledge of a female to whom you are not joined in lawful marriage."

What the hell is this all about?

"Sir?"

"And that, on the other hand, the lady in question is married. Not to you, of course."

Christ, he knows about Helene! And he's crocked! And pissed, otherwise he would not be calling at three o'clock in the morning.

"Sir?"

"I am about to ask you a question. I want you to carefully consider your answer before giving it."

"Yes, sir."

"Officer Payne, have you been conducting an illicit affair with Mrs. Helene Stillwell?"

Matt did not reply, because he was absolutely sure that whatever answer he gave was going to get him up to his ears in the deep shit.

"You do know the lady? Helene? The beloved wife of our beloved assistant district attorney?"

"Yes, sir."

"Well, yes or no, Officer Payne? Have you been fucking Farnsworth Stillwell's wife or not?"

"Yes, sir," Matt confessed.

"Good boy!" Inspector Wohl said, and hung up.

At 5:51 A.M., it was visually pleasant on the 5600 block of Sylvester Street, east of Roosevelt Boulevard not far from Oxford Circle. It had snowed, on and off, during the night, and the streets and sidewalks were blanketed in white. Here and there, light came from windows in the row houses as people began their day. Those windows, and the streetlights, seemed to glow as there came the first hint of daylight.

Physically, it was not quite so pleasant. The reason it had

stopped snowing was because the temperature had dropped; it was now twenty-six degrees Fahrenheit, six degrees below freezing. There was a steady northerly wind, powerful enough to move the recently fallen powder snow around.

Officer Richard Kallanan, of the three-man Special Operations team charged with protecting the residence and person of Mr. Albert J. Monahan, had found the wind and the blowing snow particularly uncomfortable during his turn on foot patrol around the Monahan residence. His ears and nose were perhaps unusually sensitive to cold. He had tried walking his route both ways, passing through the alley from Bridge Street to Sanger Street in a northeast direction, and then down Sylvester in a southwestern path, and the reverse. He could detect no difference in perceived cold.

It was a cold sonofabitch in the alley, no matter which way he walked, and he was, therefore, understandably pleased when he turned onto Sylvester Street one more time and saw that there were now two substantially identical dark blue Plymouth RPCs at the curb, one house up from Monahan's house.

Their relief had arrived.

A couple of minutes early, instead of a couple of minutes late. Thank God!

Kallanan picked up his pace a little, slapping his gloved hands together as he moved. As he passed the replacement RPC, he waved and glanced in the window. The side windows were covered with ice, and he could not make out any of the faces inside.

Not that it would have mattered. Kallanan was a relative newcomer to Special Operations, transferred in from the 11th District, where he had spent six of his seven years on the job, and he had not yet had time to make that many new friends.

He could see enough, however, to notice that two of the guys in the relief car were wearing winter hats, Renfrew of the Royal Canadian Mounted Police hats.

They're going to need them.

When Kallanan reached his RPC, he knocked on the window, and Officer Richard O. Totts, who was sitting in the front passenger seat, turned and reached into the back and opened the door for him. Kallanan glanced at the relief car, and gave its occupants a cheerful farewell wave. The driver, a black guy whose window was clear, waved back. Kallanan got in the backseat and pulled the door closed.

"Jesus, it's cold out there," he said.

"I think there's a little coffee left," Officer Duane Jones, who was behind the wheel, said. Totts handed a thermos bottle into the backseat. Kallanan unscrewed the top, which was also the cup, and as Duane Jones got the car moving, he emptied the thermos into it. There was not much coffee left in the thermos.

"Hungry, Kallanan?" Jones asked.

"What I would like is a cup of hot coffee. With a stiff shot in it. There's nothing in here."

"I know a place," Totts offered.

"I'm going to turn in the car first," Jones said. "I hear Pekach is a real sonofabitch if you get caught drinking."

"Hey, we've been relieved," Kallanan said.

"We're still in the goddamn car," Jones said. "You can wait."

At 6:06 A.M., Special Operations Radio Patrol Car W-22 (Radio Call, William Twenty-Two) carrying Officers Rudolph McPhail, Paul Hennis, and John Wilhite turned right off Castor Avenue onto Bridge Street, and then right again on Sylvester Street.

"I don't see the car," Officer Wilhite, who was driving, said. "You don't suppose they took off without waiting for us?"

"Shit, we're only a couple of minutes late," Officer Hennis said.

"Hey, Monahan's house is all lit up," Officer McPhail said, from the backseat.

The radio went off:

"BEEP BEEP BEEP. 5600 block Sylvester Street. Report of shooting and hospital case. Civilian by phone."

"BEEP BEEP BEEP. 5600 block Sylvester Street. Report of shooting and hospital case. Civilian by phone."

"Holy shit!" Officer Hennis said.

Officer Wilhite picked up the microphone.

"William Twenty-Two, in on that. On the scene. There is no other car in sight at this location."

The three of them literally leaped out of the car and ran as fast as they could toward the residence of Albert J. Monahan.

"Wohl," Staff Inspector Peter Wohl, his mouth as dry as the Sahara Desert, said into the phone at his bedside.

"Inspector, this is Lieutenant Farr. We have a report of a shooting and hospital case at Monahan's."

"What?"

"We have a report of a shooting and hospital case at Monahan's house."

"Did they get Monahan?"

"I think so."

"On my way. Notify Captains Sabara and Pekach, Lieutenant Malone, and Sergeant Washington. Have them meet me there."

"Yes, sir."

"And check with the people sitting on Payne. Send a Highway car there, in any event."

"Yes, sir."

Wohl hung up without saying anything else, kicked the blankets off himself, and got out of bed.

TWENTY-FIVE

"Inspector," the Emergency Room physician at Nazareth Hospital said, "I don't know why this man died—I suspect he suffered a coronary occlusion, a heart attack—but I am sure that he wasn't shot. Or for that matter, suffered any other kind of a traumatic wound."

Wohl looked at her in disbelief. She was what he thought of as a pale redhead, as opposed to the more robust, Hungarian variety. She was slight and delicate, with pale blue eyes. Probably, he guessed, the near side of forty.

"Doctor, we have an eyewitness who said she *saw* him *being* shot. His *wife*. She said she saw the gun, heard a noise, and then saw her husband fall down."

He received a look of utter contempt.

The doctor pulled down the green sheet that covered the now naked remains of Albert J. Monahan, leaving only the legs below the knees covered.

"There is no wound," she said. "Gunshots, as you probably know, make at least entrance wounds. So do knives. Will

380

you take my word that I have carefully examined the body? Or would you like me to turn him over?''

"What about the head?''

"I checked the head.''

"Doctor, what about a very small caliber wound? A .22. That's less than a quarter of an inch in diameter?''

"Closer to a fifth of an inch, actually,'' the doctor said dryly. "Let me tell you what happened: The cops in the van brought this man in here. They said he had been shot. A superficial examination showed no wound. But—there was time; he was dead on arrival—and though I had no obligation to do so, I checked for a wound. I was thinking .22. We get a lot of them in here. There is no puncture wound of any kind. Sorry.''

"And you think he had a heart attack?''

"Your guess is as good as mine. The autopsy will come up with the answer, I'm sure.'' She picked up the green sheet. "Seen enough?''

"Yes, thank you.''

She pulled the sheet up over Albert J. Monahan.

More than enough. I'm going to remember this one a long time. This one I'm responsible for. The phrase is "dereliction of duty.''

Jesus H. Christ, what's going on around here?

A Highway Patrolman pushed open the swinging door.

"You said to tell you when Washington got here, Inspector.''

"Thank you, Doctor,'' Wohl said.

She responded with a just perceptible nod of her head.

When he stepped into the corridor he saw Jason Washington walking down it toward him, and Tony Harris turning off into a side corridor.

"What's he doing here?'' Wohl snapped.

"He's going to talk to the widow,'' Washington said evenly. "He knows the hospital priest. The chapel is down that way. Or do you mean, 'what's *he* doing here'? The answer to which is that until I hear differently from you, he works for me. I am under the assumption that means I say where and when.''

"I'm sorry,'' Wohl said after a moment. "I'm on edge. I picked last night to tie one on.''

"You look like hell,'' Washington said.

"I have just been informed that there are no puncture wounds in the body—''

"There have to be," Washington interrupted him.

"—the doctor says she thinks he probably had a heart attack."

"Wilhite told me that Mrs. Monahan told him she saw him being shot. By a cop."

"He's one of those who came on duty?"

Washington nodded.

"Where is he, where are they, all of them, the three going off duty, now?"

"At Bustleton and Bowler."

"I want them separated," Wohl said.

"Sergeant Carter was on the scene. I told him to keep the two groups—the three going off and the three coming on—apart. Or do you mean separated from each other?"

"I would be happier with separated from each other, but I suppose it's too late for that now."

"You think they really had something to do with this?"

"I honest to God don't know what to think. But something, goddammit, went wrong."

"Well, let's go get you a fried egg sandwich."

"What?"

"You need something in your stomach. Besides black coffee. The only food, in my experience, that hospital cafeterias can't screw up is a fried egg sandwich."

"I'll eat later."

"I told Tony to come to the cafeteria after he's talked to Mrs. Monahan. Before I go charging off anywhere, I want to hear what Tony says."

Wohl looked at him.

"Peter, come on. What you have to do is calm down."

"Okay," Wohl said after a moment. "You're probably right."

"A little Sen-Sen might be in order too," Washington said. "And I hope you have an electric razor in your car."

"That bad, huh?"

"What was the occasion?"

"Stillwell got me alone at Dave Pekach's—*Martha Peebles's*—house. There was a little party. They're going to get married. Anyway, he told me that he's getting appointed a state assistant DA. He offered me a job as his chief investigator."

"You've lost me somewhere," Washington said as they entered the cafeteria. "Go find a table. I'll get it."

Wohl sat down at a table, then spotted a soft drink machine. He went to it and deposited coins and got a can of 7-Up, which he drank down quickly. The cold produced a sharp pain in his sinus.

He remembered, as he pressed his fingers against his forehead, the telephone call he had made to Matt Payne sometime during the evening.

"Oh, *shit!*" he said aloud.

He deposited more coins and carried a second can of 7-Up back to the table.

Washington appeared carrying a tray with two mugs of coffee and four fried egg sandwiches wrapped in waxed paper on it.

Wohl took one. When the waxed paper was open his mouth salivated.

Jesus Christ, of all the times to tie one on!

"What, if anything, I think I have to ask, has been done about notifying anybody else?" Washington asked. "Specifically, the commissioner?"

"Mike Sabara called Lowenstein and Coughlin. I told him to ask Lowenstein to notify the commissioner, and I told him to tell both of them that I am trying to find out what the hell happened."

"Then you're not in as bad shape as you look," Washington said.

"Oh, yes, I am," Wohl said.

"You'll feel better with something in your stomach and some coffee," Washington said.

Wohl had eaten two fried egg sandwiches, emptied the second can of 7-Up, and had sipped half his mug of coffee before Tony Harris came into the cafeteria.

"Good morning, Inspector," he said.

That's pretty formal. That's because of the ass-chewing I gave him yesterday about the evils of alcohol. What Detective Harris is now thinking is, What a fucking hypocrite is Inspector Wohl.

"Get anything out of Mrs. Monahan, Tony?" he asked.

"She said he wasn't sleeping well. At about six o'clock, he got out of bed to take a piss. This apparently woke her up. On the way back to bed, he heard something outside on the street. He pushed the curtains aside, looked out, and told her 'the cops have just changed again,' or words to that effect. Then he got back in bed. Then the doorbell rang. He went down to open it. She told him to stay in bed, she would see what they wanted. He went anyway. She got out of bed and put a robe on, because she knew that whenever the cops knocked on the door, Monahan would offer them coffee, and she wanted to make it. So she got to the head of the stairs in time to see him peek through the peephole in the door. Then he took the chain off the door, and opened it. A cop started to come inside. He took a gun from his coat pocket and shot him. Then he closed the door and went away. She went down the stairs, saw that he, Monahan, was unconscious, and called the cops.''

"The number we gave her or Police Emergency?'' Washington asked.

"Police Emergency. She said our number was next to the bed, and she used the phone in the kitchen.''

"She get a good look at the cop?''

"White guy.''

"Would she recognize him if she saw him again?''

"She doesn't know; she doesn't think so. I think she means that. I mean, I don't think she would be afraid to point her finger at the doer.''

"Did she see the two cars outside?'' Wohl asked.

"No. *He* looked out the window. *He* said 'the cops have changed again.' I think you have to figure he saw the two cars. Otherwise how would he know they were going off and coming on?''

"You couldn't get more precise times out of her?'' Washington asked.

"No. 'Around six.' ''

"She said she saw the gun?''

"Right.''

"And saw him shoot it?''

"Right. And then he fell.''

"There are no puncture wounds in the body,'' Wohl said.

"There would have to be.''

"The doctor says she looked. The doctor says she thinks he died of a heart attack.''

"What the hell?''

"Get on the radio, Tony,'' Washington ordered. "Tell the lab people to *really* look for a bullet—how many shots did she say she heard?''

"One. Said it sounded like a .22.''

"Yeah," Washington said. "Tell the lab people to look very carefully for a bullet hole. In the carpets, in the furniture."

'You think the medical examiner will find the wound, Jason?" Wohl asked.

"I have no idea what he'll find. But if Mrs. Monahan said she heard a shot—"

"Where are you going to be?" Harris asked.

"The inspector and I are going to talk to the cops who were on the job."

"There's bullshit in there somewhere," Tony said as he got up from the table. "The cops going off the job say they were relieved. The cops coming on the job say there was nobody there when they got there."

"Tony," Washington said. "Check with the district and see what their RPCs who rolled by there just before six saw. And the same from Highway. I'll be at Bustleton and Bowler for the next hour or so."

Harris nodded his understanding and walked out of the cafeteria.

"What was that you were saying before about Stillwell?" Washington asked.

"He's being appointed a deputy attorney general for corporate crime," Wohl replied. "He told me last night. He wants me to become his chief investigator."

"Are you going to take it?"

"Last night, it was all I could do to keep myself from telling him to go fuck himself. Now, after this, I may need the job."

"That's why you tied one on?"

"He said he doesn't think we can get a conviction. And that was before we lost Monahan. But he did say that the feds are going after Payne."

"I don't understand that."

"You ever hear of the Coalition for Equitable Law Enforcement? Something like that, anyway?"

"Yeah. I know who they are."

"They have requested that the Justice Department investigate the shooting of Charles David Stevens, alleging that it violated his civil rights."

"And the feds are going along with it?"

"According to Stillwell, they are," Wohl said. "But to answer your question, Jason, I don't know why I got drunk. But at the time, it seemed like a marvelous idea."

"I don't think Matt's got anything to worry about. That was an absolutely justified shooting; Stevens had shot at him—*hit* him—before Matt shot."

"Tell that to the Coalition for Equitable Law Enforcement."

"I don't know what, if anything, this means, but I just remembered hearing that they—the Coalition—were just about out of business, going broke, when Arthur Nelson rescued them with a substantial donation."

"That figures, knowing Nelson's interest in equitable law enforcement," Wohl said bitterly. "Jesus, what a field day that sonofabitch is going to have with this!"

"I hadn't even thought about that," Washington said, shook his head, and then asked, "You know what's going to happen now?"

"Those sleaze-balls are going to walk."

"You're going to the Athletic Club, where you will take a steam bath, followed by a shave and haircut."

"Am I?"

"You're going to have to face Czernich and the mayor, and soon. Don't give Czernich the opportunity to point out to Carlucci that you were hung over. I'll try to get to the bottom of which cops were where and when. And by then, maybe the medical examiner can tell us what happened to Monahan."

"He got shot, is what happened to Monahan," Wohl said. "Because I fucked up his protection."

"Wait until we sort it out before you start kicking yourself. Right now, go sweat the whiskey out of you."

"A good long shower will do as well as a steam bath," Wohl said. "Besides, I've got to go home anyway to dress properly before I meet the firing squad."

"Then don't answer your phone. Or the radios in your car."

Wohl nodded, and then pushed himself up from the table.

In the ten minutes Peter Wohl had been in his car en route from his apartment to Special Operations, there had been three calls for W-William One.

That meant, he believed, that the police radio operator had been instructed, most likely by the Hon. Taddeus Czernich, commissioner of police, but possibly by the Hon. Jerry Carlucci, mayor of the City of Philadelphia, to keep trying to locate Staff Inspector Peter Wohl until you find him.

He had not responded to the calls for W-William One because he was absolutely sure that the message for him would be to immediately report to the commissioner. It was bad enough that Monahan had been killed while he was charged with his protection; he didn't want to face Czernich and/or the mayor and have to tell him that although Mrs. Monahan said she saw a cop shoot him, there were no wounds in the body, or that the two groups of cops who were supposed to be sitting on Monahan told conflicting stories and he wasn't sure who was telling the truth.

There had also been two calls on the Supervisor Band that he had listened to with half a mind. They were not intended for him. Someone was trying to reach I-Isaac Seventeen. The only reason he paid any attention to the calls at all was because, in the happy, happy days of yore when he had not been W-William One, commanding officer of the Special Operations Division, he had been I-Isaac Seventeen, just one more simple staff inspector.

I wonder who I-Isaac Seventeen is now, and I wonder why W-William Seven wants to talk to him.

Jesus H. Christ! As far as turning my brain back on is concerned, that shower didn't do me a goddamn bit of good.

He grabbed the microphone.

"W-William Seven, I-Isaac Seventeen."

"Isaac Seventeen, can you meet me at the medical examiner's?"

Even with the frequency clipped tones of the radio, Jason Washington's deep melodic voice was unmistakable.

"Isaac Seventeen, on the way."

Wohl tossed the microphone onto the seat beside him, braked sharply, and then made a wide sweeping U-turn, tires squealing in protest, and headed for the medical examiner's office.

Jason wouldn't want me there unless he has learned something.

The ME probably found the bullet puncture that damned redhead couldn't find. It's not much, but it's something!

Jason Washington was sitting in his car outside the medical examiner's office when Wohl pulled into the parking lot. There was a space next to him. Wohl pulled into it, and then got in Washington's car.

"I suspect when you walk in there," Washington said,

"there will be a message for you to call the commissioner immediately. So let's take a minute here."

"They've been calling me on the radio every three minutes," Wohl said. "That Isaac Seventeen business was clever, Jason, thank you."

"It will prove to be clever if Czernich, or somebody else who remembers you used to be Isaac Seventeen and will run to Czernich, wasn't listening to the radio."

"I thought of that too. I owe you another one, Jason."

"I talked to the cops who were sitting on Mr. Monahan," Washington said, cutting him off. "I think they're all telling the truth."

"How can that be?"

"A guy named Kallanan was taking his turn walking around the house just before six. I happen to know him. When I did my civic duty in the Black Police Officer's Association, I worked with him. I was treasurer when he was secretary. Good man."

"Okay. I'll take your word."

"He said it was a couple of minutes before six when he came out of the alley and started down Sylvester Street. He said that the relief RPC was already there. He said he couldn't see into the relief RPC clearly—the side windows were mostly frozen over—but he remembers that two of the guys inside were wearing—what do you call those hats with earflaps?"

"I know what you mean."

"Okay. Two guys were wearing winter hats, for lack of a better word. And that the driver was black. He could see that well."

"He didn't recognize anybody?"

"No. It was still pretty dark. The windshield was fogged over. He saw what I just told you."

"Okay."

"The other two guys in the car getting relieved didn't say anything except that there was a car. When Kallanan got in the car, they drove off. They're either all much better liars than I think is credible, or they're telling the truth."

"And the relief car?"

"The guy driving was John Wilhite. He said they were a little late—"

"Why? Did he say?"

"They stopped at a McDonald's to get their coffee thermoses

filled. They had to wait until they made coffee. He said it was five, six minutes after six when they got to the scene. And there was no car there.''

Wohl shrugged.

"The other two guys in the relief car were a guy named McPhail and a guy named Hennis. They're white. So is Wilhite.''

"And Kallanan said the guy driving the relief car was black?''

"Right.''

"And he said it was a couple of minutes *before* six when the relief car got there? And Wilhite says he was five, six minutes *late* getting there? Which means we have ten minutes that needs explaining.''

"Scenario, Peter: The doers show up at five minutes to six, pretending to be the relief RPC. The guys on the job, who are expecting relief, see an RPC and think they're relieved and drive off. When they are around the corner, somebody gets out of the RPC, rings Monahan's doorbell, shoots him, gets back in the car, and they drive off. A couple of minutes after that, the real relief RPC shows up.''

"W-William Seven,'' the radio went off.

Washington looked at Wohl, who gestured for him to reply.

"William Seven,'' Washington said to his microphone.

"William Seven, have you a location on William One?''

Washington again looked at Wohl for instruction. Wohl nodded yes.

"I'm at the medical examiner's. William One is en route to this location.''

"William Seven, advise William One to contact C-Charlie One by telephone as soon as possible.''

"Will do,'' Washington said. "I expect him here in about ten minutes.''

"W-William One. W-William One,'' the radio said. Washington reached to the controls and turned it off.

"Was it an RPC?'' Wohl asked. "Or did Kallanan just presume it was an RPC because it was a four-door Ford or whatever?''

"He says there was no question in his mind that it was an RPC,'' Washington said. "A new one. One of ours. I think, consciously or subconsciously, he would have picked up on it if it wasn't a bona fide RPC.''

"Jesus, you know what we're saying, Jason?" Wohl said.

"I'm not saying anything yet," Washington said.

"Mrs. Monahan said she saw a *cop* shoot her husband," Wohl said.

"Yeah, but the doctor said she could find no puncture wounds. Let's find out about that first, before we start saying anything."

He opened his door.

"What's going on here?"

"The ME called me. He's an old pal. He said I wasn't going to believe what he had to show me."

"Did you ask him if he found an entrance wound?"

"Just before he told me I wasn't going to believe what he had to show me," Washington said as he got out of the car.

Chief Inspectors Dennis V. Coughlin and Matt Lowenstein were in the office of Police Commissioner Taddeus Czernich when Staff Inspector Peter Wohl came into it. The mayor was not. Wohl wondered where he was.

The odds are that in the next five or ten minutes, either Lowenstein or Coughlin will be ordered to temporarily assume command of Special Operations, pending the naming of a permanent new commanding officer.

"Good morning, sir," Wohl said.

"You're a hard man to locate, Wohl," Czernich said.

"I'm sorry about that, sir."

"Sorry won't cut it, Wohl," Czernich said. "You know that someone with your responsibilities can't simply vanish from the face of the earth for three hours."

"Yes, sir."

"You're not going to try to tell me you weren't aware I had sent out a call for you?"

"I am now, sir."

The door opened and Mayor Carlucci walked in, drying his hands on a paper towel.

Everybody stood up.

The mayor finished wiping his hands, looking around for a wastebasket, and, finding none, carefully laid the towel in Czernich's OUT basket and turned to Wohl.

"My mother used to tell me if you looked hard enough, you could always find something nice about anybody," he said. "I can find a few nice things about you, Peter. For one thing, you're here. That took some balls; I wouldn't have been surprised if you had just mailed in your resignation. And you look remarkably crisp and well turned out for someone who, I am reliably informed, arrived at the scene of the Monahan shooting looking and smelling as if he had spent the night on a saloon floor."

Wohl forced himself to meet the mayor's eyes. Their eyes locked for a moment, and then the mayor looked away.

"No denial?" he asked softly.

"I drank too much last night, sir."

"The third nice thing I have to say about you is that you seemed to be able to instill a high, hell, incredibly high, level of loyalty in people who work for you. It took a lot of balls from Jack Malone, especially considering the trouble he's in already, to march into my office and tell me that if anyone was to blame for this colossal fuckup, it was him, not you."

"He did what?" Czernich asked indignantly.

"You heard what I said," the mayor said. "And if you're thinking about doing anything to him for coming to see me, forget it."

"The responsibility is mine, Mr. Mayor," Wohl said, "not Lieutenant Malone's."

"Yeah, that's what I told him," Carlucci said. "Okay, Peter, you're here. Tell me what the fuck happened."

"All I can do is tell you what I know so far, sir."

Carlucci sat down on the edge of Czernich's desk and made a "come on" gesture with both hands.

"A few minutes before six this morning, an unmarked car pulled up behind the unmarked car on protection duty outside Mr. Malone's home. In the belief their relief had arrived, the officers on duty drove away—"

"If you had used Highway Patrol as I told you to," Commissioner Czernich said, "none of this would have happened!"

"We believe that as soon as the RPC going off duty turned the corner, an individual in police uniform—"

"Answer the commissioner's question, Peter," the mayor said.

"I wasn't aware that it was a question, sir."

"Don't add insolence to everything else, Peter," the mayor said.

"I didn't use Highway because I thought using Special Operations officers was a more efficient utilization of manpower. And because I didn't want a Highway car parked there all night, every night.''

''But you do now admit that was faulty judgment?'' Czernich said.

''No, sir. I do not. I would do the same thing again. And I don't think it would have made a bit of difference if a Highway car had been given the job. The same thing would have happened.''

''Now, that's bullsh—''

''He answered your question, Tad,'' the mayor interrupted. ''Now let me ask one: What, if it was still your responsibility, would you do to the cops who took off before they were properly relieved?''

The question took Wohl by surprise. He tried to shift mental gears to consider it.

''They took off without checking to see that the cops who were relieving them were really cops. That got Monahan killed, and makes the entire Department look ridiculous,'' the mayor said.

''I don't think I'd do anything to them, sir. I hope you don't. If I had been in that car and saw another car with uniformed cops in it show up when I expected a car with uniformed cops in it to show up, I would have presumed I had been relieved.''

''And you would have been wrong.''

''Malone's plan was pretty thorough. I reviewed it. There was nothing in it about having the cops on the job check the IDs of the cops relieving them. That's my fault. Not Malone's and certainly not theirs.''

The mayor shrugged, but said nothing. He made another ''come on'' gesture with his hands.

''We believe,'' Wohl continued, ''that as soon as the RPC, the one going off the job, turned the corner, an individual wearing a police uniform rang Mr. Monahan's doorbell, and when Mr. Monahan answered the doorbell, he shot him, if that's the correct word, with a stun gun.''

''What?'' Chief Lowenstein asked incredulously. ''What did you say, 'stun gun'?''

''What the hell is a stun gun?'' the mayor asked.

''What it is, Jerry,'' Chief Coughlin said, ''is a thing that throws little darts at you. There's wires, and when it hits you, you get shocked. It's supposed to be nonlethal.''

"You know what this thing is?" Carlucci asked him incredulously.

"They had a booth at the IACP (International Association of Chiefs of Police) Convention," Chief Coughlin said. "They demonstrated them. They're supposed to be used places where you don't want to fire a gun."

"And Monahan was shot with one of these things?" the mayor asked.

"That's what the medical examiner believes, sir," Wohl said. "Mr. Monahan died of a heart attack. The ME thinks it was caused by getting hit with a stun gun. There are two small bruises on his chest."

"How come the ME knows about these things?" the mayor asked.

"They've been trying to sell them to us," Coughlin said.

"We buy any of these things, Tad?" the mayor asked.

"I would have to check, Mr. Mayor."

"There are three at the range at the Academy," Wohl said. "On loan from the dealer, or the manufacturer, I'm not sure which."

"Let me get this straight: You're telling me Monahan was shot by a cop with a Mickey Mouse Buck Rogers stun gun we borrowed from somebody?"

"No, sir. I checked with the Academy. The ones out there are inoperative; they're waiting for the manufacturer, or the dealer, to come fix them."

"So where did the one who shot Monahan come from?" the mayor asked, and then, before Wohl could frame a reply, thought of something else: "I thought Coughlin just said they're nonlethal?"

"They're supposed to be, Jerry," Coughlin replied. "That's what they said at the convention. They're supposed to knock you on your ass for a couple of minutes, but they're not supposed to kill you."

"Monahan's dead," the mayor said.

"They're not classified as firearms, Mr. Mayor," Wohl said. "So they're available on the open market. I called Colosimo's. They said they didn't have any, never had, but they had heard that a place in Camden had them, and some store in Bucks County. I've got people checking that out."

"How do we know Monahan was shot by a cop?" the mayor asked.

"We don't. Mrs. Monahan said that she saw a police officer take a gun from his coat—"

"These things look like guns?"

"I don't know, sir. I've never seen one."

"In dim light, or if you don't know all that much about guns," Coughlin said, "it would look, maybe, to Mrs. Monahan, like a gun."

"Do they make any noise? Where do they get the electricity to shock you?"

"They go 'splat,' " Coughlin said. "Or like that. Not like a .38."

"Like a .22, Chief?" Wohl asked.

"Something. Sure. It could be mistaken for a .22."

"Mrs. Monahan said it sounded like a .22," Wohl said.

"Why would they use something like this?"

"So there wouldn't be the sound of a gun going off," Lowenstein said.

"If it makes as much noise as a .22, then why not use a .22?" the mayor asked. He did not wait for a reply, but asked another question: "What is it, Peter? The guy who shot Monahan with this thing, the people in the car, were they cops or not?"

"They had an RPC, Mr. Mayor. An unmarked RPC."

"How do we know that? And if so, where did they get it?"

"We *don't* know. But Washington said, and I think he's right, that if it wasn't an RPC, I mean if it was just a similar Ford, the cop who walked past it would have picked up on that, either consciously or subconsciously: The tires would have been wrong, it wouldn't have had an antenna, or the right antenna—"

"So if it was a bona fide car, that makes it look as if a cop, cops, were the doers, doesn't it?" Carlucci interrupted.

"That sounds entirely credible," Wohl said. "As to where it came from, it probably came out of the parking lot at Bustleton and Bowler."

The mayor turned to Lowenstein and pointed a finger at him.

"I want those bastards, Matt!"

"Yes, sir," Lowenstein said softly, coldly, "so do I."

Carlucci turned back to Wohl. "What I'm thinking now is that it would be best, until he can give some real thought to your replacement, that we have Mike Sabara fill in for you. Is there something wrong with that?"

"No, sir. Sabara is a good man."

"Is there some way you can put off going to Harrisburg for a day or two? I'd like you to be available to Lowenstein."

"I'm not going to Harrisburg," Wohl said.

Carlucci looked at him in surprise, and then the look seemed to turn to anger.

"That's strange, Peter," he said. "Not half an hour ago, your pal Farnsworth Stillwell was on the phone. He wanted to be sure there would be no hard feelings about you going with him. He said you really didn't want to go, and that to get you he had to offer you a hell of a lot of money."

"I saw him last night. He offered me a job as his chief investigator. I told him I'd have to think it over, and I'd get back to him before he had his press conference this morning."

"He told me you had accepted. Period."

"I never thought of accepting. The reason I didn't call him this morning to tell him was that I was busy."

"Look at me, Peter," Carlucci said. Wohl met his eyes. "Now tell me again, when did you decide?"

"When he made the offer," Wohl said evenly. "I was afraid I would say something I would regret if I said anything last night."

Carlucci looked at him intently for a full thirty seconds before he spoke again.

"Okay. That obviously changes things," he said, finally, and then looked around the table. "Since Inspector Wohl is not resigning from the Department, there is no need to name a replacement for him at Special Operations at this time—"

"Mr. Mayor!" Czernich said.

"—temporary or otherwise," Carlucci went on coldly. Then he looked at Wohl. "There will be, Peter, unless you get this mess straightened out. *Capisce?*"

"Yes, sir."

"Keep me informed," the mayor said, and got up and walked out of the room.

TWENTY-SIX

Officer Foster H. Lewis, Jr., sat, as quietly and as inconspicuously as possible, on a folding steel chair in the small office that housed the Special Investigations Section of the Special Operations Division. He was very much afraid that he would, at any moment, be ordered out of the room on some minor errand or other, and he very much wanted to hear what was being said in the room.

The entire staff of the Special Investigations Section, that is to say Sergeant Jason Washington, Detective Anthony Harris, and himself, was in the room.

The night before, Officer Lewis had spent just about an hour making up an organizational chart for the Special Investigations Section using a drafting set he had last used in high school. There were three boxes on the chart, one on top of the other. The uppermost enclosed Sergeant Washington's name. The one in the middle read, Det. Harris, and the one on the bottom, PO Lewis. Black lines indicated the chain of authority.

It was sort of, but not entirely, a joke. Every other bureaucratic subdivision of the Special Operations Division had an organizational chart. It had been Tiny's intention, when Sergeant Washington saw the new organizational chart thumbtacked to the corkboard and, as he almost certainly would, asked, *"What the hell is that?"* to reply, *"We may be small, but we're bureaucratically up to standards."*

Tiny Lewis had come to believe there was a small but credible hope that he could manage to stay assigned to the Special Investigations Section rather than find himself back in uniform and riding around in one of the Special Operations RPCs, which was the most likely scenario.

For one thing, the Officer Magnella murder job was no closer to a solution than it had ever been, and since it was the murder of a cop, it would continue to be worked. Tony Harris would continue to need his services as an errand runner. For another, now that they were officially caught up in the bureaucracy, there would be paperwork, that which was now being done by Inspector Wohl's administrative sergeant. He could take that over. Certainly the Black Buddha wouldn't want to do it, nor Tony Harris. If he could make himself useful, his temporary assignment just might become permanent.

And my God, what a way to see how detectives worked! Even Pop says Tony is nearly as good as Washington, and everybody knows Washington is as good as they come.

It hadn't gone exactly as planned. The Black Buddha had come into the office to find Tiny waiting for him, nodded at him idly, and then looked at the corkboard.

"What the hell is that?"

"That's our organizational chart."

"Jesus Christ!" Washington had offered contemptuously before asking, "Is there any coffee?"

"Yes, sir."

That was, of course, because of what had happened to Monahan. Washington, almost visibly, was thinking of nothing but that. The only other thing he had said before Harris came into the office was, as he pointed to the phone, "Wohl, Sabara Pekach, and nobody else. Lowenstein and Coughlin too."

"Yes, sir."

Running telephone interference had provided the excuse to stay in the office and watch them brainstorm the job. It had been absolutely fascinating to Tiny, as much for the way the two of them worked together as for the various scenarios they came up with.

They seemed to have a telepathic, or at least a shorthand, means of communication. They exchanged ideas with very few words, as if both knew the way the other one's brain worked.

And Tiny got to listen.

"From the beginning," Washington had begun. "The firebomb."

"Somebody knew the Highway car was sent there."

"And why."

"Off the air?"

"No."

"Payne's car bothers me."

"Could have been anybody."

"Anybody who knew (1) Porsche (2) where he lived."

"Oh."

"Back to somebody with access."

"They could have been watching Monahan's house."

"Different people driving by."

"Too many drive bys."

"Back to somebody with access."

"Somebody pretty sure of his own smarts."

"The stun gun?"

"Why didn't they just pop him?"

"Hold that one a minute."

"No noise?"

"They could have hit him with an ax."

"They didn't want to kill him?"

"Hold that one too."

"They didn't give a shit when they blew the watchman away."

"Maintenance man. Not watchman."

"Did they think the firebomb would not be lethal?"

"Are they?"

"Hold that one too."

"Why don't burglars go armed?"

"Because breaking and entering isn't murder one."

"Christ, they already committed murder."

"Define 'they.' "

"The ones who hit Goldblatt & Sons Credit Furniture & Appliances, Inc."

"What if we had caught the guy with the firebomb."

"Huh?"

"What would it be? Not more than assault. Maybe even creating a public nuisance."

"Hold *that* one."

"Defining 'they' again. Are those clowns in the bathrobes smart enough to stage what happened this morning?"

"Not getting their hands on an unmarked car."

"Back to someone with access."

"That means someone here."

"Someone here would be too smart to rob Goldblatt's: no money."

"Back to the burglar. What happened at Goldblatt's was potentially murder caused in connection with another felony. What the hell?"

"Where did the money come from for Giacomo?"

"What the hell are they after?"

"I thought about that. More robberies, banks, maybe, with witnesses scared off by what happened at Goldblatt's."

"Back to the goddamn Liberation Army."

"Back to defining 'they.' Are the Goldblatt doers smart enough for the press releases?"

"The organized telephone calls to Payne?"

"There are now two kinds of 'they.' The ones who are calling the shots—"

"Including setting up the clowns to rob Goldblatt's."

"I can't see anybody here doing that."

"We have somebody here. That's a given."

" 'They' is now three. The sleaze-balls at Goldblatt's; somebody here; and somebody calling the shots for the first two. Somebody with enough money to hire Giacomo."

"That would be the ILA."

"The ILA is bullshit. There is no ILA."

"Hold that too."

"They knew the firebomb wasn't good for murder; they knew the stun gun—"

"They *thought* the stun gun—"

"—would be nonlethal. Somebody here would think that."

"And cover his ass."

"They would have convinced Monahan that police protection or not they could get to him whenever they wanted to."

"But if they hadn't killed him, he would have had a face."

"A face wouldn't do him much good if it wasn't a cop's face."

"Bingo!"

"It's an opening. Not 'Bingo.' ''

"We're talking about a white face here, by the way. She said it was a white guy she saw shoot him."

"Interesting."

"It could be a light-skinned Cuban or something."

"Not Cuban. The white doesn't fit, but not Cuban. Very few Muslims, make-believe or otherwise, among the Cubans. Or for that matter, Latinos."

Both Washington and Harris fell silent for what seemed like a very long time, but was probably no more than sixty seconds.

Finally Washington raised his head and looked at Officer Foster H. Lewis.

"What are you thinking?" Harris asked.

"I am thinking I have a task for Officer Lewis."

"Yes, sir?"

"I want you to check with the corporal. Get his sheets on unmarked cars for yesterday. Check the incoming mileage against the outgoing today."

Tiny Lewis realized he had absolutely no idea what Washington wanted. As he was trying to frame a reply that might just possibly make him look like less of an ignorant asshole than he felt himself to be, Washington correctly read the expression on his face.

"What I'm looking for, Foster," he said patiently, "is a discrepancy between the mileage recorded when the driver of the unmarked car turned it in yesterday, and the mileage recorded when the car was taken out today."

"Unscrew the speedometer cable. Takes ten seconds," Harris said.

"Do you understand now, Foster?"

"Yes, sir."

"Tiny, then contact everybody who took an unmarked RPC out of here this morning," Harris said. "Ask them if there was any indication that it hadn't sat out there in the snow and ice all night."

"Unless somebody here is driving the car he took to Goldblatt's."

"Sergeant," Tiny said hesitantly.

"Come on, Foster, pay attention!"

"I went out to warm up my car when I got here. Did either of you drive it last night?"

"I gather somebody had?" Jason Washington asked softly.

"Bingo!" Harris said.

Washington reached for the telephone.

"Lieutenant Lomax, please," he said when his party answered. "Sergeant Washington is calling."

Tiny Lewis understood enough of the one side of the conversation he heard to know that Lieutenant Lomax had told Sergeant Washington that it would be best to leave the car where it was; that if that was going to be impossible, that next best was to have it towed to the nearest police garage; and that in no event should the car be driven or entered again.

Sergeant Washington returned the phone to its cradle.

"Officer Lewis," he said, "you will now go stand by the hood of the car until a police wrecker comes to haul it off. If you somehow could convey the impression that it has a mysterious malady, fine. But in no event let anyone touch it, much less get inside."

"Yes, sir."

Assistant Special Agent in Charge (Criminal Affairs) Frank F. Young came into the morning Senior Staff Conference ten minutes late.

"Sorry to be late, Chief," he said as he took a chair at the table that butted against Special Agent in Charge Walter F. Davis's desk and made a vague but unmistakable gesture of dismissal to Special Agent F. Charles Vorhiss, who had been filling in for him.

Davis waited until Vorhiss had left the room before replying, "It's all right, Frank, we know what difficulty you have getting up before noon."

Not quite sure whether Davis was cracking witty or had some other agenda, Young said, "I was just having the most fascinating conversation with Agent Matthews, who *was* out carousing until the wee hours."

"With the cops, you mean?"

"In the FOP," Young said.

"We were, just coincidentally, talking about the police," Davis said, and slid a copy of the Philadelphia *Ledger* across the desk to him. "Have you seen this?"

"No," Young said, and since he suspected he was expected to, he read the front-page story.

ASSASSINS GET PAST POLICE TO MURDER WITNESS AGAINST ILA

By Charles E. Whaley
Ledger Staff Writer

Albert J. Monahan, 56, was shot to death before his wife's eyes early this morning at his home in the 5600 block of Sylvester Street according to a highly placed police official who declined to be identified.

Monahan was shot with a small-caliber weapon, according to the same police official, when he opened his door to an assassin who had somehow gotten past three officers of the "elite" Special Operations Division that was charged with his round-the-clock protection.

Staff Inspector Peter F. Wohl, commanding officer of the Special Operations Division, which was formed, reportedly at the orders of Mayor Jerry Carlucci, late last year to combat the growing crime in Philadelphia, was "not available to the press" for comment.

Monahan, who was employed by Goldblatt & Sons Credit Furniture & Appliances, Inc., was scheduled to appear before the Grand Jury next Monday. Assistant District Attorney Farnsworth Stillwell was to seek an indictment for murder against six men for a shooting death during a robbery at the South Street furniture store. Monahan reportedly had positively identified seven men presently being held in the Detention Center as being involved.

"Prosecution now seems unlikely," the police official said, "with the death of Mr. Monahan, and Mr. Stillwell off the case." He was apparently referring to the appointment, announced today, of Stillwell to the staff of the state attorney general in Harrisburg. (See "Governor Names Stillwell As Corporate Crime Prosecutor," Page B-1).

Police have thrown up a barrier of silence around the incident. Police Captain Michael J. Sabara, deputy commander of Special Operations, the only senior police official willing to speak officially to the press at all, would say only that "the incident is under investigation and no information can be released at this time."

Sabara also refused to discuss rumors circulating throughout the Police Department that the Justice Department is investigating Officer M. M. Payne, Inspector Wohl's administrative assistant. During the arrest of the eight men charged in the Goldblatt robbery, Payne shot to death one of the alleged bandits, Charles David Stevens. It has been said the Justice Department is investigating allegations that Payne, who has something of a reputation for being too quick to use his pistol, exceeded Police Department criteria governing the use of force. If the allegations are true, Payne could be charged with violating Stevens's civil rights, a federal offense.

"Jesus!" Young said. "I wonder how that happened?"

"How about gross incompetence?" Glenn Williamson, A-SAC (Administration), asked rhetorically.

"I would think it's a case of having underestimated the opposition," SAC Davis said. "What do we have on the ILA? Did you check with Washington?"

"There's three of them," A-SAC (Counterintelligence) Isaac J. Towne said. "One in New York, one in Chicago, and one in Berkeley, California. There is no known connection between the three, and no known connection between any of them and anyone in Philadelphia."

"Have we got anybody in with them?"

"In all three. That's where we got what I came up with."

"Any of them ever into anything like this?"

"They're mostly into protest marches," Towne said. "Talk and protest marches."

"I'd like to help Wohl if I could," SAC Davis said.

"There was something I heard—" Towne said, stopped, and then went on. "I heard that Wohl was going with Farnsworth Stillwell. As his chief investigator."

"Really?" Davis asked.

"He might as well," Young said. "I'll bet Carlucci throws him to the wolves."

"You think that 'unnamed police official' was Carlucci?"

"I think it was somebody close to Czernich. Maybe even Czernich himself."

"Not Czernich," Davis said. "Czernich wouldn't do that, unless Carlucci told him to. But somebody close to Czernich—"

"If Carlucci isn't behind it, and finds out who the big mouth is, he's in more trouble than Wohl."

"I don't think anyone's in more trouble than Wohl," Davis said. "How good was your source about Wohl going with Stillwell?"

"I just heard it. I can't even remember where. Maybe on one of those radio talk shows driving to work."

"See what you can find out for sure, Isaac, will you please?" Davis said.

"Yes, sir," Towne said.

"I'll tell you what I can see," Davis said. "Armed robberies of banks, with witnesses afraid to testify because of this case, because of what happened to Mr. Monahan."

"You really think so, Chief?" Young asked.

"I think it's a credible possibility," Davis said. "I think this could be a dry run for something like that."

"Well, there goes our bank robbery solution rate," A-SAC Williamson said.

"I wasn't trying to be funny, Glenn," Davis said.

"Chief, neither was I," Williamson said. "I'm very much afraid you're absolutely right."

"I hope not," Davis said.

It was evident to the others that Davis did not violently object to being told he was absolutely right.

"This isn't exactly on the same subject—" Young said.

"But?" Davis prodded.

"I told you the reason I was late was because I was talking with Jack Matthews. He heard something last night that might, just might, affect one of our ongoing investigations."

"Which one?"

"Bob Holland."

"Oh, Jesus, that's all we need! We're getting pretty close to the end of that, aren't we?"

"At the cost of I don't like to think how much money and man-hours," A-SAC Williamson said, "I have been assured that we are beginning to see light at the end of the tunnel."

"Well, spit it out, Frank, what did young Matthews hear?"

"Nothing specific. But what he did hear made him think he should bring me in on it. He went drinking with young Payne, his bodyguard, and another young cop—"

"What the hell is *that* all about?" Williamson interrupted.

"He went out drinking with the cops? I've been telling my people to maintain a polite, cordial, but distant—"

"I sent him," Davis said, annoyance in his voice. "Okay, Glenn? Go on, Frank."

"Well, toward the end of the evening, when Matthews mentioned that he was working on interstate auto theft, he said the ears of both Payne and one of the cops—Mc-Something—perked up, and they started asking all sorts of questions about how the Bureau runs a car theft investigation. From the nature of their questions, Jack thought that they could be talking about Bob Holland's operation."

"What kind of questions?" A-SAC Towne asked.

"Why don't we go to the source?" SAC Davis said. He picked up his telephone. "Carolyn, would you please ask Special Agent Matthews to come in here?"

"Who's that?" Officer Robert Hartzog said into the microphone of the new intercom on the wall of Matt Payne's kitchen.

"Inspector Wohl."

"Be right there, Inspector," Hartzog said. He then went down the stairs two at a time.

Wohl appeared a moment later at the head of the stairs, carrying Hartzog's shotgun.

"I told him to take a couple of laps around Rittenhouse Square," Wohl said, resting the shotgun against the closet door. "And how are *you* this morning, Casanova?"

"I heard about what happened," Matt said. "I'm sorry."

"For me or Monahan?"

"Both."

'I'm sorry for Malone and Monahan, and for me. I'm even sorry for you. Everybody's sorry for someone else."

"Why are you sorry for me?" Matt asked.

"I would desperately like to have a cold beer," Wohl said, as if he hadn't heard the question. "For purely medicinal purposes."

"Help yourself," Matt said, gesturing toward the kitchen. "Bring me one too, please."

"You want a glass?" Wohl called the kitchen.

"Absolutely. A good beer, like a decent wine, needs to breathe."

"Oh, *God!*"

"It's true," Matt said.

Wohl came into the living room with two bottles of Tuborg, glasses sitting upside down on their necks.

"And there is a way to get the beer from the bottle to the glass," Matt said, demonstrating. "One pours the glass approximately half full by decanting against the side of the glass, and then, at the precise moment, allowing the incoming liquid to fall into the middle, thus providing the proper head."

He looked at Wohl, smiling. Wohl did not return the smile.

"You're going to be investigated by the FBI, for the Justice Department, for violating the civil rights of Charles David Stevens."

"I know. The FBI told me last night."

"They were here already?" Wohl asked, surprised.

"They sent a young FBI agent, Jack Matthews, to tell me. On the QT."

"How nice of the FBI," Wohl said. "I wonder why they are being so friendly?"

"I've been wondering the same thing myself."

"I wouldn't worry about this, Matt."

"You know the joke?"

"What joke?"

"The doctor about to perform major surgery looks down at the patient and says, *'I wouldn't worry about this,'* and the patient looks up and says, *'if I wasn't lying here, I wouldn't be worried either.'* "

"Well, I mean it. It's a defense tactic, a sleazy one, but that's all it is."

"I was worried about it," Matt said. "But I just got off the telephone with Colonel Mawson. He said he's going to sue the—what is it?—Coalition for Something?"

"Equitable Law Enforcement."

"He's going to sue them for ninety-nine million dollars, the minute the FBI actually shows up here. I think he's delighted it happened."

Wohl smiled.

"I had a few too many drinks last night."

"The Tuborg will fix that," Matt said.

"I shouldn't have made that early morning call."

"Why don't we both forget it? I just hope, among other things, that the knowledge won't make it awkward for you with Stillwell. How the hell did you find out, anyhow?"

"Why should it be awkward for me?"

"In Harrisburg, I mean."

"I'm not going to Harrisburg."

"That's not what it said on the radio. The radio said you had been appointed chief investigator to Stillworth, who was just appointed to some bullshit position with the attorney general."

"The radio is wrong. Never believe what you hear on the radio. For that matter, never believe what you read in the newspaper, especially the *Ledger*."

"Really?"

"Dave Pekach proposed to Martha Peebles. Surprising no one at all, she accepted. She had a few of his friends, Mike Sabara and his wife, Jack Malone, and me, plus Mr. and Mrs. Farnsworth Stillwell in for a little intimate supper."

"And that's where you found out?" Matt asked. "Christ, how?"

"Your *paramour*—is that the word?"

"For the sake of discussion only, it will do."

"Your *paramour*, as I said, was there. She sounded very much like a lady who left erotic messages on your answering machine. Being the clever fellow I am, I put two and two together. And being the horse's ass I seem to be when I'm drinking, I—I called you."

"Christ, does anybody else know?"

"I don't think so. But that wasn't the smartest thing you ever did, Matt."

"You ever hear that a stiff prick has no conscience?"

"How deep are you in with her?"

"It happened just once," Matt said. "She was at a party downstairs. She saw my gun and got turned on by it. She was a little drunk."

"Are you going to pursue it?" Wohl asked, and then, before Matt could reply, asked, "What do you mean she got turned on by your gun?"

"It was a little frightening. She wanted to know if it was the gun I used on the serial rapist. It aroused her."

"Well, *are* you going to pursue it?"

"What do you do to get out of something like this?"

"You thank God the lady's leaving town. In the meantime, don't answer your telephone."

"Anything like this ever happen to you?"

"You mean a gun fetishist?"

"I mean a married woman."

"Yeah. Once. It was very painful."

Matt picked up his glass and leaned back in the leather armchair, looking thoughtfully into his beer.

I wonder why I told him that? Wohl thought. *I damned sure never told anybody else.*

"I don't want to sound like I didn't know what I was doing, but I didn't actually seduce her," Matt said.

"No man has ever seduced a mature woman," Wohl said. "And probably very few virgins have ever been seduced. The way it works is that *they* decide who *they* want to have take them to bed, and then *they* arrange to be seduced."

Matt looked up at him.

"You really believe that?"

I don't know if I do or not. It sounds plausible. But what I was really trying to do was cheer him up. More than that, to point him onto Ye Olde Straight and Narrow.

Why the hell am I doing that? What the hell am I doing here, anyway? I could have told him about the FBI investigation on the phone.

The answer, obviously, is that I am very fond of this kid. He is, I suppose, the little brother that I never had. So what's wrong with that?

"It sounds plausible," Wohl said with a grin.

"So I'm not on your shit list?"

"You're not on mine, but *I'm* apparently on everybody else's."

"They're not blaming you for what happened?"

"It's a question of who had the responsibility. That's spelled WOHL."

"You couldn't be expected to sit outside his house yourself," Payne argued. "If it's anybody's fault, it's Jack Malone's."

"Malone works for me," Wohl said. "Whatever he does, or doesn't do, is my responsibility."

"Loyalty down and loyalty up, huh?"

"Is something wrong with that?"

Matt shrugged and looked uncomfortable.

"Come on, Matt, out with it."

Payne met his eyes.

"Did you tell Malone to lay off trying to catch Bob Holland?"

"Not specifically," Wohl replied. "I'm sure he got the message, though.'' And then he understood the meaning of Payne's question. ''What do you know that I don't, Matt?''

''I promised him if I decided to tell you, I would tell him first.''

''This isn't the Boy Scouts. You can't have it both ways.''

''Charley caught him surveilling Holland's body shop, the one up by Temple.''

''What do you mean, caught him?''

''McFadden—off duty, he had just dropped Margaret off at work at Temple—''

''Margaret being his girlfriend?''

''Right. So he saw this old car with somebody in it parked near Holland's body shop. And he checked it out. It was Malone. He, Malone, told Charley not to tell anybody about it.''

''Which proves what?''

''The night you had me measuring the school building, Malone showed up there. Charley was with me. He offered to buy us a cheese-steak, and I brought him here. Both of them. And he admitted that what he was trying to do was catch Holland.''

''And you decided not to tell me, right?''

Matt nodded.

''I don't know what I would have done if I hadn't gone to play Dick Tracy and gotten myself shot, but that night, I told Malone I was going to sleep on it, that I would probably decide I had to tell you, but if I did, I would tell him first.''

''You must have had a reason,'' Wohl said, more than a little annoyed. ''You work for me, getting back to that loyalty business.''

''He convinced the both us that Holland is a thief,'' Matt said.

''You and McFadden, of course, being experts in the area of car theft.''

''Open the goddamn door!'' the intercom speaker erupted. ''Michael J. O'Hara is gracing these crummy premises with his presence.''

''Oh, shit!'' Wohl said, even though he had to smile. ''The last guy in Philadelphia I want to see is Mickey.''

''You want to hide in the bedroom while I get rid of him?''

''No,'' Wohl said, after a moment's hesitation. ''I've always thought, said, Mickey can be trusted. Let's put it to the test.''

He walked quickly to the stairwell, and down it, to let O'Hara in.

TWENTY-SEVEN

"I must be getting old," Michael J. O'Hara said to Inspector Peter Wohl as Wohl handed him a bottle of Tuborg. "I should have guessed you would be here."

"I'm not here, Mickey. You didn't see me."

O'Hara looked at him intently for a moment, and then shrugged and nodded his agreement.

"Okay. Neither of us are here. But if we were here, and I asked you, on or off the record, 'How do you think you're going to like Harrisburg?' what would be your off-the-record, just-between-us-boys reply?"

"*On* the record, I'm not going to Harrisburg."

"That's not what it said—what *he* said, *he* being Farnsworth Stillwell—on the radio."

"As I was just saying to Casanova here, you should never believe everything you hear on the radio, or read in the newspapers, especially the *Ledger*."

"Give me a for example."

"I just gave you one. I never told Stillwell that I would take that job."

411

"If I were to write that—'*Staff Inspector Peter Wohl today emphatically denied that he ever intended to resign from the Police Department to become chief investigator for Farnsworth Stillwell, newly appointed deputy attorney general for corporate crime*'—it would make Stillwell look pretty silly."

"How about leaving out the phrase '*to resign from the Police Department*'?"

"How about the making him look silly part?"

"I don't think that would reduce me to tears," Wohl said.

"Is it that bad, Peter? You're really thinking of resigning?"

"We were talking about not always believing what you read in the newspapers. You want another for example?"

"Yeah."

"The records of the medical examiner, so far as I understand it, are public records. If you were to go down there, and pay the small fee—I think it's two dollars—they would give you a copy of Mr. Albert J. Monahan's death certificate. I think you might find that very interesting."

"Why?"

"Why don't you go spend the two dollars?"

"If I didn't know better, I'd think you were trying to get rid of me," O'Hara said.

"Perish the thought. But trust me, Mickey, I think you'd find the death certificate interesting."

"He's dead, right?" O'Hara asked.

"He's dead."

"So what would I find interesting? What did they do, shoot him with a cannon? He wasn't shot? Some jungle bunny threw a spear at him? What?"

"For two dollars, you could find out," Wohl said.

"I can find out cheaper than that," O'Hara said.

He leaned over and picked up the telephone on the table beside Matt's chair. He draped the handset over his shoulder, and then dialed a number.

"Dr. Phane, please. Mickey O'Hara . . .

"Oh, bullshit. Tell him he owes me one."

He covered the mouthpiece with his hand. "Interesting," he observed, "the bastard doesn't want to talk to me. . . .

"Charley, how the hell are you? . . .

"Well, just put her on hold, all I have is a couple of questions. . . .

"Tell me about Albert J. Monahan. . . .

"Yeah, I know he's dead. What did they shoot him with? . . .

"What are you telling me, Charley? . . .

"And that's what's going on the death certificate? . . .

"Charley, if I print this and it turns out it's not true, I would be very unhappy. It is for that reason I have been recording this call. Just so you can't deny having told me what you just told me."

O'Hara shrugged, hung the handset on his shoulder again, and dialed another number.

"Would you believe that the Most Exalted Poo-Bah of the Knights of Columbus just told me to go fuck myself?" he asked, in hurt innocence, and then his party answered.

"O'Hara," he said. "Are you ready to copy? . . .

"Slug: ILA Witness Dead of Natural Causes, Says Medical Examiner. By Michael J. O'Hara. In an exclusive interview with this reporter, Philadelphia County Medical Examiner Dr. Charles F. Phane refuted reports in another newspaper—break. I'd like to say the Philadelphia *Ledger*, but you'd better run it past legal before you do."

"—in another newspaper that Mr. Albert J. Monahan was shot to death, allegedly by persons connected with the so-called Islamic Liberation Army. Dr. Phane said that a thorough autopsy of Mr. Monahan's body has convinced him, and other medical personnel of his staff, that Mr. Monahan had died of a cardiac arrest, commonly called a heart attack.

"Dr. Phane, who personally conducted the autopsy, also said that tests had been run that ruled out the possibility of poisons.

"Quote Mr. Monahan's heart just stopped beating, Unquote Dr. Phane said. Quote. He had a medical history of heart trouble and it finally took his life. Unquote.

"Got that? . . .

"Yeah, I'm sure. If I wasn't sure, I wouldn't have called it in."

Mickey put the handset back in the cradle, and then set the telephone back on the table.

"Okay, Peter. So you tell me why Mrs. Monahan told me she saw her husband getting shot."

"This has to be off the record, Mickey."

"Off the record."

"I think she did see someone—"

"A cop? She said, *'a white cop.'* "

"—someone, probably a Caucasian, in a police uniform, shoot her husband. But what he was using was a stun gun, not a real one."

"One of those things that shocks people?" Mickey asked. "No shit?"

"There were bruise marks, plus slight indications of electric burns, on his chest."

"Phane didn't say anything about that."

"Phane is a very careful man, Mickey."

"You don't *have* the stun gun, do you?" O'Hara challenged. "This is a *theory*?"

"It's a pretty good theory," Wohl said.

"You tell me why it's a good theory."

"We don't think they were trying to kill Monahan, just scare him."

"I have no idea what you're talking about," O'Hara said.

"I'll tell you what we think this whole thing is about, and where we are, but if you print it, you can really screw things up. Not only for me, but for a lot of other people."

"You prick!" O'Hara said. "You know that after you told me that, I couldn't use it."

"Fuck it," Matt Payne said. "The risk is too great, don't tell him."

Mickey turned to look at him in what looked like hurt surprise. "For the rest of your life, I will misspell your name," he said.

He turned at Wohl. "Does *he* know what's going on?"

"No. He's just worried about me."

"Okay, Peter," O'Hara said after a moment. "Boy Scout's Honor." He held up three fingers as Boy Scouts do when giving their word of honor. "I won't use any of this until you tell me I can."

It took Wohl ten minutes, during which Mickey O'Hara asked a very few questions, all of which struck Matt as being penetrating.

"Okay," Mickey said, finally. "So what are you doing here drinking beer with Wyatt Earp? Why aren't you out catching—better still, shooting by accident, or at least running over—this rogue cop of yours?"

"Two reasons," Wohl said. "For one thing, I think I would probably get caught if I did. More importantly, Jason Wash-

gton asked me to make myself scarce until five o'clock. That's
hat I'm doing.''

"Can I stick around?''

"I wish you wouldn't.''

"Well, and all this time, I thought we were buddies,''
'Hara said. "How would you feel about me interviewing Ar-
hur X? Getting his *Islamic* slant on this?''

"Will he talk to you?''

"Yeah, I think so. He likes being in the newspapers.'' He
aw the look on Wohl's face. "Relax, I won't give anything
way.''

"If I thought you would, I wouldn't have told you what I
id.''

"I just had a better idea,'' O'Hara said. "Fuck Arthur X. I
now what he's going to say. I'm going to see Sam Goldblatt
nd maybe Katz too.''

"Who?'' Matt asked.

"Sam Goldblatt, of Goldblatt's furniture,'' O'Hara replied.
'Ol' Mr. I-have-to-think-about-my-wife-and-children. The one
vho covered his ass about these scumbags by having his eye-
ight conveniently fail. Phil Katz is Goldblatt's nephew.''

"Oh,'' Matt said, and then asked, "why?''

" 'Mr. Goldblatt, would you tell me how you feel about the
eople who killed both poor Mr. Cohn and now poor Mr.
Monahan escaping punishment because you have bad eyesight?
My one point three million readers would like to know. In case
hey wanted to buy a washing machine, or something, and
vanted to make sure they were buying it from somebody who
vas always thinking about his wife and children.' ''

Wohl chuckled. "I really think you would do that.''

"You'd better believe it.''

"I'll tell you what I did do,'' Wohl said. "When Goldblatt
and Katz walked out of their houses this morning, they found
a Highway RPC waiting for them. Highway's going to sit on
both of them for the next couple of days, at least.''

"To protect them? Or to remind them they need protection?''

"Both.''

"Mr. Goldblatt, considering what happened to poor Mr.
Monahan, do you think the police are going to be able to protect you from these people you weren't able to see well enough
to identify?''

''If you added, 'and your family,' '' Wohl said, ''that migh not be a bad question to ask.''

''Consider it asked,'' O'Hara said.

He stood up, shrugged into his fur-collared overcoat, fin ished off his bottle of beer, and went down the stairs.

At five minutes past four, just after Officer Charles McFadde had relieved Officer Frank Hartzog on the protection detail o Officer Matthew M. Payne, the doorbell rang.

''Who's there?'' McFadden asked, through the intercom.

''Sergeant D'Angelo.''

''You know a Sergeant D'Angelo, Inspector?'' McFadde asked Wohl.

''Yeah. Let him in.''

''Be right down,'' McFadden said, and went down the stairs

The face that first appeared at the head of the stairwell moment later was that of the Hon. Jerry Carlucci, mayor o the City of Brotherly Love. He was followed by a burly, curly haired man in his late twenties.

''I didn't know anybody lived up here,'' the mayor though aloud, and nodded at the occupant, Officer Payne, as he looke around.

''What the hell is this all about, Peter?'' he asked.

''Chief Lowenstein said he would be here at four,'' Woh said. ''He must have been delayed.''

''That's not what I asked,'' the mayor said, but he did no pursue the question. He looked at Matt.

''How's your leg, son?''

''Pretty good, sir. Thank you.''

''I don't suppose there's any coffee?''

''I can make some in just a minute,'' Matt said, and starte to get out of his leather armchair.

''Al, make coffee,'' the mayor ordered.

Sergeant D'Angelo went into the kitchen.

''Coffee's in the cabinet right over the machine,'' Mat called.

''Got it,'' D'Angelo called back.

The telephone rang.

''Hello?'' Matt answered it.

''Chief Lowenstein. Is Carlucci there?''

''Mr. Mayor,'' Matt said. ''Chief Lowenstein for you, sir.''

Carlucci snatched the phone from Payne's hand.

"Lowenstein, what the hell's going on? . . .

"How did that happen? . . .

"I'll be damned," he said, and hung up.

He looked at Wohl.

"That was Lowenstein. He's at the district attorney's. That's why he's late."

"Yes, sir."

"Mr. Samuel Goldblatt just identified from photographs all of the doers of the Goldblatt job, and is prepared to go before the Grand Jury on Monday. And, *and*, get this: Tom Callis just called Giacomo, as a professional courtesy, and informed him he will personally prosecute."

"That's good news, sir," Wohl said.

"Did you know about this, Peter?"

"I'd heard that another attempt to get Mr. Goldblatt to testify would be made, sir."

"Stop the bullshit, Peter, what do you know about this sudden change of heart?"

"Chief Lowenstein told me that he was going to have a talk with Mr. Goldblatt, sir. And I believe that Mickey O'Hara saw him, Goldblatt, today too."

"O'Hara? What about O'Hara?"

"He was here earlier, sir."

"He was here? How is it, Peter, that every sonofabitch and his brother but the police commissioner and me knew where you were?"

"I wasn't aware you were looking for me, sir."

"Czernich was looking for you, and he couldn't find you. Or so he told me."

"Chiefs Coughlin and Lowenstein knew I was here, sir. And so did Captain Sabara."

"I don't like it a goddamn bit the way the three of you treat Czernich like the enemy," Carlucci said. "It has to stop. You understand me?"

"Yes, sir."

"Now, what about O'Hara?"

"Mr. O'Hara led me to believe he was going to ask Mr. Goldblatt and the nephew, Katz, about how they felt about these people going to walk with Monahan dead."

"You got him to do that?"

"It was Mickey's idea, sir."

"Bullshit," the mayor said.

The telephone rang again, and Matt answered it.

"Is that you, Matty?" Chief Inspector Dennis V. Coughlin asked.

"Yes."

"Is the mayor there? Lowenstein?"

"Chief Lowenstein is on his way here from the district attorney's office."

"Who is that?" the mayor asked suspiciously.

"Chief Coughlin, sir."

"Give me the phone," he ordered sharply. Matt handed it over.

"What the hell is this all about, Denny?"

Matt couldn't hear what Coughlin replied.

"If the both of you aren't here in ten minutes, we will adjourn this meeting to the commissioner's office. Capisce?" Carlucci said, and hung up.

He turned to Wohl.

"I don't suppose you're going to tell me what the hell is going on around here?"

"I'd prefer to wait until Chief Lowenstein is here, sir."

"In numbers, there is strength, huh?" Carlucci said unpleasantly. "Where the hell is that coffee, Al?"

"It's almost through, sir," Sergeant D'Angelo said.

"Let me ask you something else, Peter," Carlucci said. "Are you conducting an investigation of Bob Holland?"

"No, sir."

"Strange. The FBI thinks you are. Davis called Czernich and asked him. Czernich told him he would ask you about it. You better have a goddamn good answer when he does. Auto theft is none of your business.

"That sonofabitch!" Charley McFadden said.

The mayor looked at him. McFadden, realizing that his mouth had run away with him, looked stricken.

"What sonofabitch is that, son?" Carlucci asked softly, menacingly. "The police commissioner or Mr. Davis of the FBI?"

"There was an FBI agent here last night, Mr. Mayor," Matt said. "We took—"

"What was he doing here? Friend of yours, what?"

"I met him yesterday," Matt said. "He came to confirm rumors that I'm going to be investigated by the Justice Department."

"For what?"

"For shooting Stevens."

"Did you know about this, Peter?"

"Yes, sir."

"How come I don't?"

"I sent a memorandum to Commissioner Czernich, sir."

Carlucci turned back to Matt Payne.

"What about the FBI agent who was here last night?"

"We went to the FOP," Matt said. "During the conversation, when he said that he was working interstate auto theft, I asked him some questions about how that works."

"Me too. I did too," Charley McFadden said.

"What Officer McFadden is suggesting is that Matthews, the FBI guy, reported our interest to his superiors," Matt explained.

" 'Our interest'?" Carlucci snapped. "Just what is 'our interest'?"

"We think Mr. Holland is involved in at least the sale of stolen automobiles," Matt said.

" 'We'? Who's 'we'?"

"Officer McFadden and myself," Matt said.

"On one hand, coming from two rookies with an exaggerated opinion of themselves, that's probably bullshit," the mayor said. "But on the other hand, the FBI wouldn't be trying to tell us to butt out unless they were onto something. Peter, you sure you don't know anything about this?"

The door buzzer went off, sparing Wohl having to reply.

"Who's there?"

"Lowenstein."

"Be right there."

"Peter," the mayor said. "I think it would be very embarrassing to the Police Department if the FBI came up with a case against Bob Holland that we didn't know anything about. You take my meaning?"

"No, sir."

"I mean I want you to find out what these two hotshots of yours think they know."

"And give it to Major Crime?"

"No. Give it to me," Carlucci said, "either these two are imagining things, or Major Crime isn't doing their job."

He then turned his attention to the stairwell, in which a

moment later Chief Inspector Matt Lowenstein's head and shoulders appeared.

"Matt," the mayor greeted him, "There better be a goddamn good reason for all this goddamn mystery."

Thirty minutes later, the mayor said, in quiet fury, "What you're telling me is that both the guy who killed Monahan with the stun gun, *and* two guys with him, *and* the miserable sonofabitch out of Bustleton and Bowler are going to get away with it? Everything?"

"We can't go to court with this, Jerry," Lowenstein said. "You can see that."

"On the bright side," Chief Inspector Dennis V. Coughlin said, "the Grand Jury will return a true bill against the doers of the Goldblatt job. And Tom Callis is convinced that he can get convictions."

"On the *dim* side, there is *nothing* lower than a cop who would do something like this, and the sonofabitch is going to get away with it!"

He glowered, in turn, at Chief Inspectors Lowenstein and Coughlin and Staff Inspector Wohl, all of whom, in turn, shrugged.

"Jesus *Christ*!" the mayor said in frustration.

"Or," Peter Wohl said. "We could just leave him where he is and watch him."

The mayor considered that a moment before replying. "No. Go ahead with this. I'll clear it with Czernich."

"Yes, sir," Wohl said.

"Maybe that's not smart, but I can't stand the thought of this bastard walking around in a Highway uniform," the mayor said. "Highway means something to me."

"It means something to me too," Peter Wohl heard himself say.

Jesus, he realized with genuine surprise, *I really meant that*.

Sergeant Jason Washington sat slouched behind the wheel of his car until he saw Sergeant Wilson Carter pull into the parking lot. Then he sat up and watched as Carter parked his car. He got out of his car and walked toward the side entrance of the building, timing himself so that he arrived there a few seconds before Carter.

"I was hoping to run into you," he said to Carter.

"Well, hey, Brother. How they hanging? What's on your mind?"

"Let's have a beer," Washington said.

"*One*," Carter said, after a just perceptible hesitation. "I have plans."

"Sure. I understand. But there's a couple of questions I'd like to ask you."

"What kind of questions?"

"More like advice questions, about what I should do about something."

"Well, then, hell, yes."

"I thought Hellman's? They have booths in the back."

"Give me thirty minutes to check out and I'll meet you there."

"Thanks, Carter, I appreciate it," Washington said, touched Carter's arm, and walked back to his car.

When Sergeant Carter walked into the back room of Hellman's Restaurant, he found Sergeant Jason Washington already there, sitting alone in a booth, his massive hand wrapped around a glass of whiskey.

"You must have a problem," Carter said as he slipped into the bench across from Washington. "Beer, little problem, whiskey, big problem."

"Big problem," Washington agreed.

Carter glanced around the room, looking for a waitress. He couldn't see one, but he saw a familiar face in another booth.

"Richard Kallanan's over there," he said, waving.

Kallanan took his hand from his glass of whiskey long enough to wave back.

A waitress appeared from the barroom. Carter waved to catch her attention.

"Cutty Sark, on the rocks," Carter ordered. "You ready, Jason?"

"Might as well."

"I thought Kallanan was one of those straight home to the wife and kiddies types," Carter said. "I don't think I've ever seen him in here before."

"I don't think he comes in here often," Washington said. "Tonight's sort of special."

"What?"

"You want to know what Kallanan's thinking right now, Carter?"

"What the hell are you talking about?"

"He's thinking, 'Christ, why didn't I recognize Carter in that car?' "

"What car would that be, Washington?"

"The car normally driven by Foster Lewis's boy, the kid we call 'Tiny,' " Washington said. "The one you drove to Monahan's house."

"That sounds like an accusation, Washington."

"Statement of fact. We picked your prints off the plastic behind the front seat. You know where I mean? Where it's flat on top? You must have touched it when you got in. Or maybe when you reached for the seat belt. We got a match on your pinky, ring and index fingers."

"I don't know what the fuck you're up to, but you could probably find my prints on half the unmarked cars in the parking lot."

"We also got your prints, heel of the hand and four fingers, on the hood of Matt Payne's pretty little Porsche."

"I must have rested my hand on it when I looked down at the tire."

"More likely when you stabbed the tires," Washington said.

"You don't really believe that?"

"Yes, I do."

"You're out of your fucking mind, Washington!"

"Kallanan is a very interesting man," Washington said. "Did you know that he's a lay reader in the Episcopal Church?"

"So what?"

"So he told me that he has to be very careful about not bearing false witness."

"Meaning what?"

"Meaning he's worried about the power of suggestion. In other words, he's afraid that when I asked him if it could have been you driving that car, and he said, *'Oh, yes. That's who it was,'* he's afraid that the reason he now recognizes you *is because* I asked him if it could have been you."

"What the hell is going on here? Are you that fucking desperate? You come up with a couple of matched prints—How many other prints matched?"

"Four sets," Washington said. "And there were prints from two people in that car that don't match any of anybody in Special Operations. We're now running them against every cop in the Department. That'll take a long time, there's six thousand odd cops. I frankly will be surprised if we get a match, but you never know.''

''I think I've had enough of this bullshit conversation,'' Carter said, and stood up and took a wad of money from his pocket.

''How do you think you're going to like it in the 6th District?''

''What's that supposed to mean?''

''You're being transferred, tomorrow, to the 6th District. Where you will work for Lieutenant Foster H. Lewis, Sr.''

''I don't know what the fuck you think you're doing, or who the hell you think you are, Washington, but I will not take a transfer to the 6th Division or anywhere else.''

''You could resign, of course. That would make a lot of people happy. But if you stay on the job, you're going to the 6th, tomorrow.''

''Because you have this nutty idea that I trashed Payne's car? Or that I was involved in what happened to Monahan?''

''There is no question in my mind that you trashed Payne's car, drove the car to Monahan's house the morning he was shot, shot Monahan with a stun-gun, and told your friends when I was going to pick Monahan up at Goldblatt's so they could throw a gasoline bomb at me.''

''You know how far you would get with this in court? They'd laugh you out of City Hall.''

''Did I say anything about taking you to court? All I said was that you were going to the 6th District.''

''You try to get me transferred, transferred anywhere, and I'll have the Black Police Officer's Association all over your ass!''

''You know how a complaint gets acted on by the Black Police Officer's Association?'' Washington asked, and then went on without waiting for a reply. ''It goes to the Executive Committee. The Executive Committee is composed of former officers. Like me, for example. And Richard Kallanan. I really don't think, Brother, that you're going to get a hell of a lot of sympathy from the Black Police Officer's Association.''

''Fuck you, Washington!'' Sergeant Carter said, tossed a five-dollar bill on the table, and walked away.

As he approached the booth occupied by Officer Richard Kallanan, their eyes met and Kallanan stood up.

Carter stopped at the booth.

"You're still the white man's slave, motherfucker!" he said.

Officer Kallanan thereupon struck Sergeant Carter in the face with his fist, causing him to fall to the floor.

Sergeant Washington rushed from his booth to restrain Officer Kallanan, but this proved unnecessary.

Officer Kallanan was already bending over Sergeant Carter, to assist him to his feet.

"I'm sorry I hit you, Carter," Richard Kallanan said. "I should have remembered what it says in the Bible, 'Judge not, lest ye be judged.' "

Sergeant Carter shook free of Kallanan's hand and walked out of the back room of Hellman's Bar & Grill.

The Philadelphia County Grand Jury returned indictments charging the seven men arrested by the police with murder in the first degree.

Between the Grand Jury indictments and the trial, Hector Carlos Estivez came to an agreement with District Attorney Thomas J. Callis under which Mr. Estivez agreed to testify against those persons charged in the robbery of Goldblatt & Sons Credit Furniture & Appliances, Inc.; the murder that occurred during the robbery; and others, in exchange for immunity from prosecution.

In sworn statements made to the district attorney, Mr. Estivez stated that it was his belief that Charles David Stevens, aka Abu Ben Muhammed, had planned the Goldblatt robbery with the advice and assistance of Omar Ben Kalif, whom he described as a black male, approximately twenty-seven years of age, with a shaven head and a full beard. Mr. Estivez stated that, in his presence, Omar Ben Kalif was identified as a member of the Philadelphia Islamic Temple.

Estivez stated that Charles David Stevens, aka Abu Ben Muhammed, had stated that should anything "go wrong" with the Goldblatt robbery, Omar Ben Kalif, and/or the Philadelphia Islamic Temple, would provide legal counsel, bail money, and other assistance.

The Philadelphia Islamic Temple, through its counsel, categorically denied any involvement of any kind whatever in the robbery/murder that took place at Goldblatt & Sons Credit Furniture & Appliances, Inc. The Temple further categorically denied that there was now, or ever had been, anyone associated with the Temple by the name of Omar Ben Kalif.

In separate trials, and as a result of plea bargaining, the remaining accused were found guilty of murder in the first degree, manslaughter in the first degree, assault, and armed robbery. Sentences ranged from life imprisonment to five years incarceration.

The Philadelphia County Grand Jury determined that the death by gunfire of Charles David Stevens at the hands of Officer M. M. Payne was an act of self-defense.

Following an investigation by the Justice Department, it was determined there had been no violation of the civil rights of Charles David Stevens by Officer Matthew M. Payne.

A suit for defamation of character and slander brought by Officer M. M. Payne against the Coalition for Equitable Law Enforcement was settled out of court for an undisclosed sum.

Sergeant Wilson Carter resigned from the Philadelphia Police Department four weeks after being transferred to the 6th District. He shortly thereafter had his name changed to Wilson X. He is now serving as personal bodyguard to Arthur X, and as head of the Fruit of Islam.

PROMINENT AUTO DEALER CHARGED IN HOT CAR RING

By Michael J. O'Hara
Bulletin Staff Writer

Robert L. Holland, prominent Delaware Valley auto dealer, was arrested this morning, following a joint FBI-Philadelphia Police investigation, and charged with 106 counts of trafficking in stolen automobiles, falsification of registration documents, and other auto-theft related charges.

"It is one more example of the fine cooperation we have learned to expect from our brother officers in the Philadelphia Police," said Walter F. Davis, Special Agent in Charge of the Philadelphia FBI office.

He had special praise for Philadelphia Police Lieutenant John J. Malone, of the Special Operations Division, who headed the police investigation.

"Malone's professionalism and dedication in a very tough investigation was inspiring," Davis said.

Philadelphia Police Commissioner Taddeus Czernich, who was with Special Agent in Charge Davis when Holland, in handcuffs, was brought to the Central Lock-Up in the Police Administration Building, said the arrest of Holland proved once again how effective a joint effort of federal and local law enforcement can be.

(Photos and additional story on Page B-1.)